[redacted]

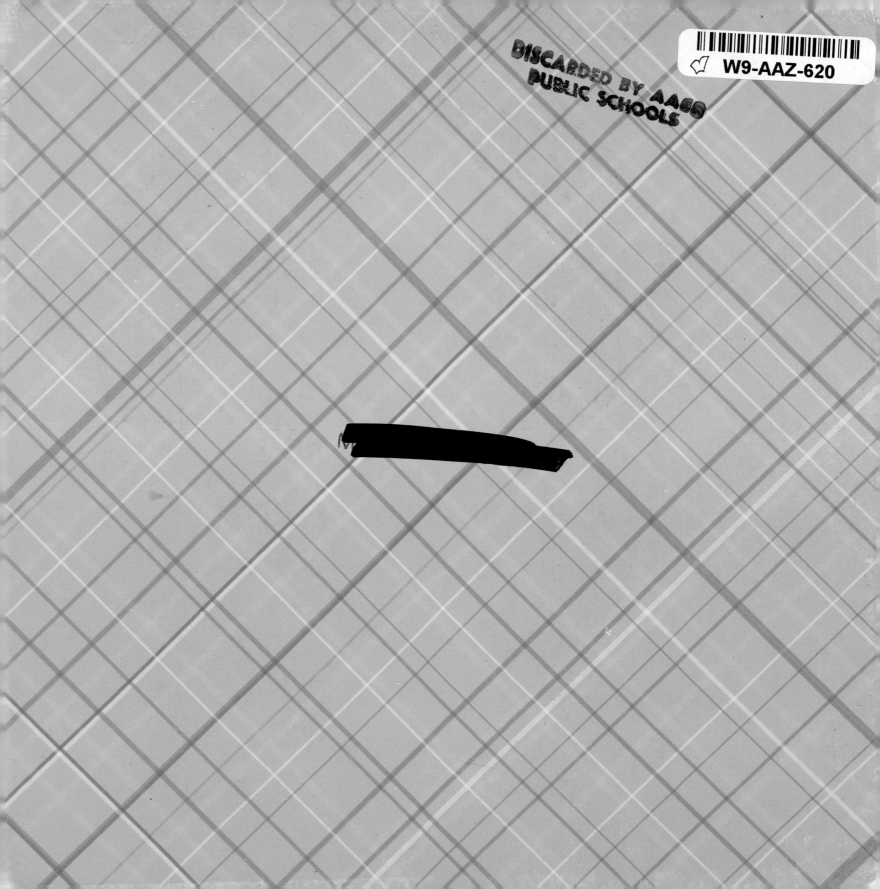

Gabby & Gator

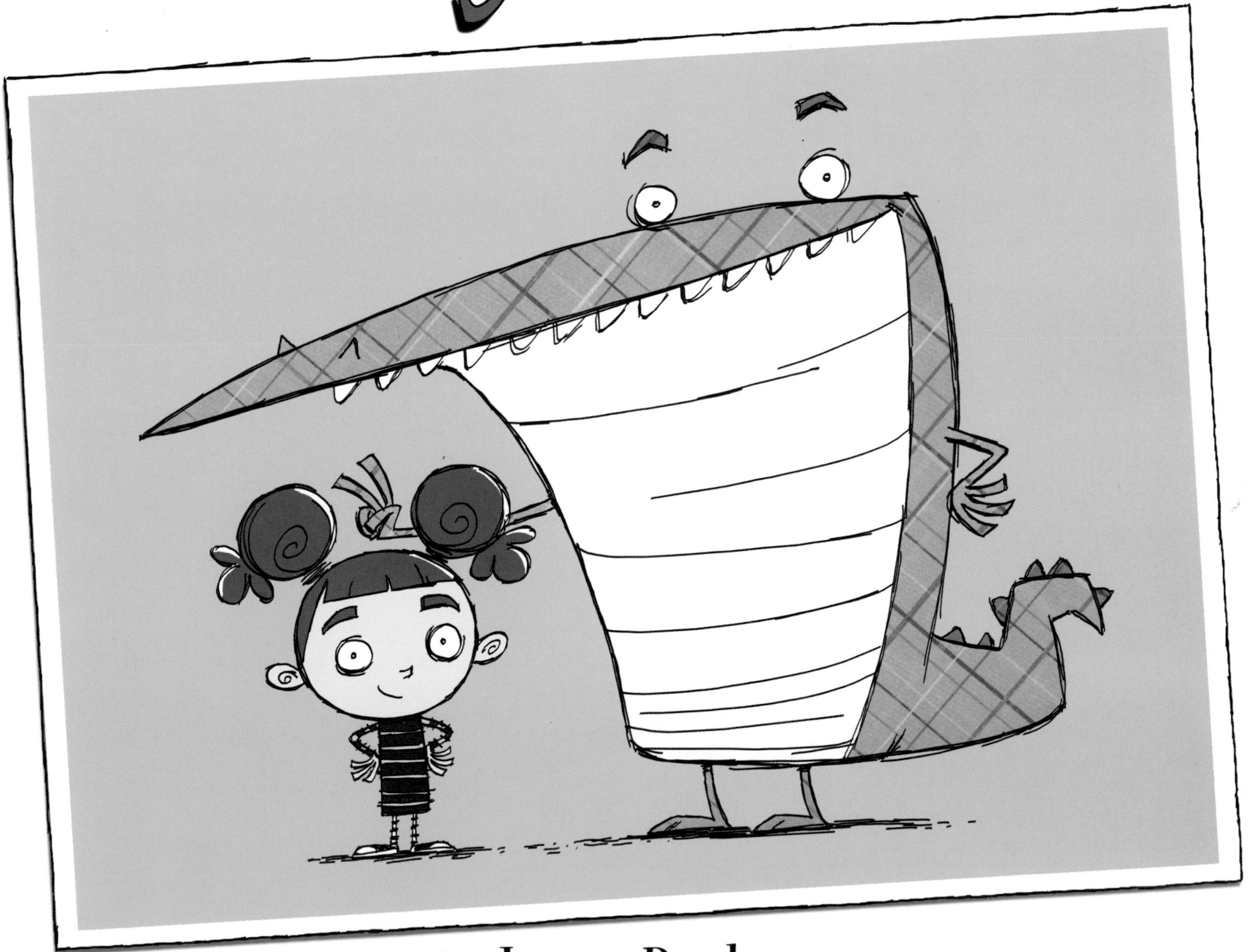

by James Burks

For Maddie, Max, and Suzanne

Yen Press
Hachette Book Group
237 Park Avenue, New York, NY 10017

www.HachetteBookGroup.com
www.YenPress.com

Yen Press is an imprint of Hachette Book Group, Inc.
The Yen Press name and logo are trademarks of Hachette Book Group, Inc.

First Yen Press Edition: September 2010

ISBN: 978-0-7595-3145-1

Library of Congress Control Number: 2010920174

10 9 8 7 6 5 4 3 2 1

SC

Printed in China

Special thanks to Bob, Frank, Allan, and Kelly for being my second, third, fourth, and fifth pairs of eyes.

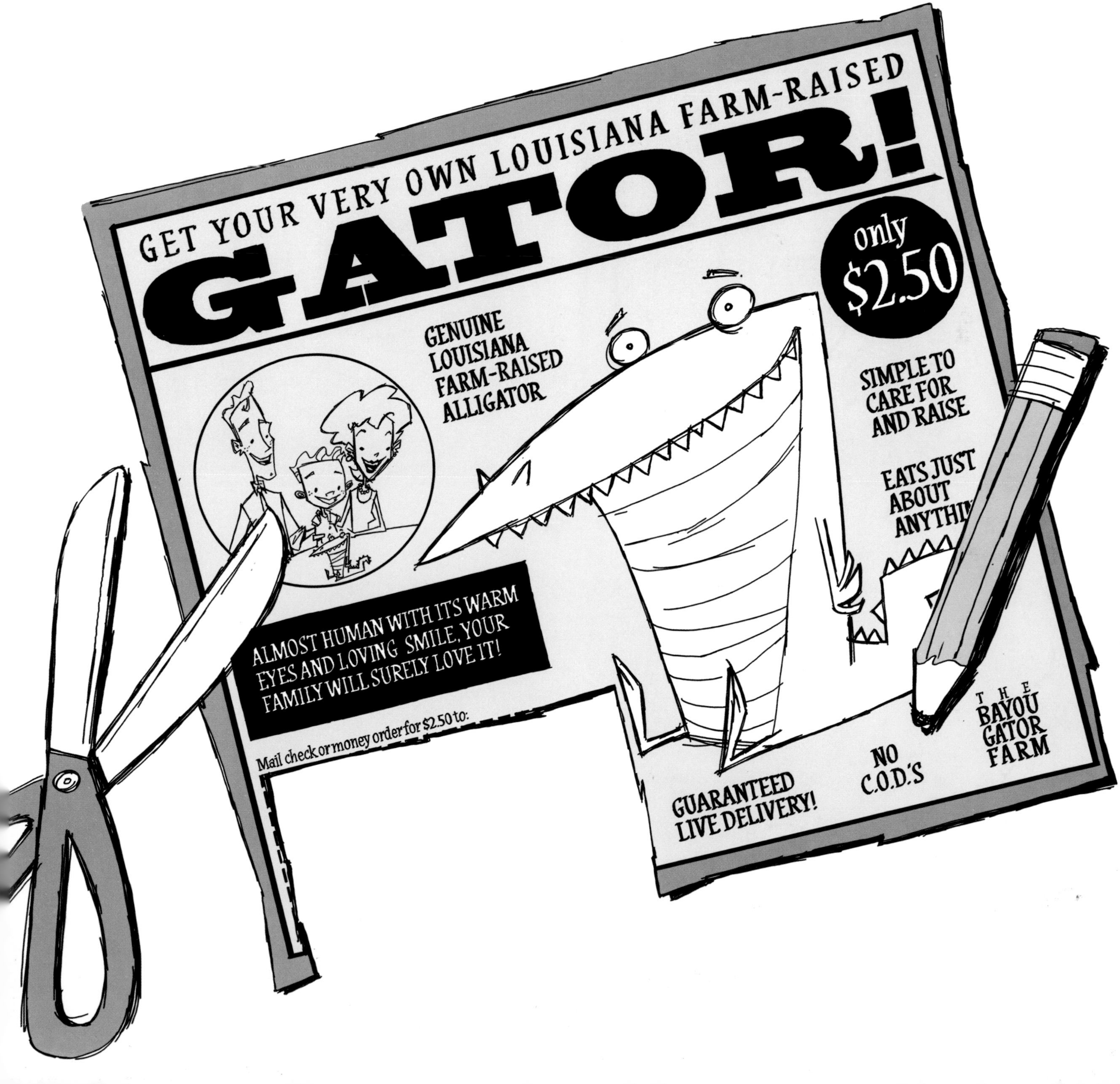
GET YOUR VERY OWN LOUISIANA FARM-RAISED
GATOR!
only $2.50
GENUINE LOUISIANA FARM-RAISED ALLIGATOR
SIMPLE TO CARE FOR AND RAISE
EATS JUST ABOUT ANYTHI
ALMOST HUMAN WITH ITS WARM EYES AND LOVING SMILE, YOUR FAMILY WILL SURELY LOVE IT!
Mail check or money order for $2.50 to:
THE BAYOU GATOR FARM
NO C.O.D.'S
GUARANTEED LIVE DELIVERY!

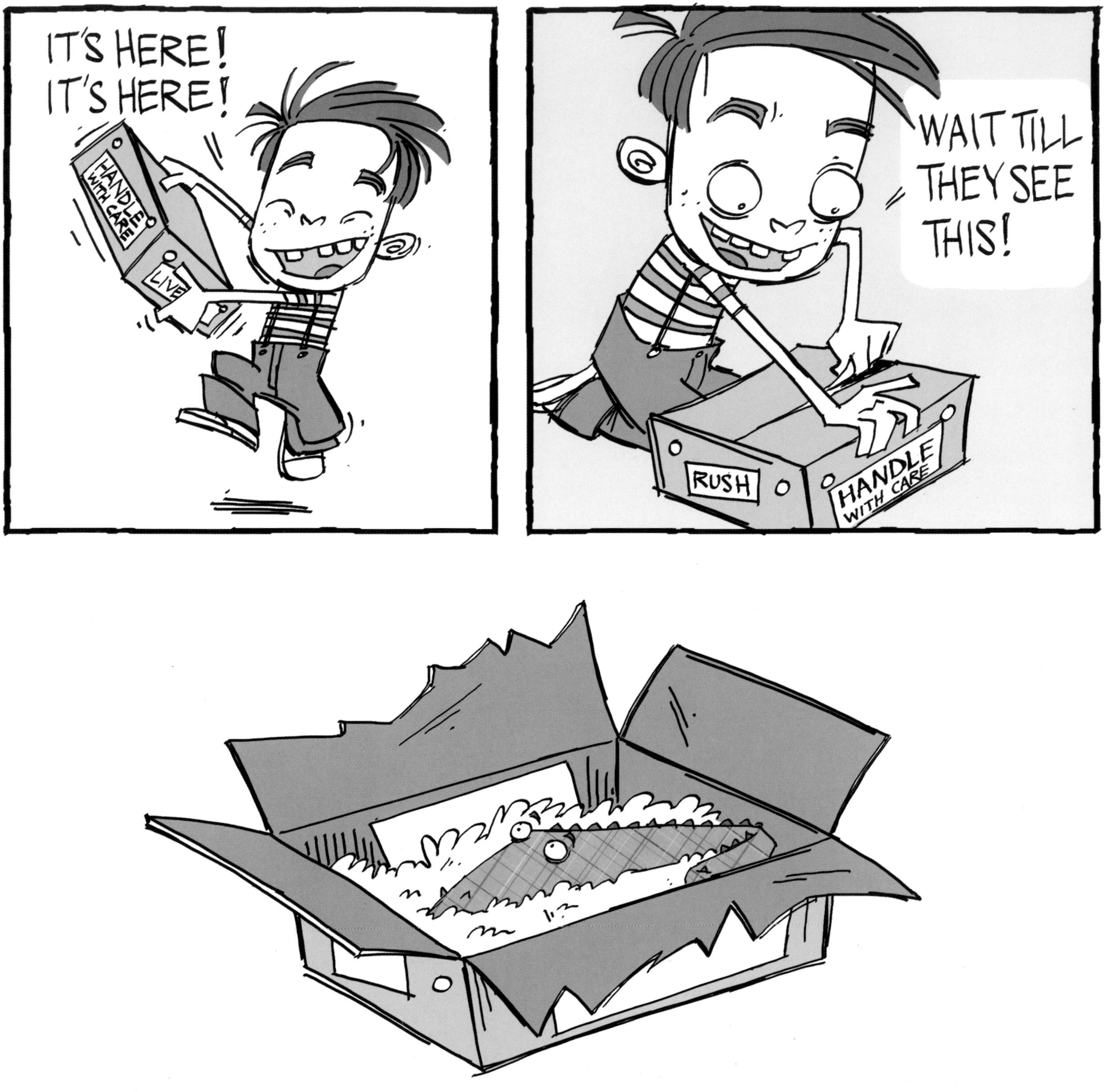
IT'S HERE! IT'S HERE!
HANDLE WITH CARE
LIVE
WAIT TILL THEY SEE THIS!
RUSH
HANDLE WITH CARE

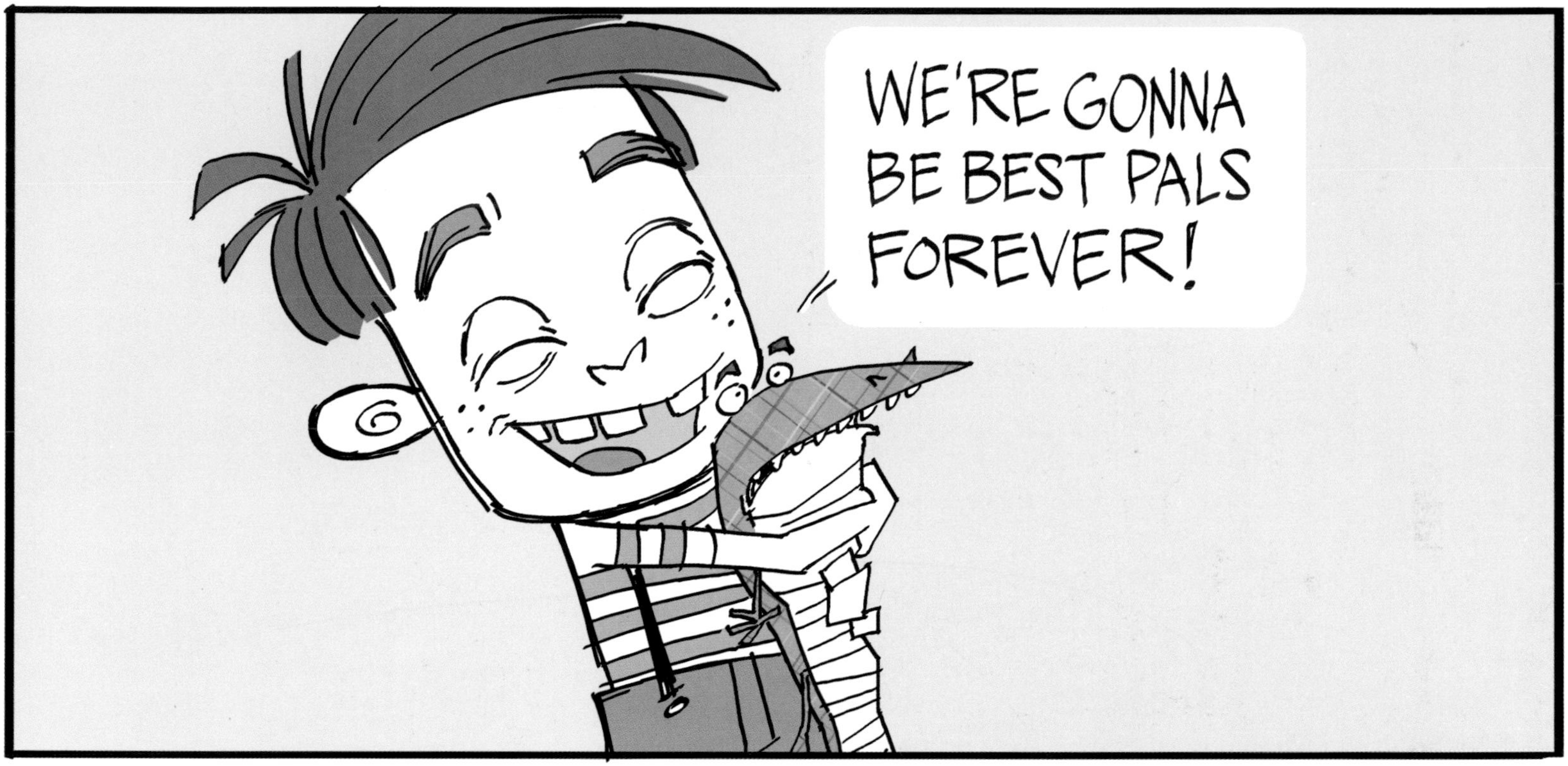
WE'RE GONNA BE BEST PALS FOREVER!

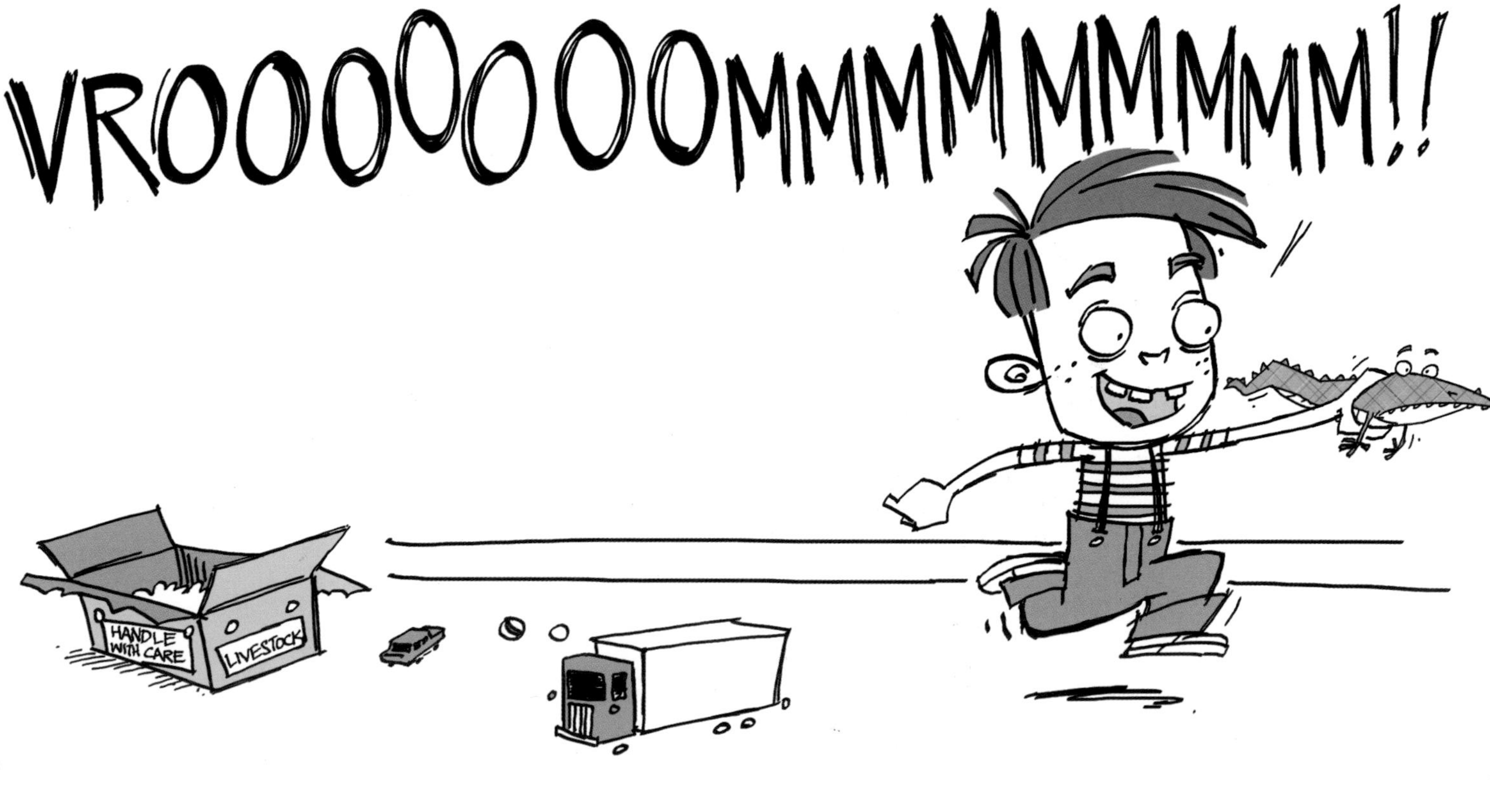
VROOOOOOOOMMMMMMMMM!!
HANDLE WITH CARE
LIVESTOCK

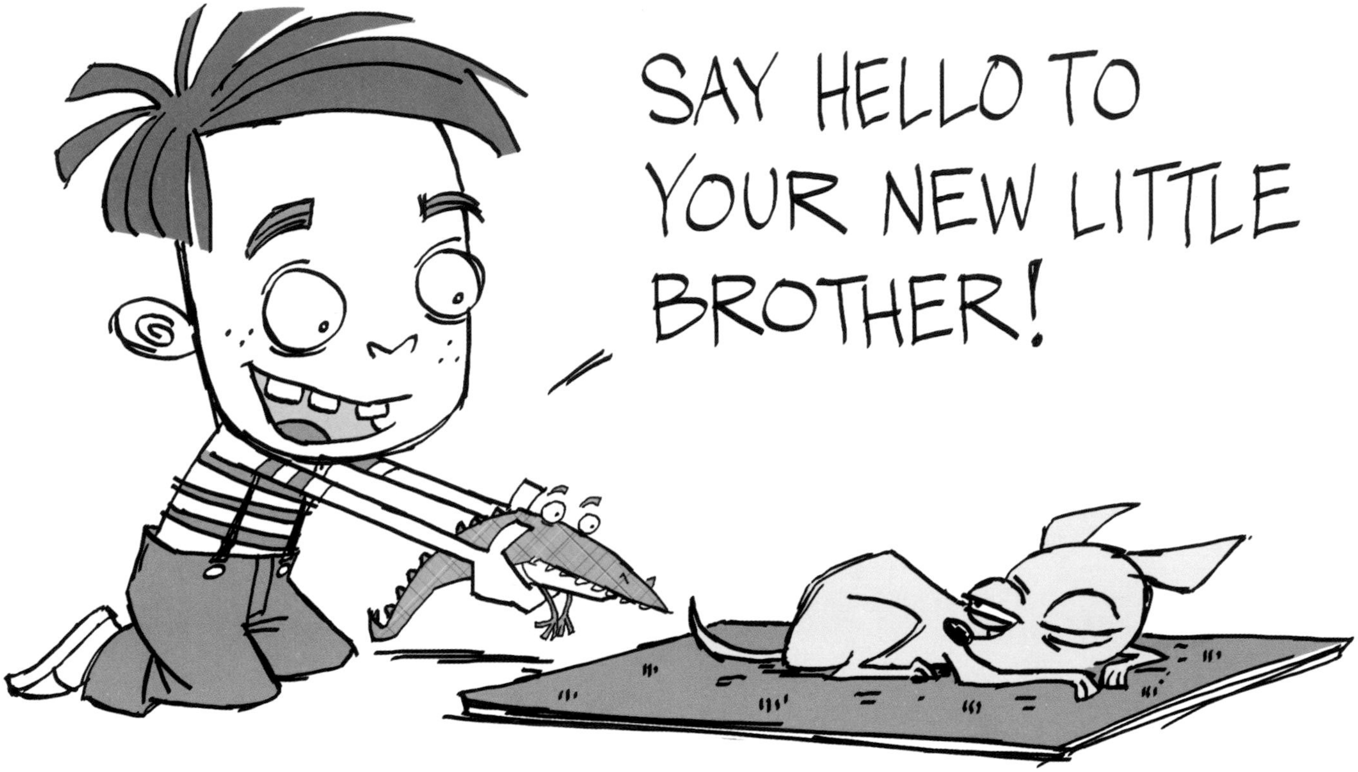
SAY HELLO TO YOUR NEW LITTLE BROTHER!

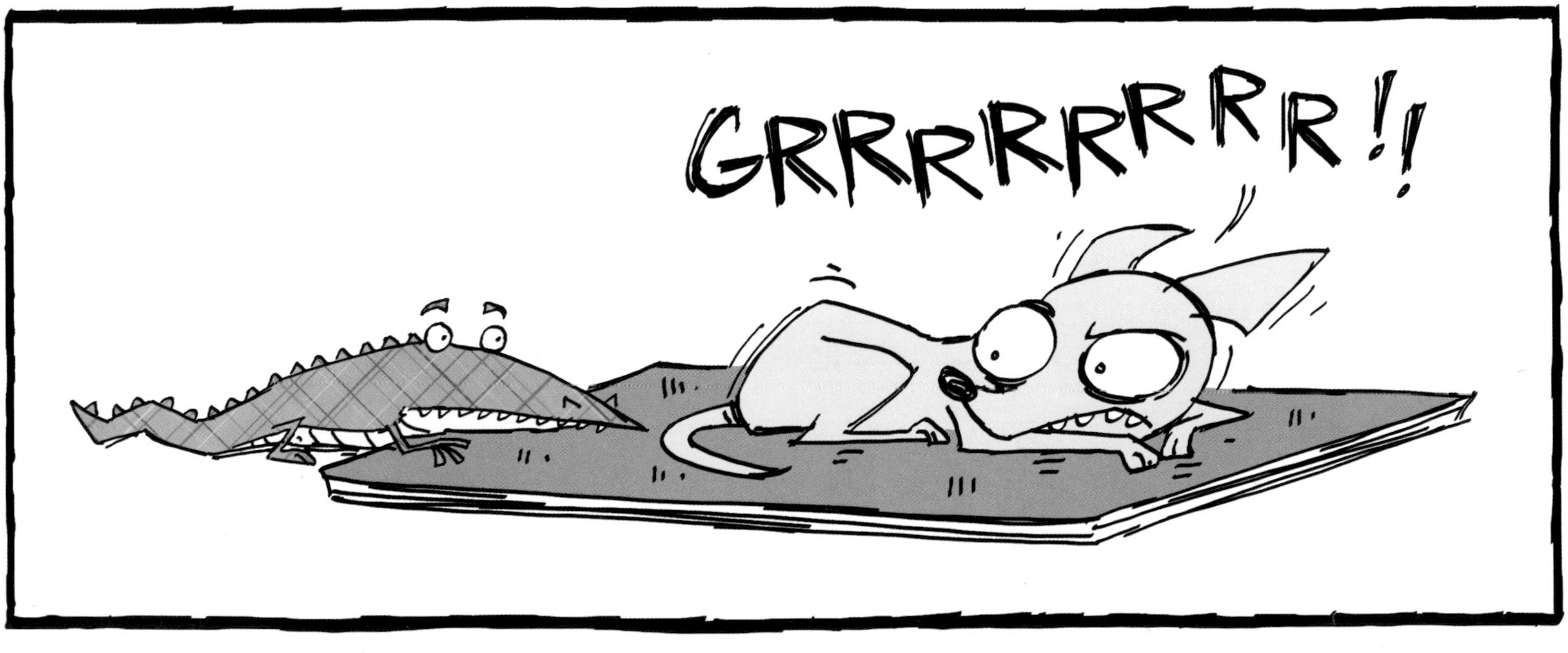
GRRRRRRRRR!!

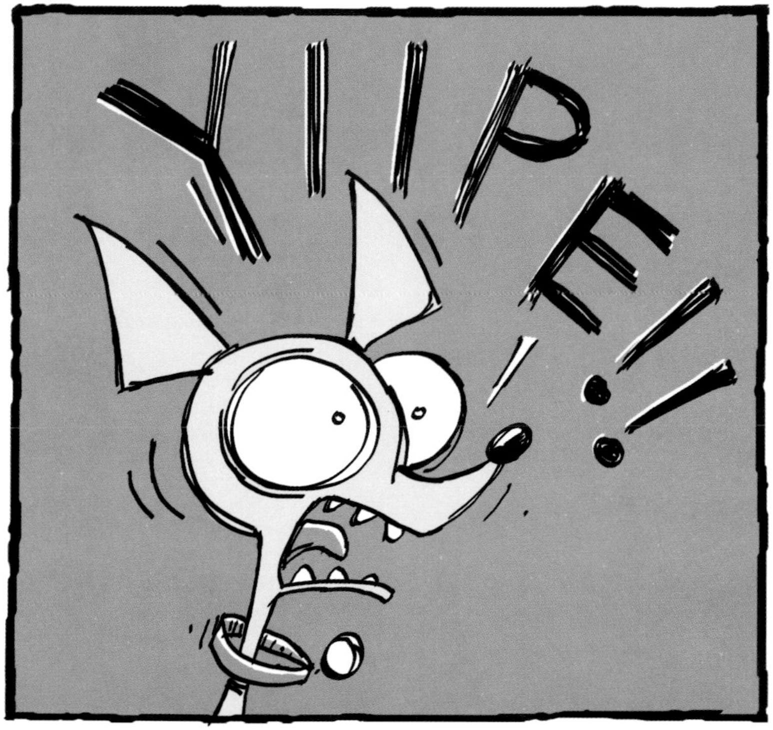
YIIPE!!
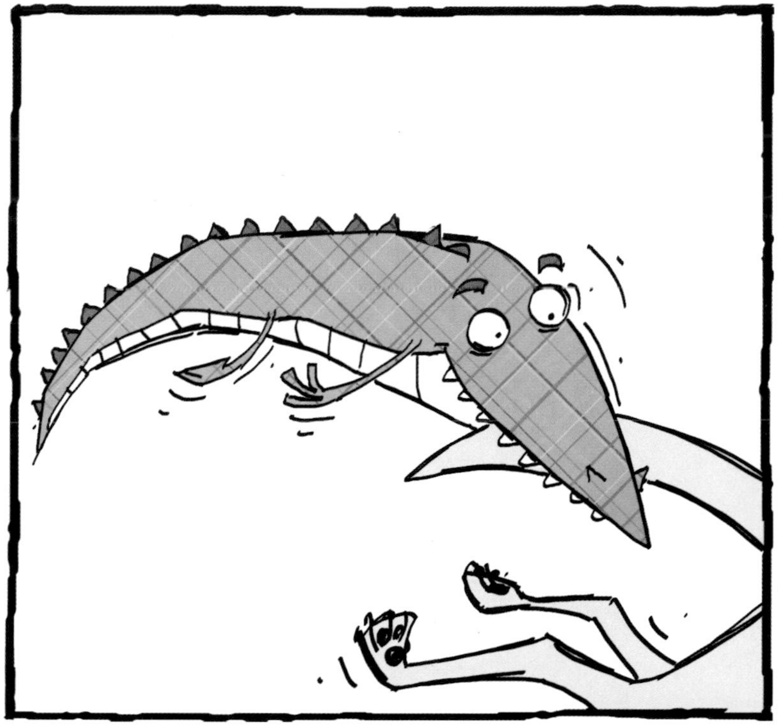
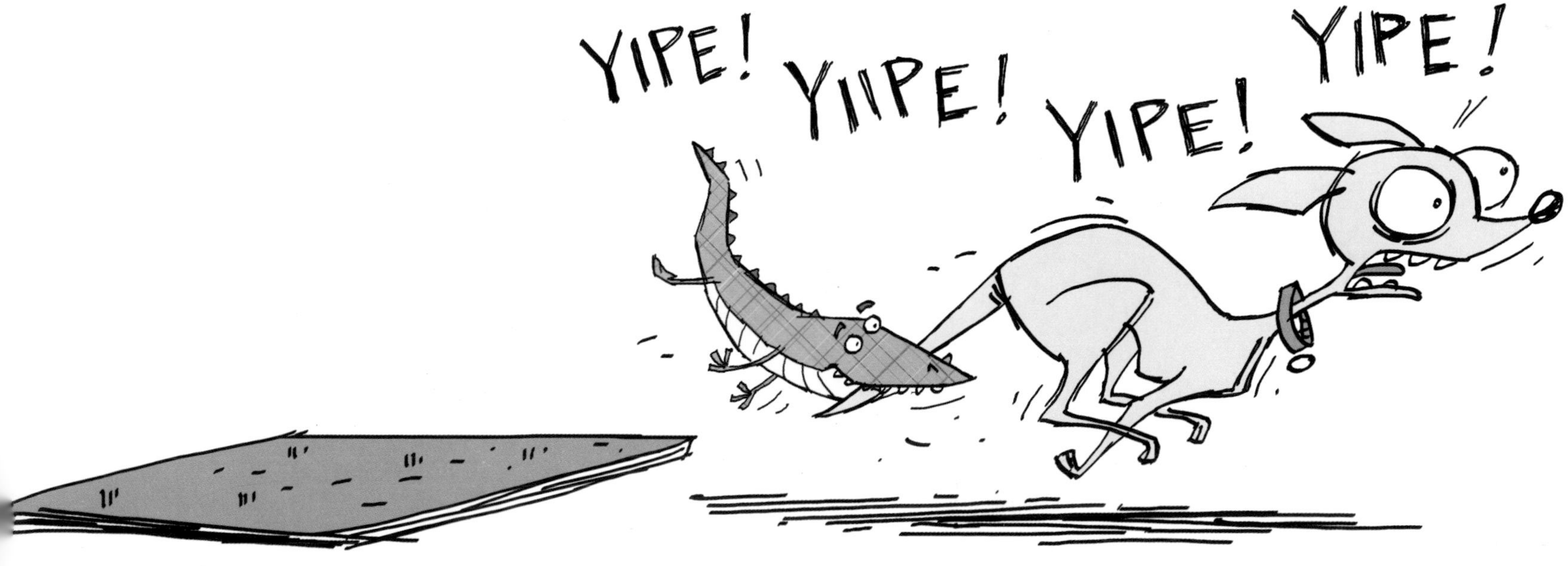
YIPE!
YIIPE!
YIPE!
YIPE!

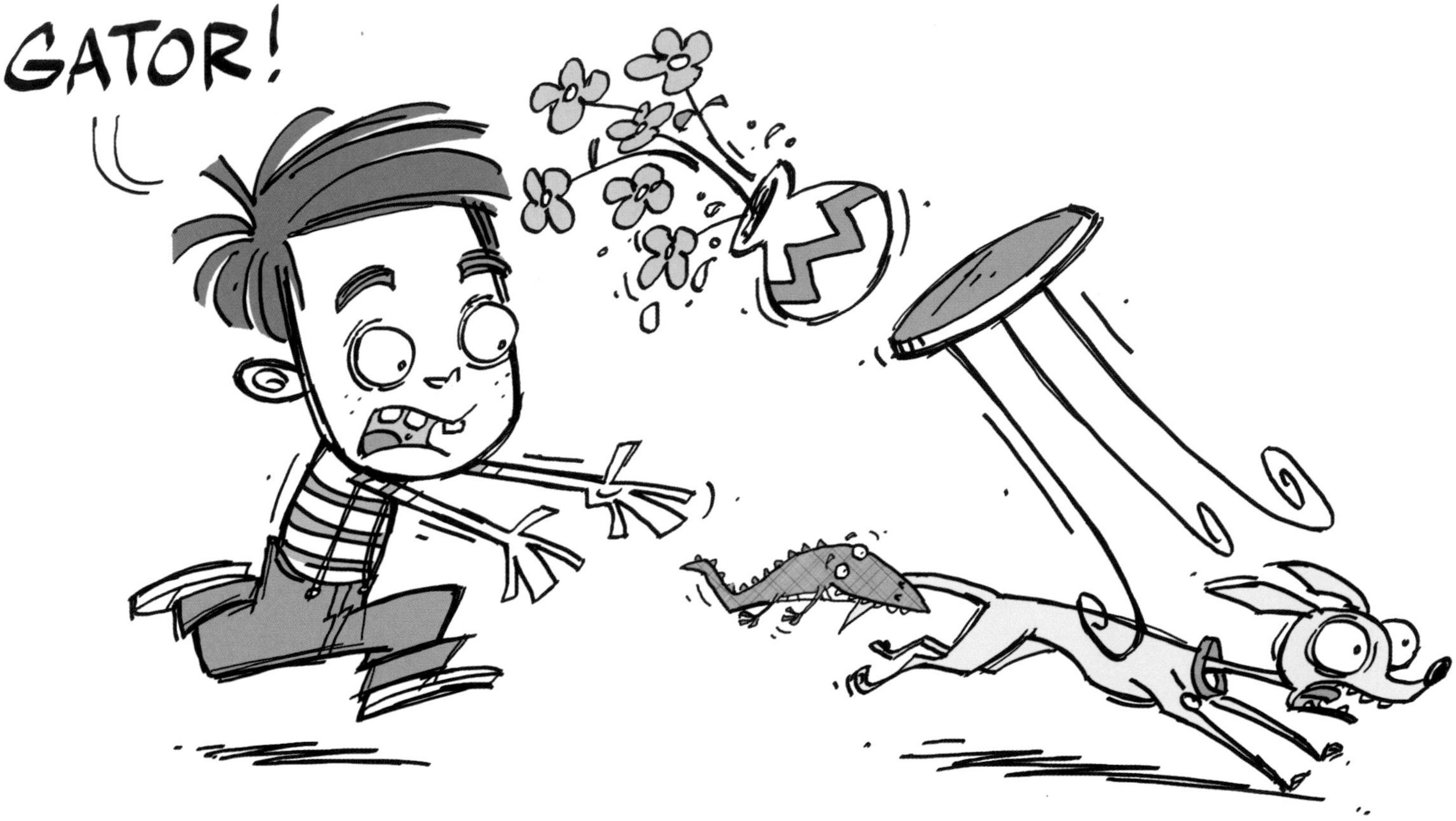
GATOR!

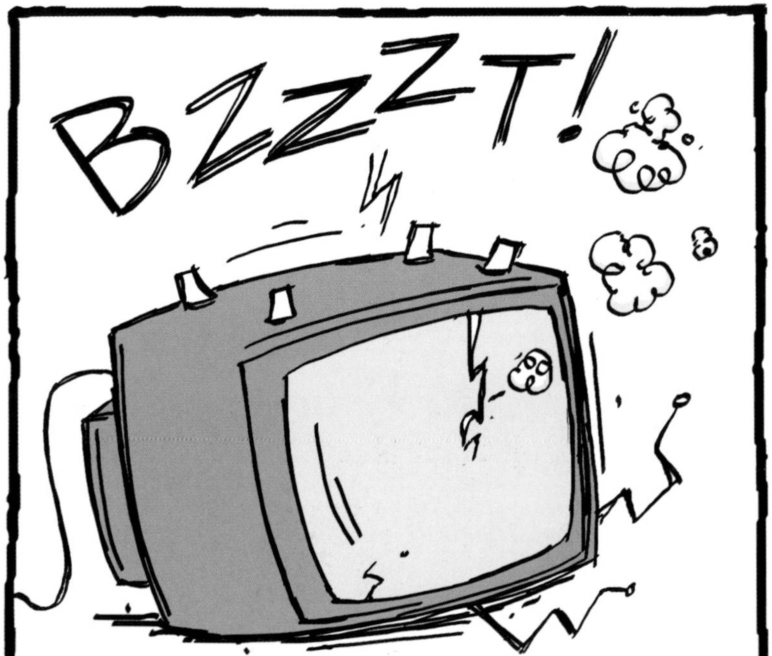
BZZZT!

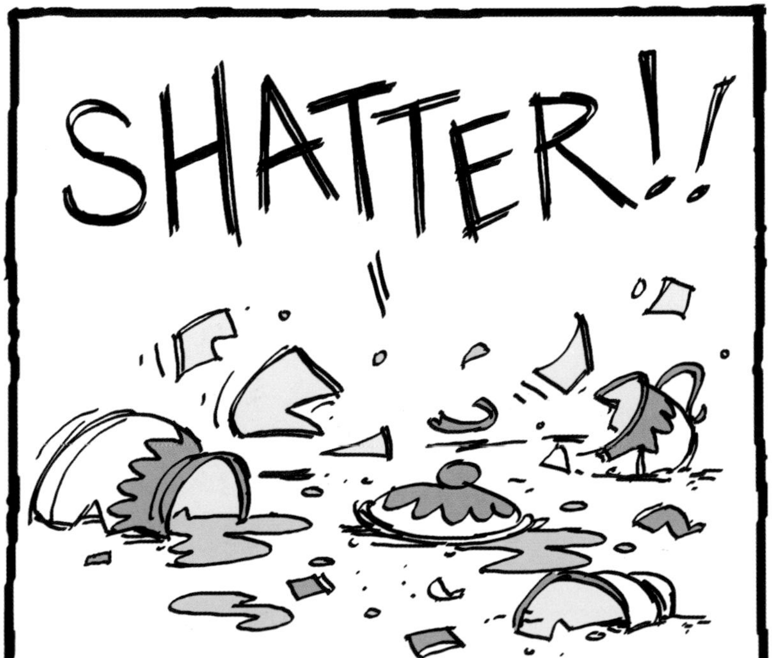
SHATTER!!

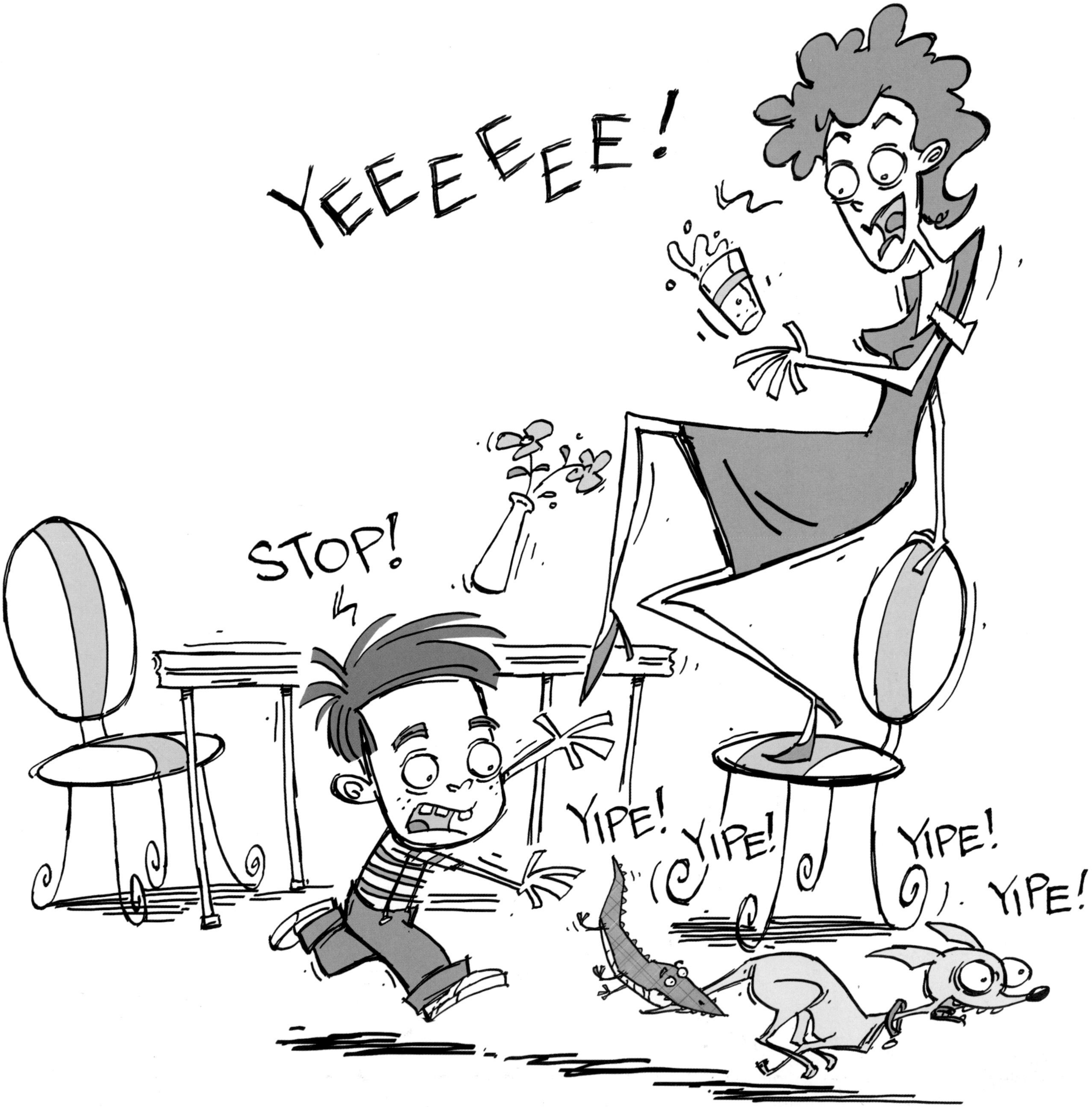
YEEEEEEE!
STOP!
YIPE!
YIPE!
YIPE!
YIPE!

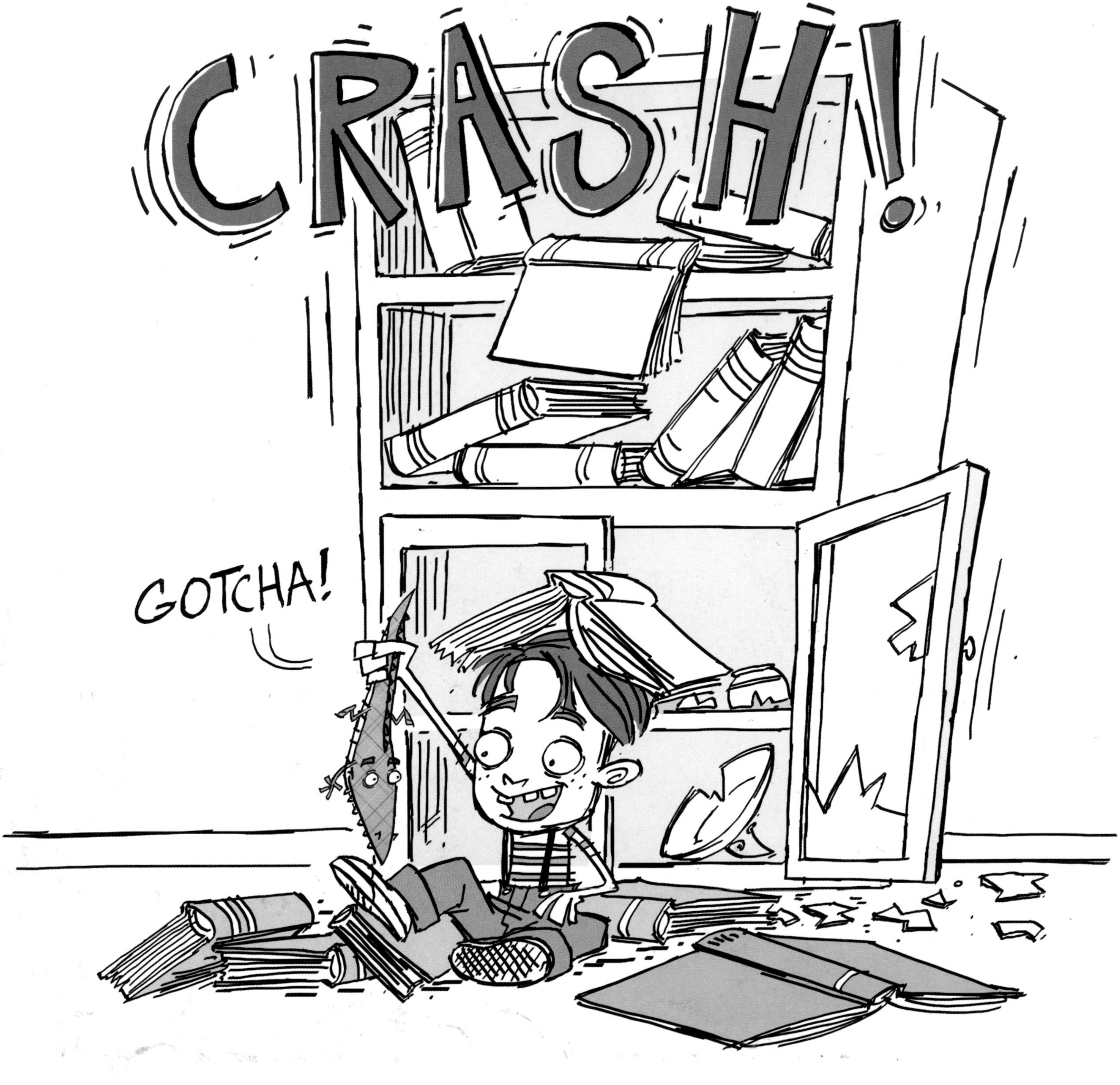
CRASH!
GOTCHA!

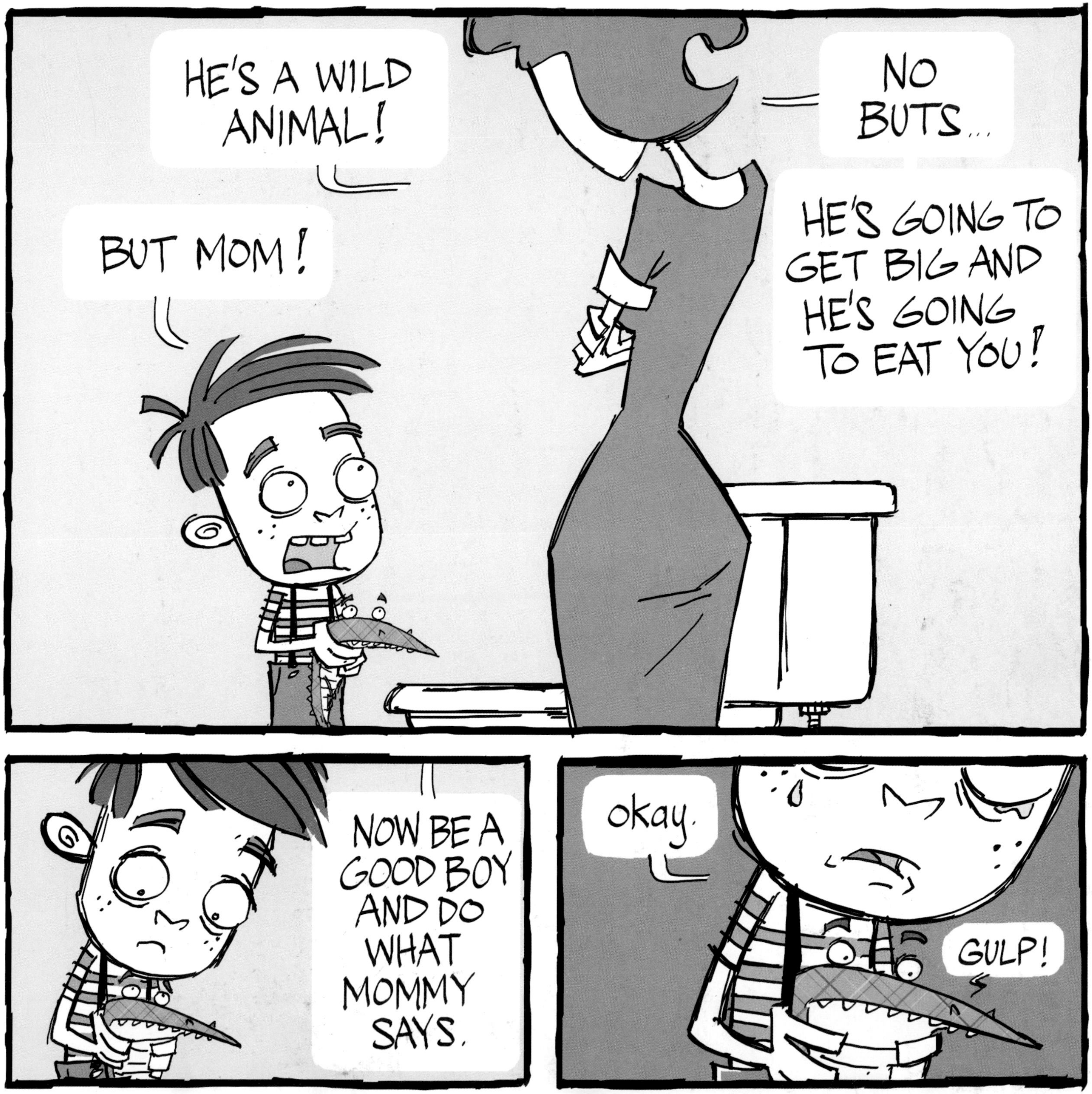
HE'S A WILD ANIMAL!
NO BUTS...
HE'S GOING TO GET BIG AND HE'S GOING TO EAT YOU!
BUT MOM!
NOW BE A GOOD BOY AND DO WHAT MOMMY SAYS.
okay.
GULP!

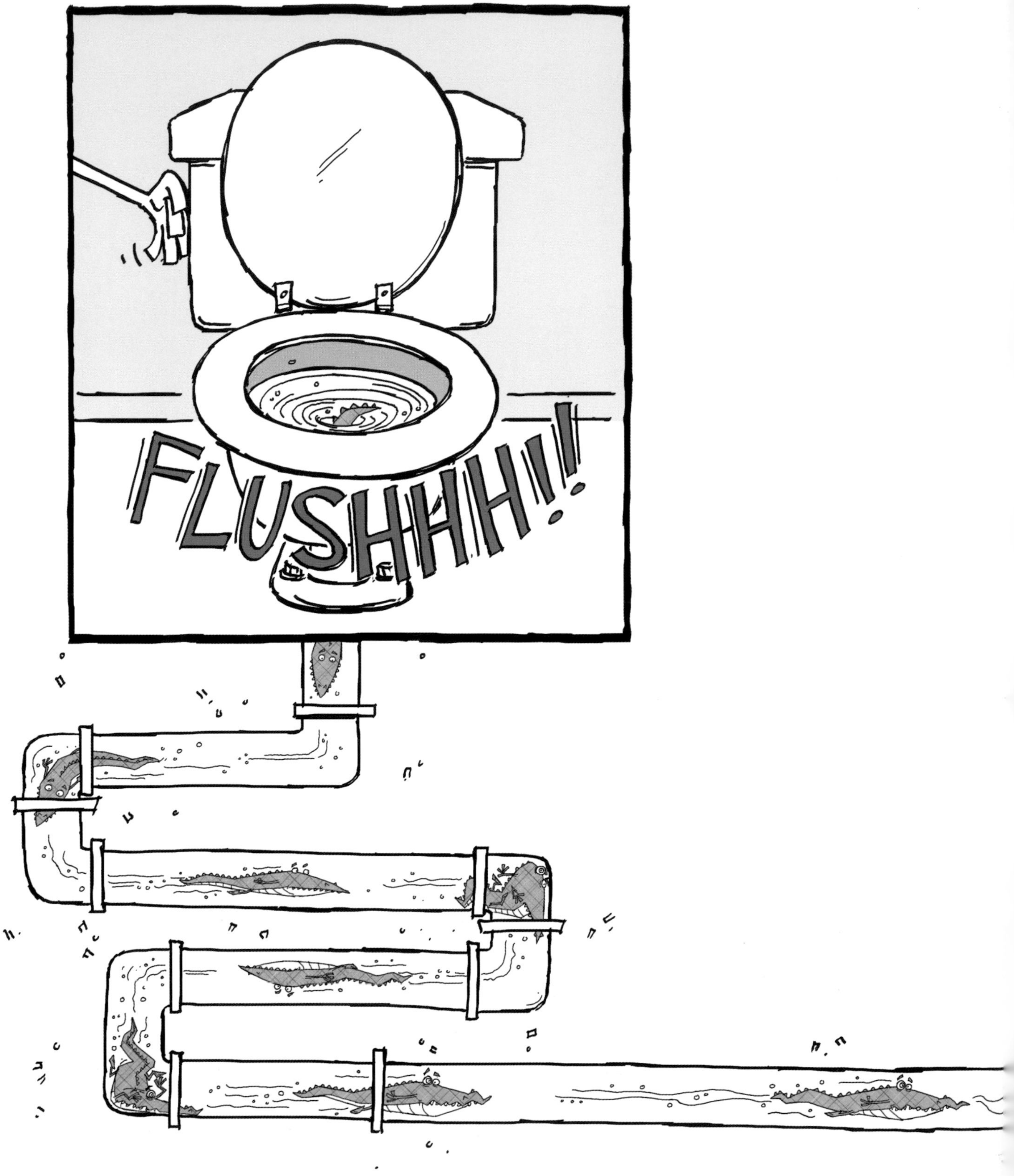
FLUSHHH!!!

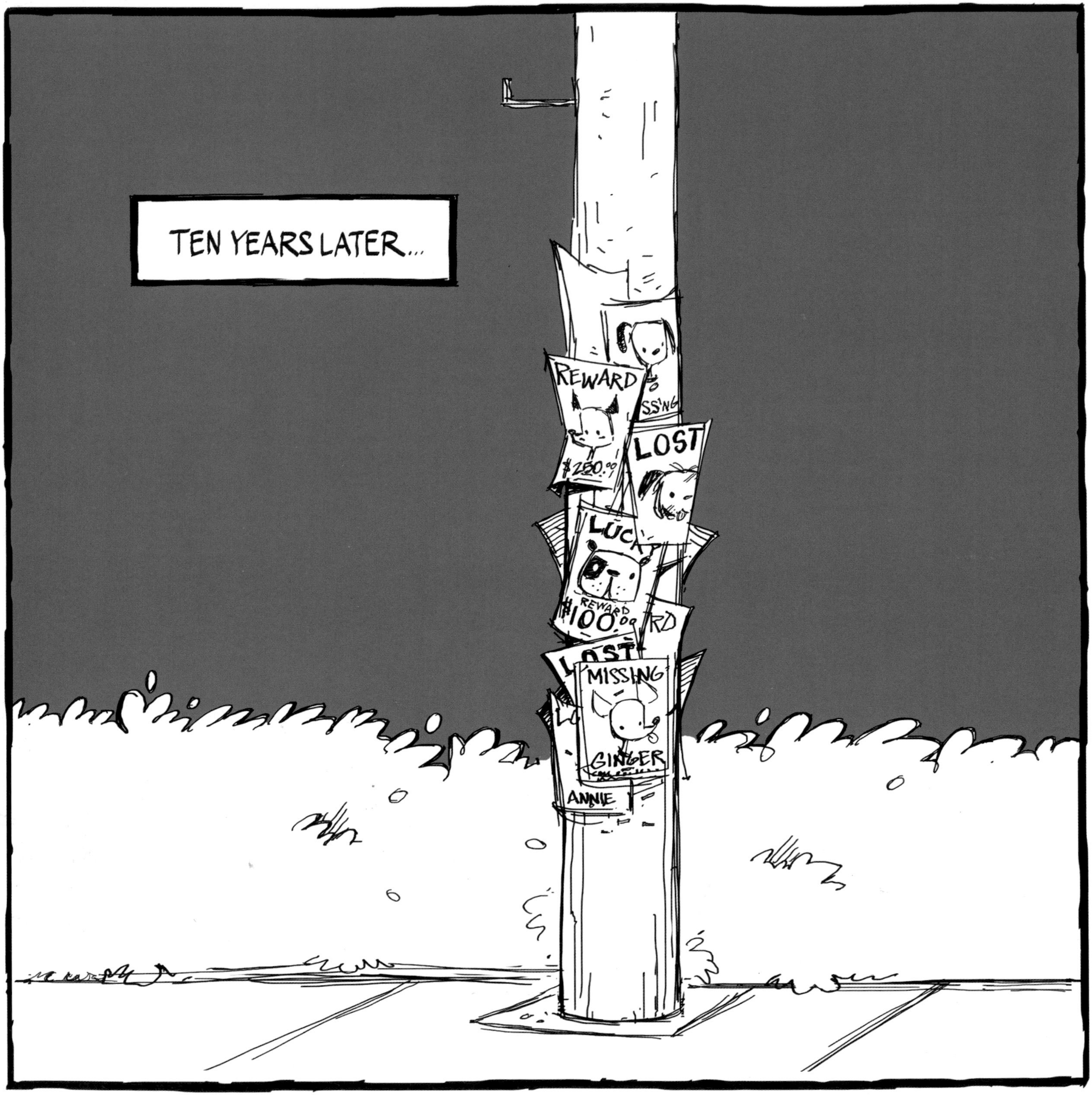
TEN YEARS LATER...
REWARD
$250.00
LOST
REWARD
$100.00
LOST
MISSING
GINGER
ANNIE

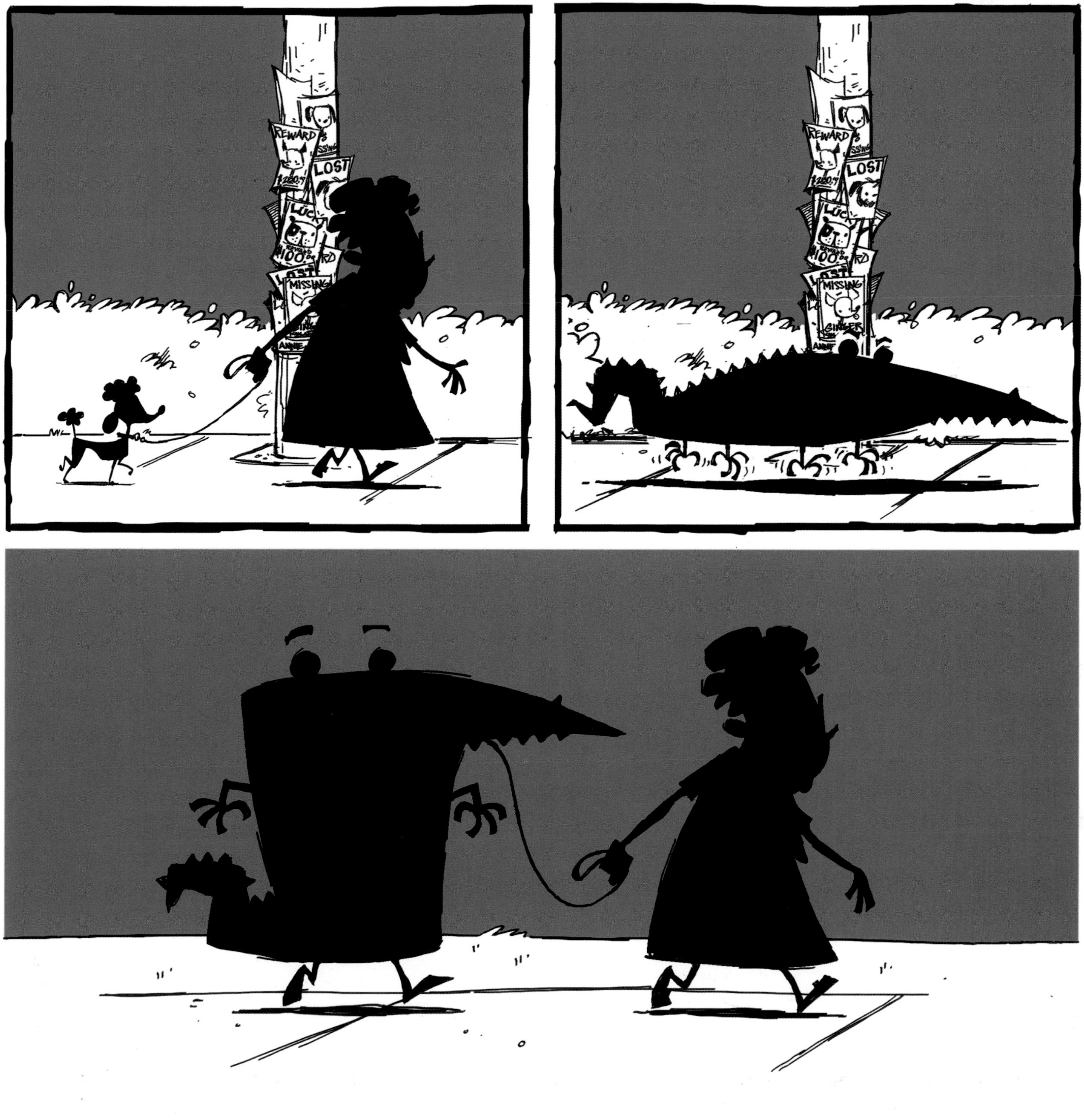

REWARD
LOST
MISSING
ANNIE
REWARD
LOST
MISSING

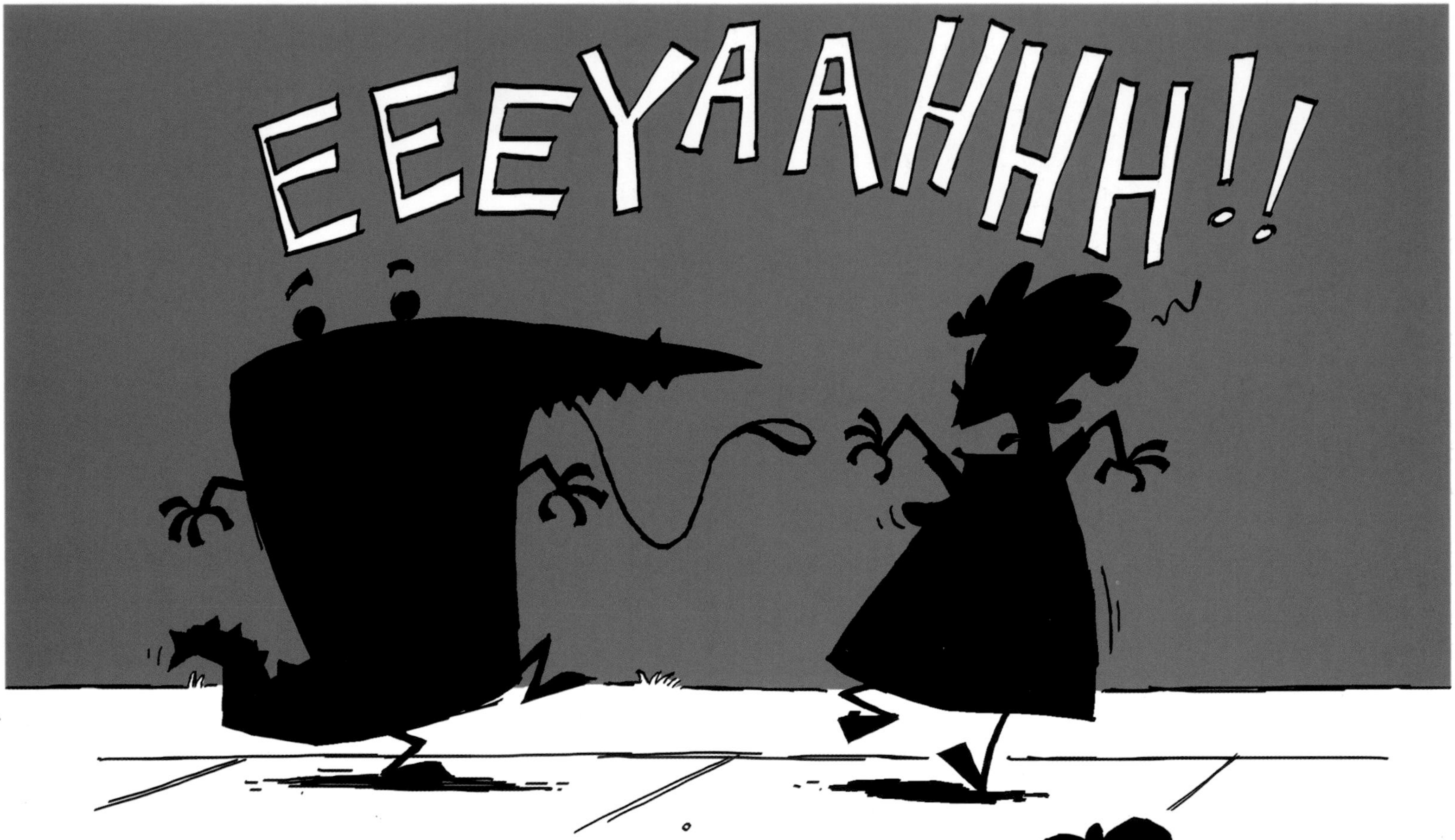
EEEYAAHHH!!

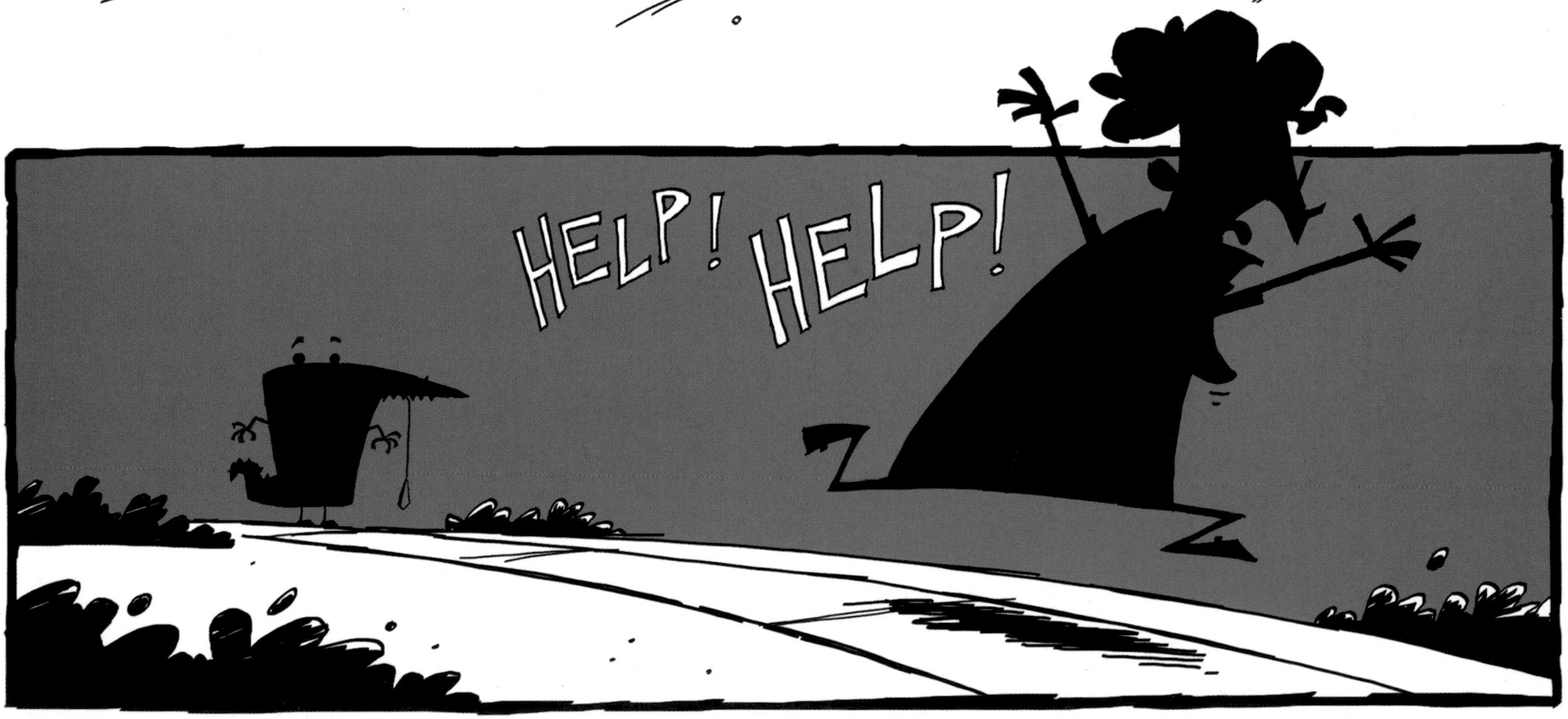
HELP! HELP!

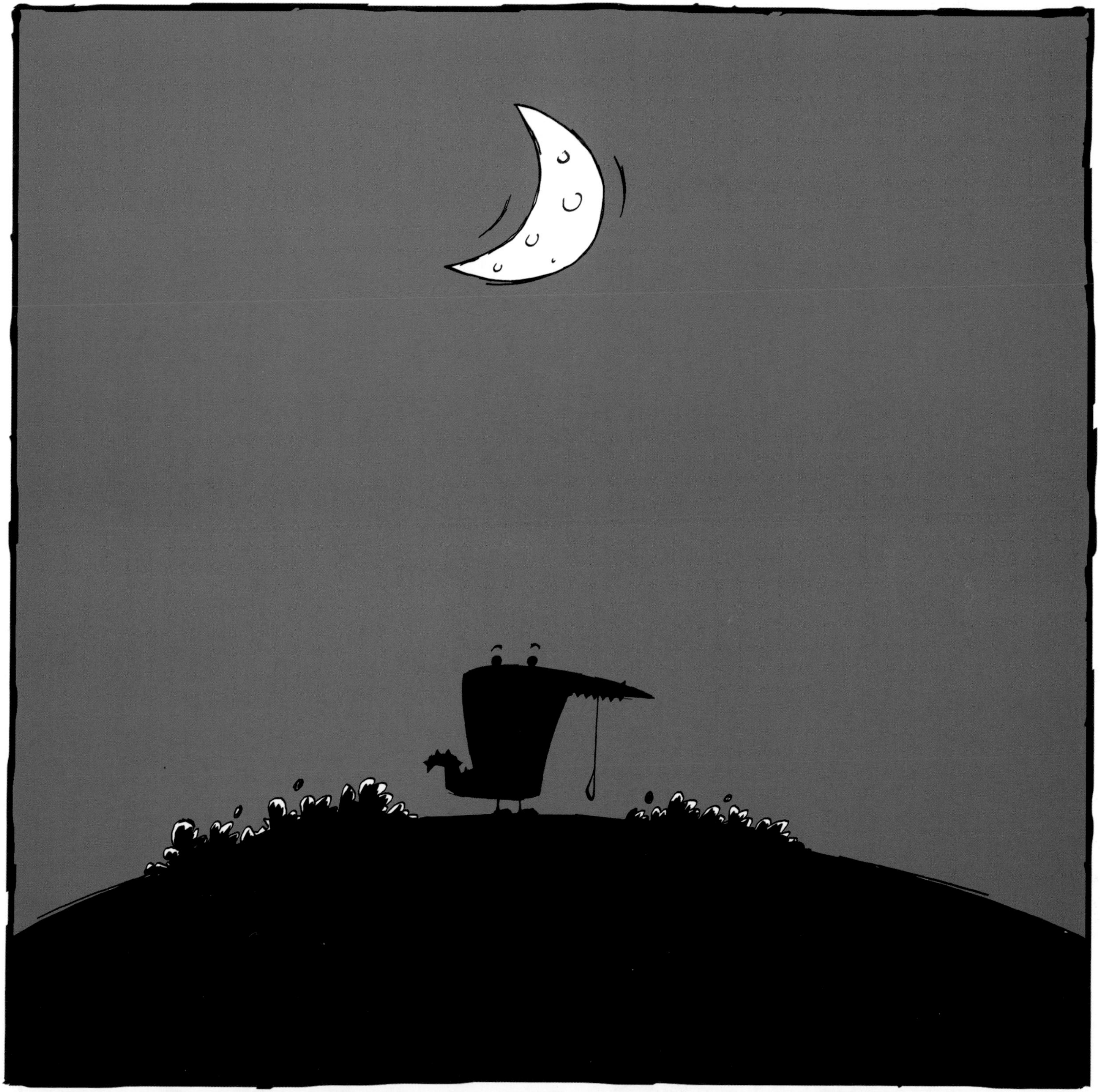

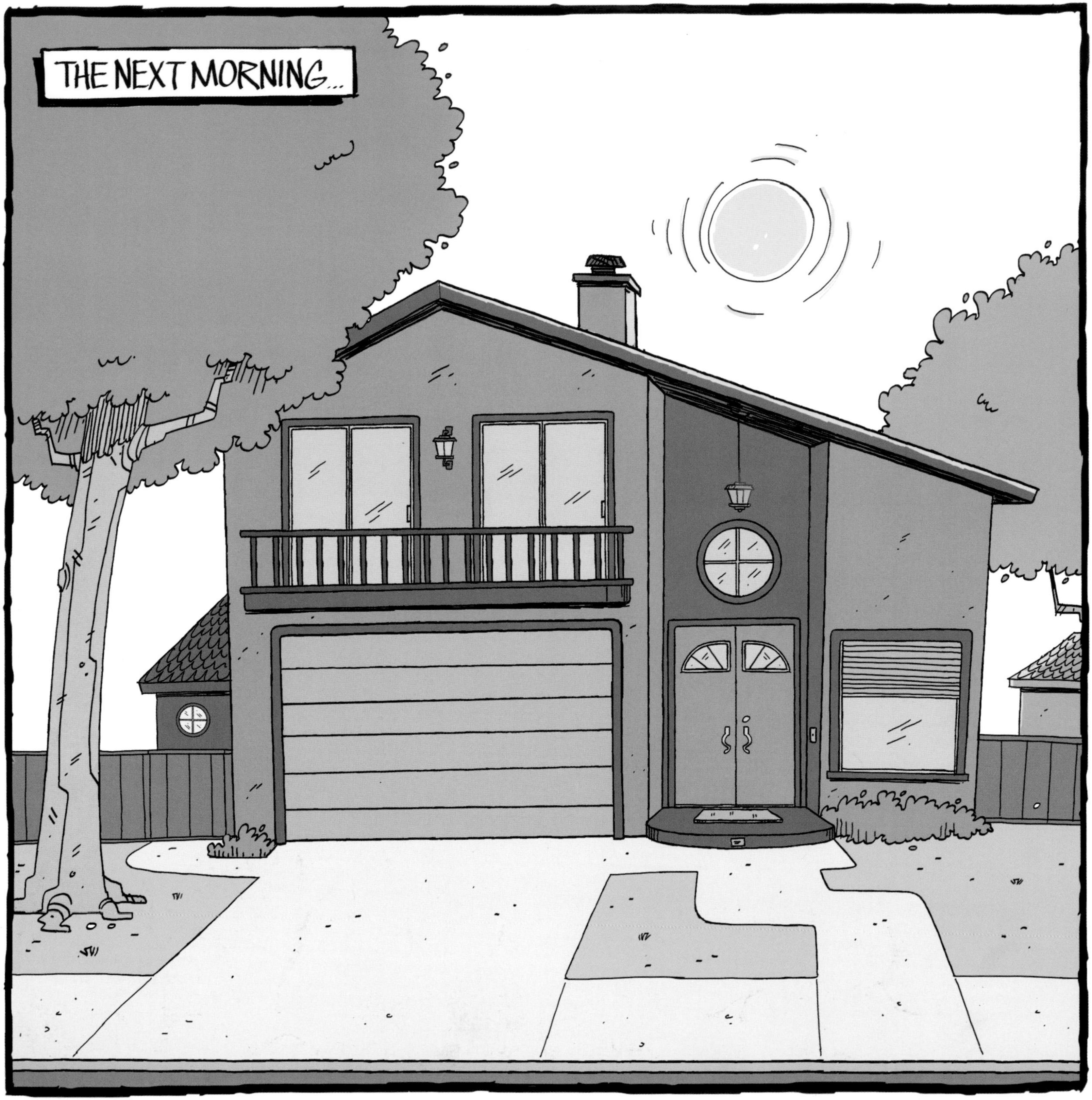
THE NEXT MORNING...

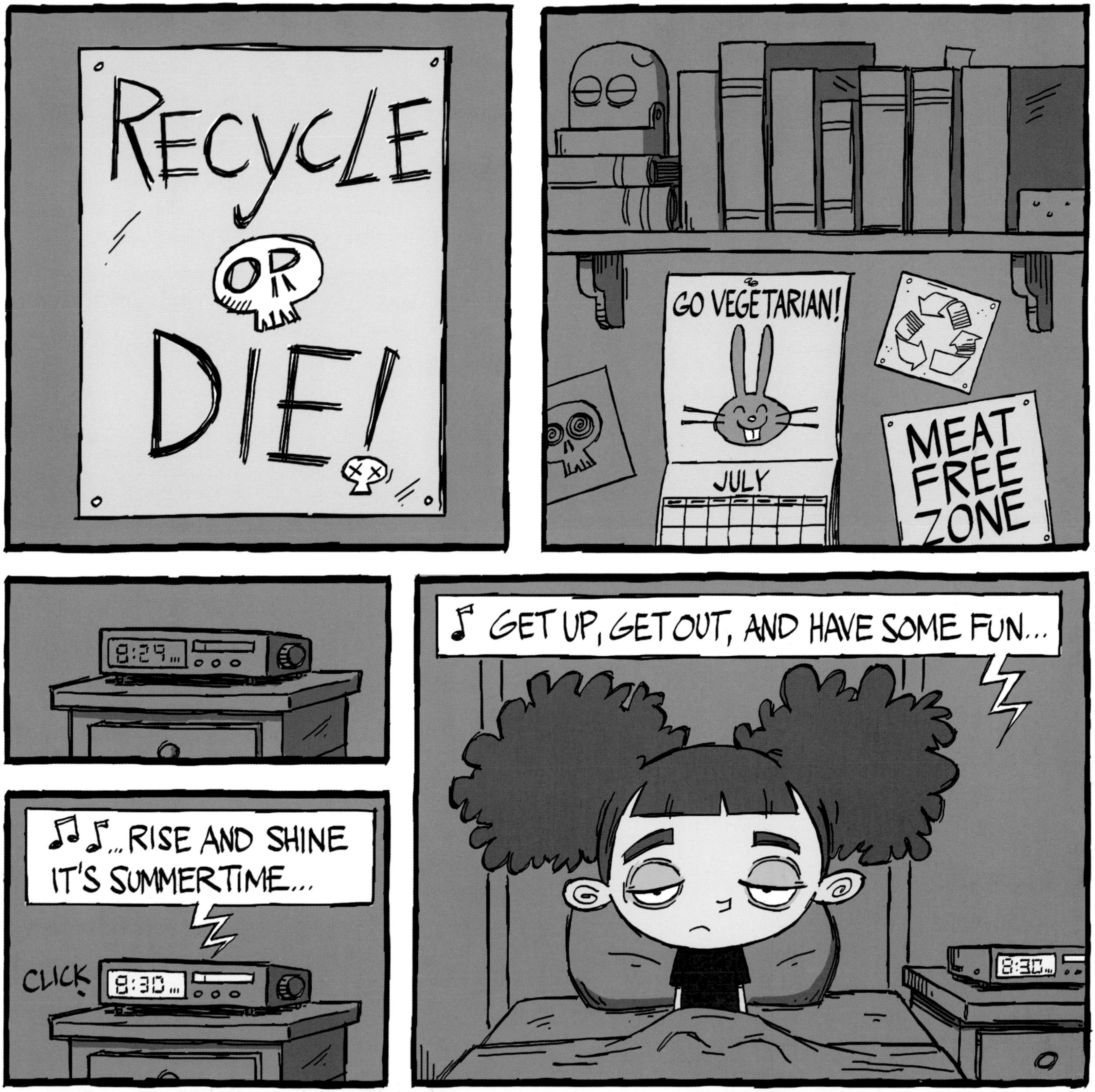
RECYCLE OR DIE!
GO VEGETARIAN!
JULY
MEAT FREE ZONE
8:29
...RISE AND SHINE IT'S SUMMERTIME...
CLICK
8:30
GET UP, GET OUT, AND HAVE SOME FUN...
8:30

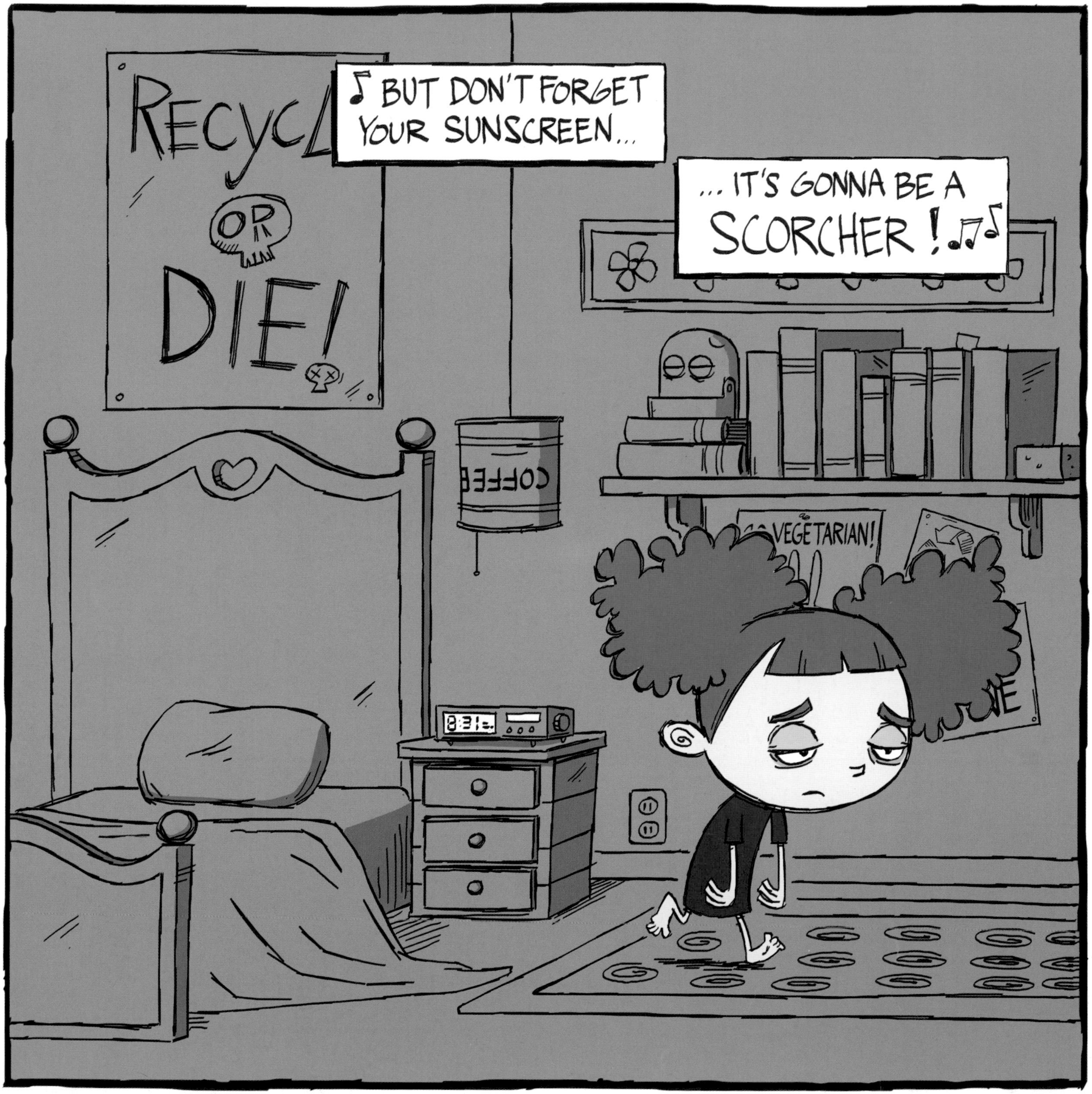
RECYCLE OR DIE!
♪ BUT DON'T FORGET YOUR SUNSCREEN...
... IT'S GONNA BE A SCORCHER! ♫♪
COFFEE
VEGETARIAN!

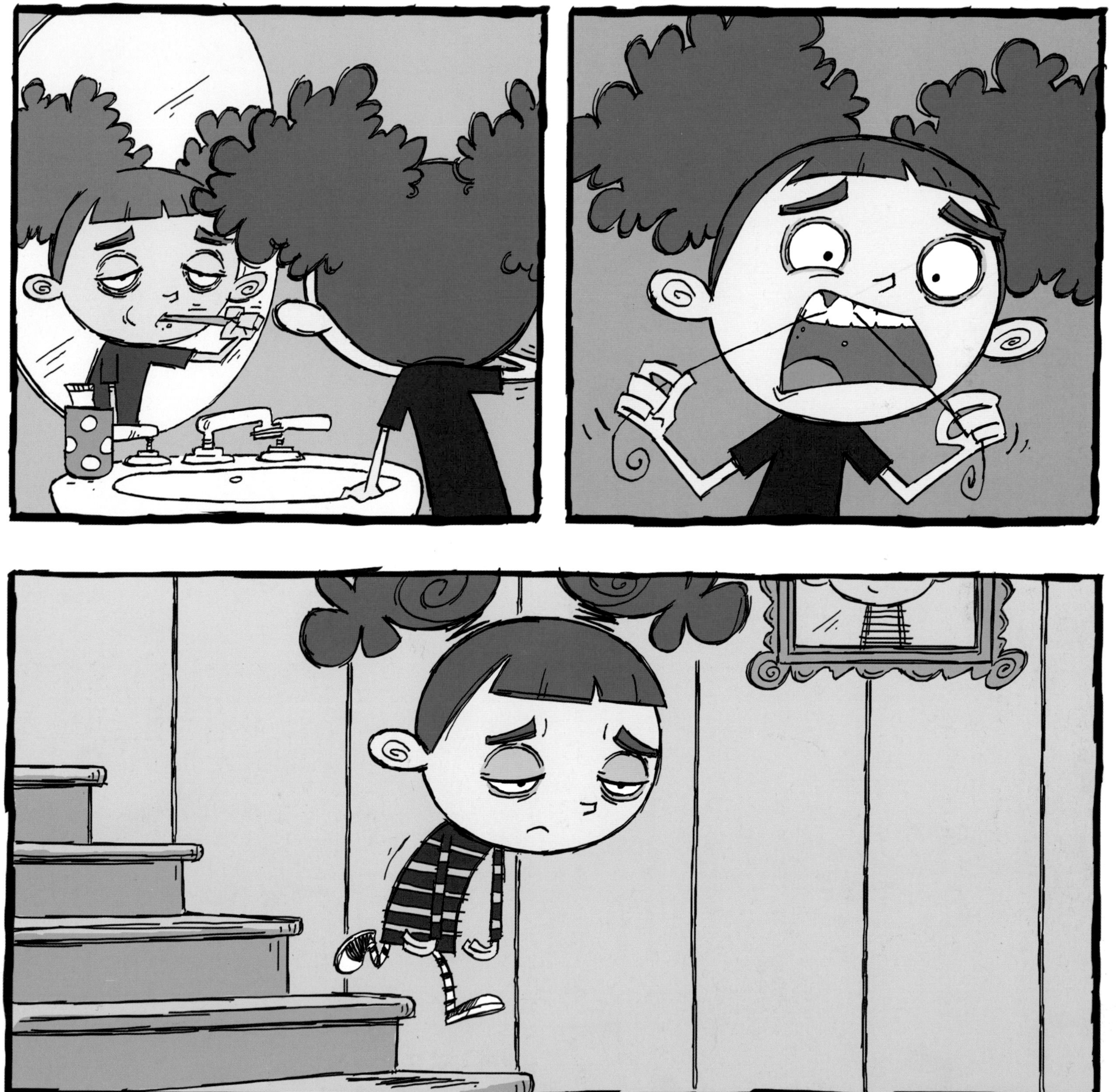

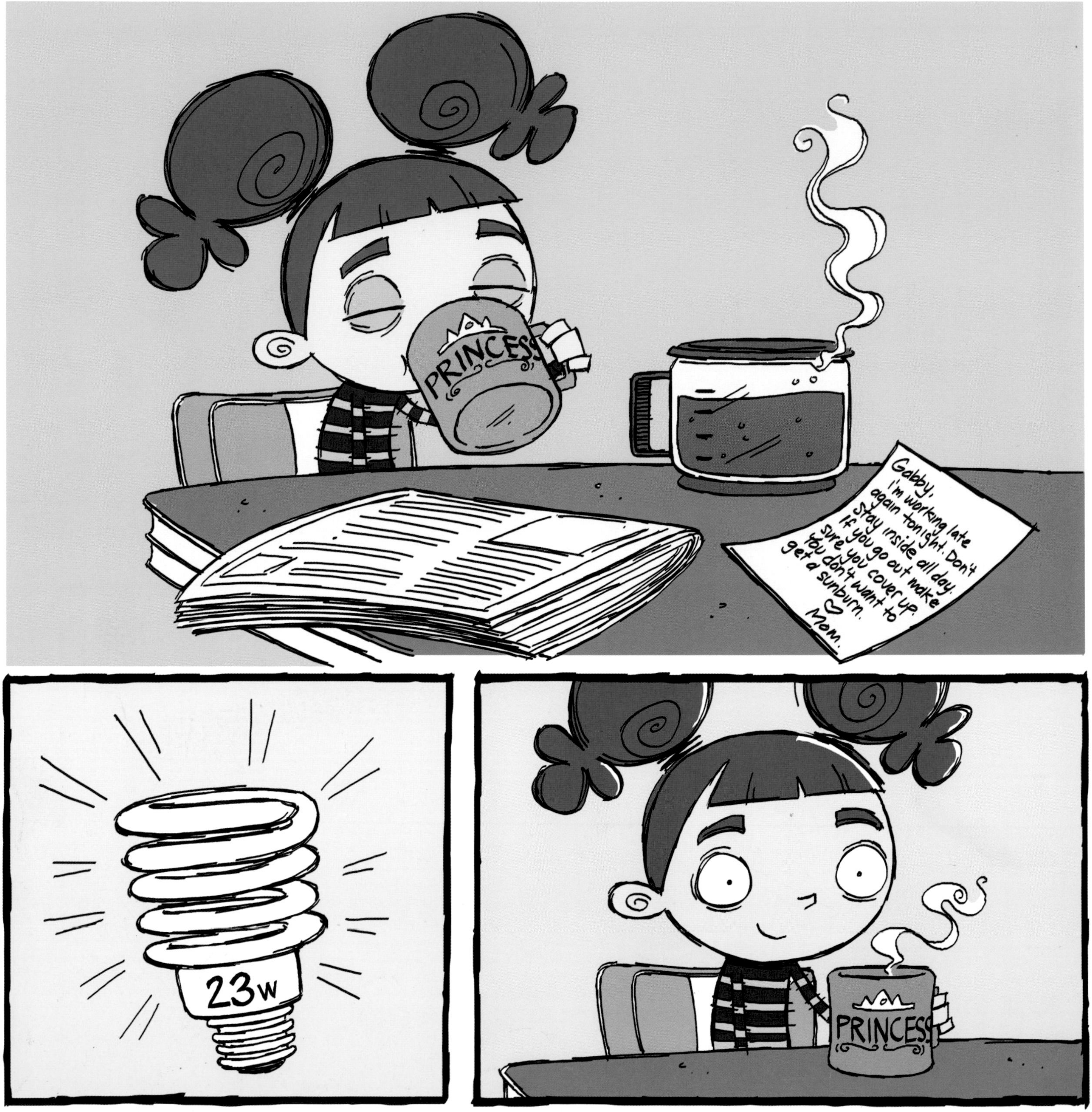
PRINCESS
Gabby,
I'm working late
again tonight. Don't
Stay inside all day.
If you go out make
sure you cover up.
You don't want to
get a sunburn.
Mom.
23w
PRINCESS

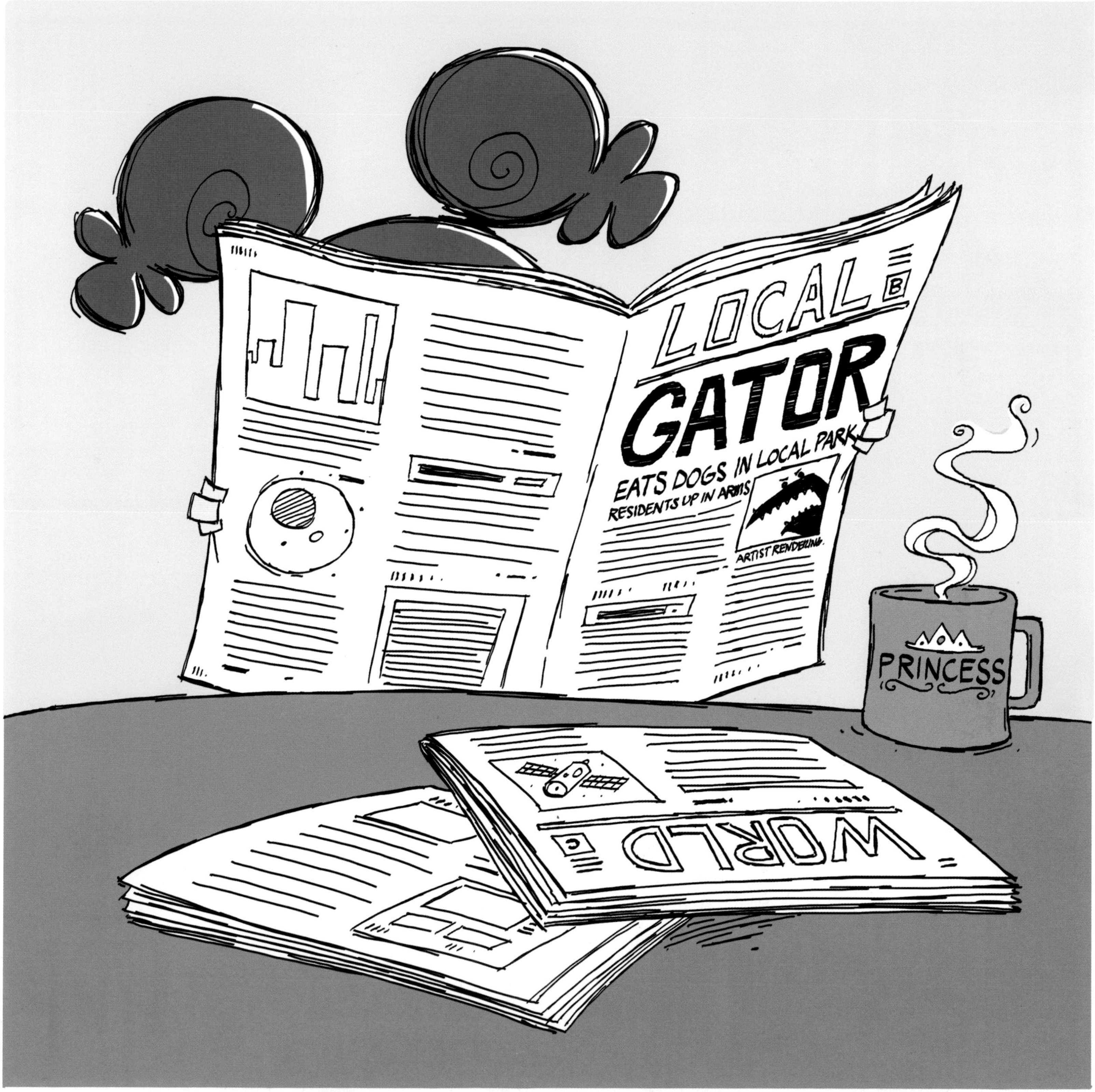
LOCAL B
GATOR
EATS DOGS IN LOCAL PARK
RESIDENTS UP IN ARMS
ARTIST RENDERING
PRINCESS
WORLD C

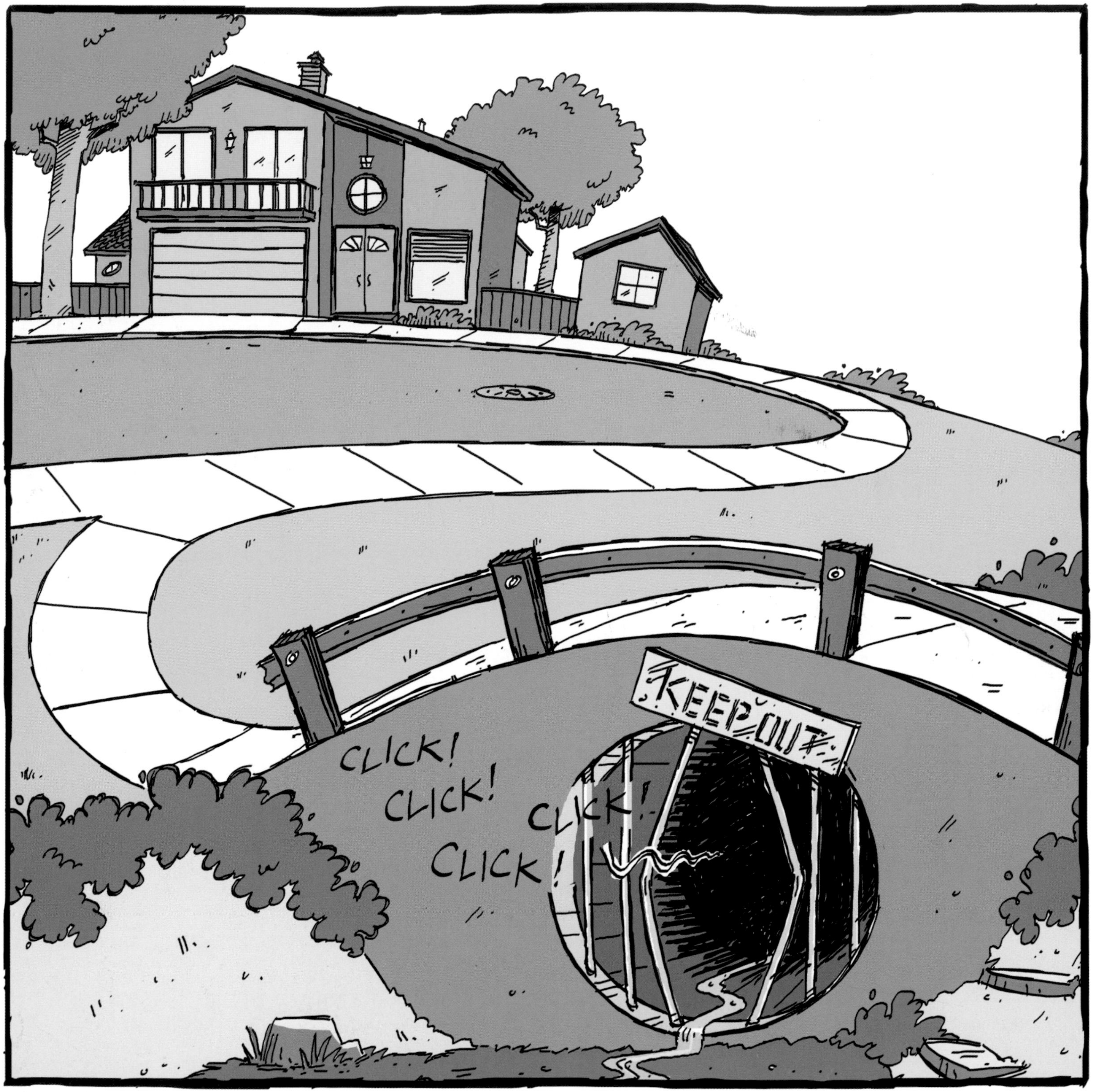
KEEP OUT
CLICK!
CLICK!
CLICK!
CLICK!

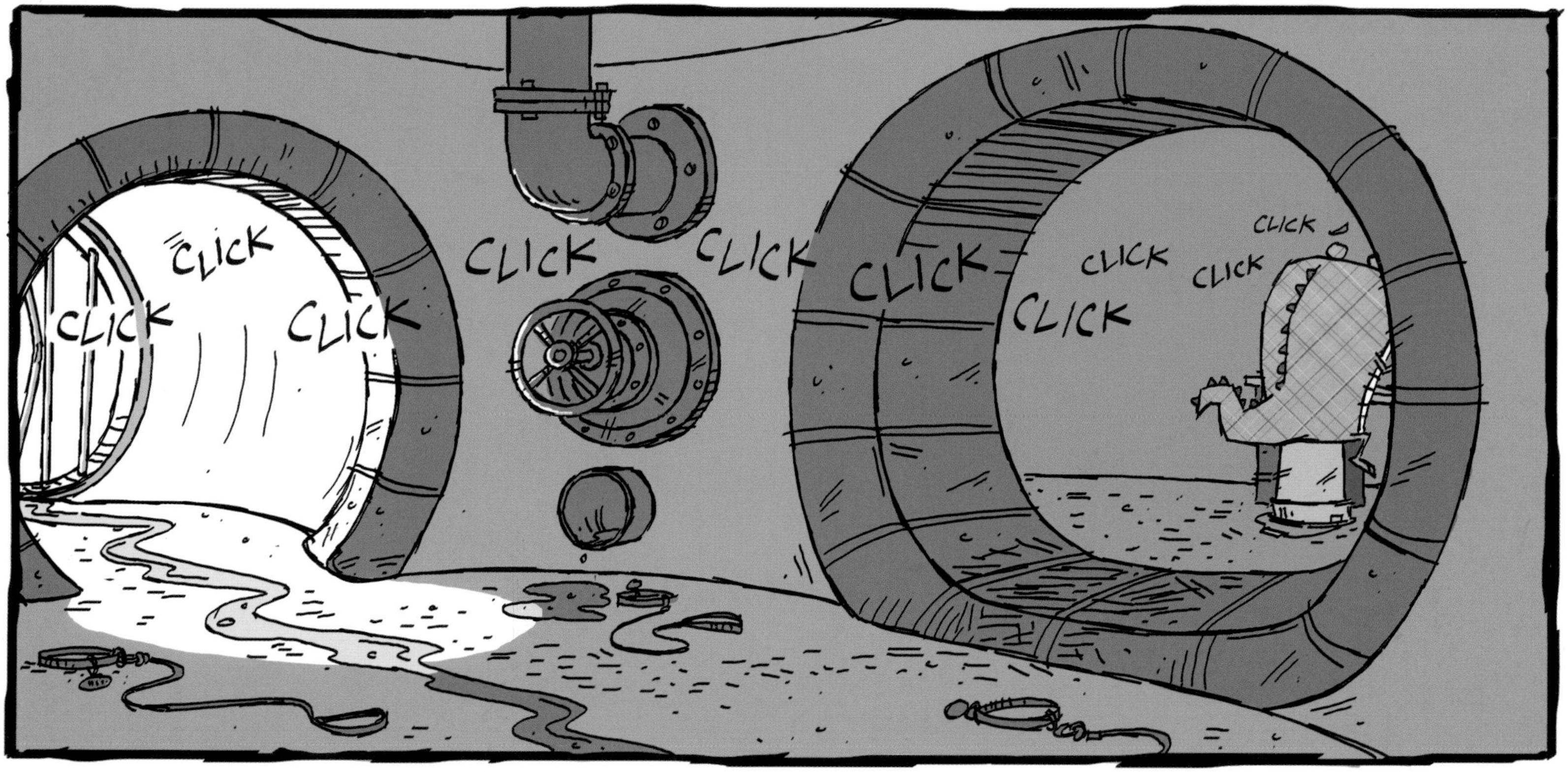

CLICK
CLICK
CLICK
CLICK
CLICK
CLICK
CLICK
CLICK
CLICK
CLICK

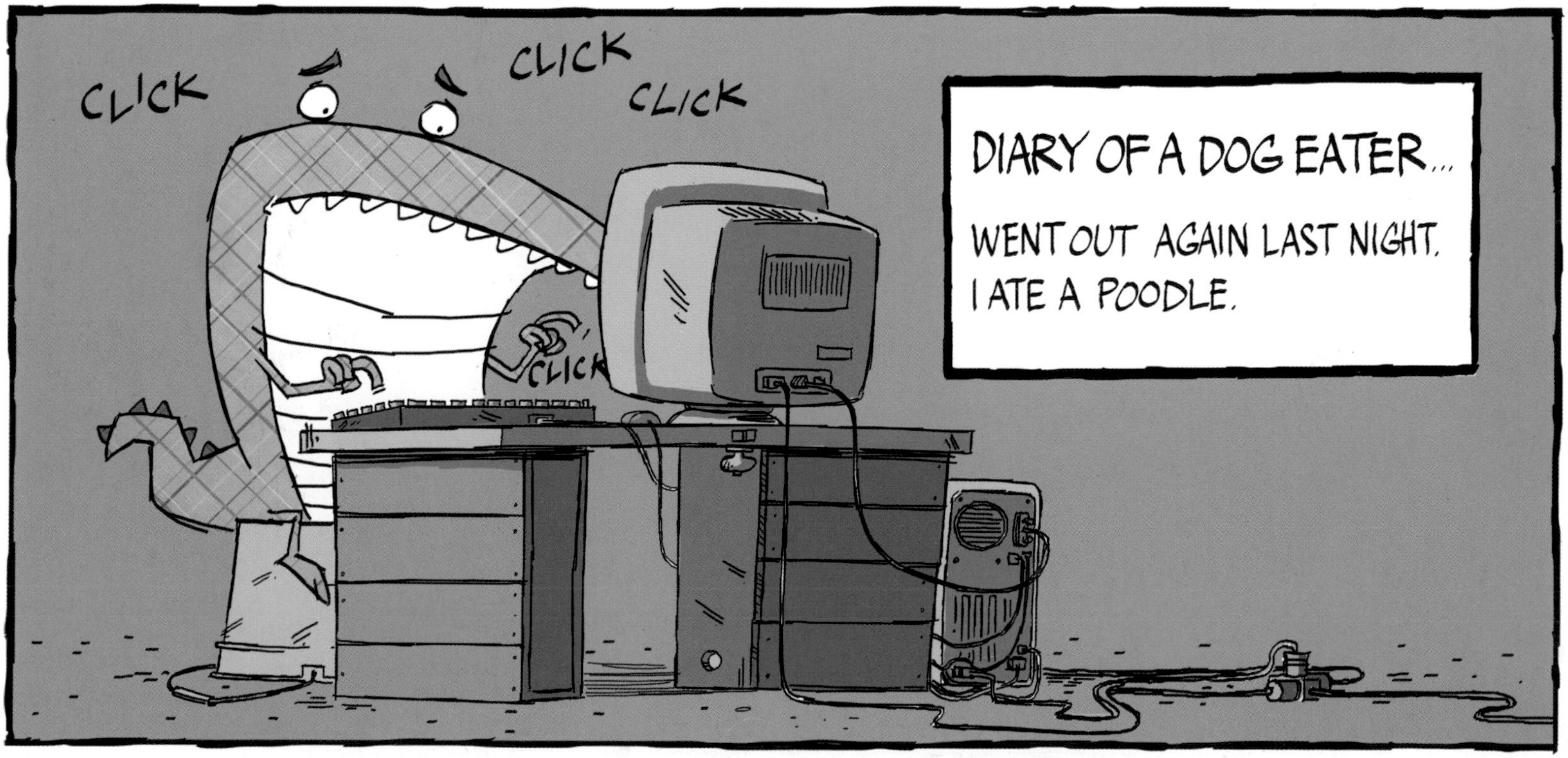

CLICK
CLICK
CLICK
CLICK
DIARY OF A DOG EATER...
WENT OUT AGAIN LAST NIGHT.
I ATE A POODLE.

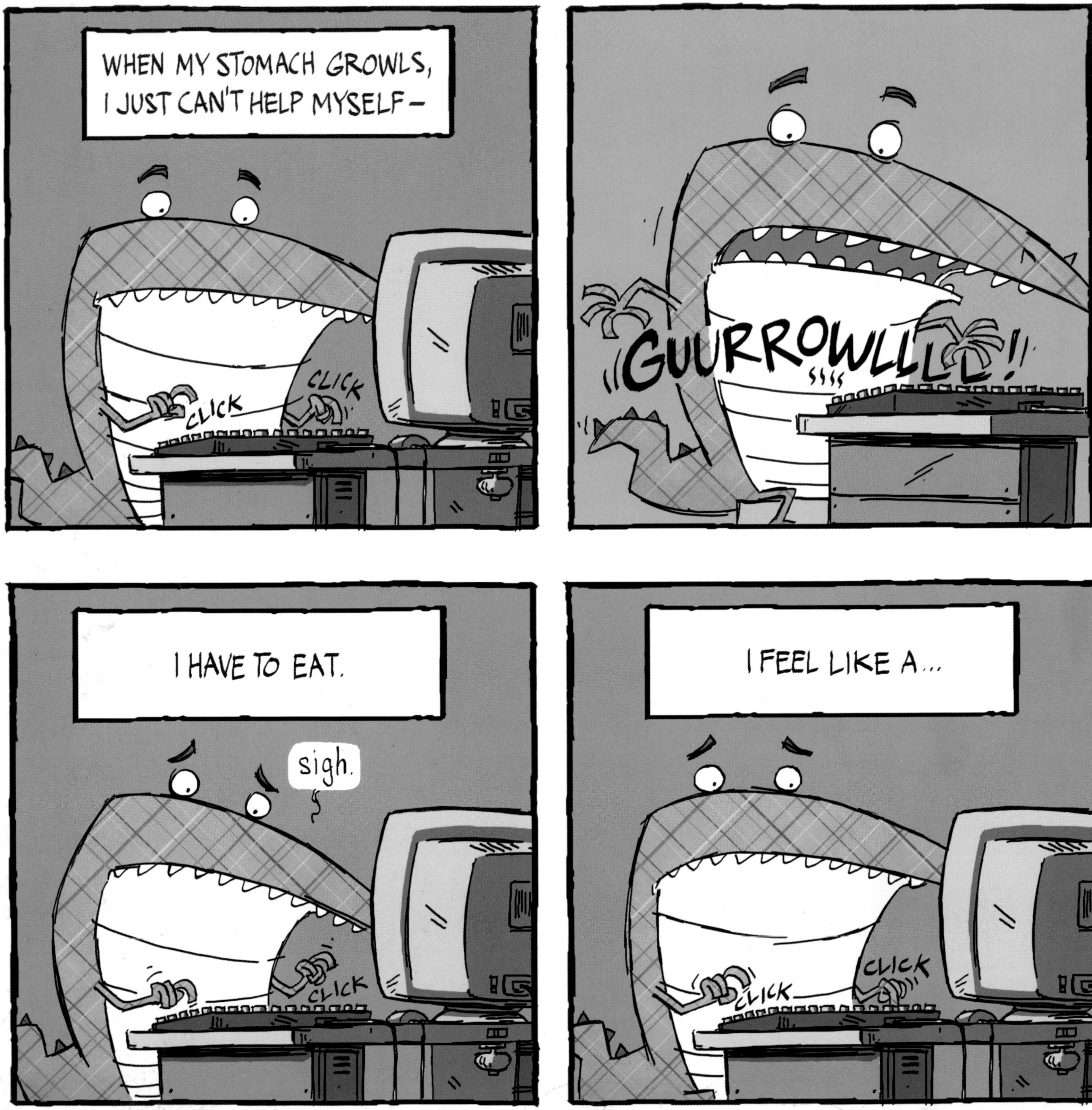
WHEN MY STOMACH GROWLS, I JUST CAN'T HELP MYSELF–
CLICK
CLICK
GUURROWLLLLL!
I HAVE TO EAT.
sigh.
CLICK
I FEEL LIKE A...
CLICK
CLICK

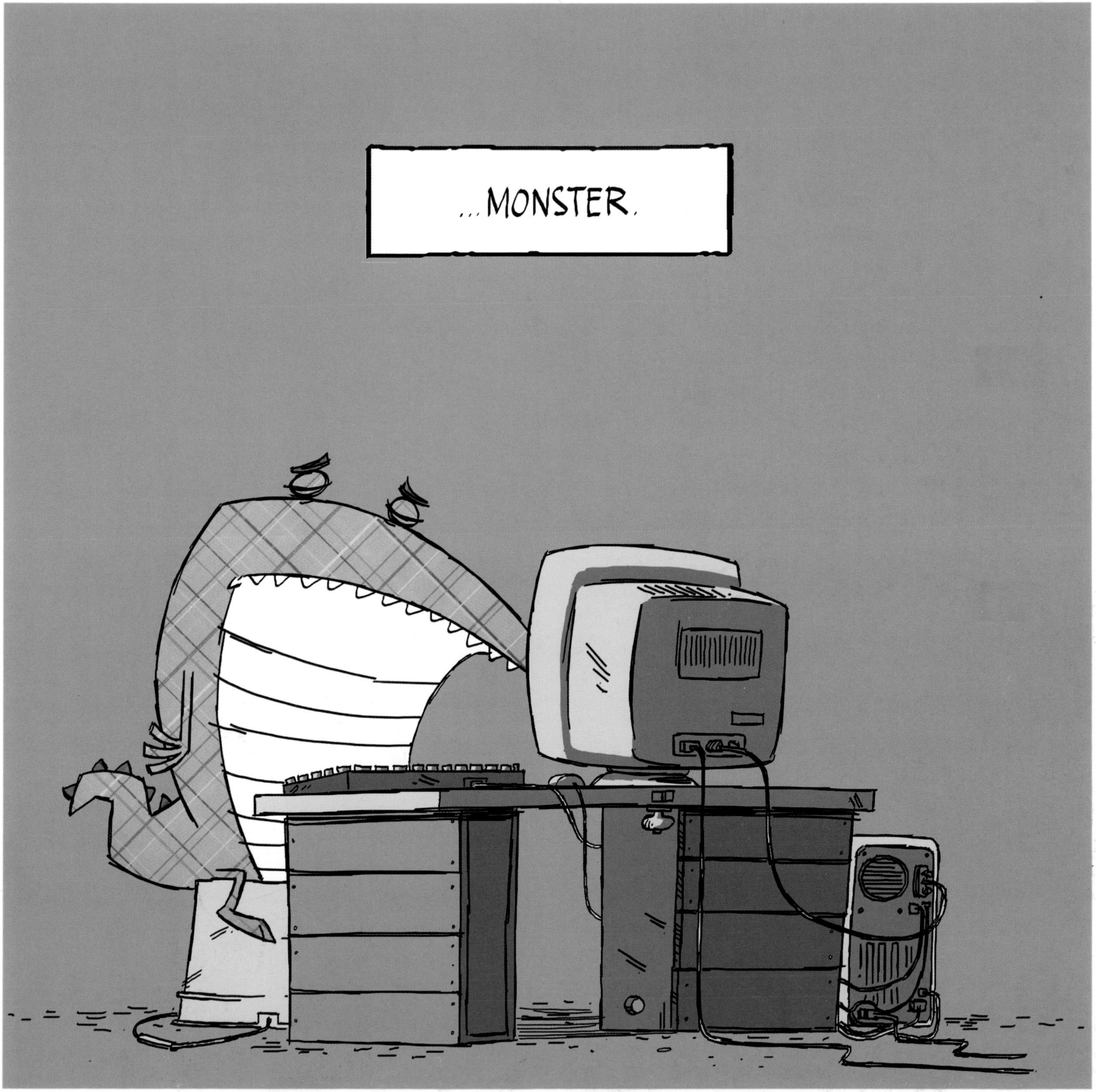
...MONSTER.

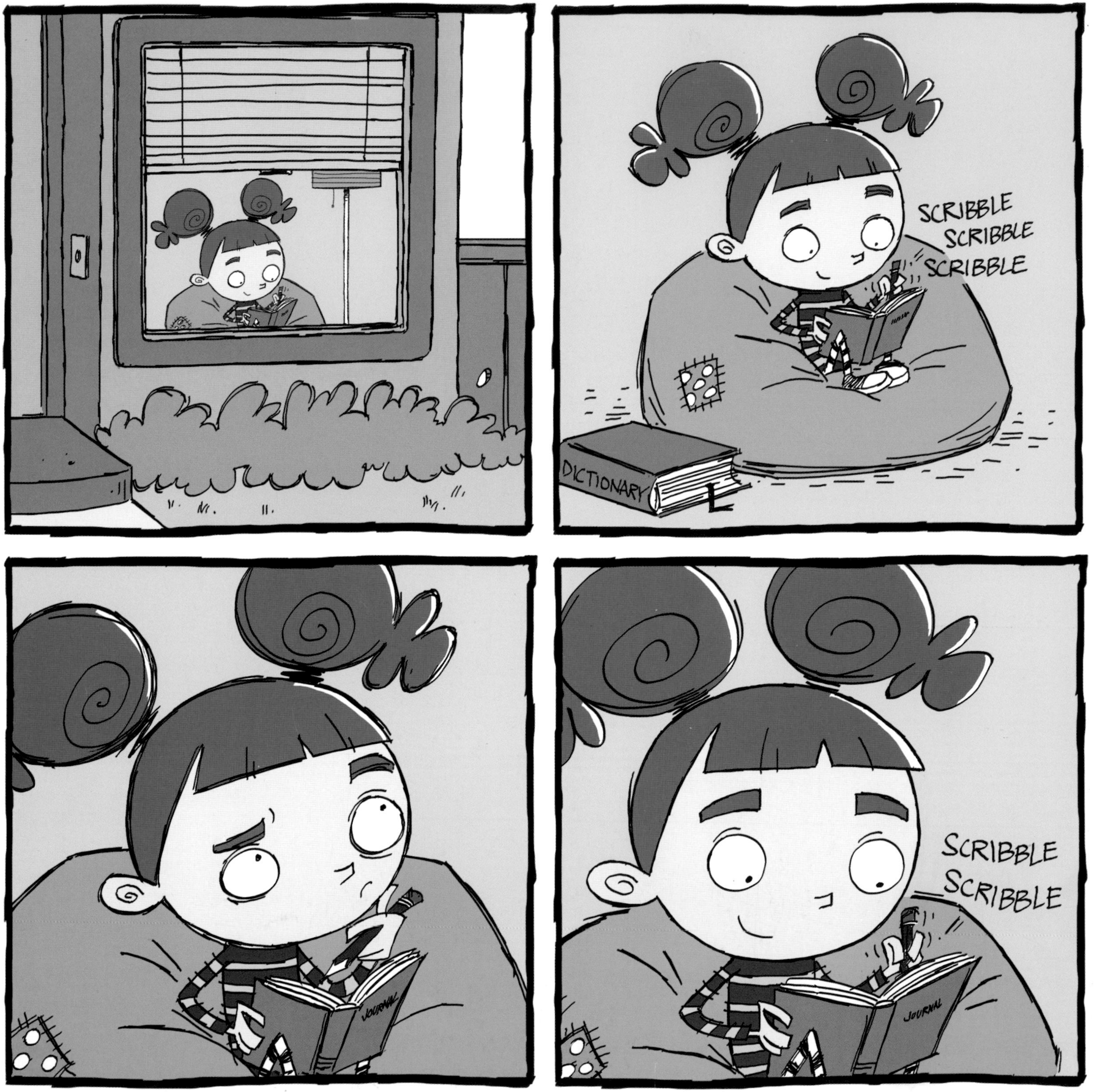
SCRIBBLE
SCRIBBLE
SCRIBBLE
DICTIONARY
JOURNAL
JOURNAL
SCRIBBLE
SCRIBBLE

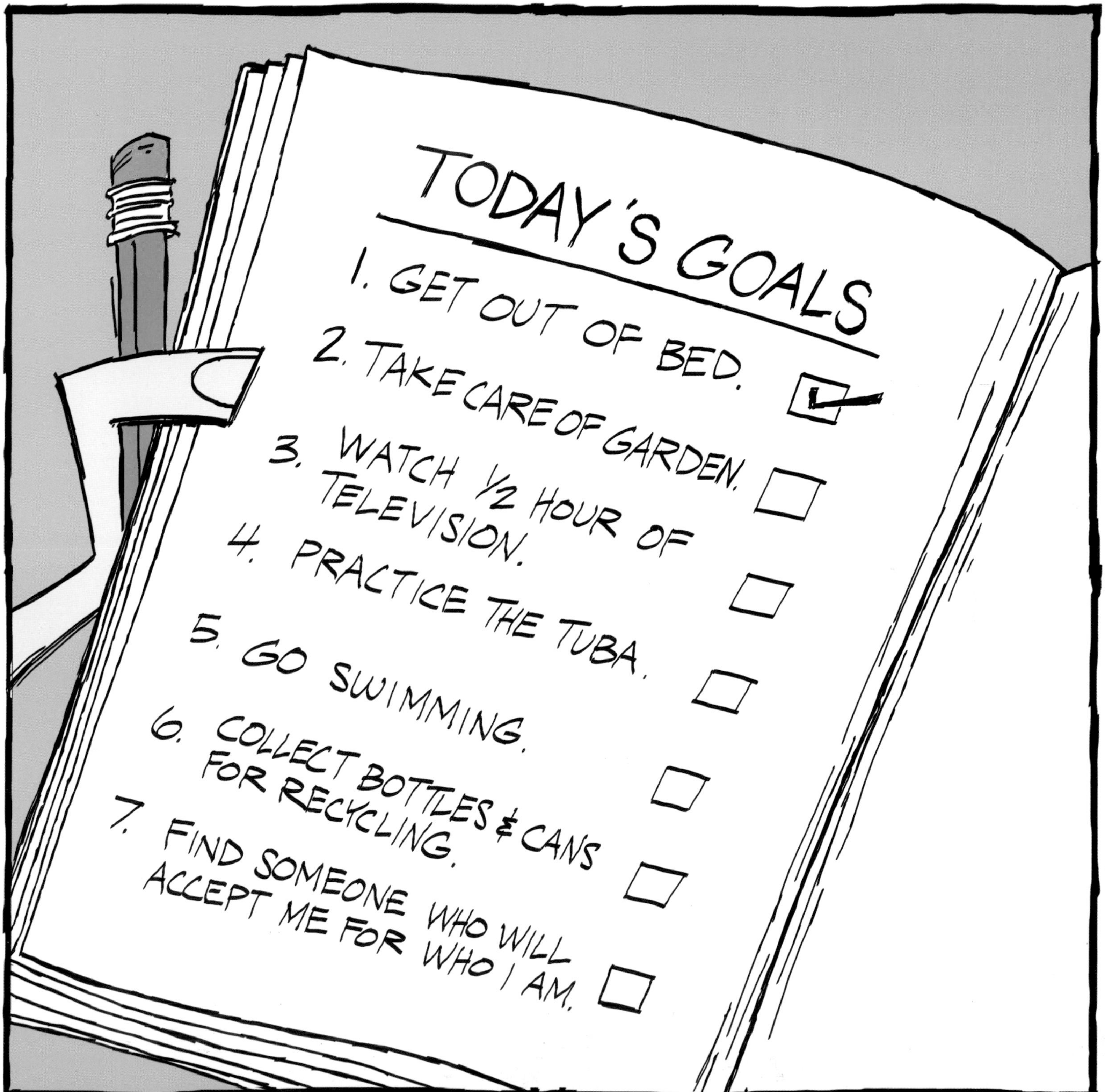

TODAY'S GOALS
1. GET OUT OF BED.
2. TAKE CARE OF GARDEN.
3. WATCH 1/2 HOUR OF TELEVISION.
4. PRACTICE THE TUBA.
5. GO SWIMMING.
6. COLLECT BOTTLES & CANS FOR RECYCLING.
7. FIND SOMEONE WHO WILL ACCEPT ME FOR WHO I AM.

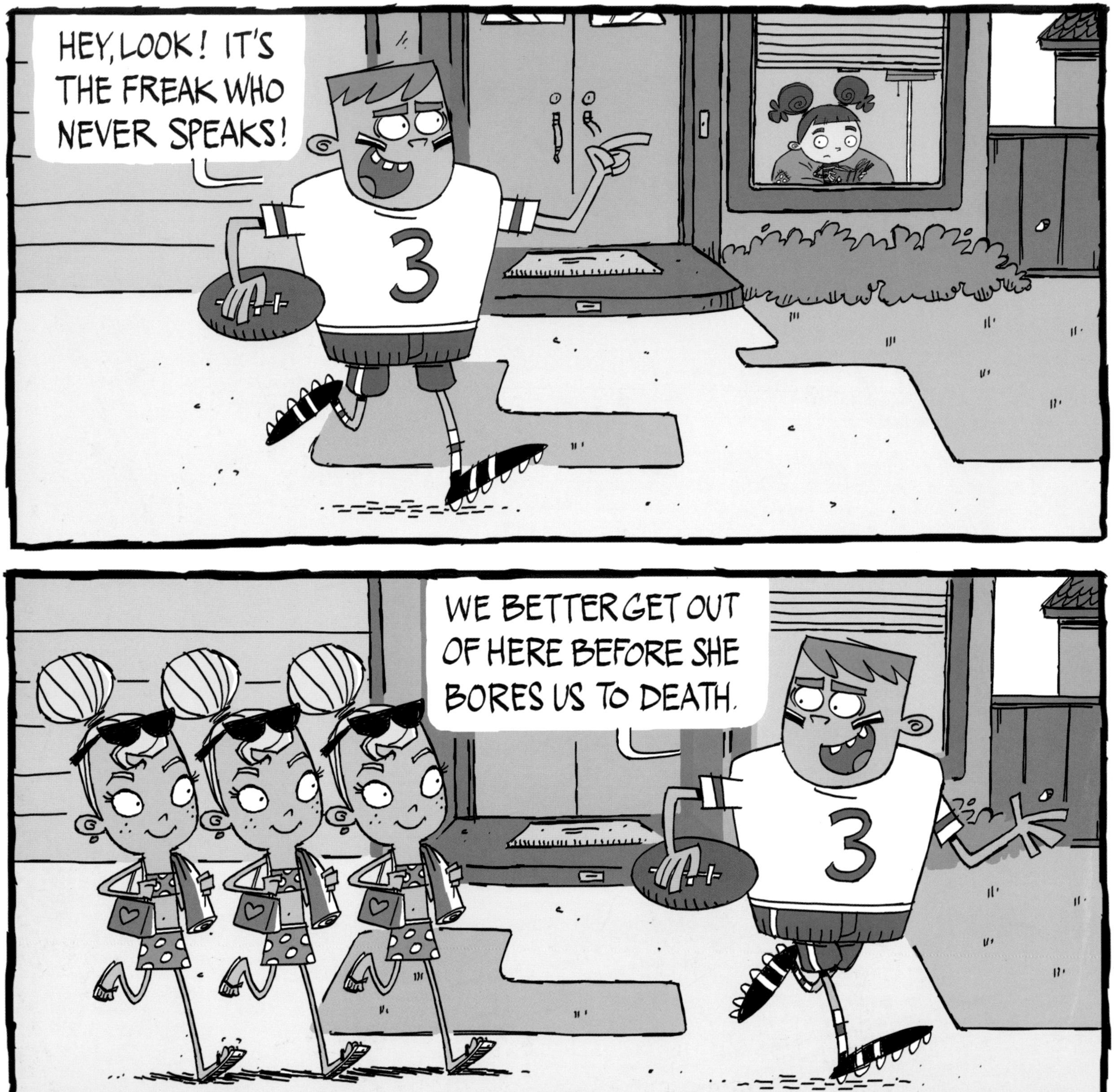
HEY, LOOK! IT'S THE FREAK WHO NEVER SPEAKS!
3
WE BETTER GET OUT OF HERE BEFORE SHE BORES US TO DEATH.
3

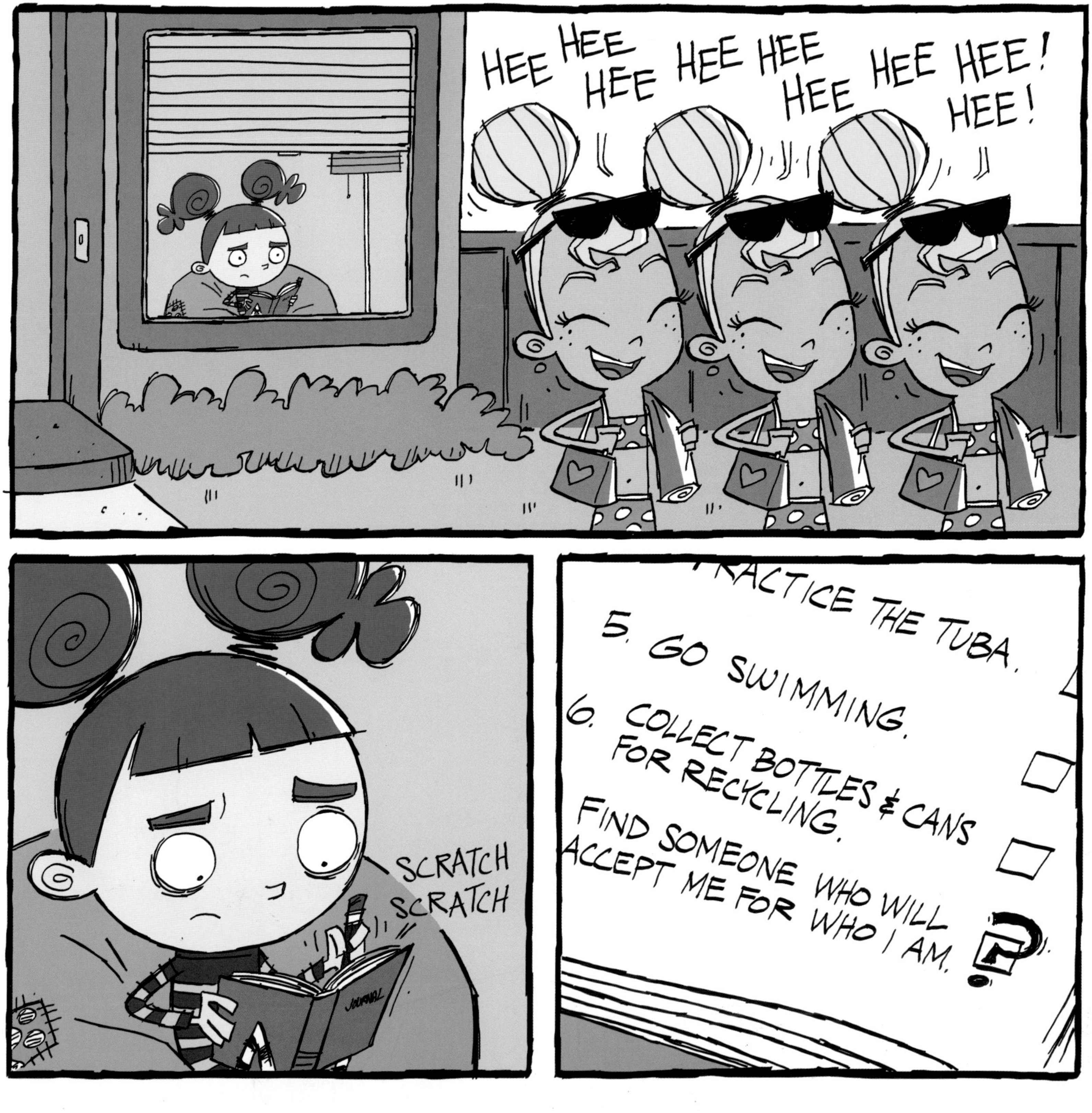
HEE HEE
HEE HEE HEE
HEE HEE HEE!
HEE!
SCRATCH
SCRATCH
JOURNAL
RACTICE THE TUBA.
5. GO SWIMMING.
6. COLLECT BOTTLES & CANS FOR RECYCLING.
FIND SOMEONE WHO WILL ACCEPT ME FOR WHO I AM.
?

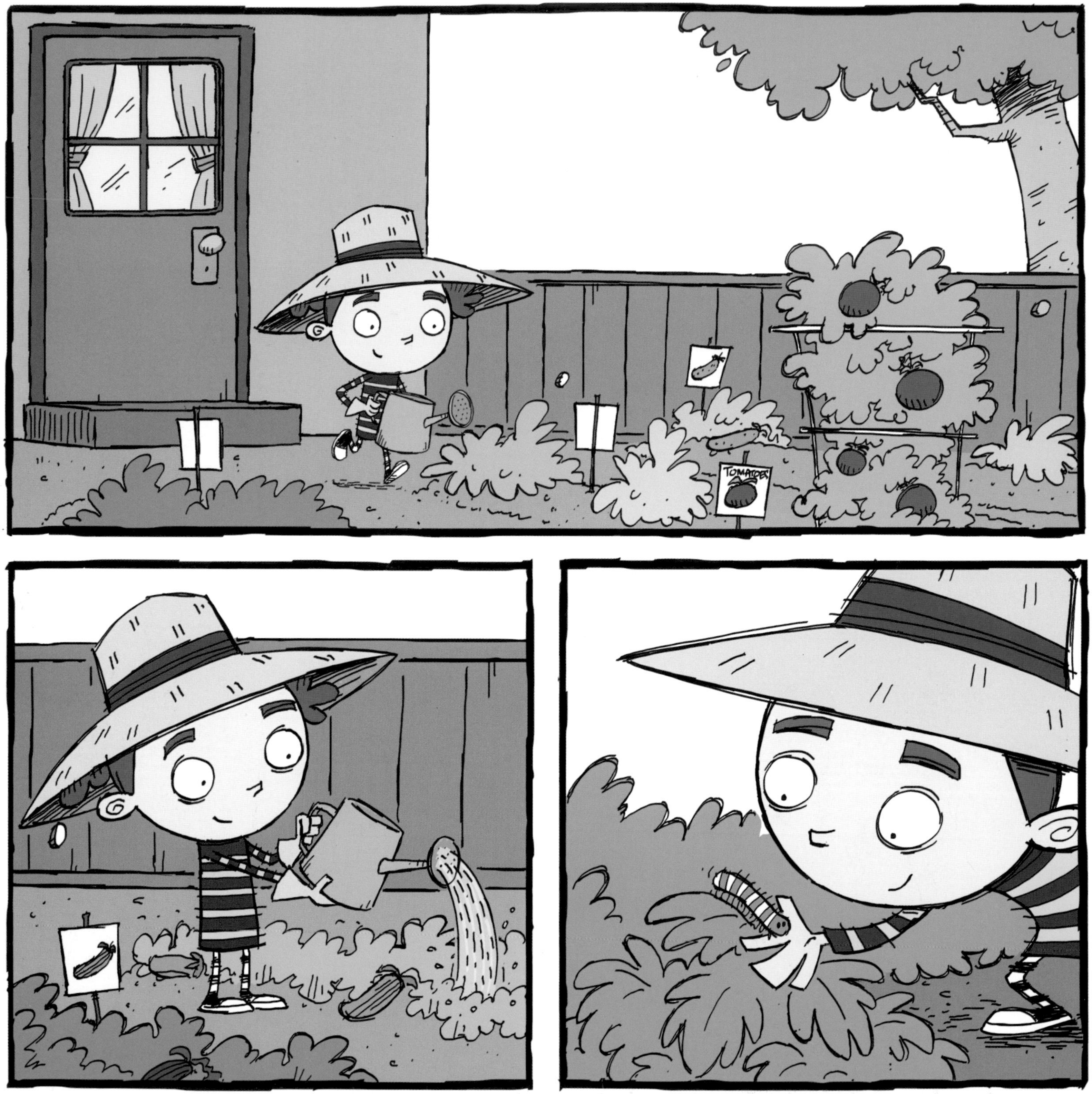
TOMATOES

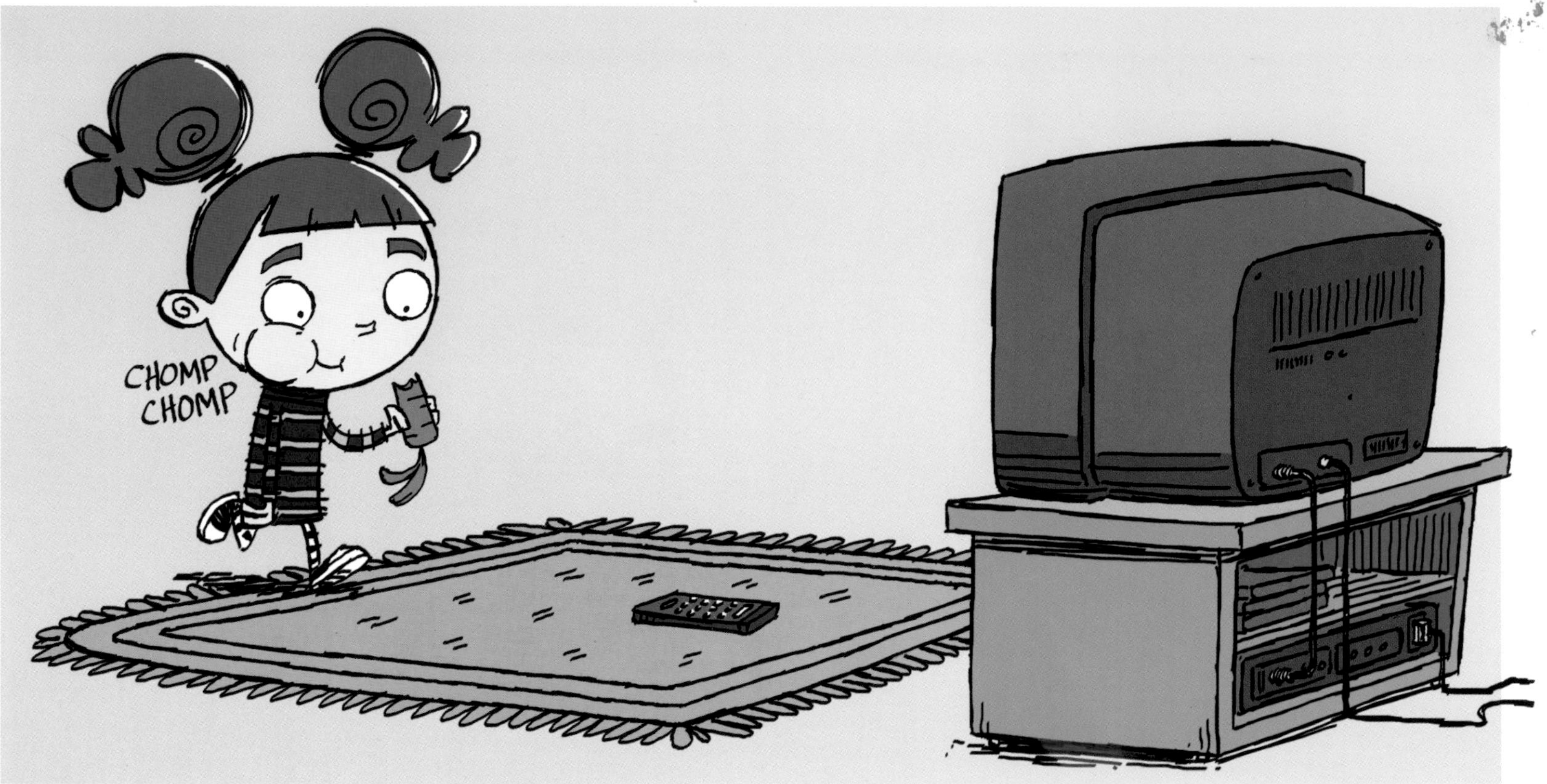
CHOMP
CHOMP

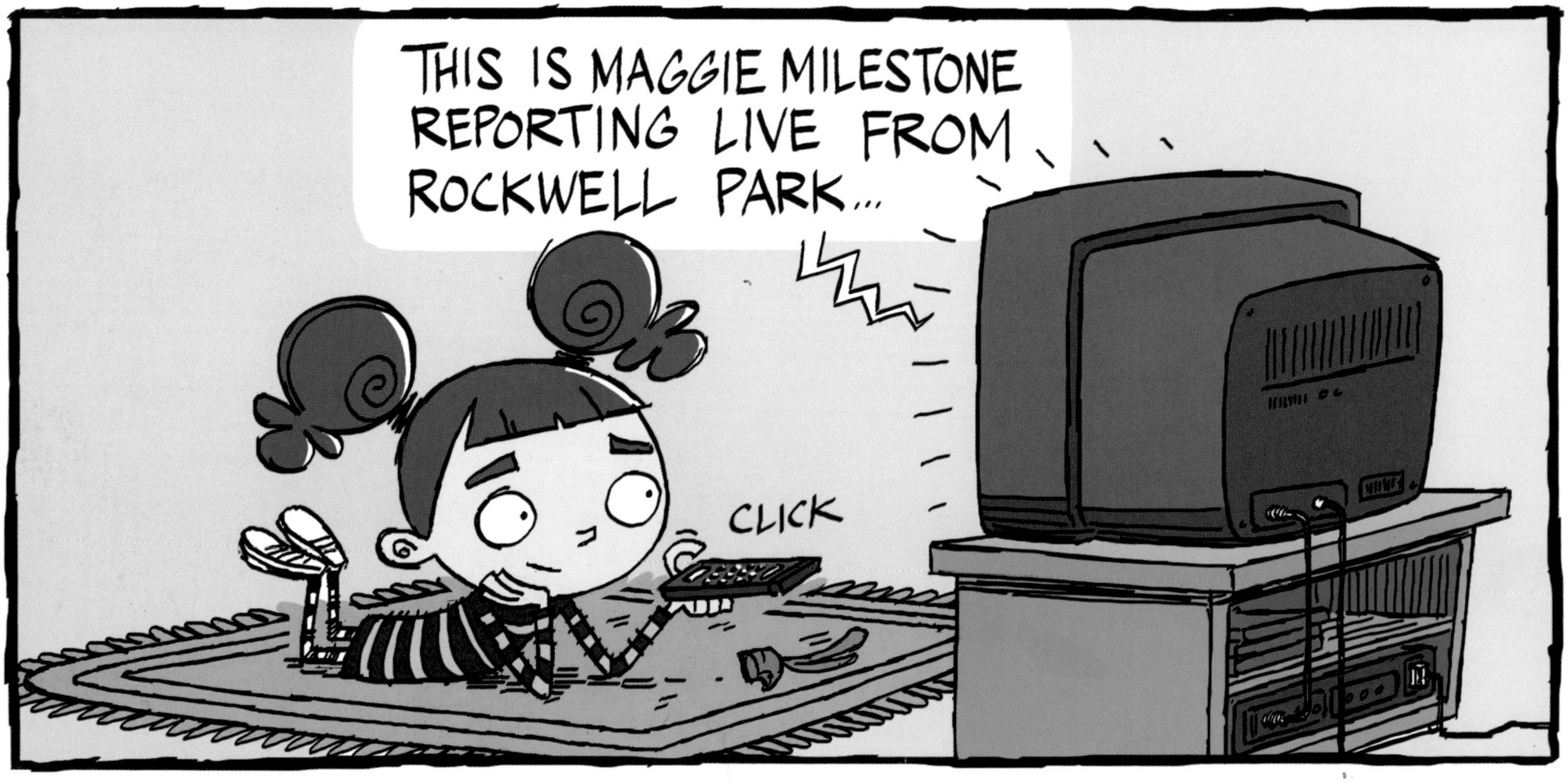
THIS IS MAGGIE MILESTONE REPORTING LIVE FROM ROCKWELL PARK...
CLICK

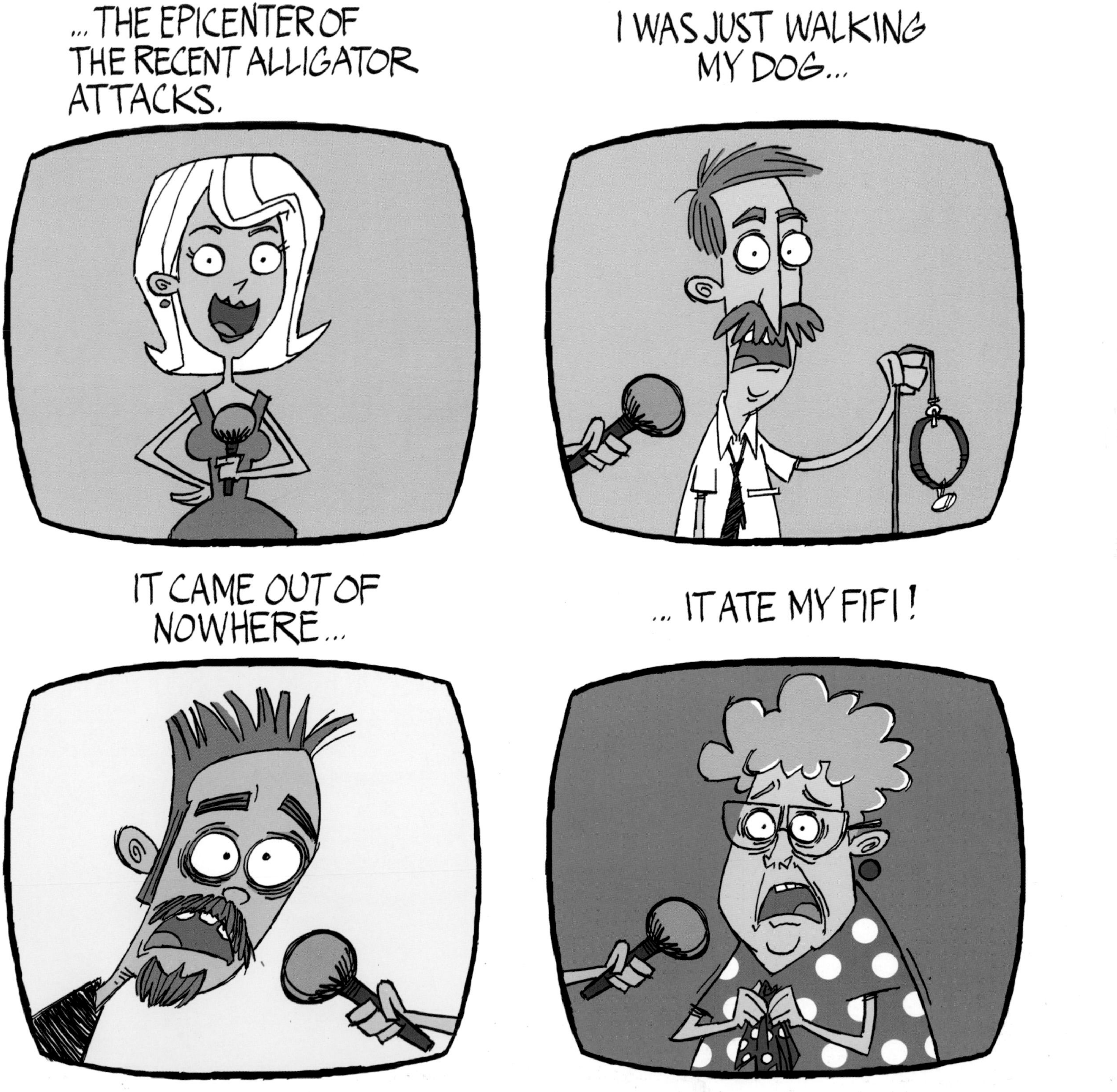
... THE EPICENTER OF THE RECENT ALLIGATOR ATTACKS.
I WAS JUST WALKING MY DOG...
IT CAME OUT OF NOWHERE...
... IT ATE MY FIFI!

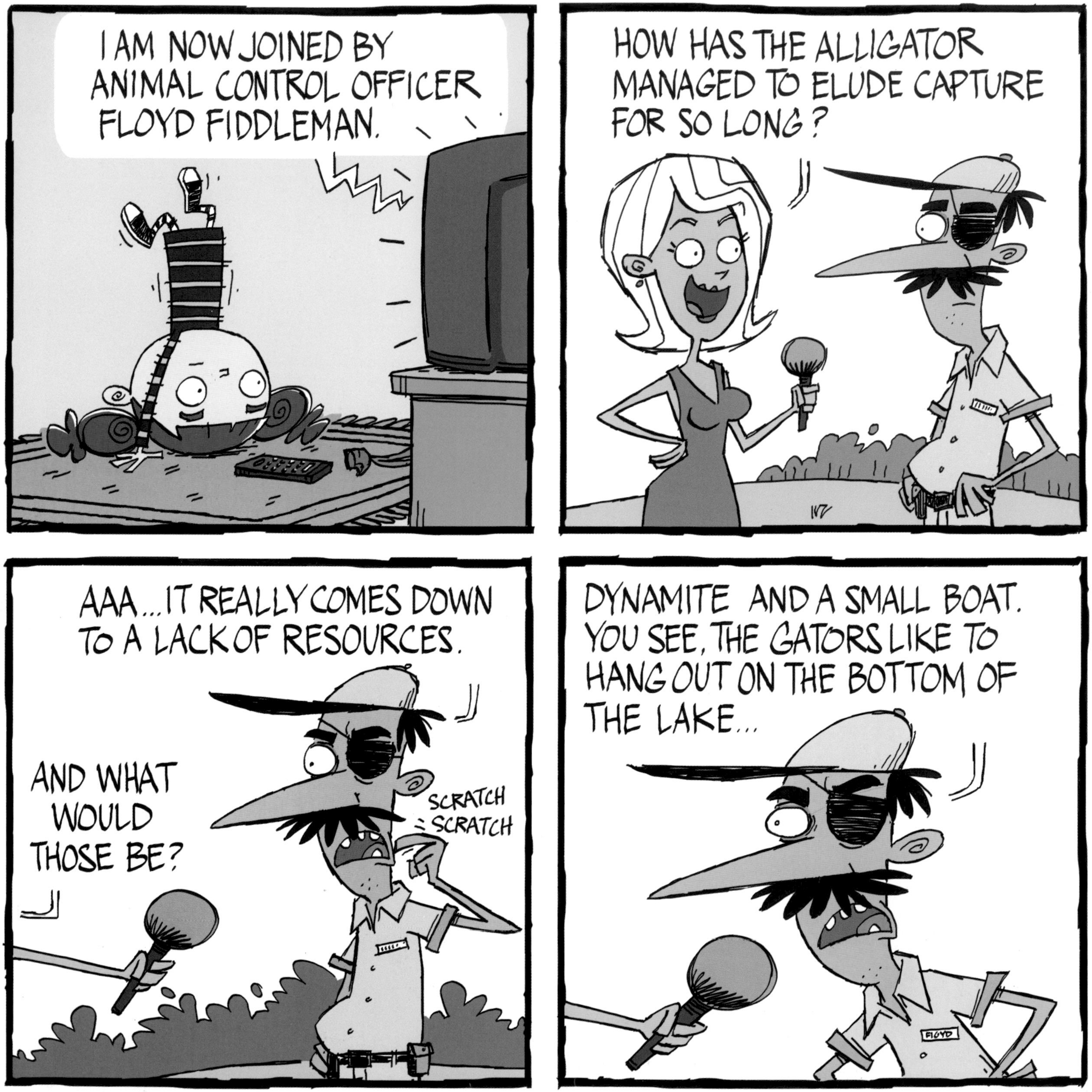
I AM NOW JOINED BY ANIMAL CONTROL OFFICER FLOYD FIDDLEMAN.
HOW HAS THE ALLIGATOR MANAGED TO ELUDE CAPTURE FOR SO LONG?
AAA... IT REALLY COMES DOWN TO A LACK OF RESOURCES.
AND WHAT WOULD THOSE BE?
SCRATCH SCRATCH
DYNAMITE AND A SMALL BOAT. YOU SEE, THE GATORS LIKE TO HANG OUT ON THE BOTTOM OF THE LAKE...
FLOYD

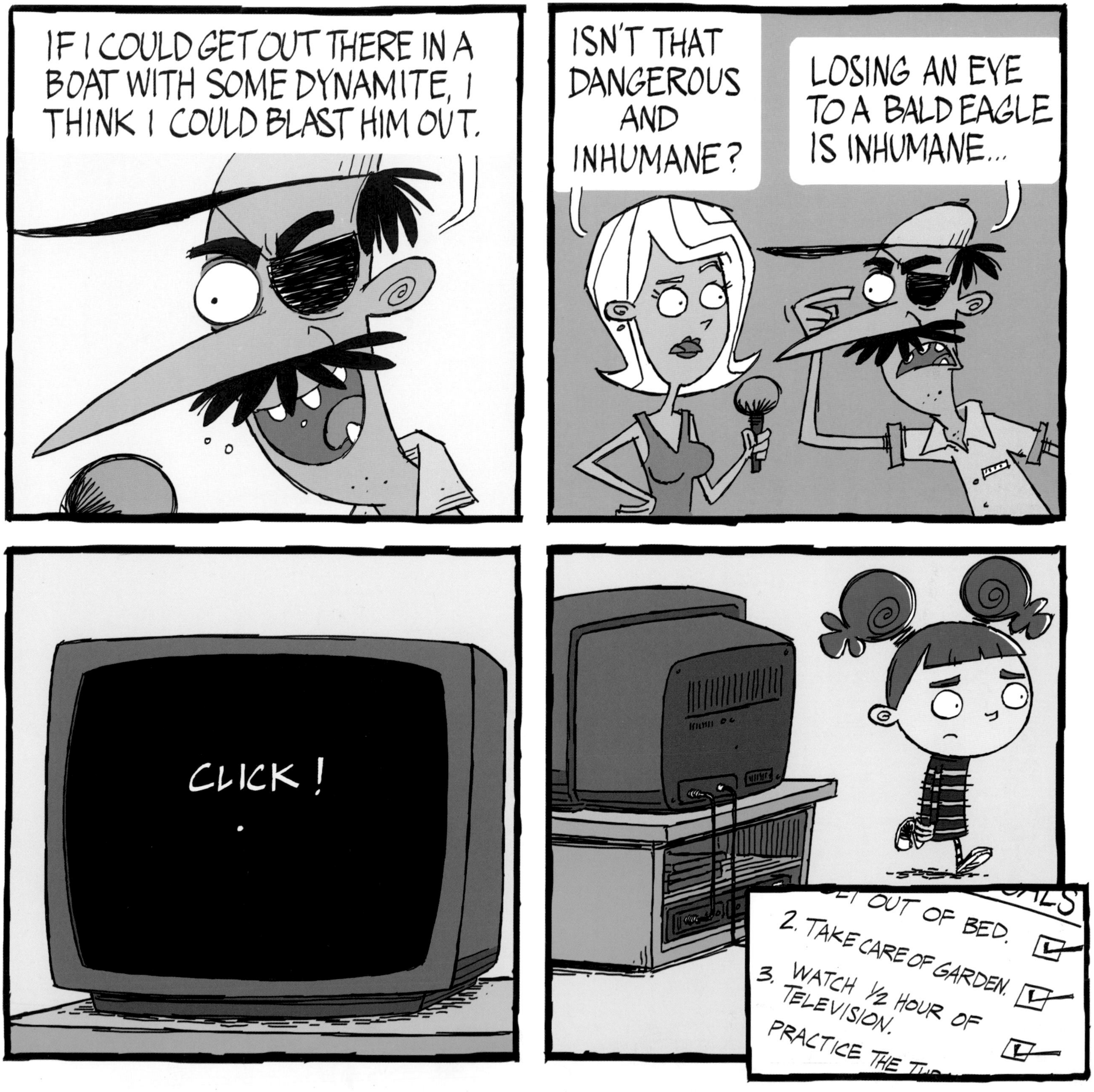
IF I COULD GET OUT THERE IN A BOAT WITH SOME DYNAMITE, I THINK I COULD BLAST HIM OUT.
ISN'T THAT DANGEROUS AND INHUMANE?
LOSING AN EYE TO A BALD EAGLE IS INHUMANE...
CLICK!
OUT OF BED.
2. TAKE CARE OF GARDEN.
3. WATCH 1/2 HOUR OF TELEVISION.
PRACTICE THE

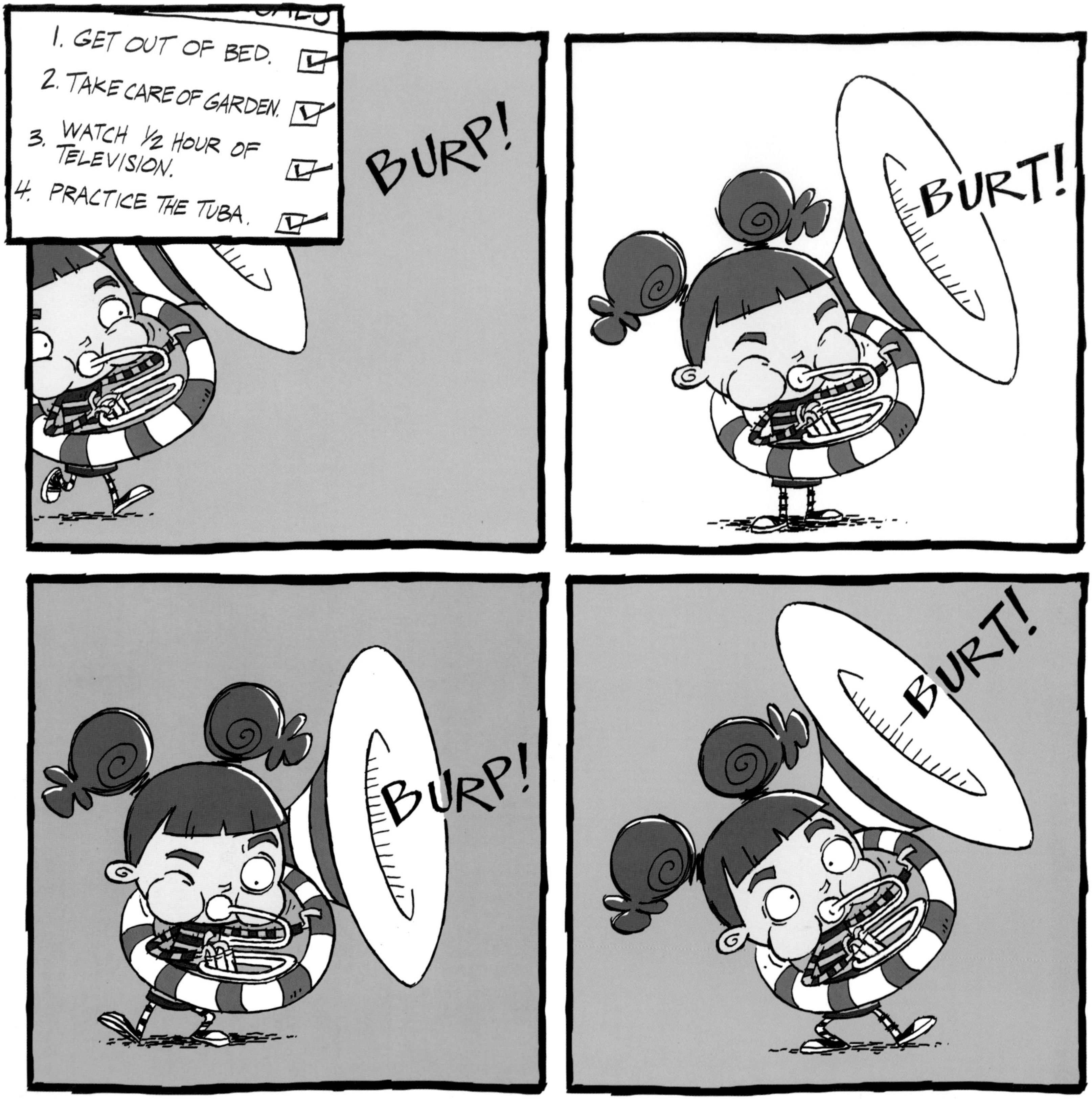
1. GET OUT OF BED.
2. TAKE CARE OF GARDEN.
3. WATCH 1/2 HOUR OF TELEVISION.
4. PRACTICE THE TUBA.
BURP!
BURT!
BURP!
BURT!

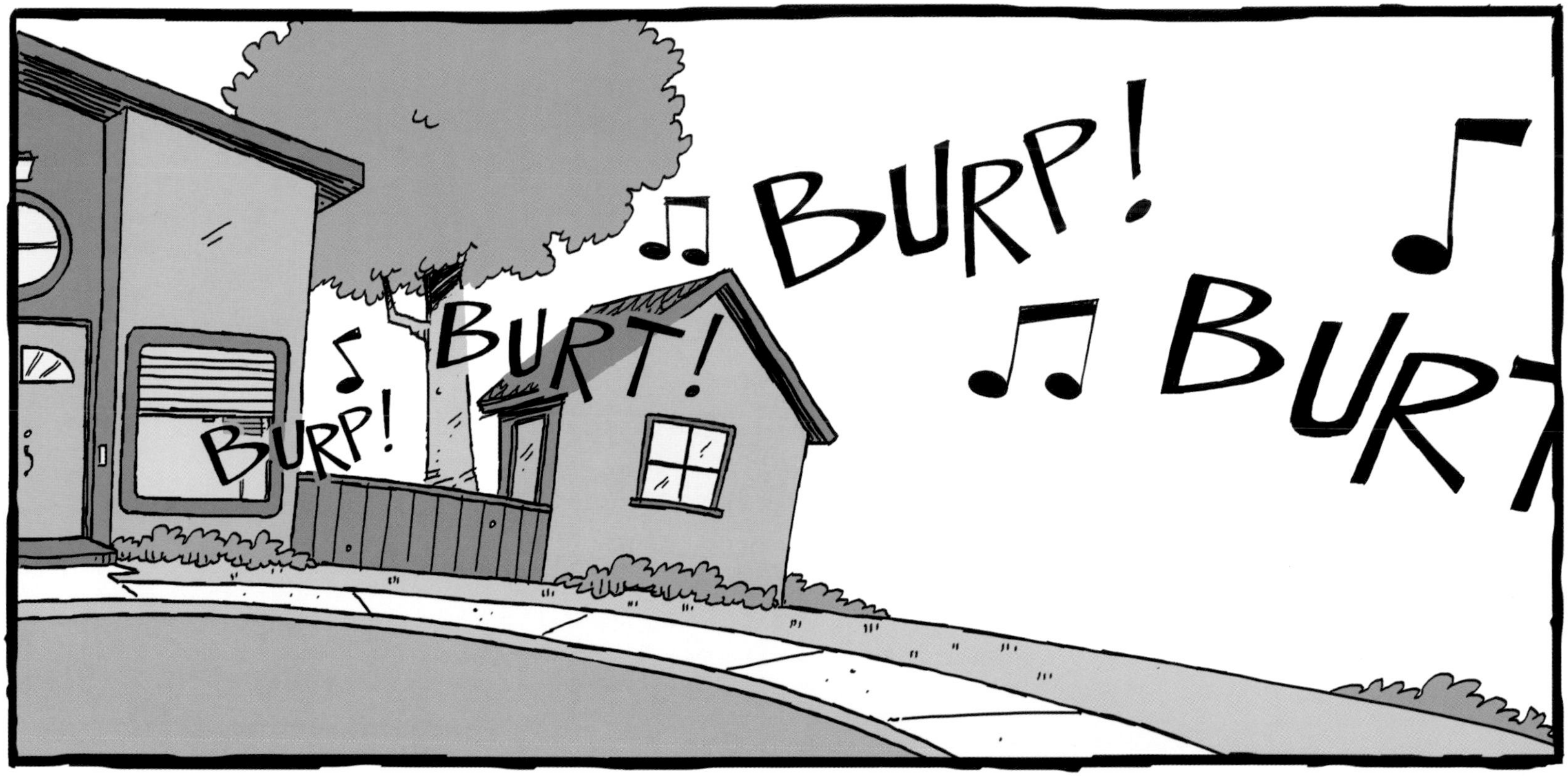

BURP!
BURT!
BURP!
BURT

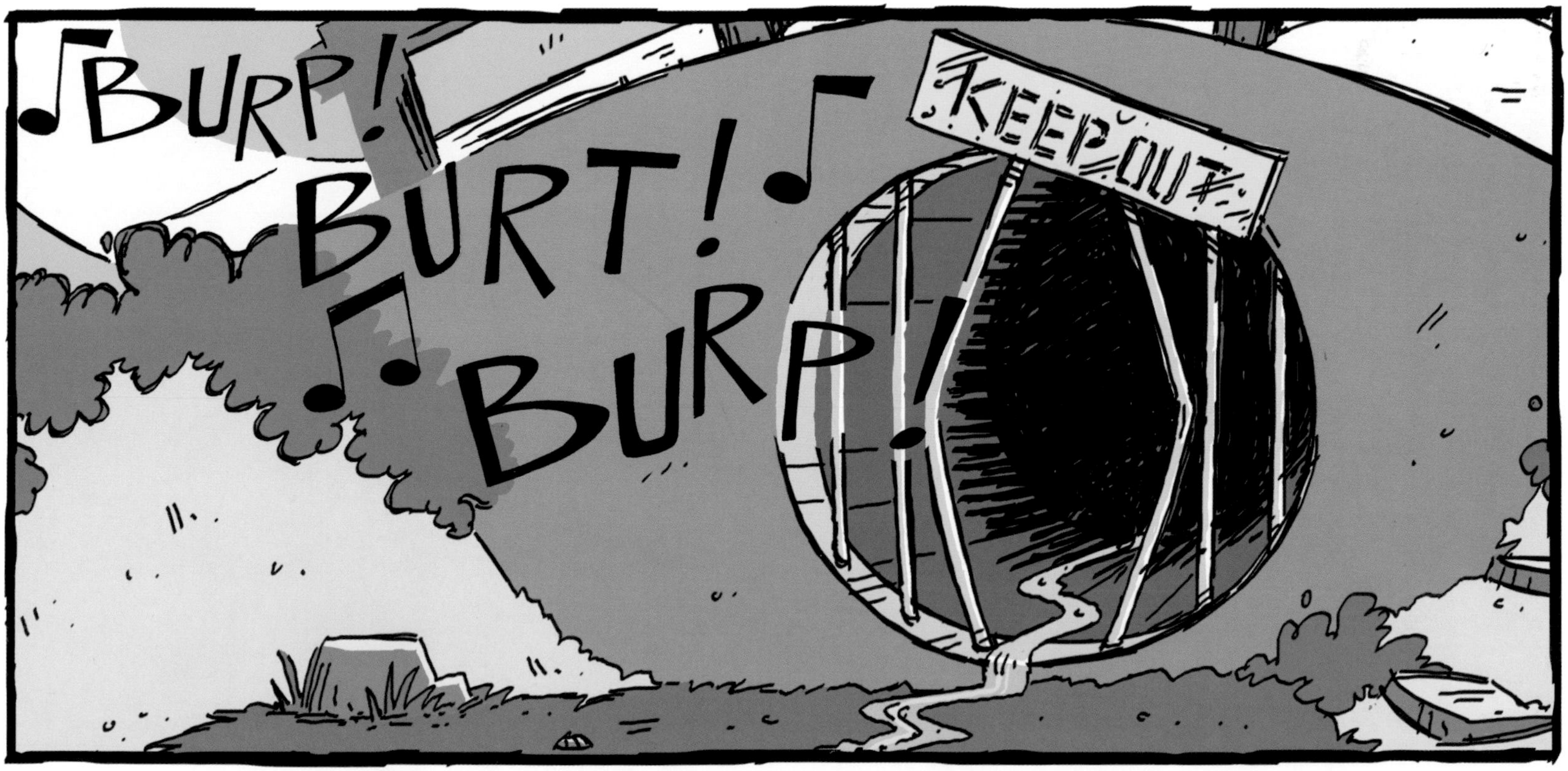

BURP!
BURT!
BURP!
KEEP OUT

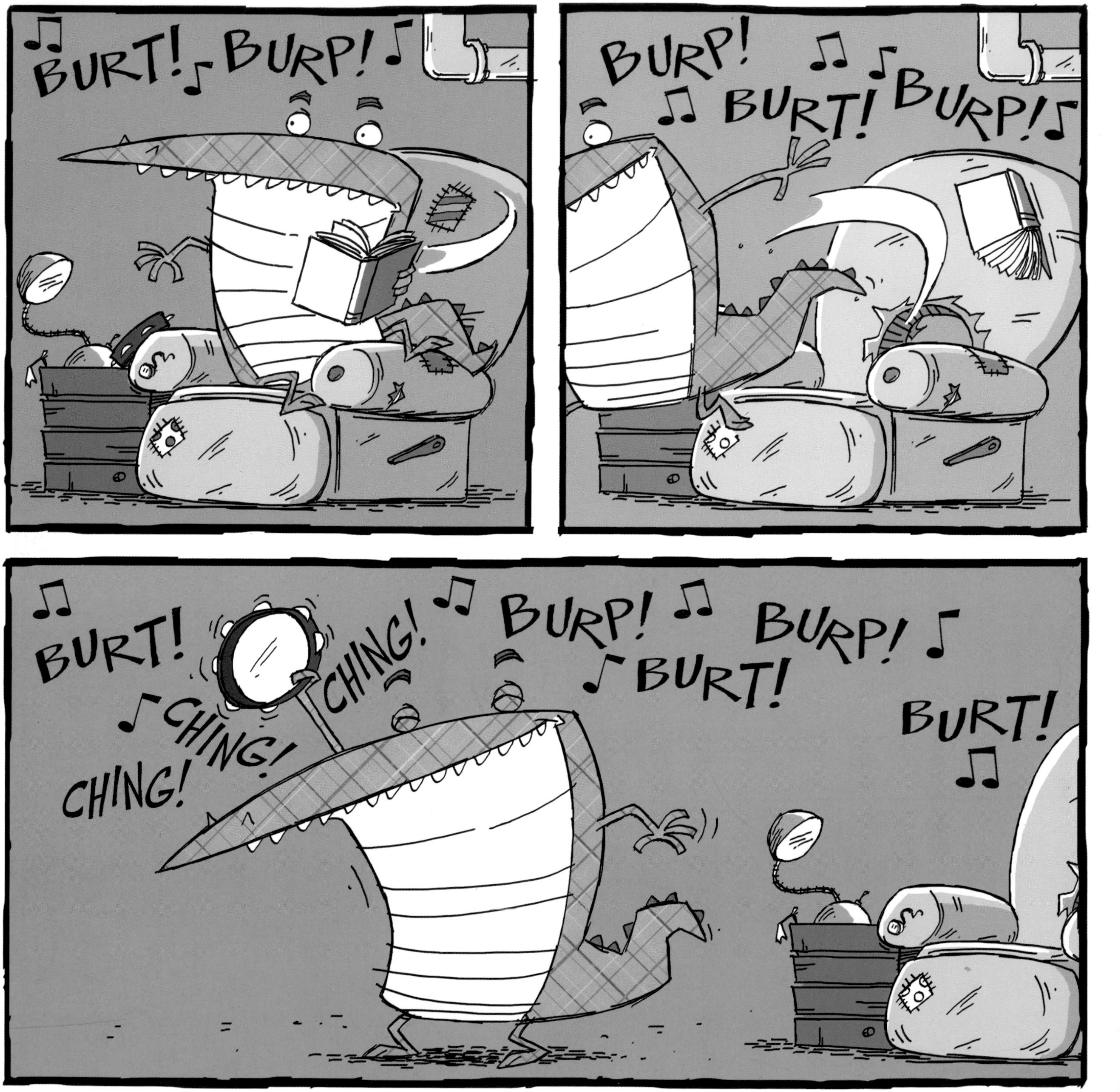
BURT! BURP!
BURP!
BURT! BURP!
BURT!
CHING!
CHING!
CHING!
BURP!
BURT!
BURP!
BURT!

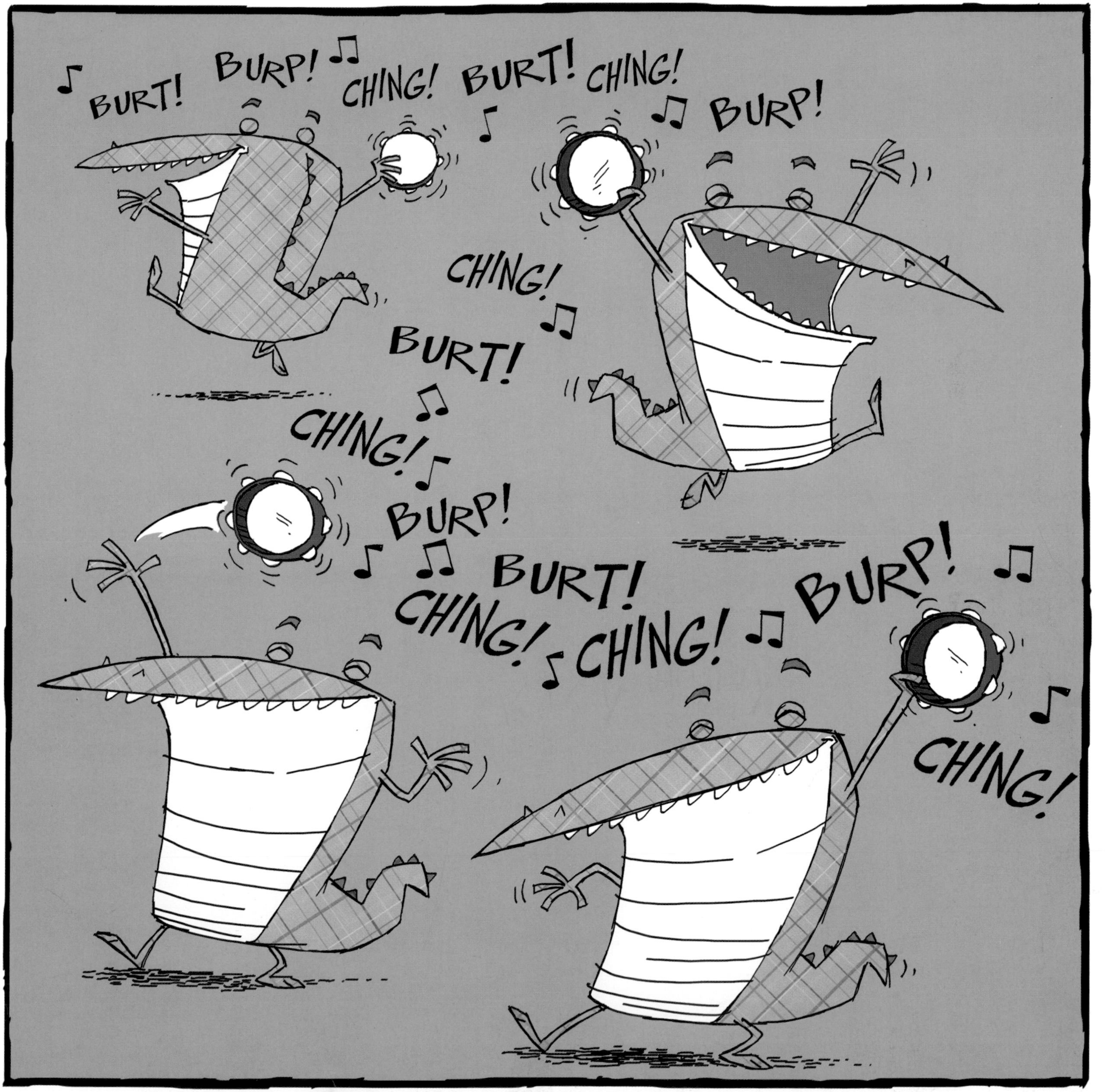
BURT! BURP! CHING! BURT! CHING! BURP!
CHING!
BURT!
CHING!
BURP!
BURT!
CHING! CHING! BURP!
CHING!

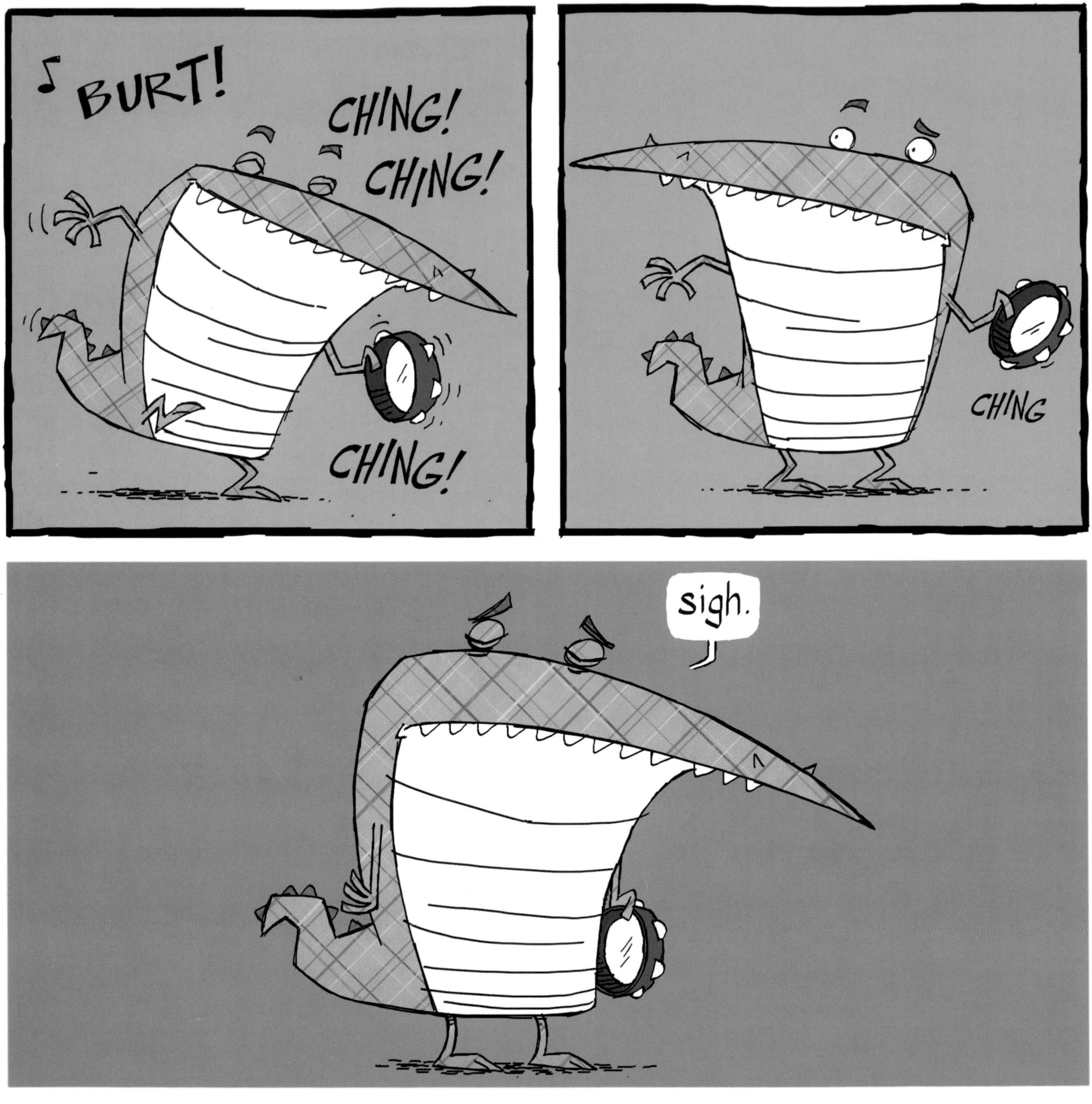
♪ BURT!
CHING!
CHING!
CHING!
CHING
sigh.

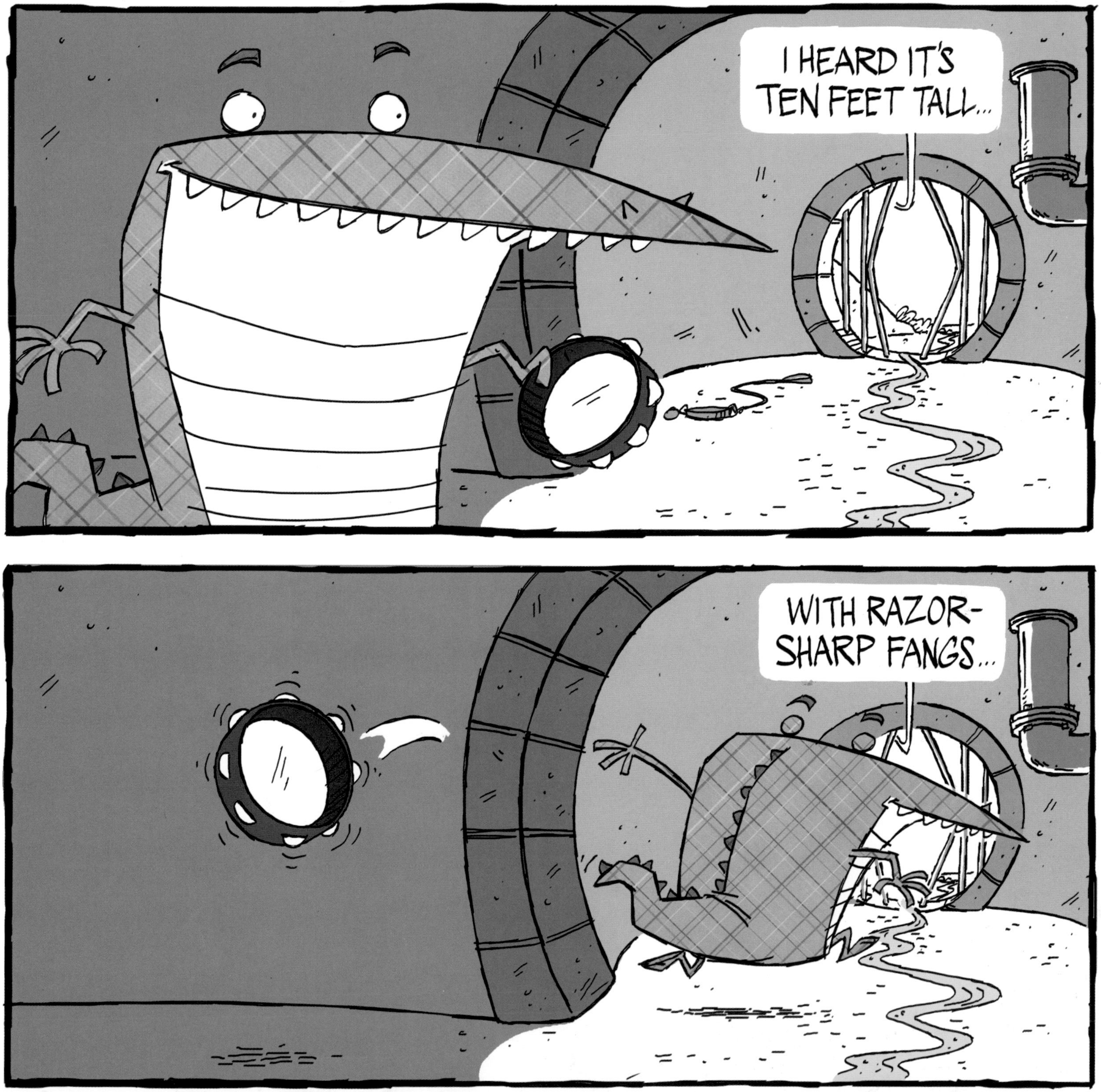
I HEARD IT'S TEN FEET TALL...
WITH RAZOR-SHARP FANGS...

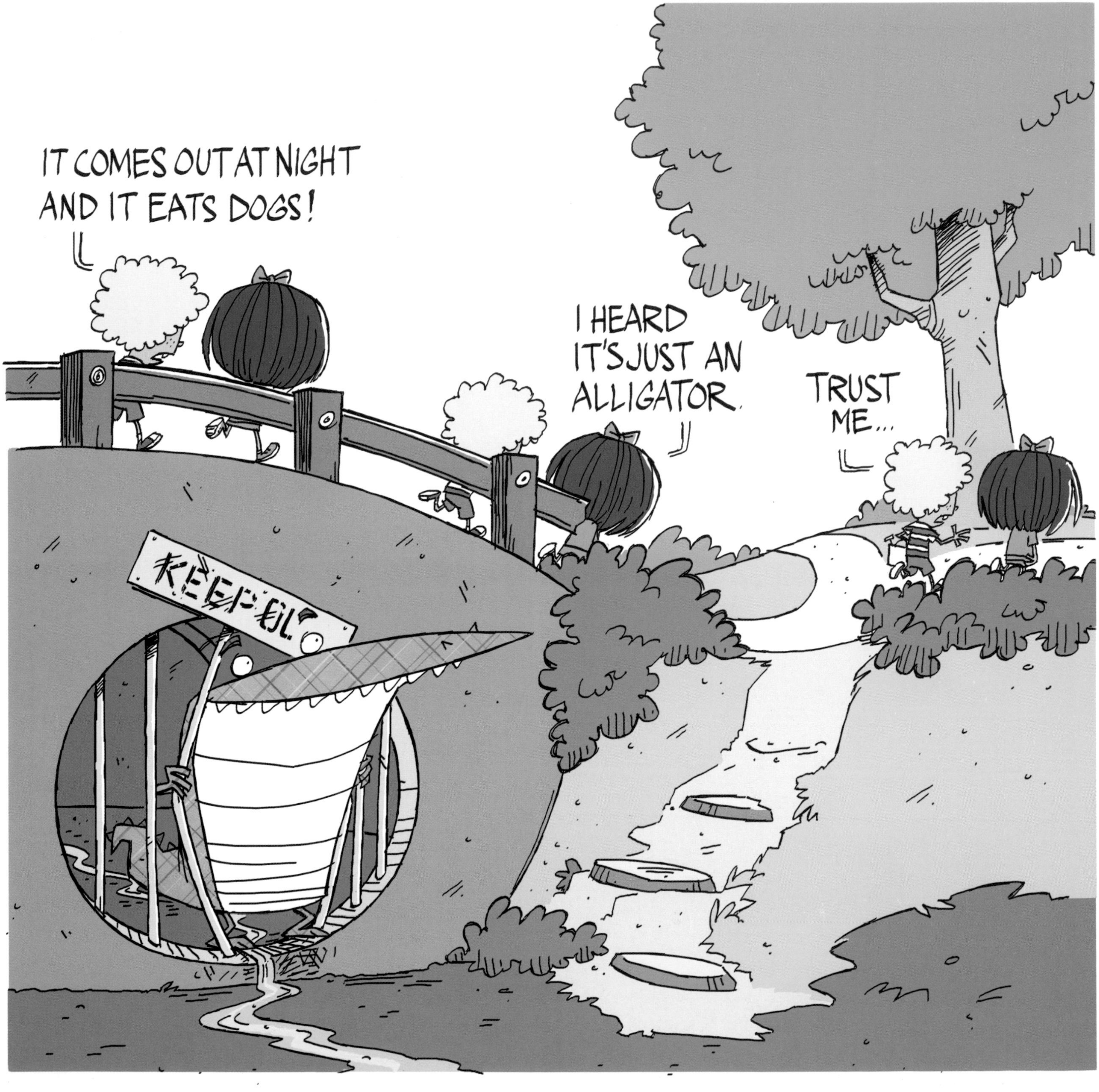
IT COMES OUT AT NIGHT AND IT EATS DOGS!
I HEARD IT'S JUST AN ALLIGATOR.
TRUST ME...
KEEP

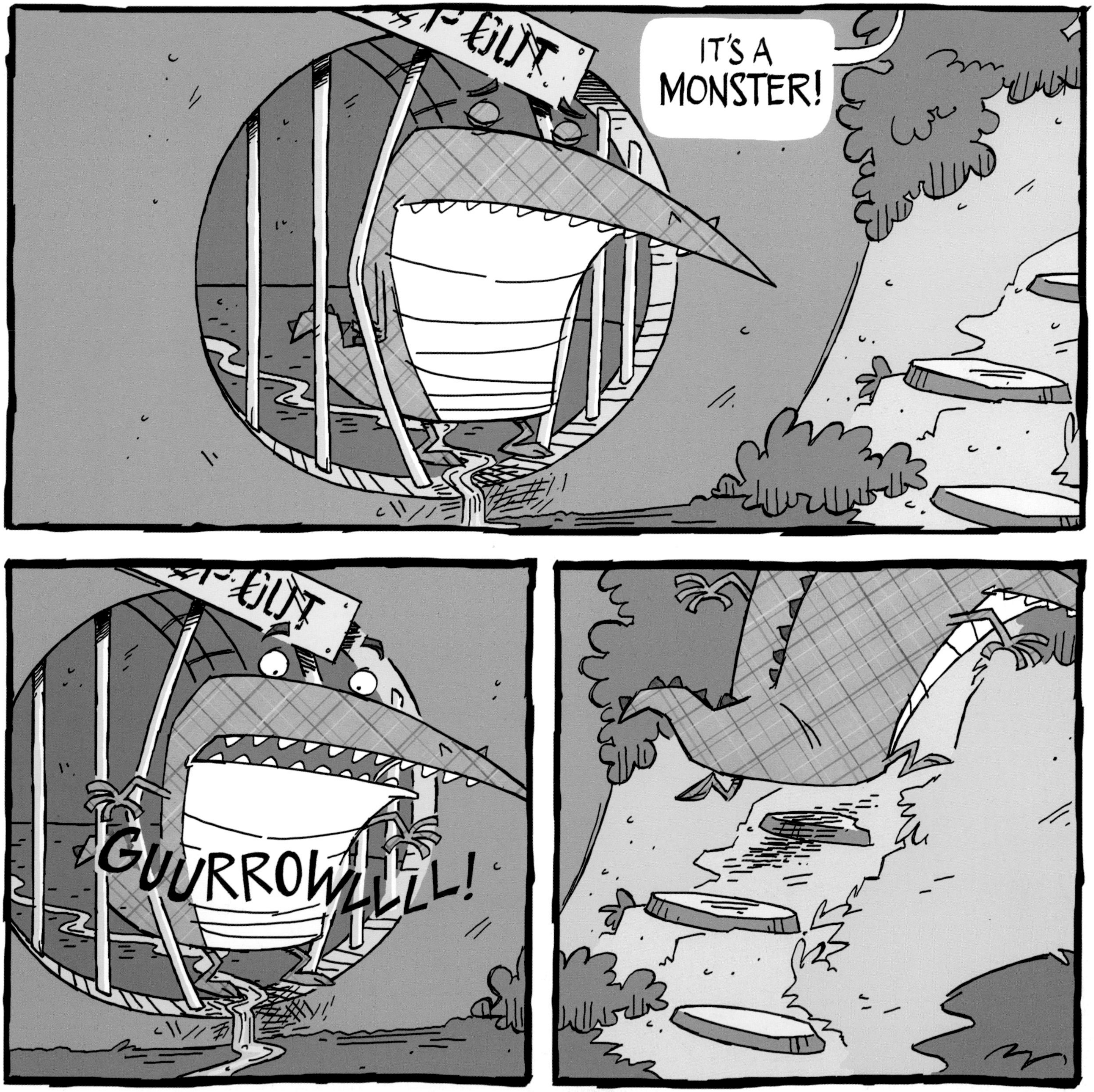
IT'S A MONSTER!
GUURROWLLLLL!

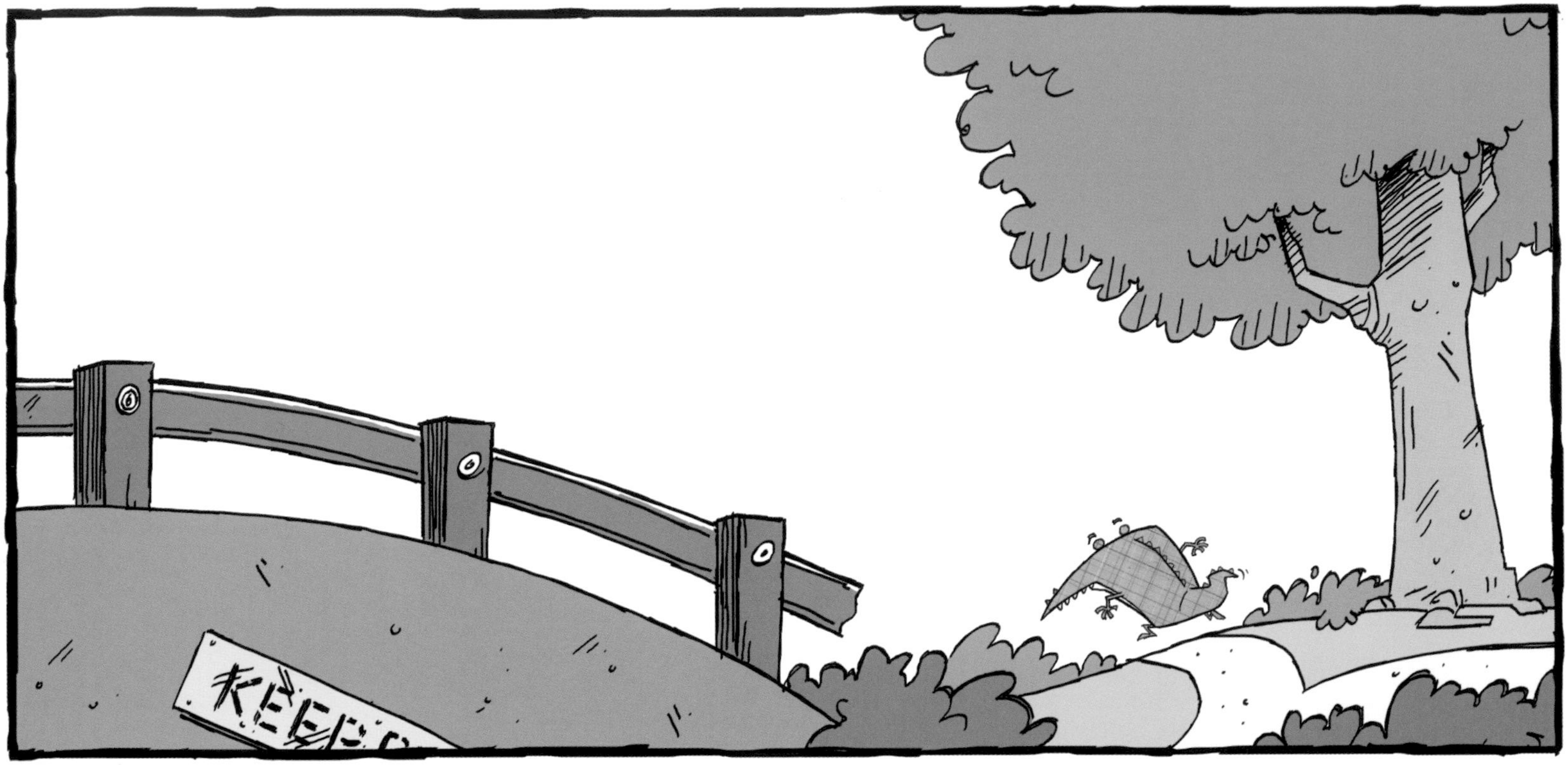

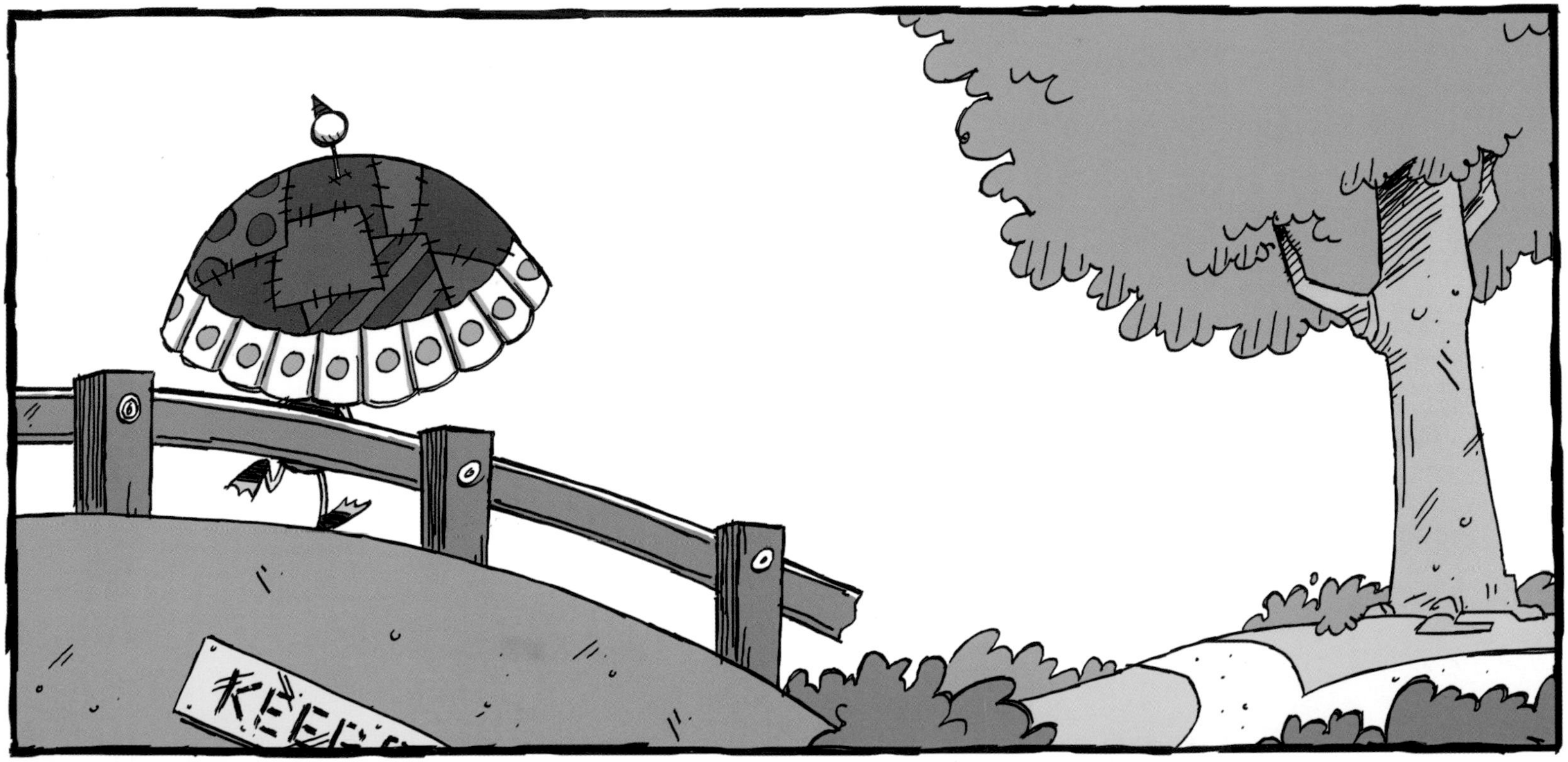

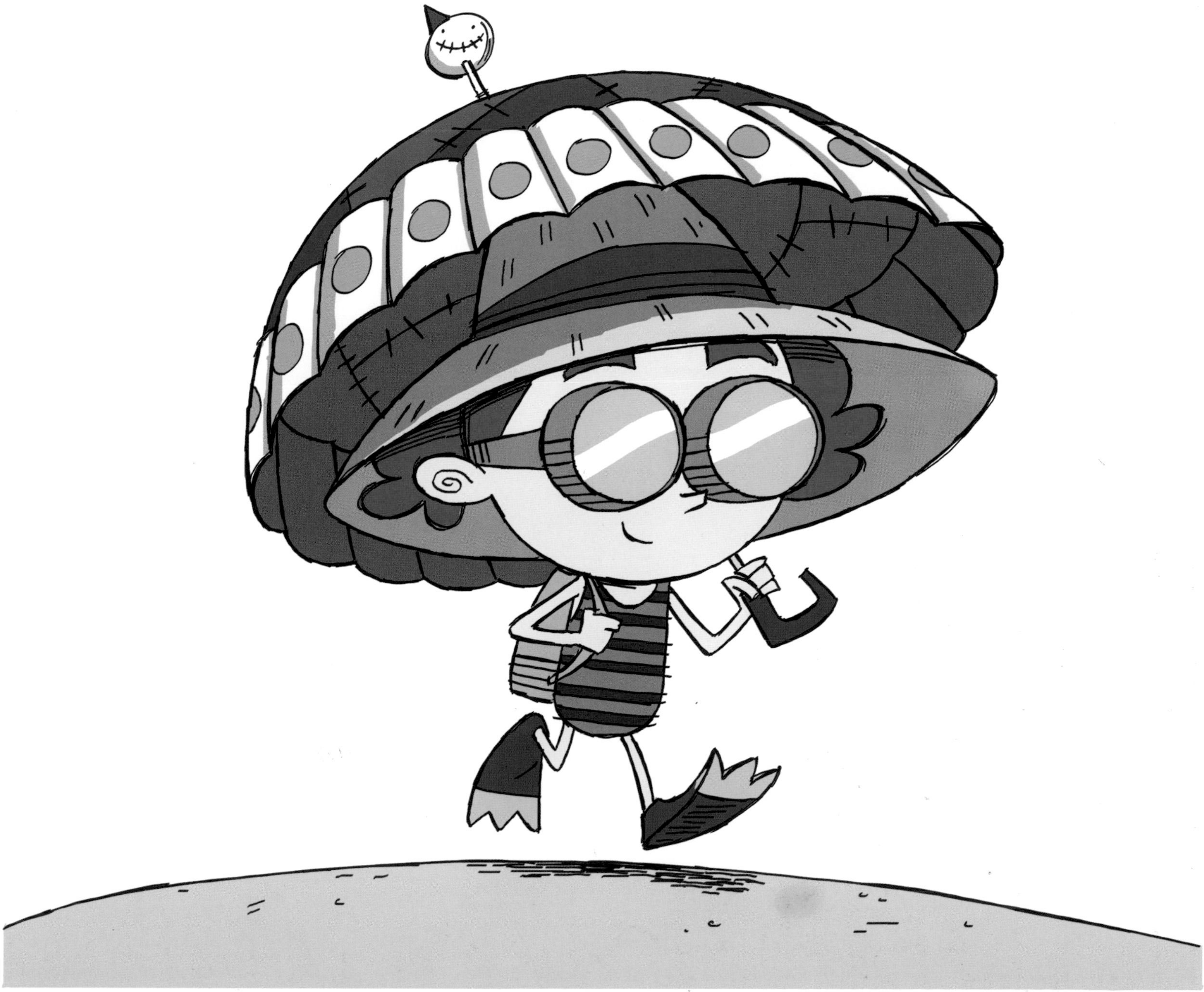

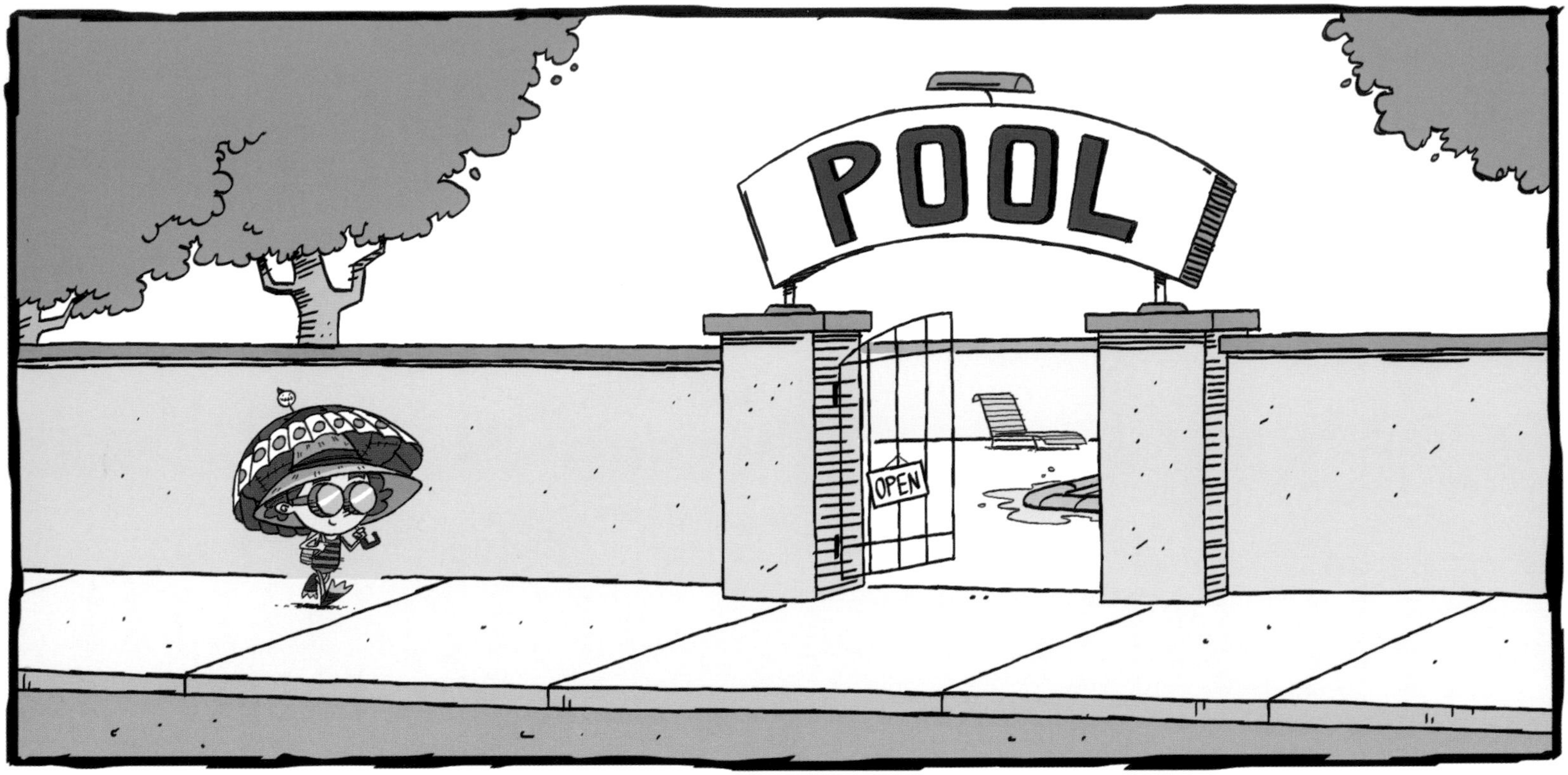
POOL
OPEN

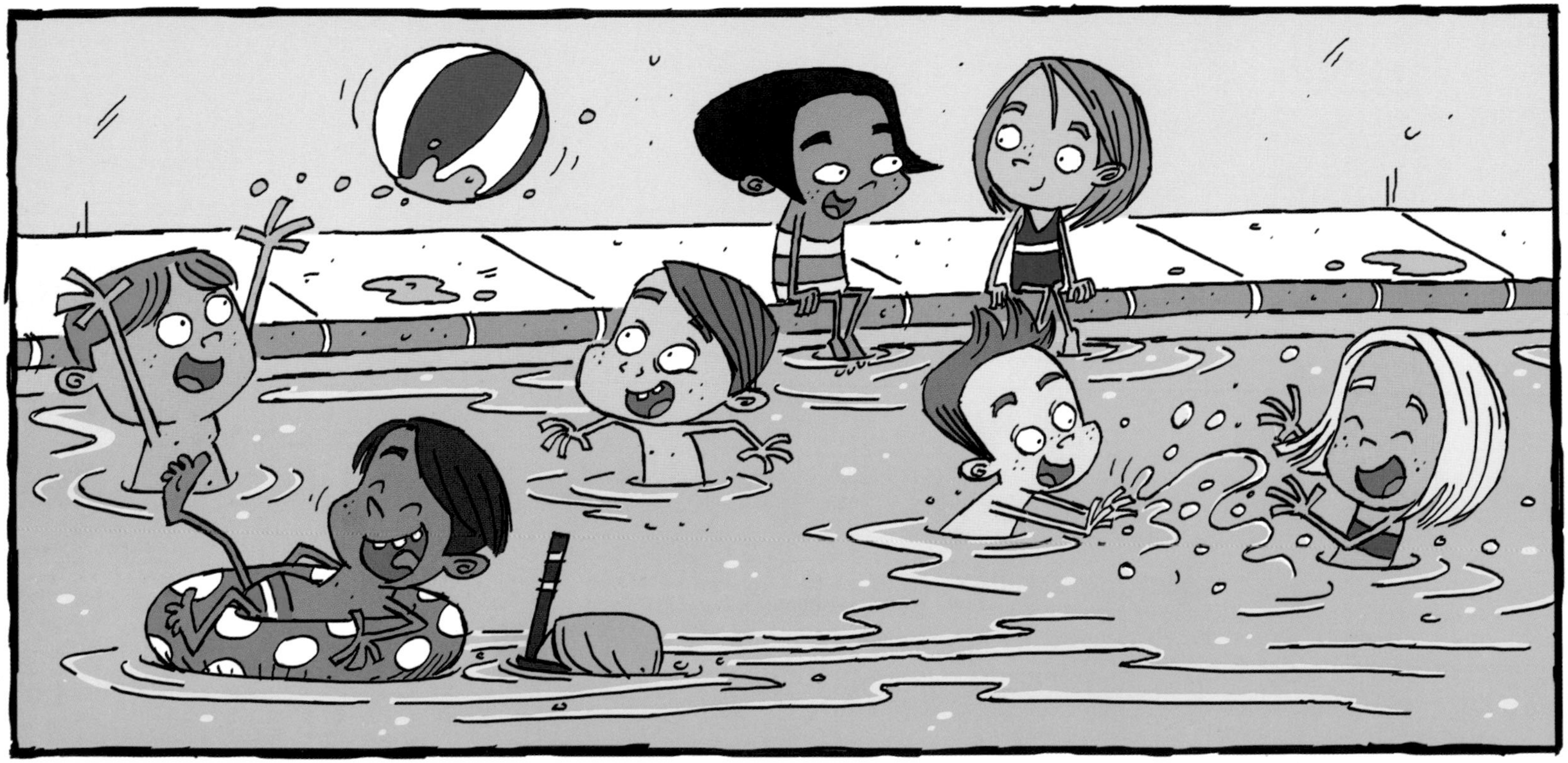

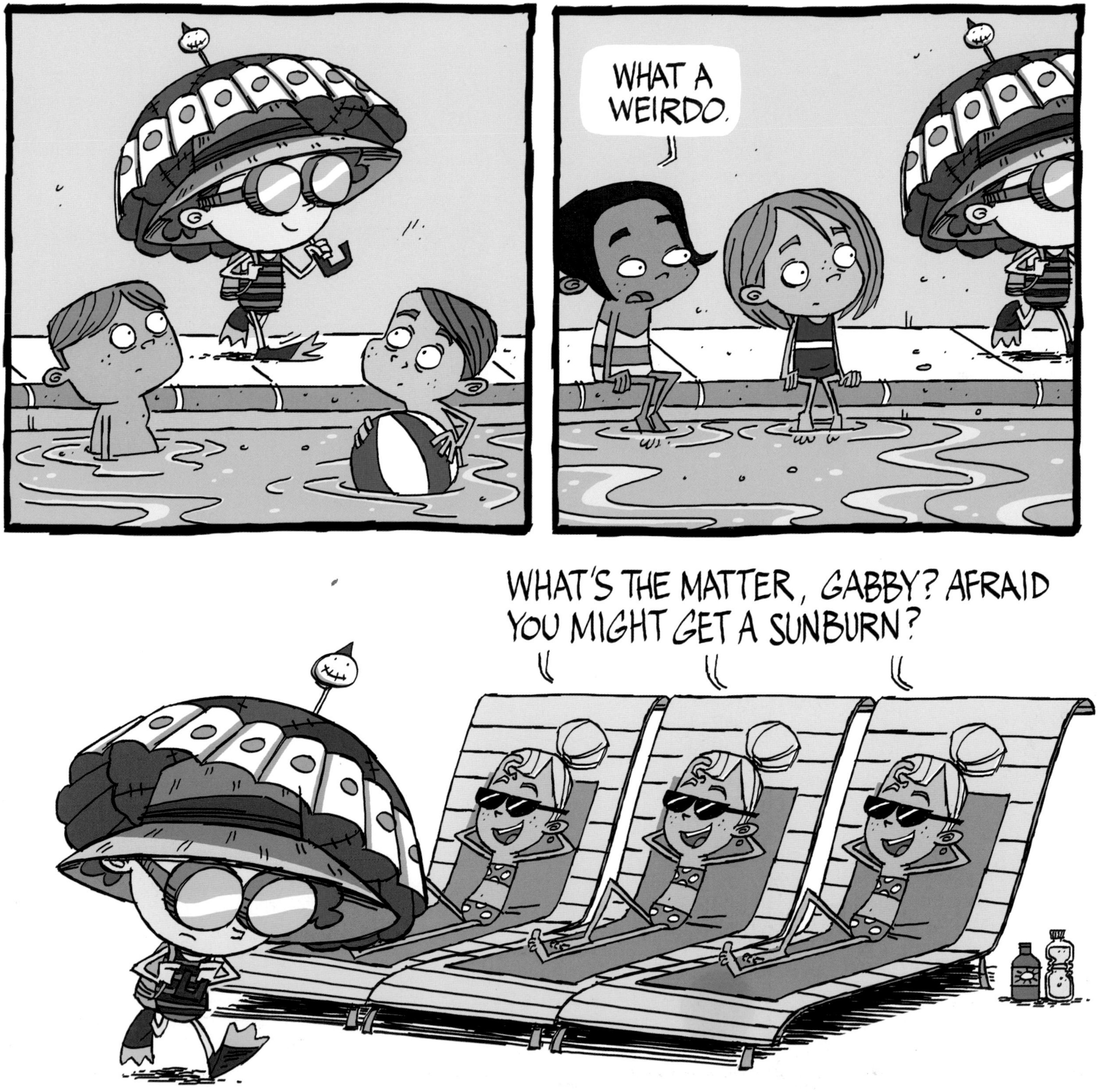
WHAT A WEIRDO.
WHAT'S THE MATTER, GABBY? AFRAID YOU MIGHT GET A SUNBURN?

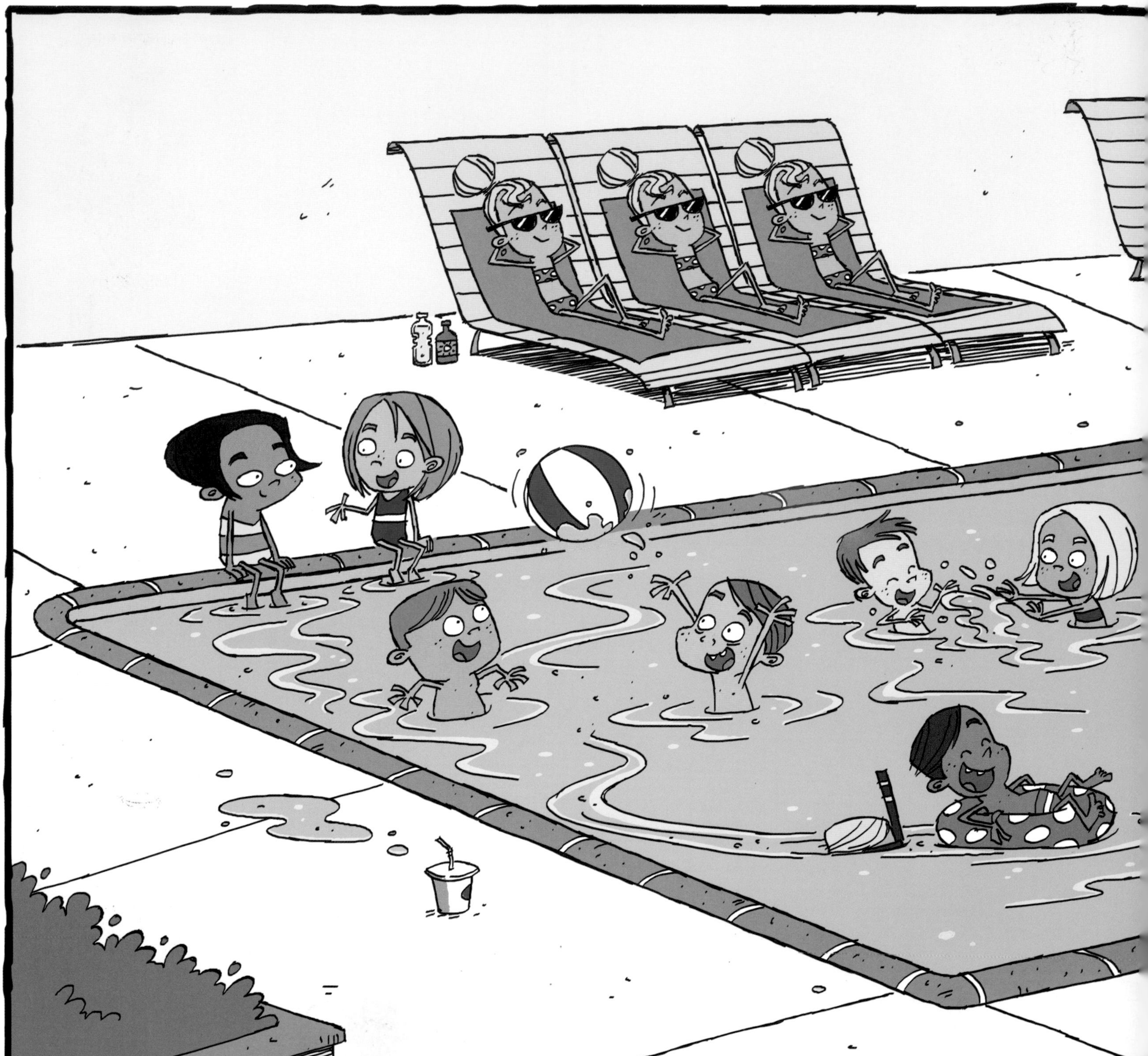

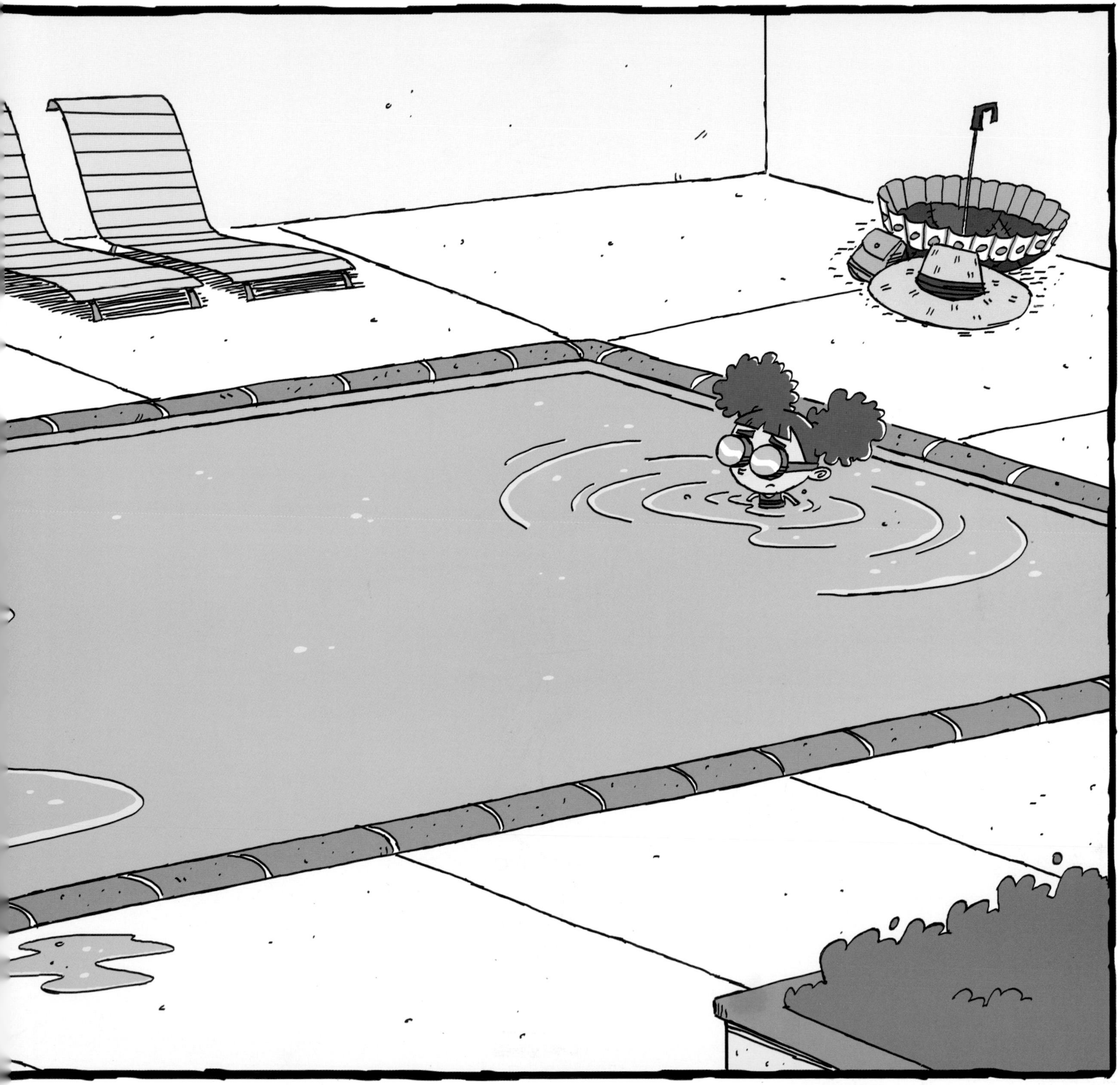

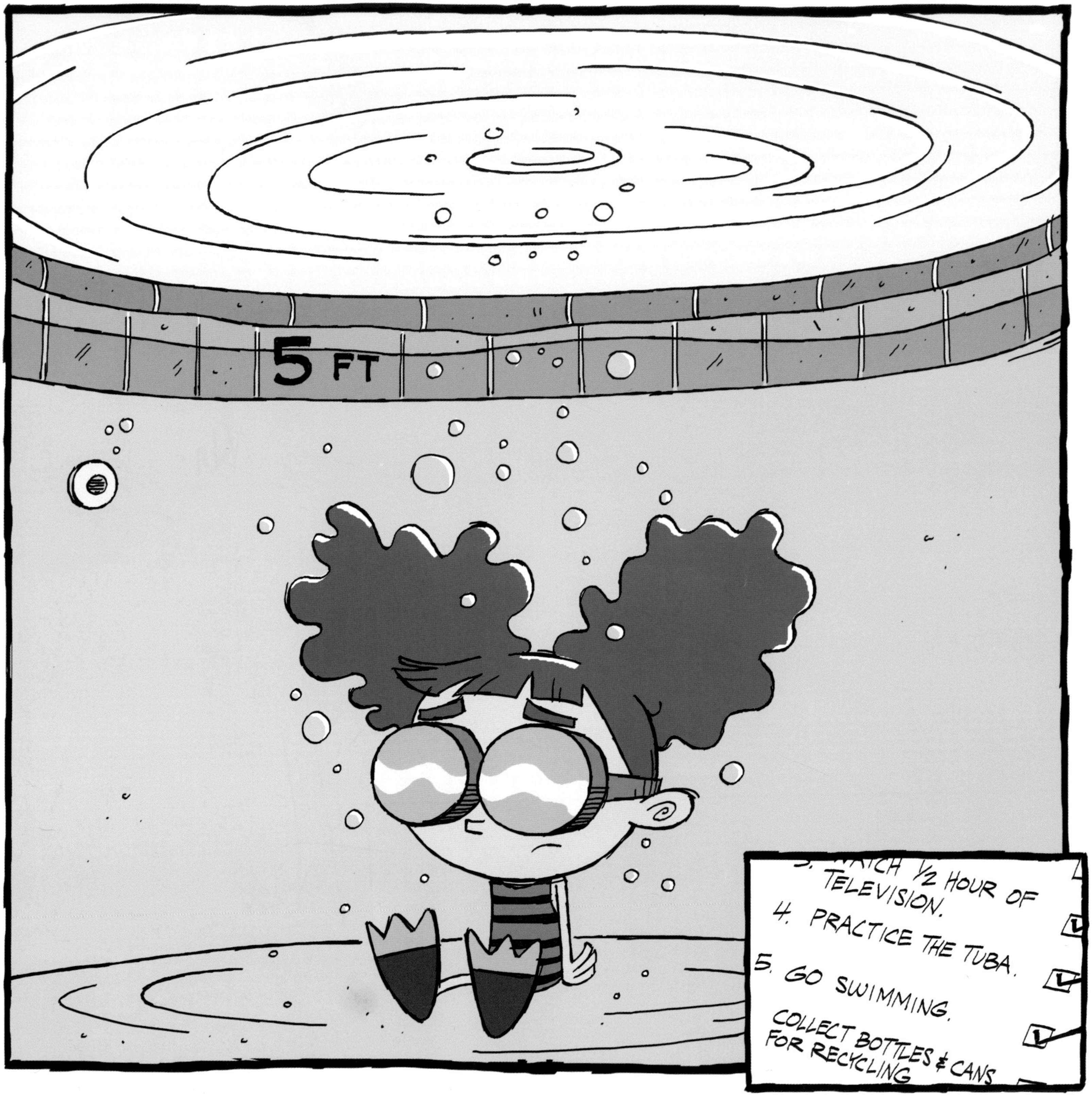
5 FT
WATCH 1/2 HOUR OF TELEVISION.
4. PRACTICE THE TUBA.
5. GO SWIMMING.
COLLECT BOTTLES & CANS FOR RECYCLING

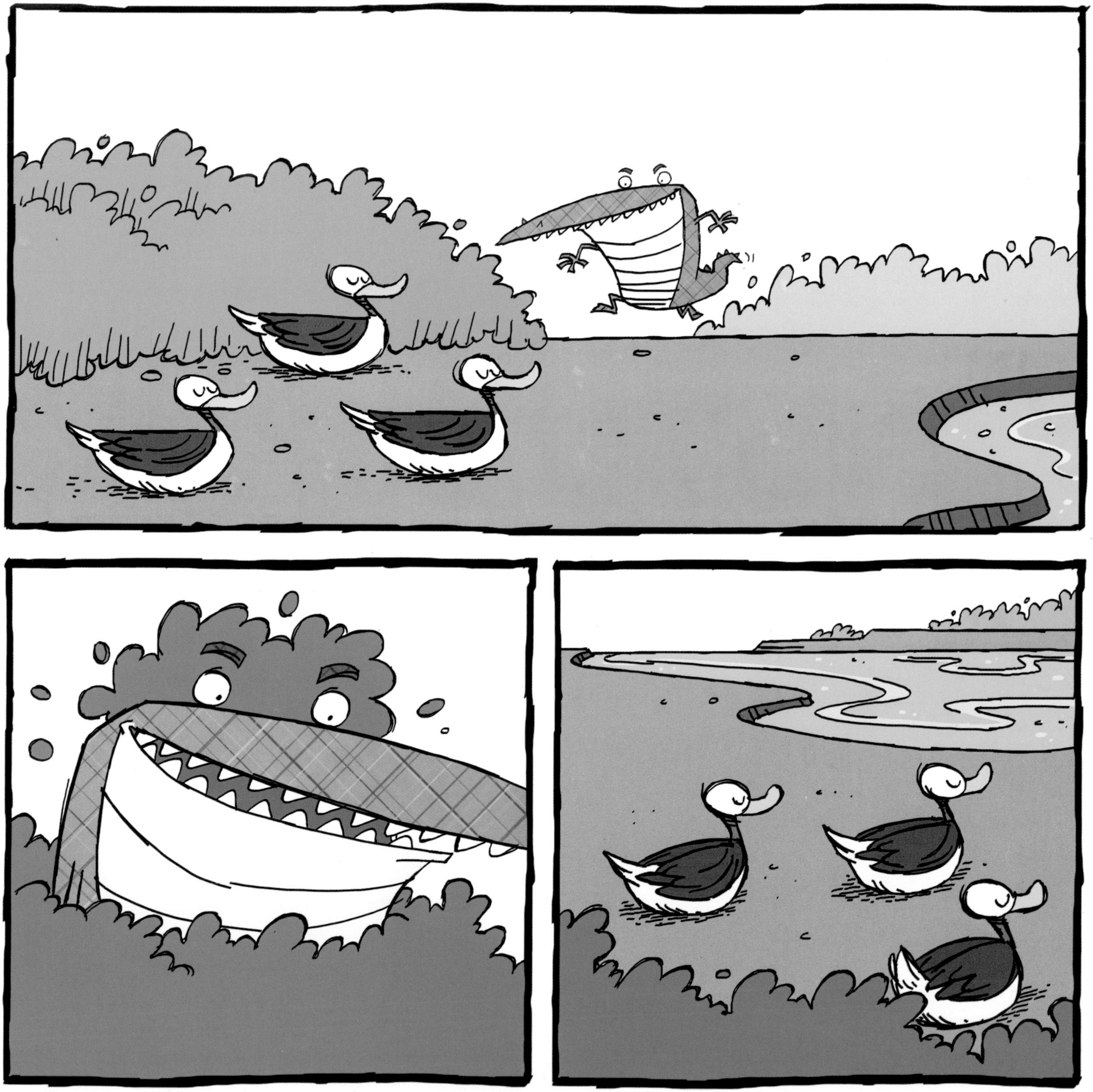

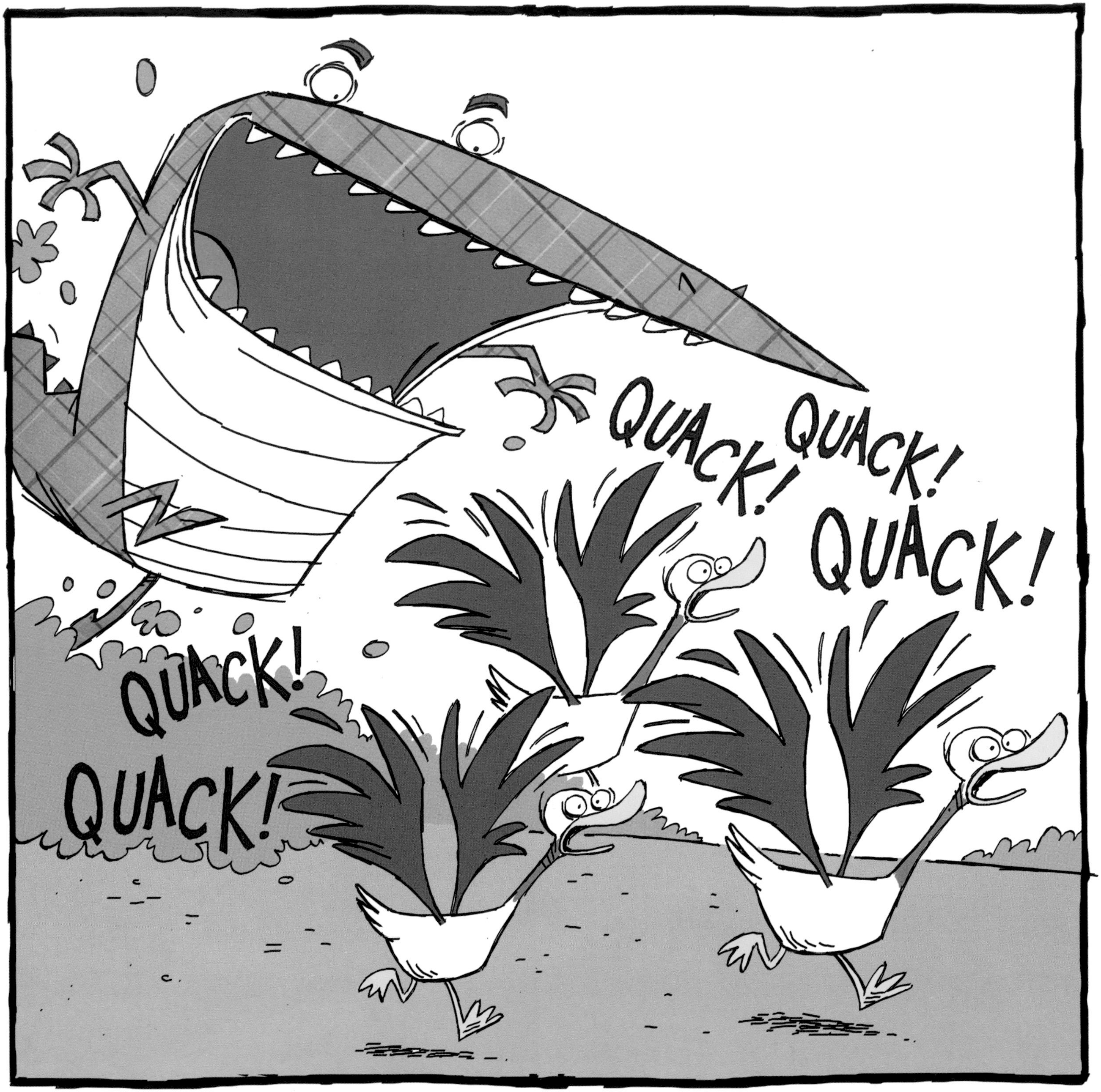
QUACK!
QUACK!
QUACK!
QUACK!
QUACK!

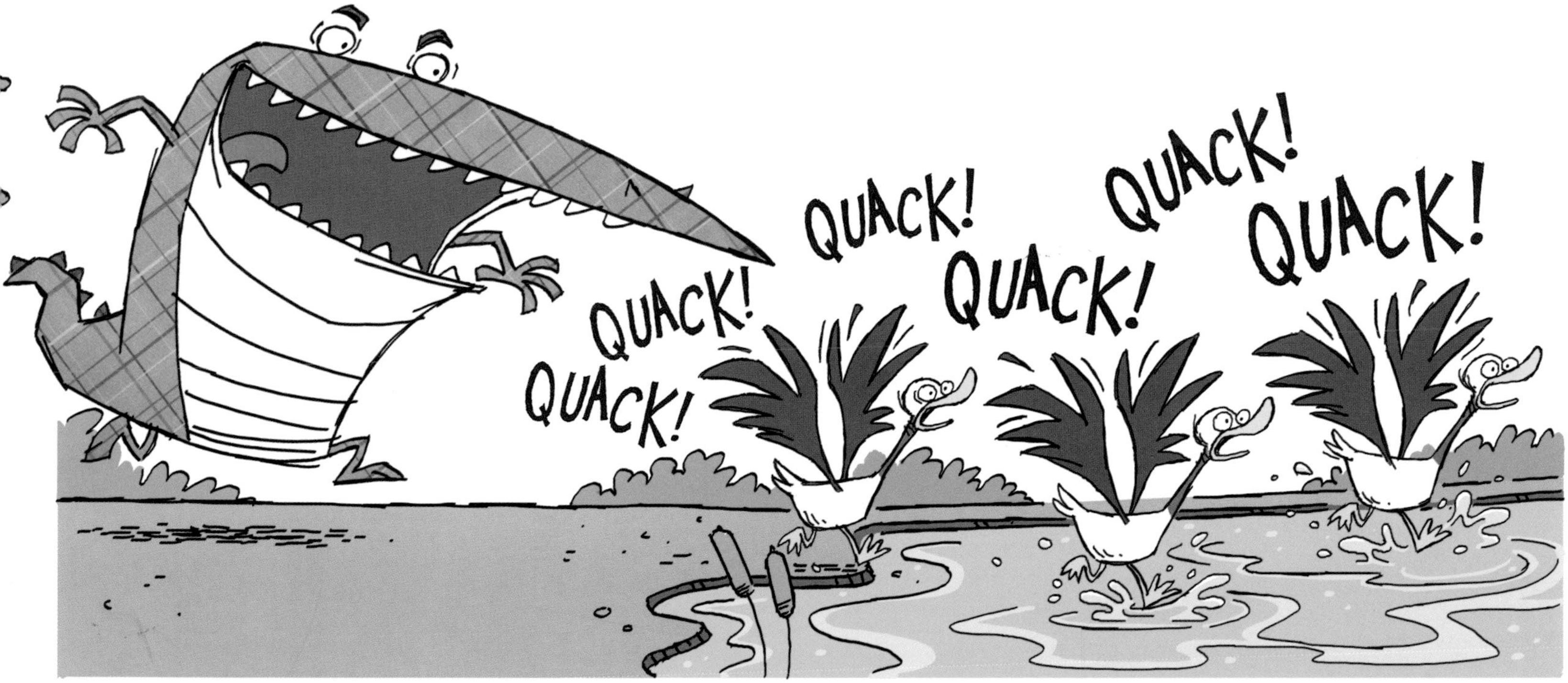
QUACK!
QUACK!
QUACK!
QUACK!
QUACK!
QUACK!

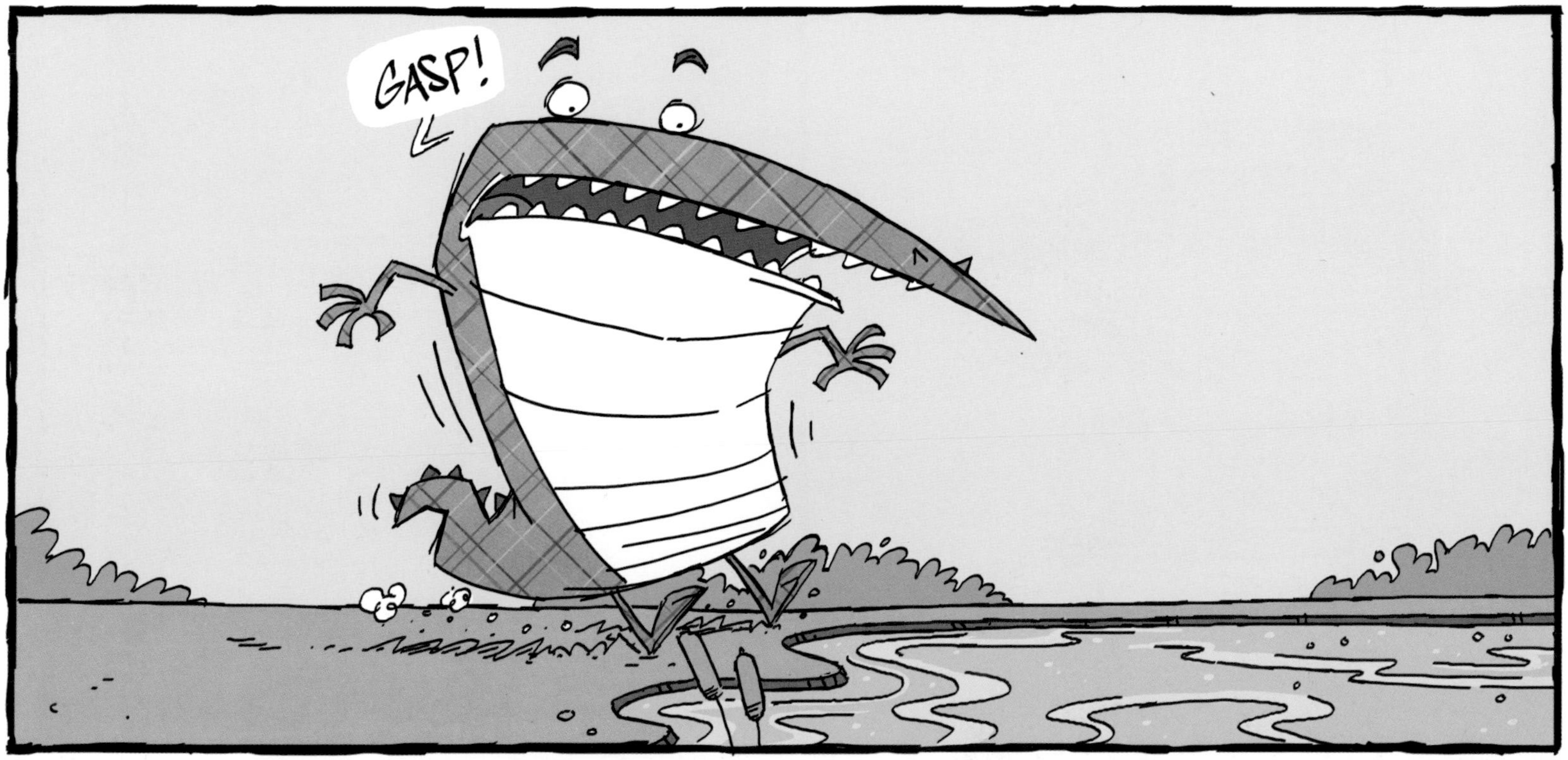
GASP!

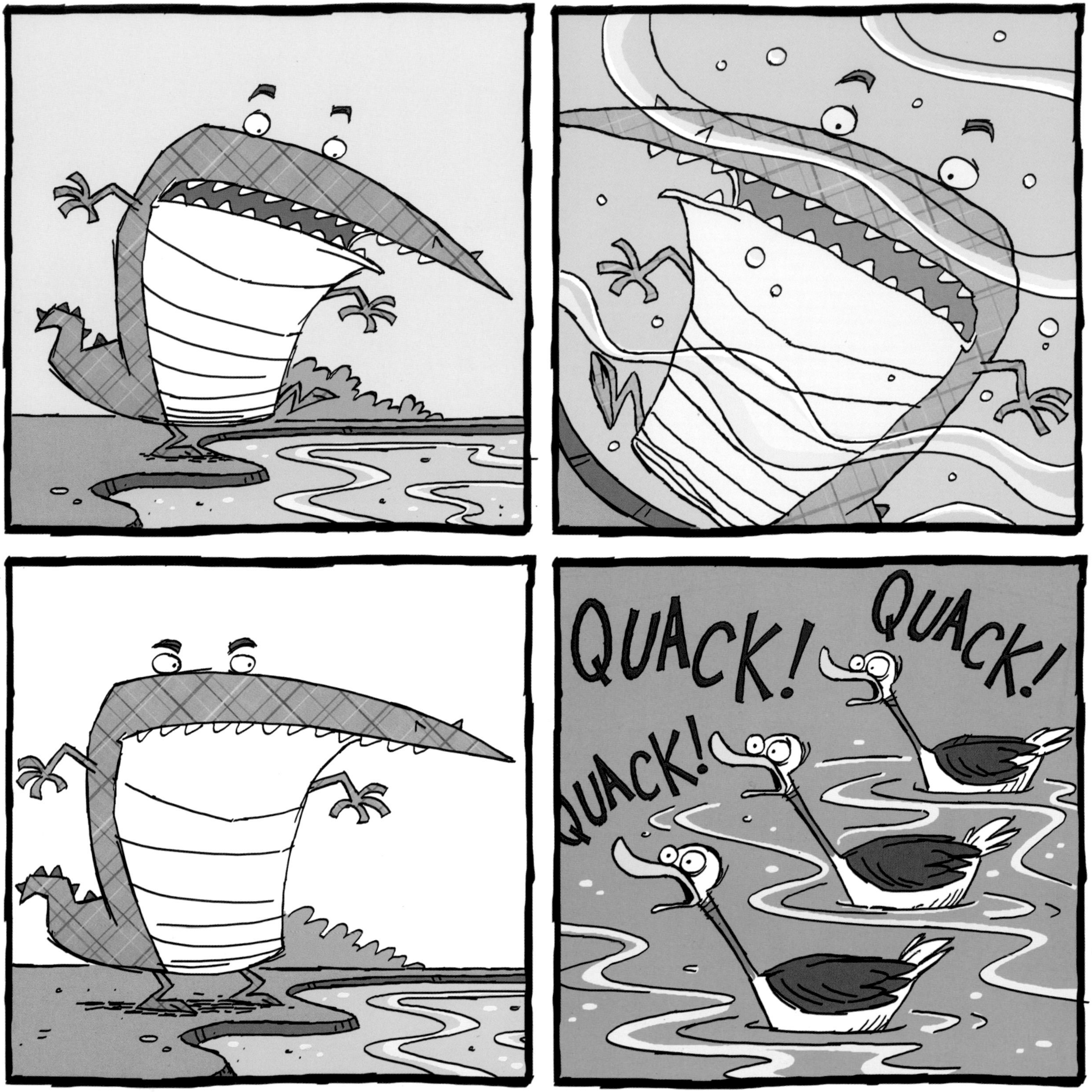
QUACK!
QUACK!
QUACK!

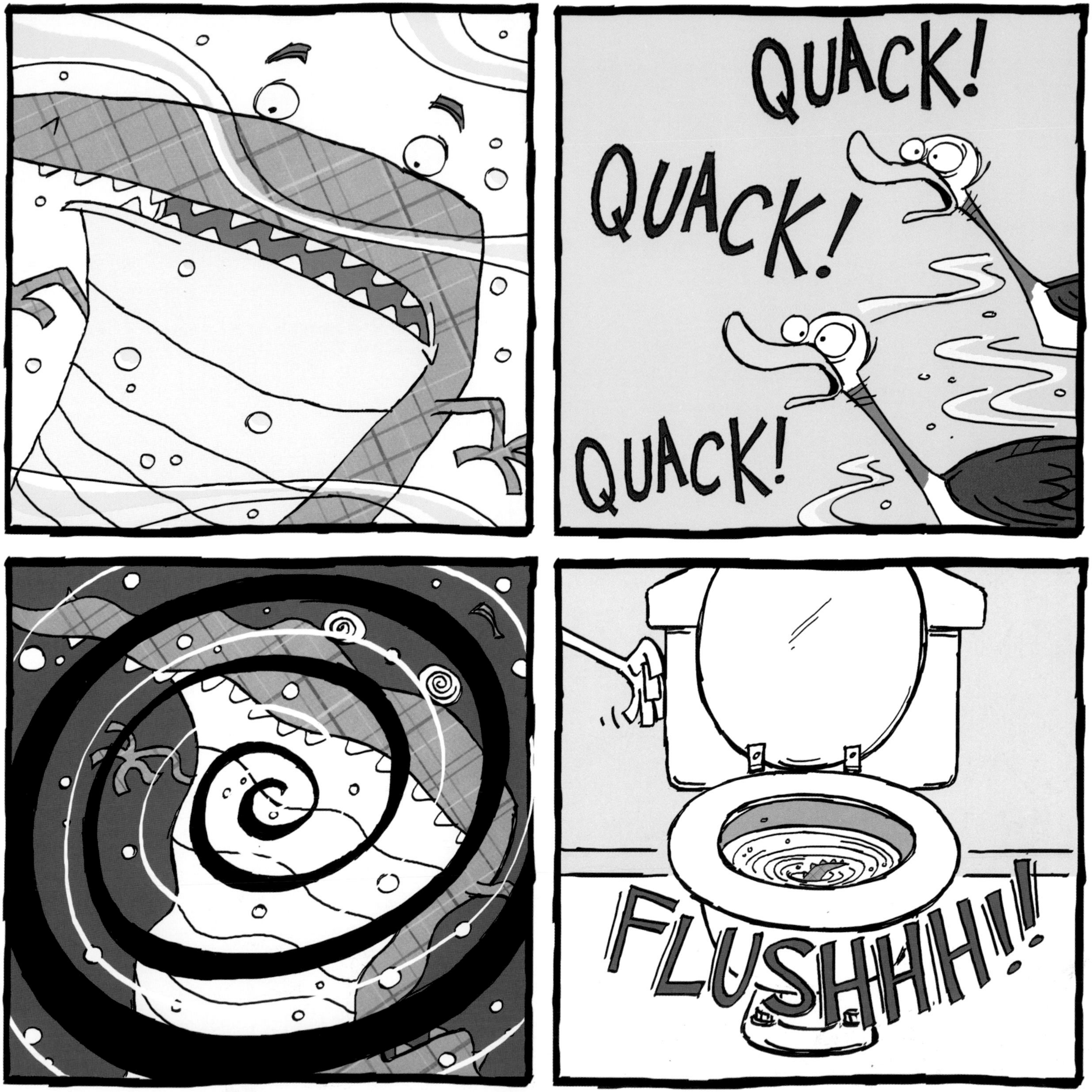
QUACK!
QUACK!
QUACK!
FLUSHHH!!

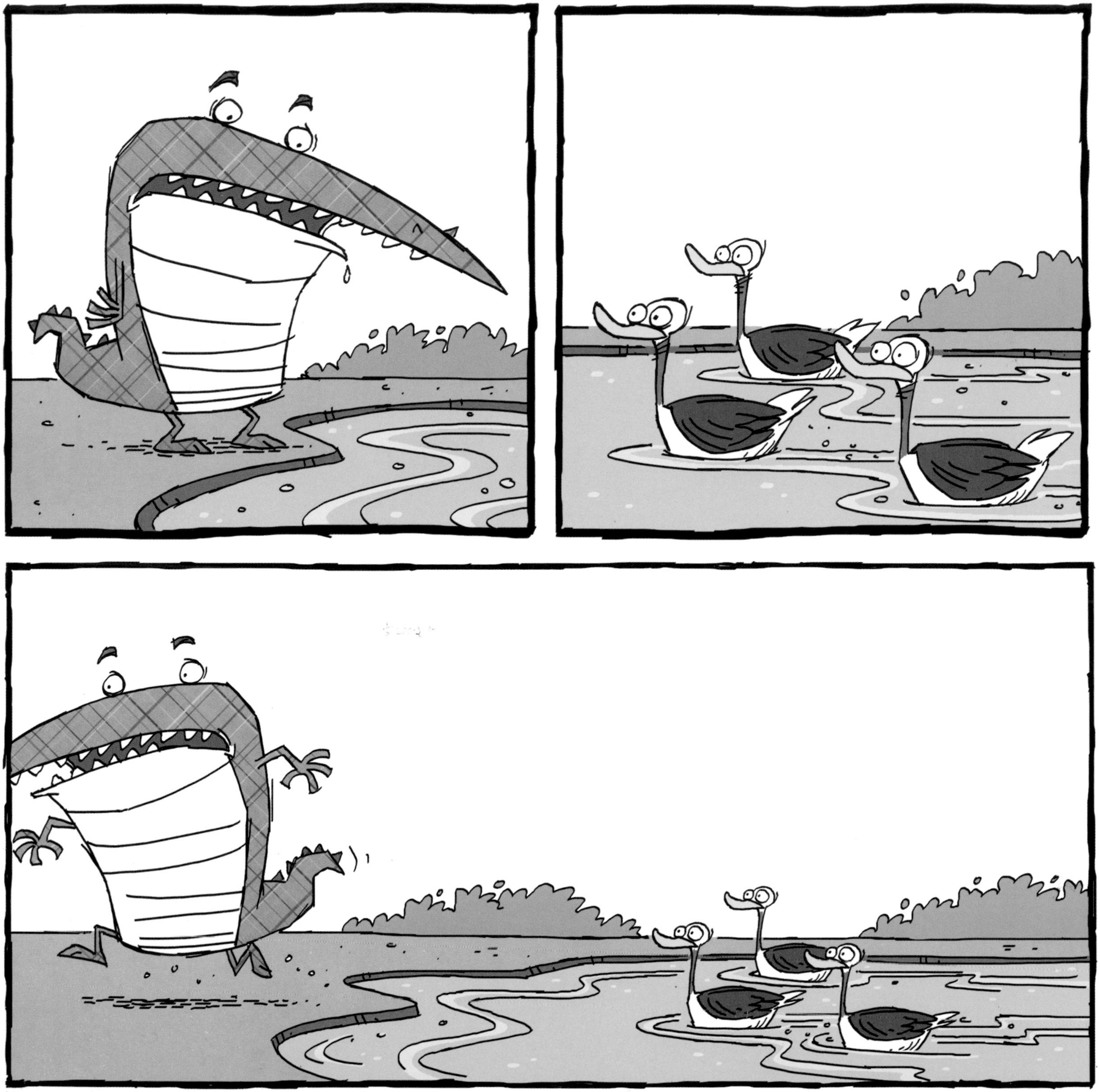

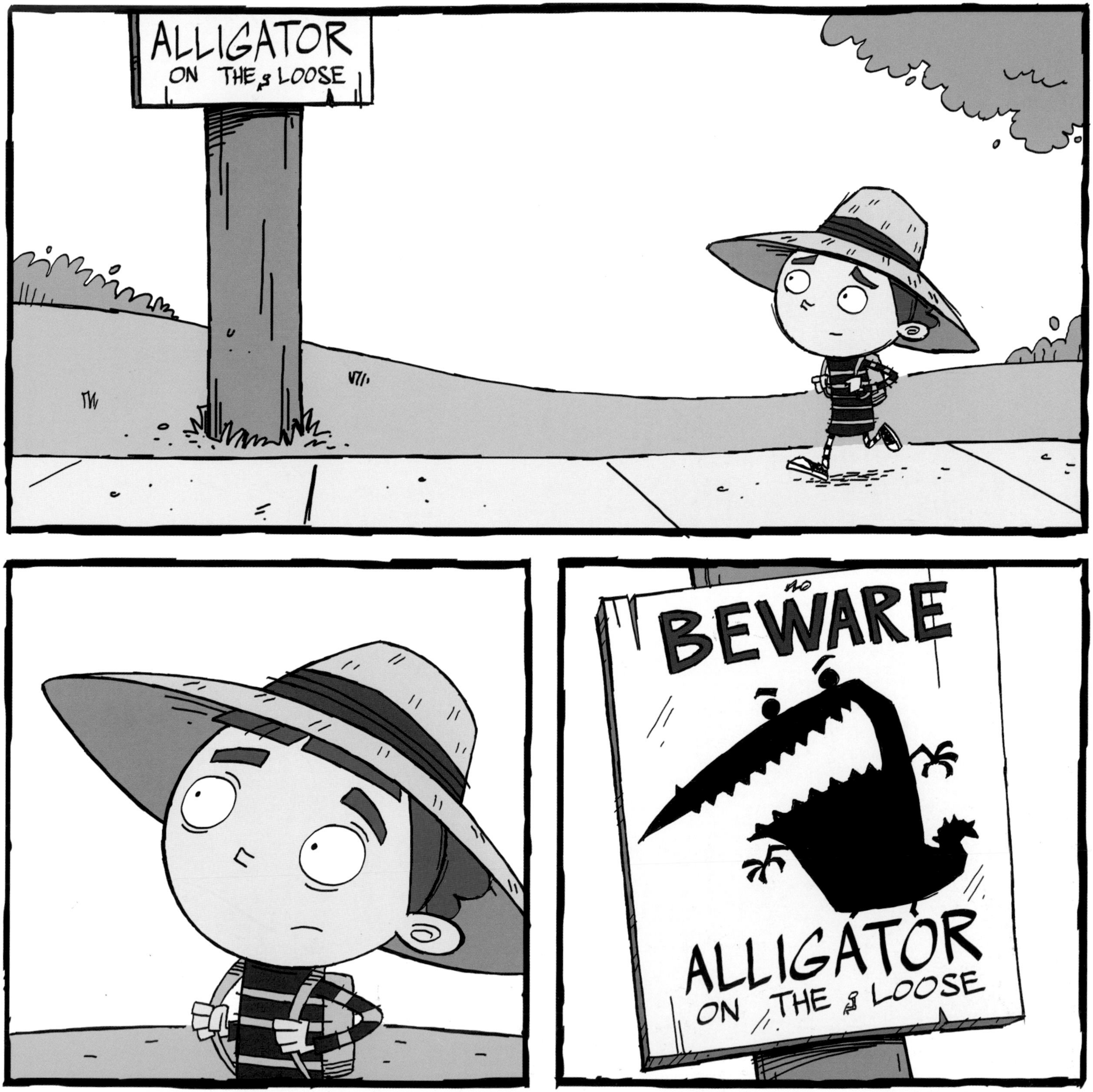
ALLIGATOR
ON THE LOOSE
BEWARE
ALLIGATOR
ON THE LOOSE

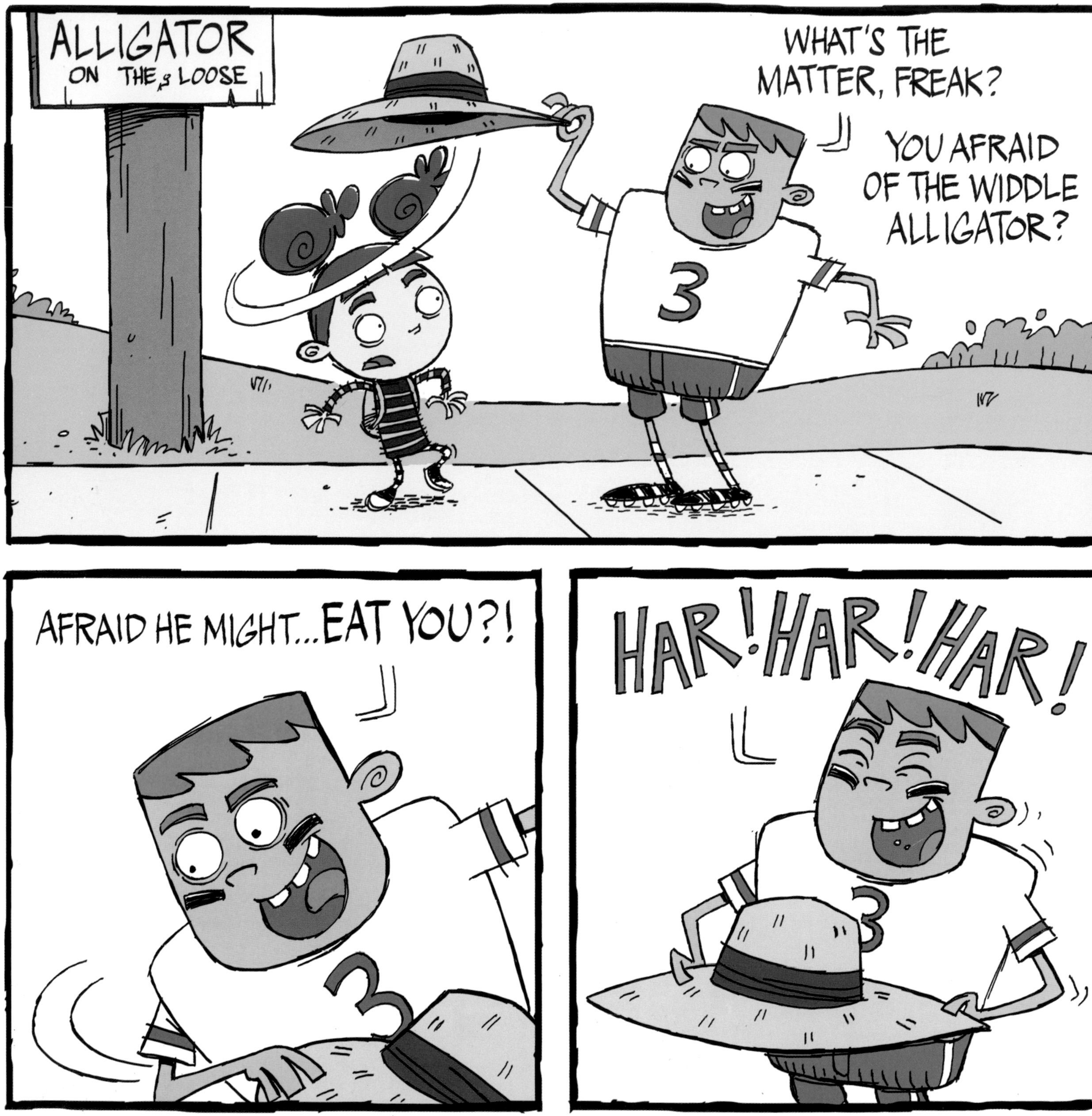
ALLIGATOR ON THE LOOSE
WHAT'S THE MATTER, FREAK?
YOU AFRAID OF THE WIDDLE ALLIGATOR?
3
AFRAID HE MIGHT...EAT YOU?!
3
HAR! HAR! HAR!
3

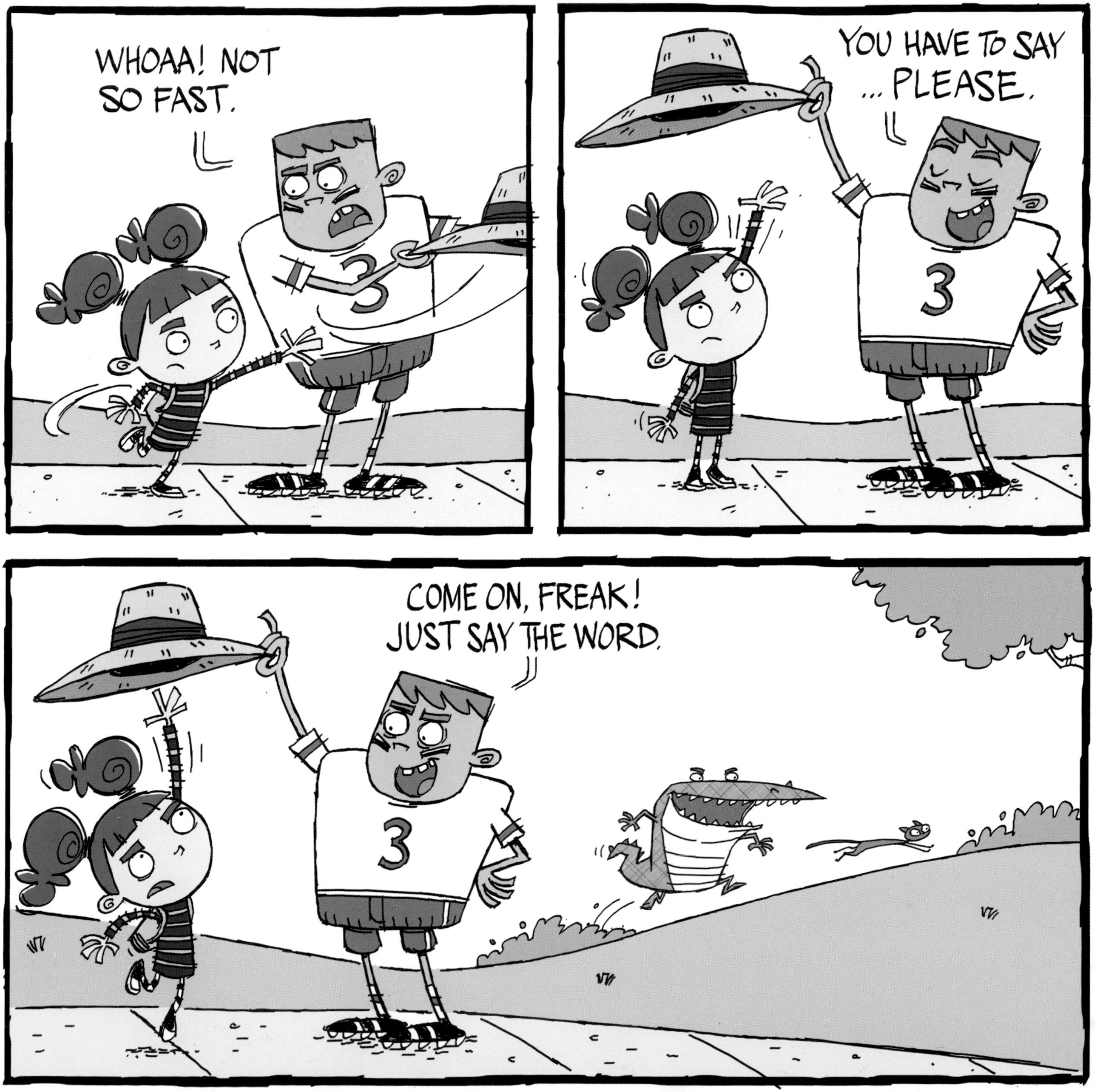
WHOAA! NOT SO FAST.
YOU HAVE TO SAY ...PLEASE.
COME ON, FREAK! JUST SAY THE WORD.

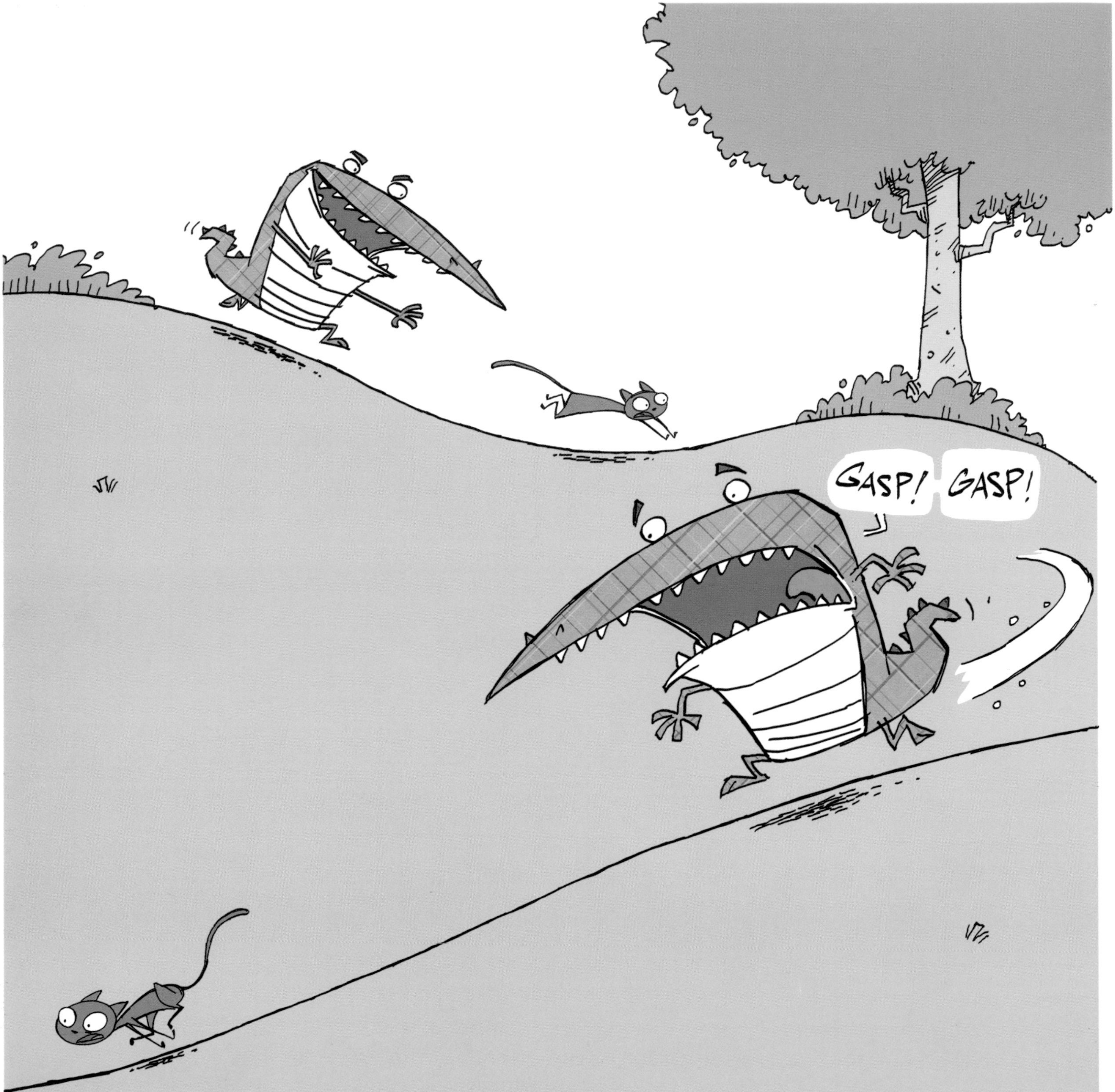
GASP!
GASP!

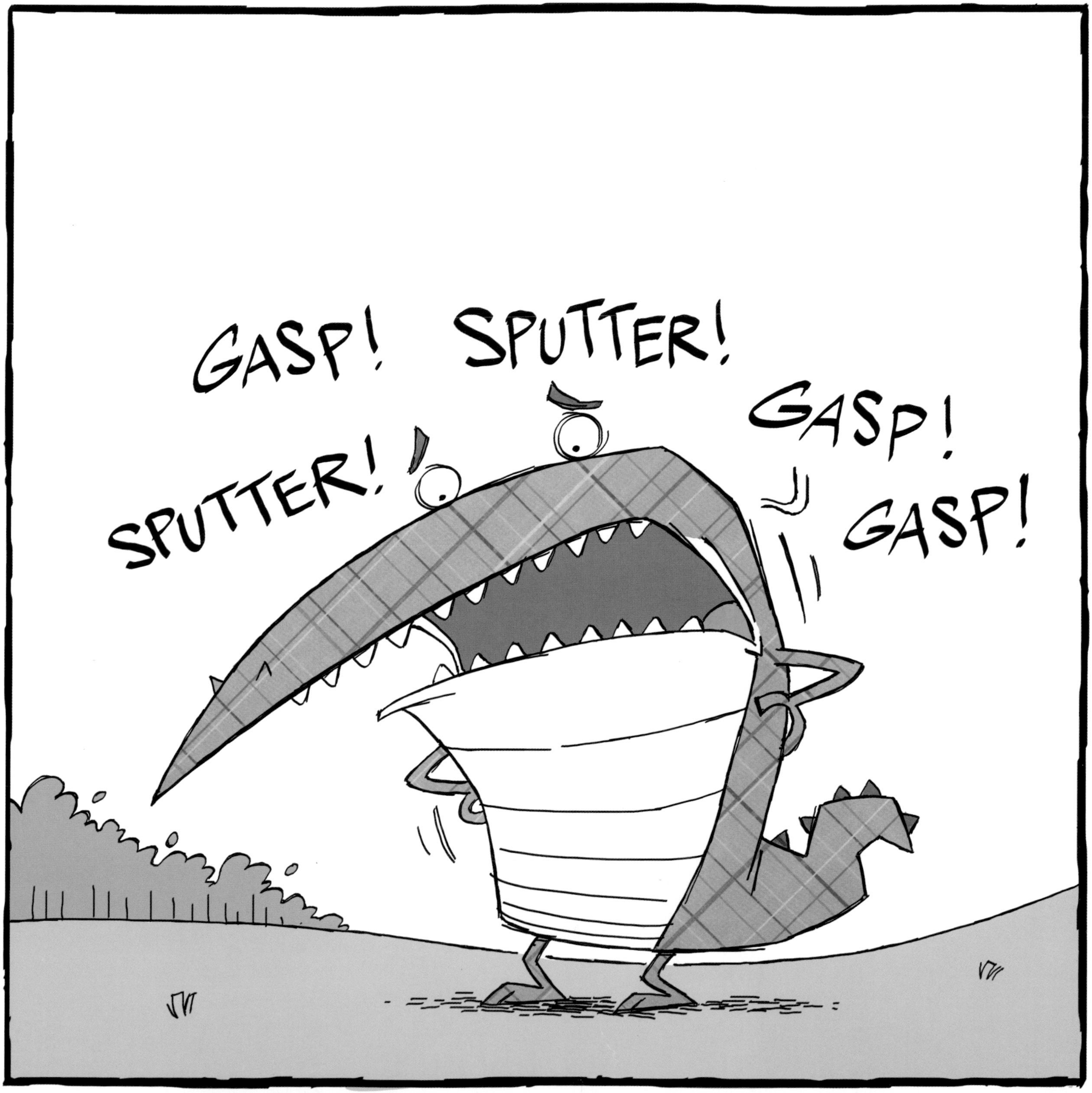
GASP! SPUTTER!
SPUTTER!
GASP!
GASP!

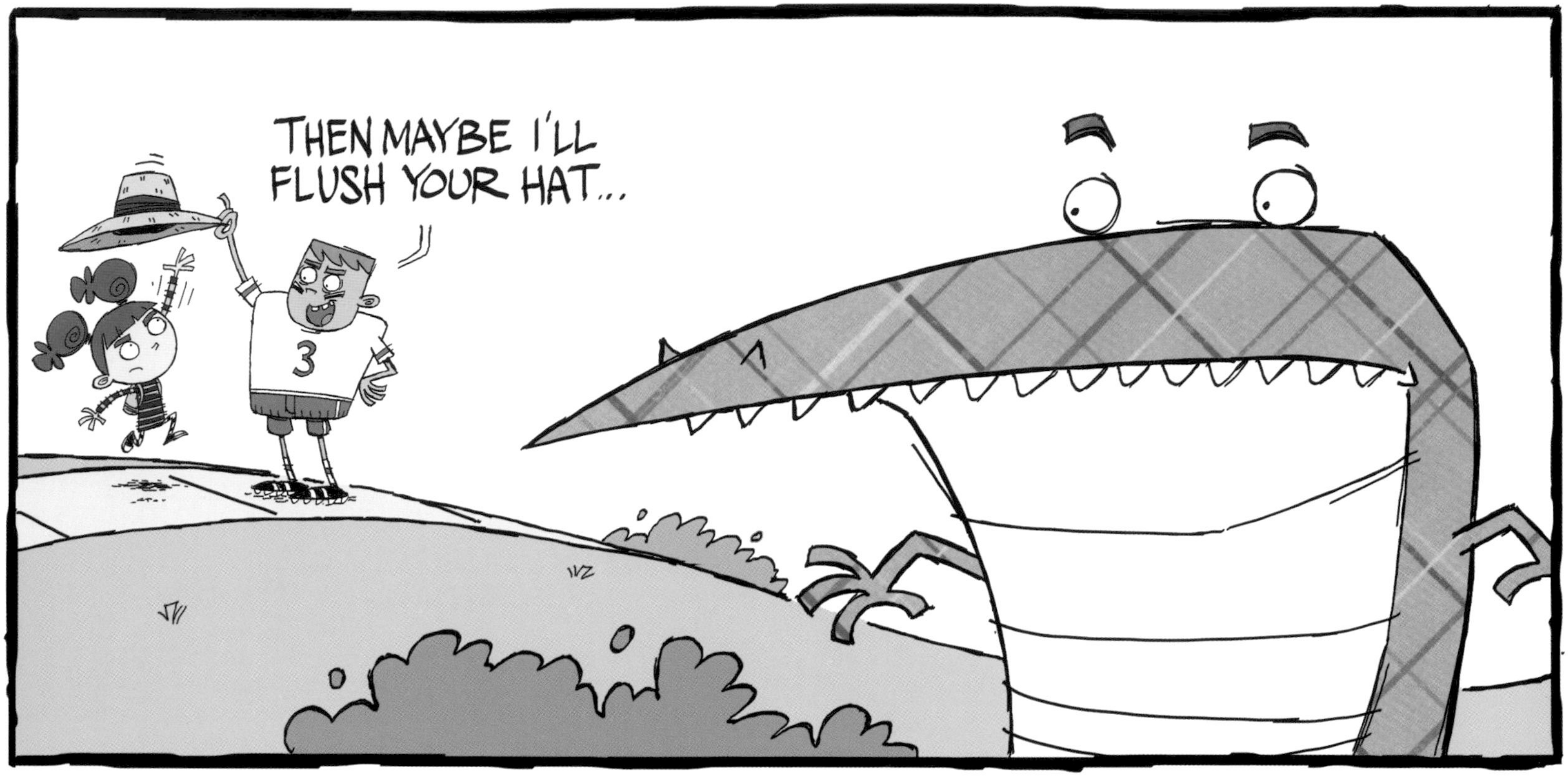
THEN MAYBE I'LL FLUSH YOUR HAT...

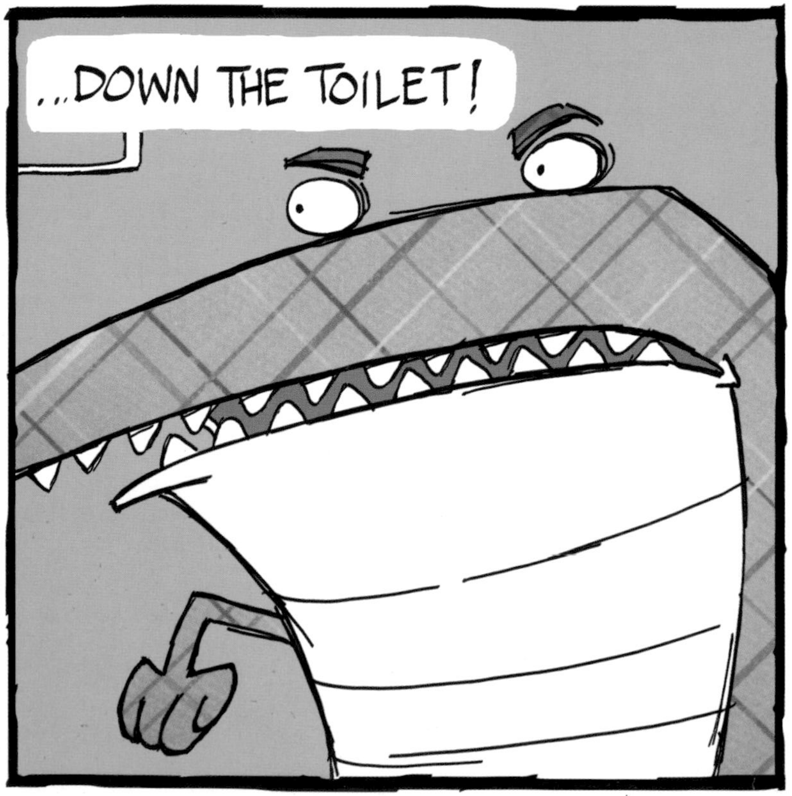
...DOWN THE TOILET!

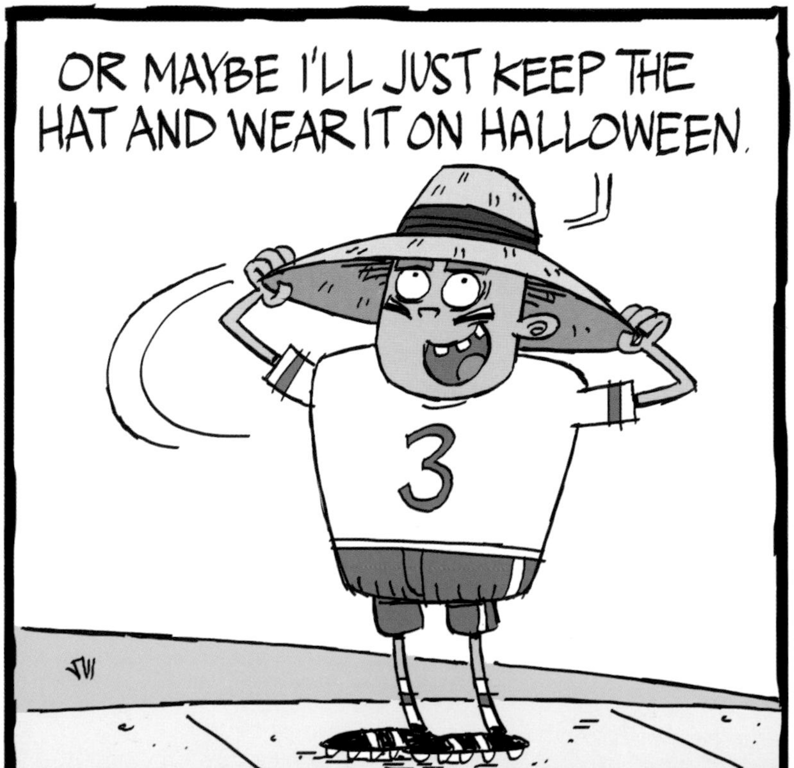
OR MAYBE I'LL JUST KEEP THE HAT AND WEAR IT ON HALLOWEEN.

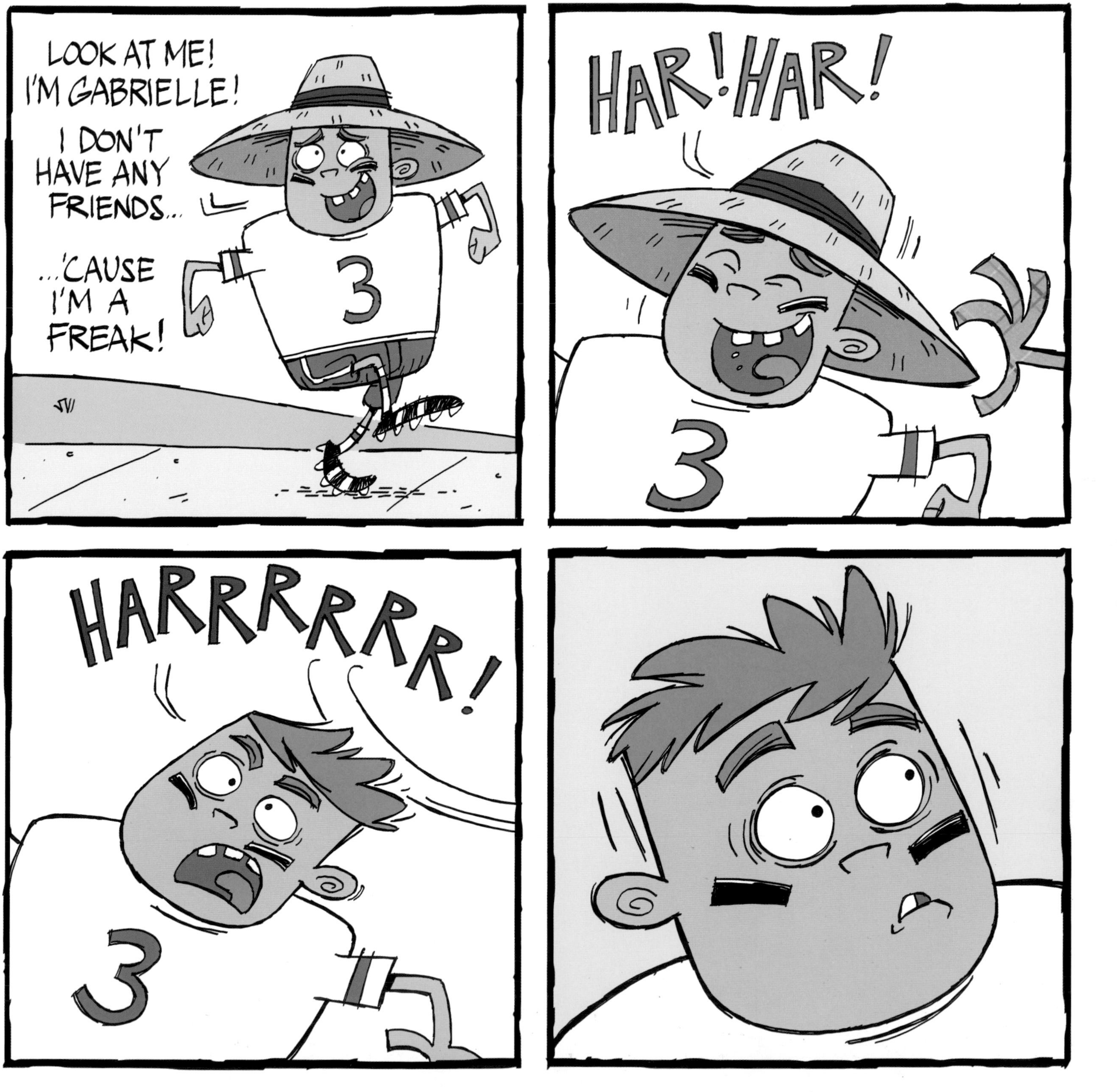
LOOK AT ME! I'M GABRIELLE!
I DON'T HAVE ANY FRIENDS...
...'CAUSE I'M A FREAK!
HAR! HAR!
HARRRRRRR!

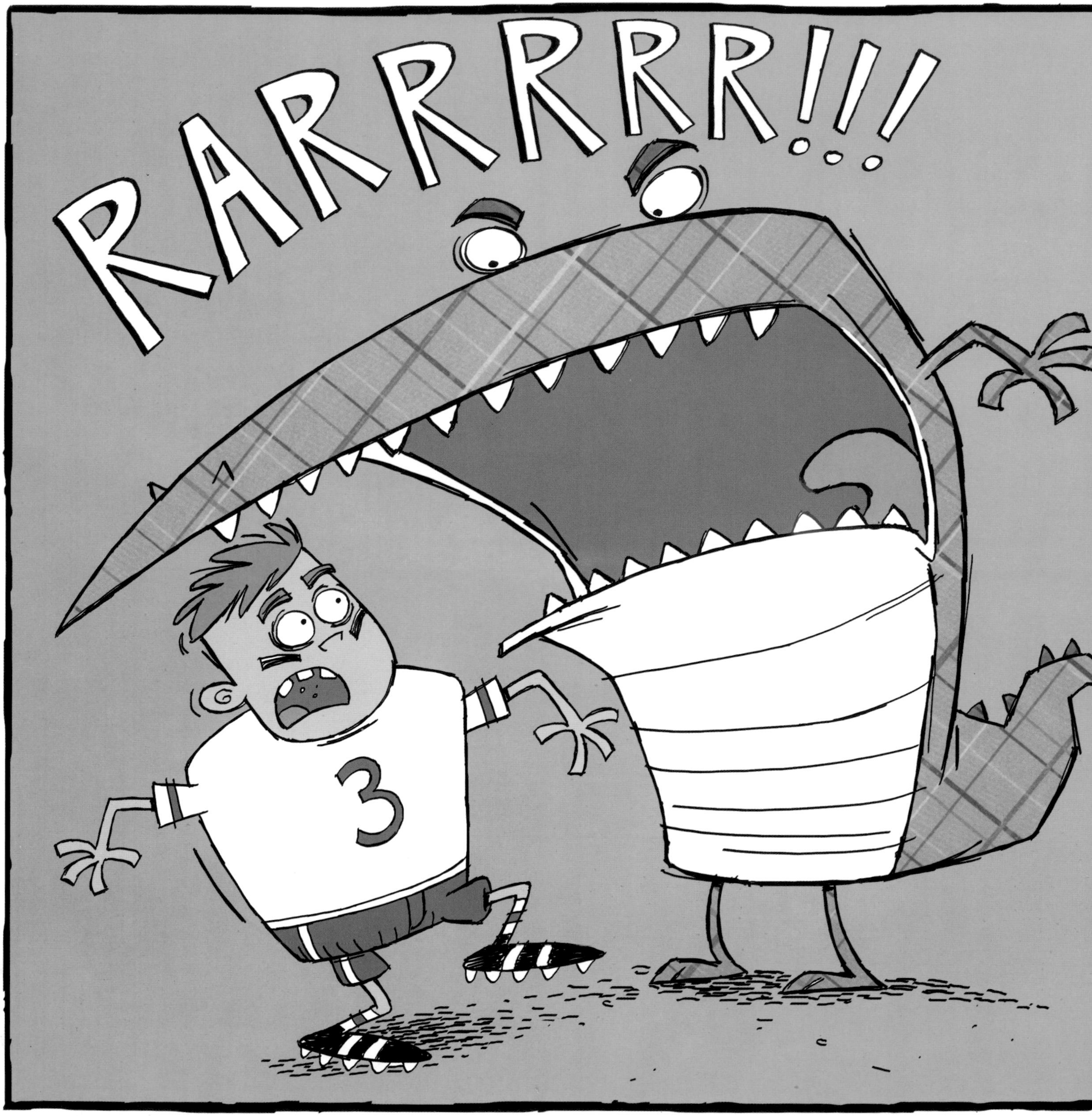
RARRRRRR!!!
3

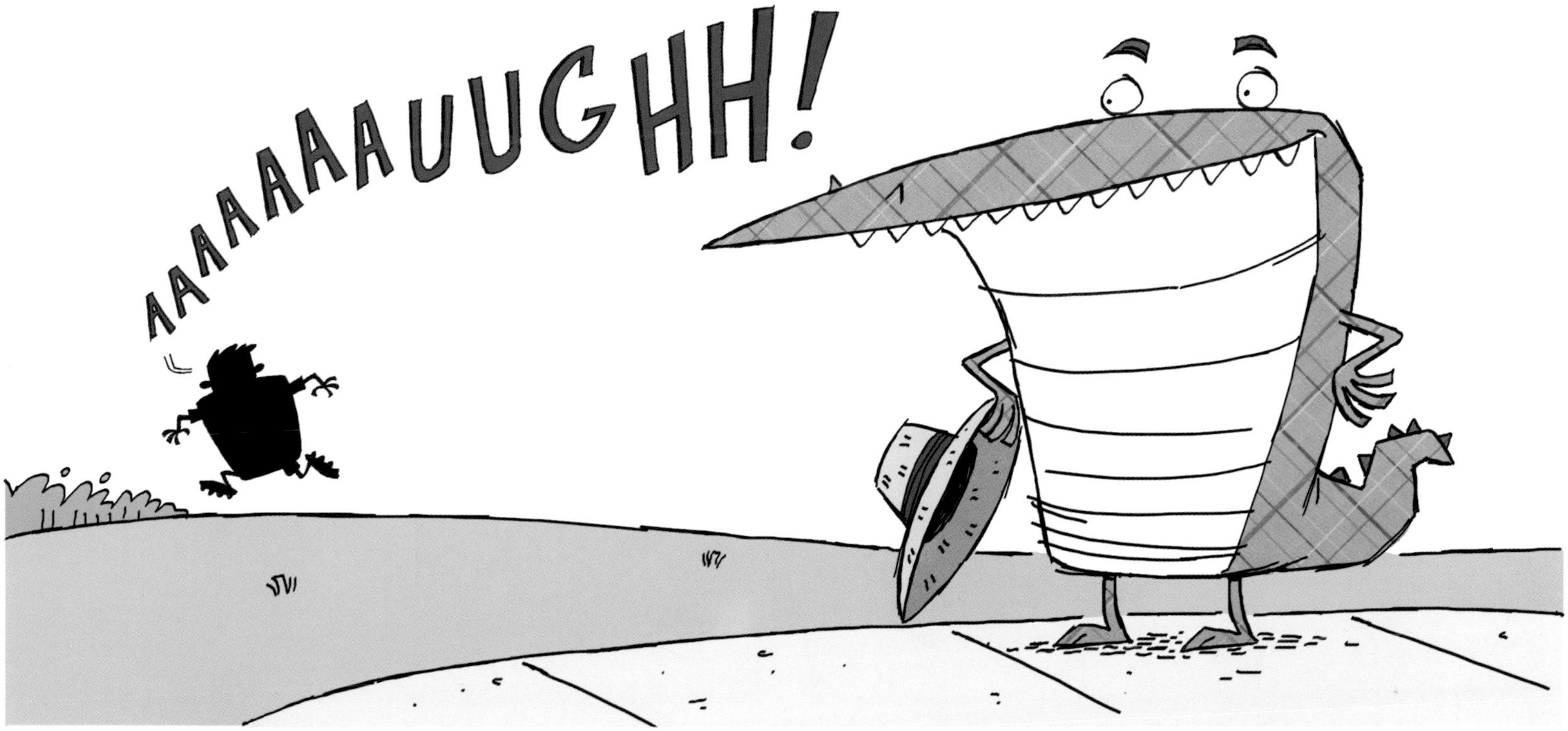
AAAAAAAUUGHH!

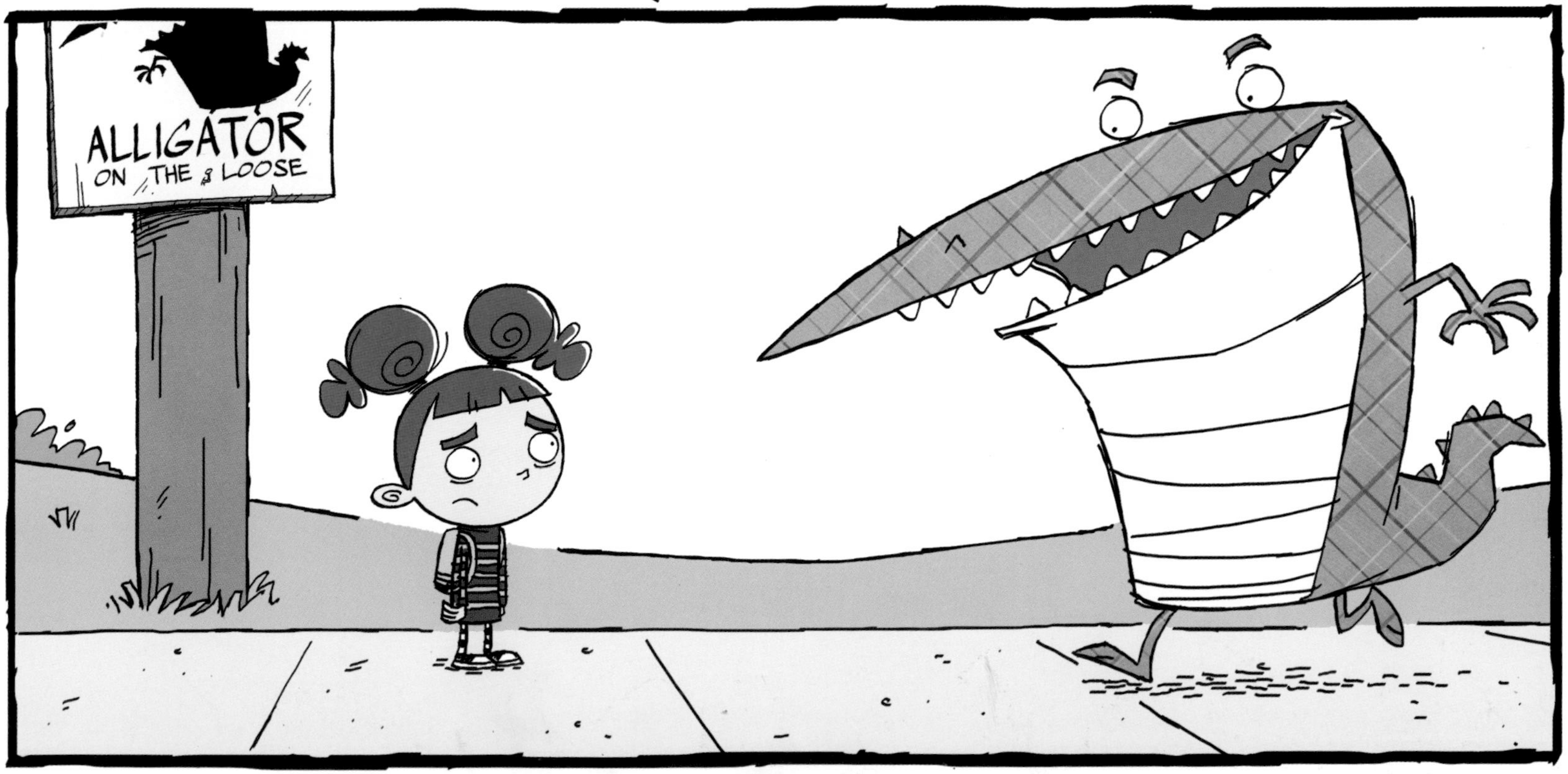
ALLIGATOR
ON THE LOOSE

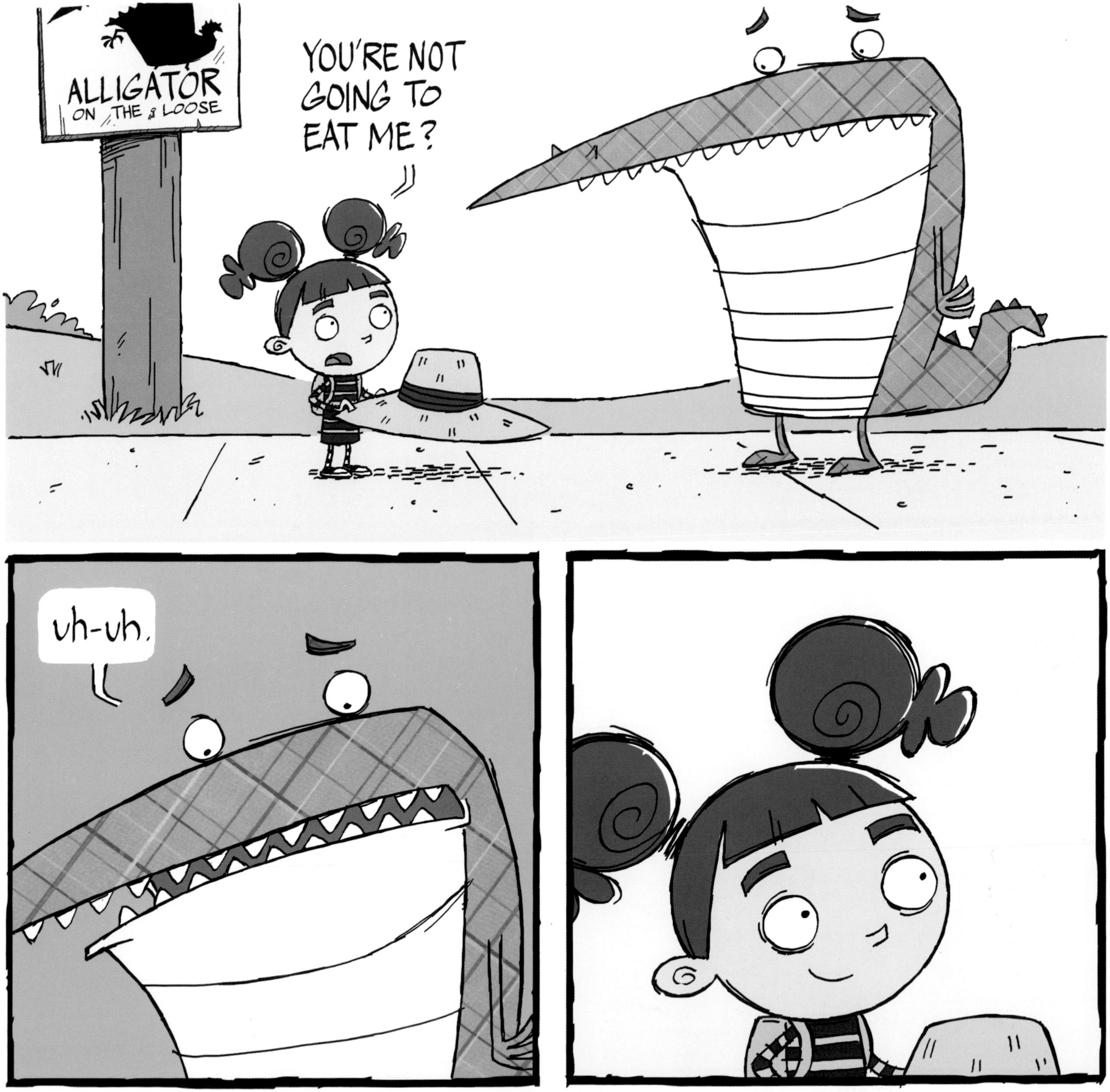
ALLIGATOR
ON THE LOOSE
YOU'RE NOT GOING TO EAT ME?
uh-uh.

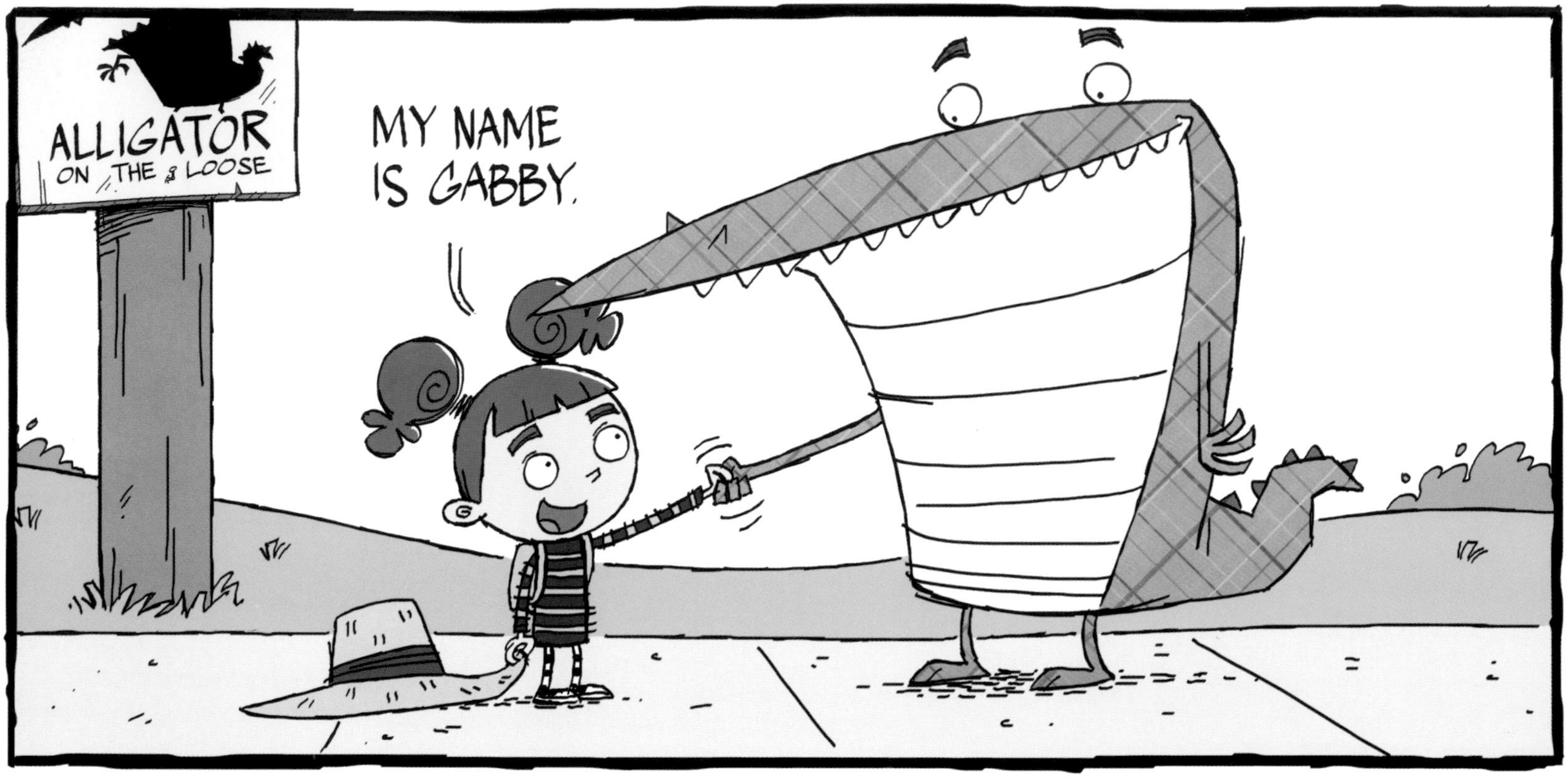
ALLIGATOR ON THE LOOSE
MY NAME IS GABBY.

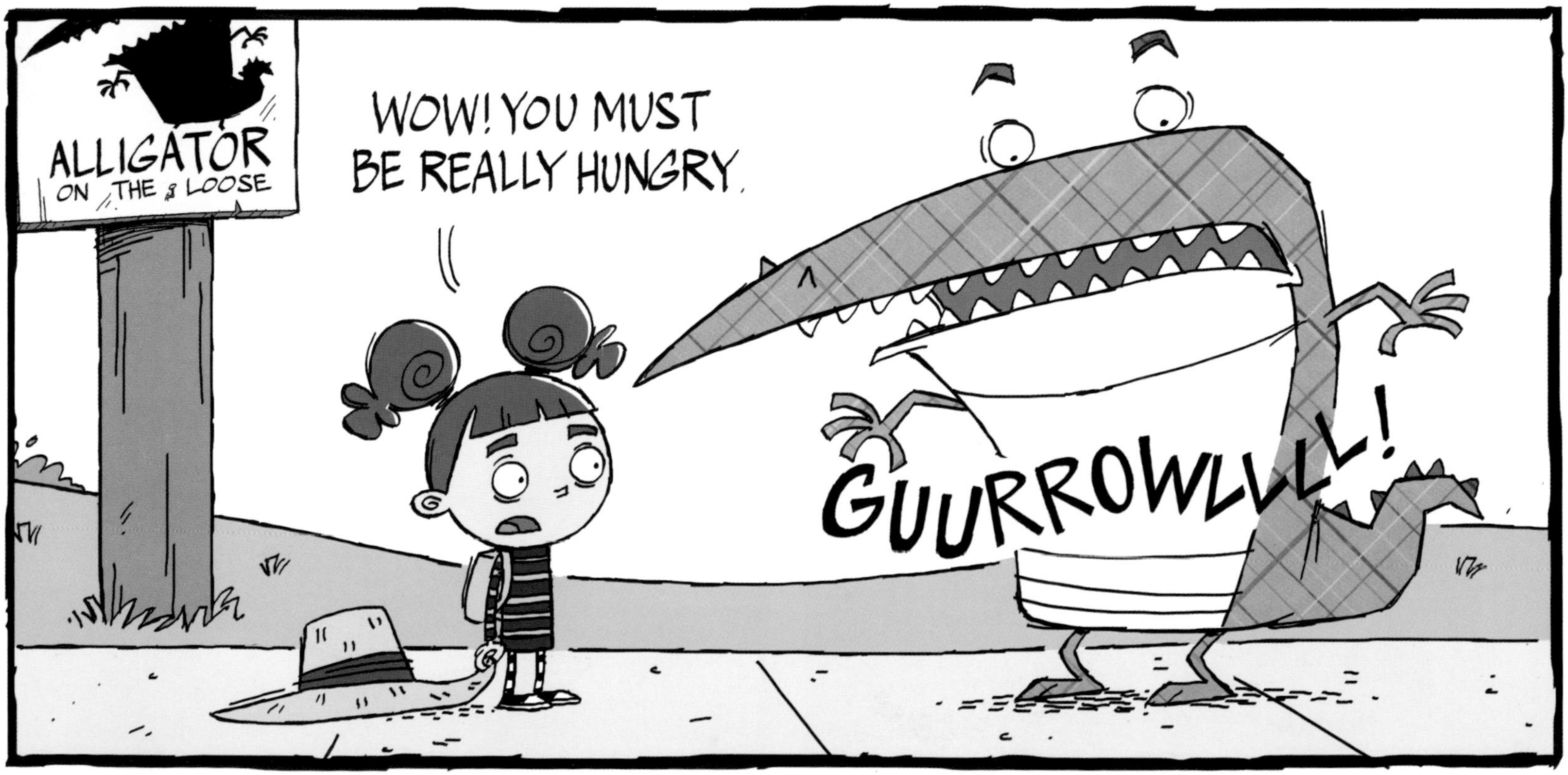
ALLIGATOR ON THE LOOSE
WOW! YOU MUST BE REALLY HUNGRY.
GUURROWLLLL!

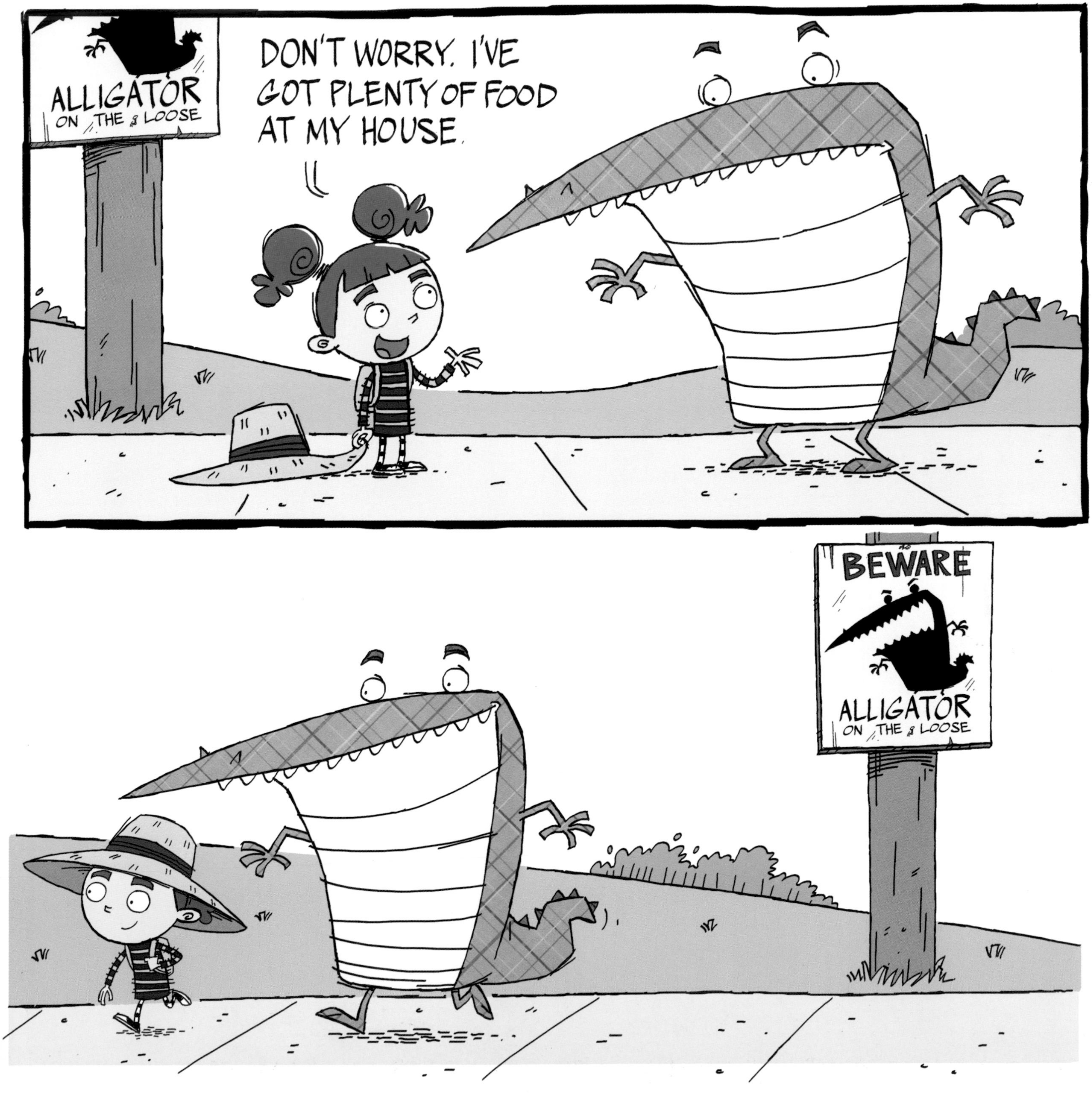

ALLIGATOR ON THE LOOSE
DON'T WORRY. I'VE GOT PLENTY OF FOOD AT MY HOUSE.
BEWARE
ALLIGATOR ON THE LOOSE

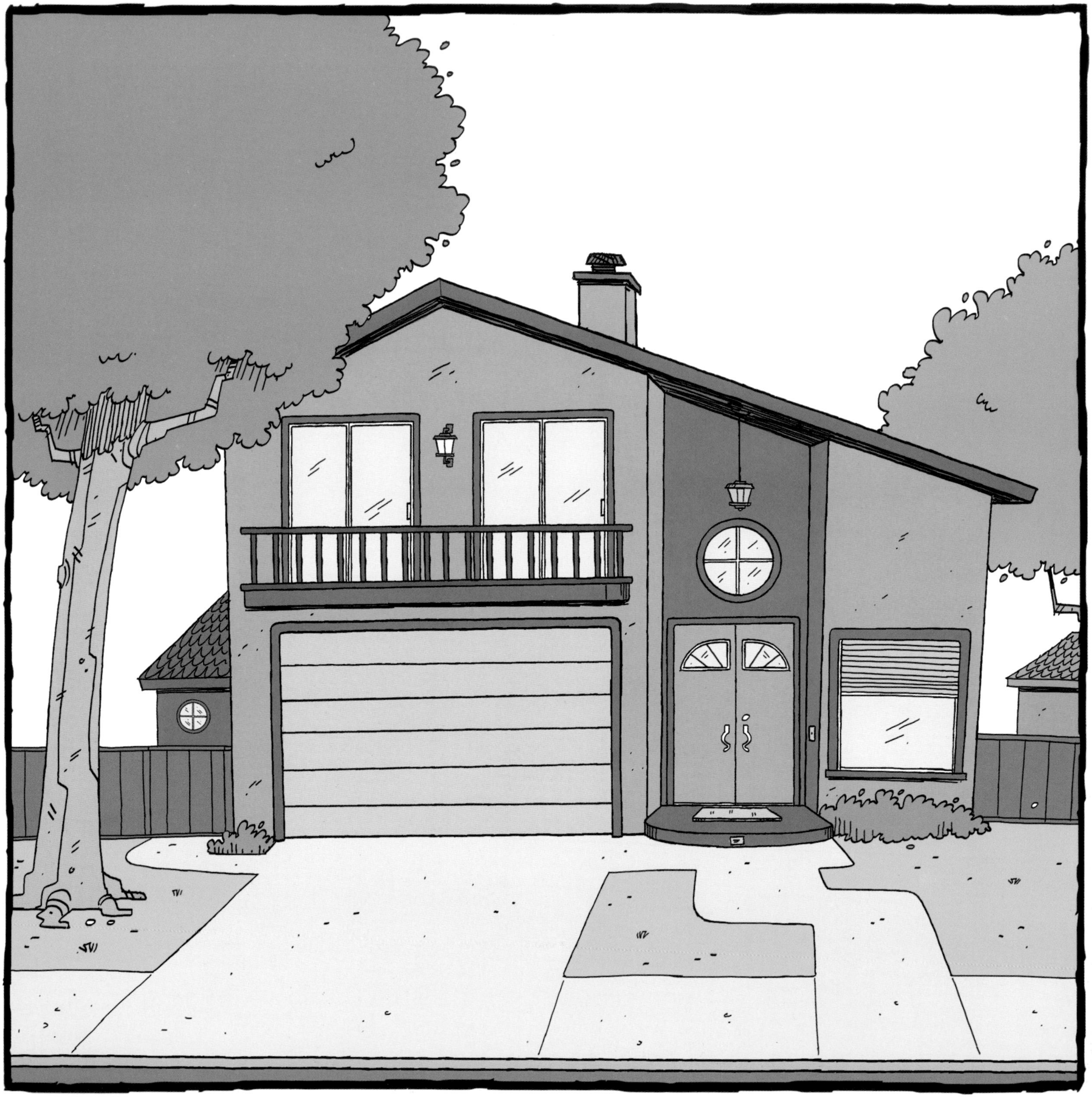

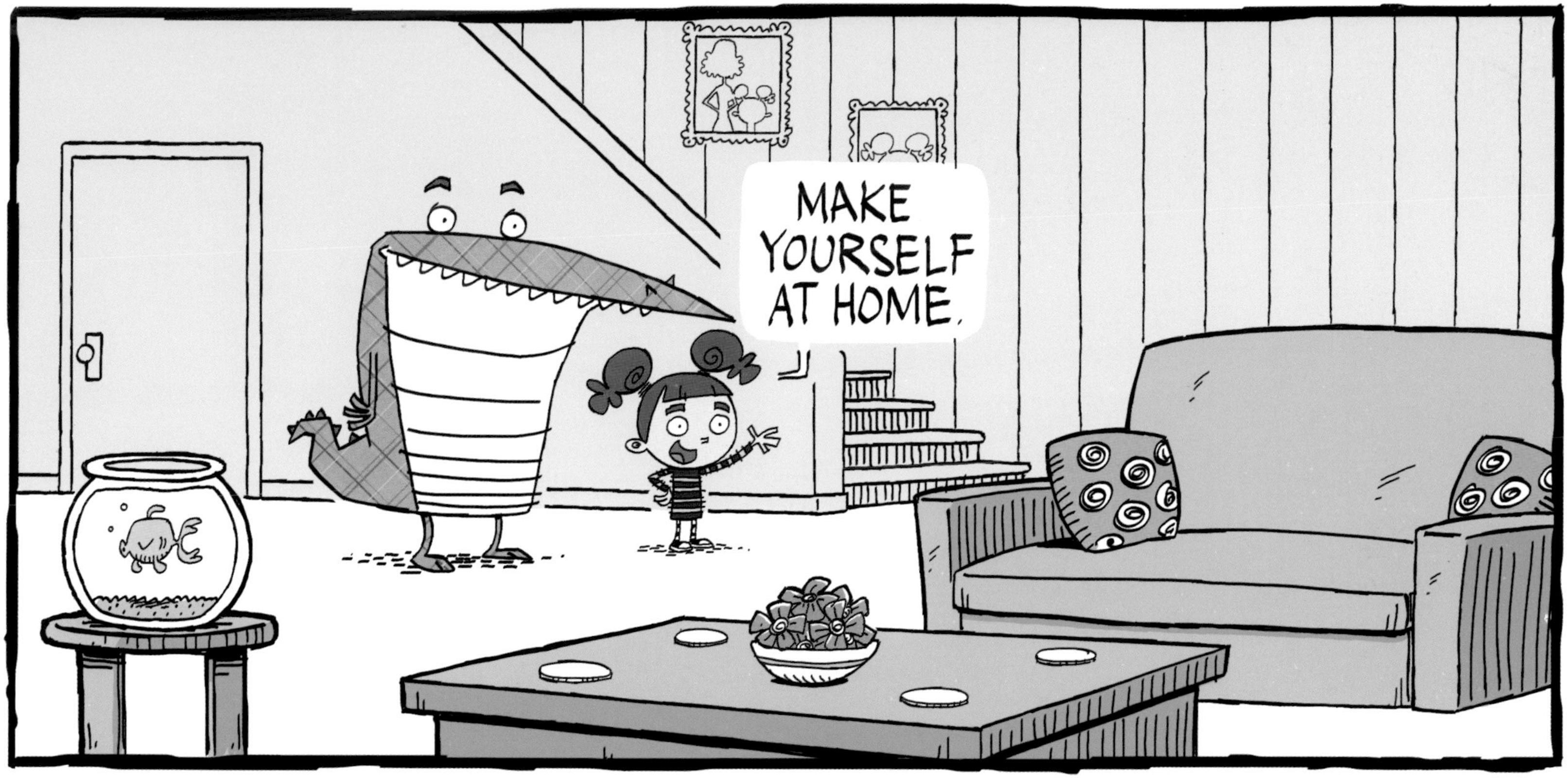
MAKE YOURSELF AT HOME.

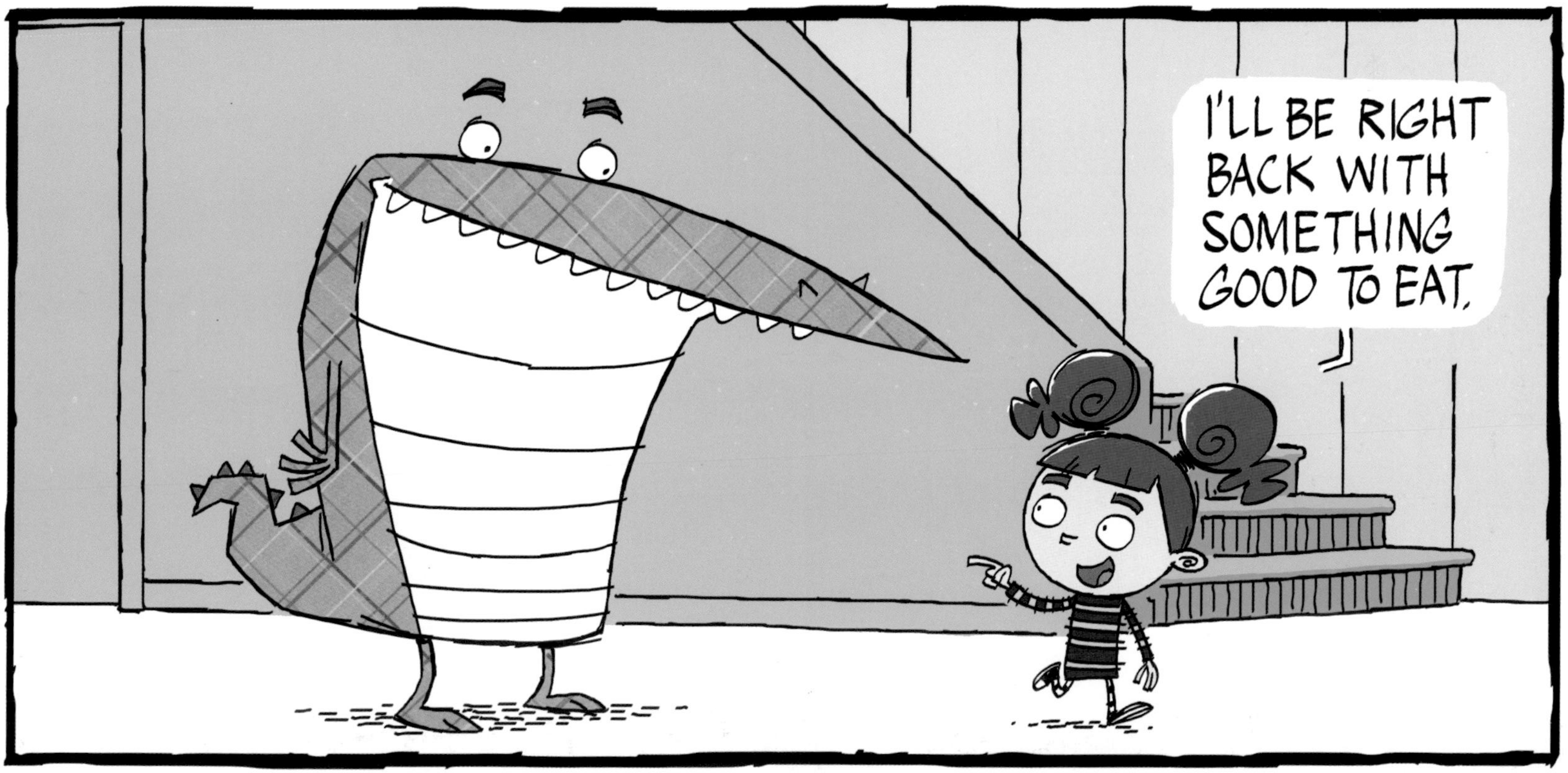
I'LL BE RIGHT BACK WITH SOMETHING GOOD TO EAT.

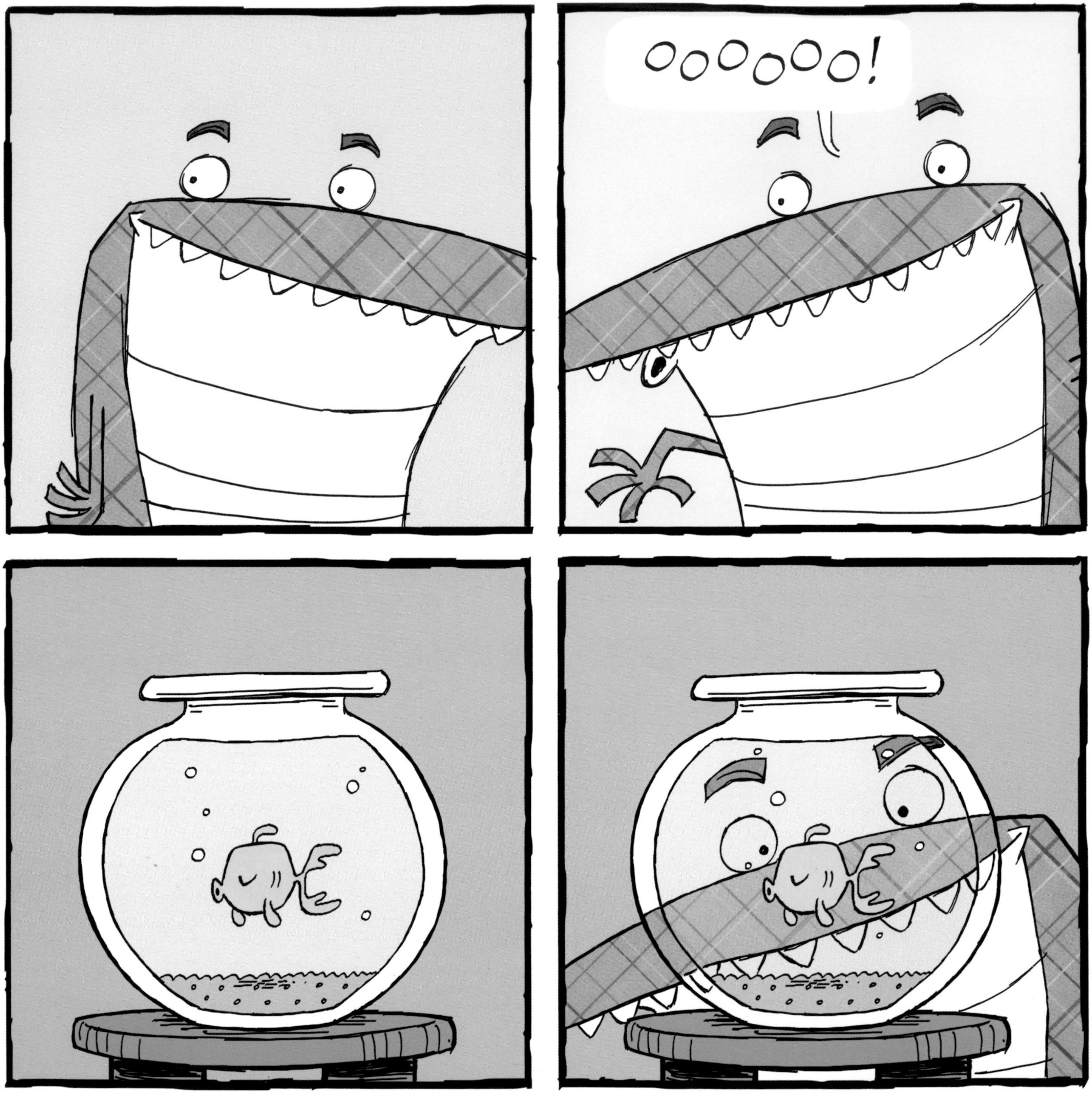
OOOOOO!

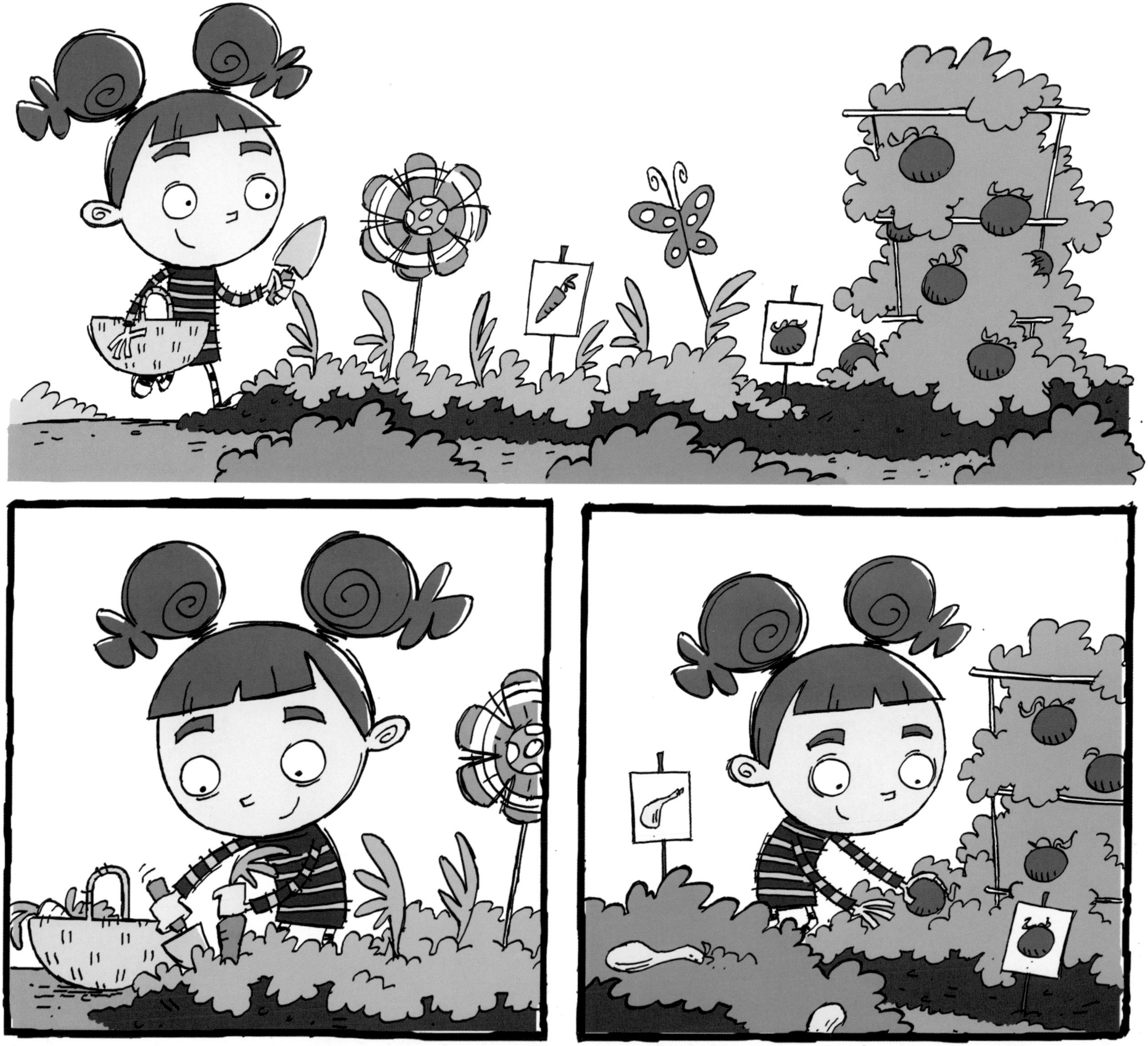

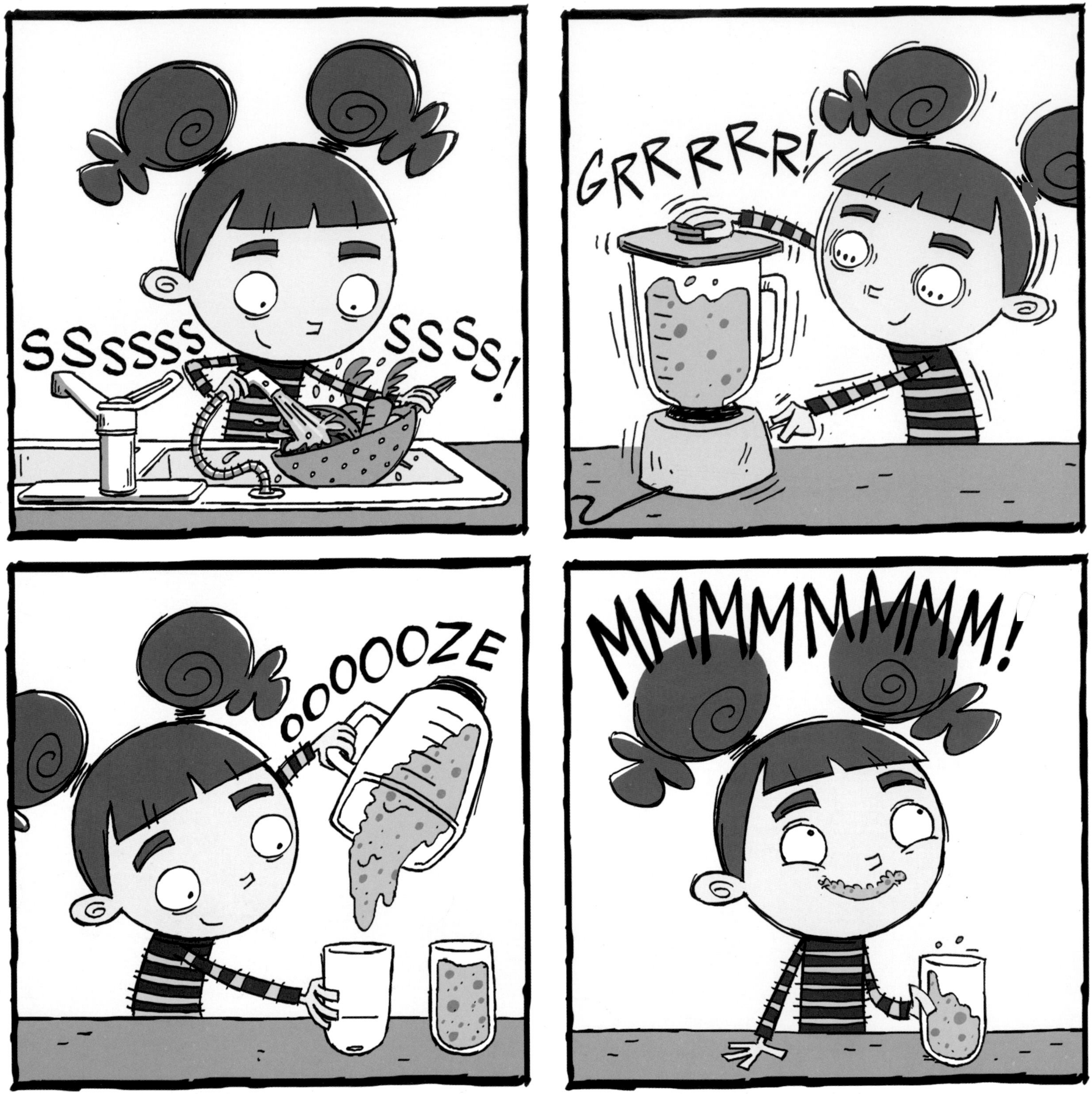
SSSSSS
SSSS!
GRRRRR!
OOOOOOZE
MMMMMMMM!

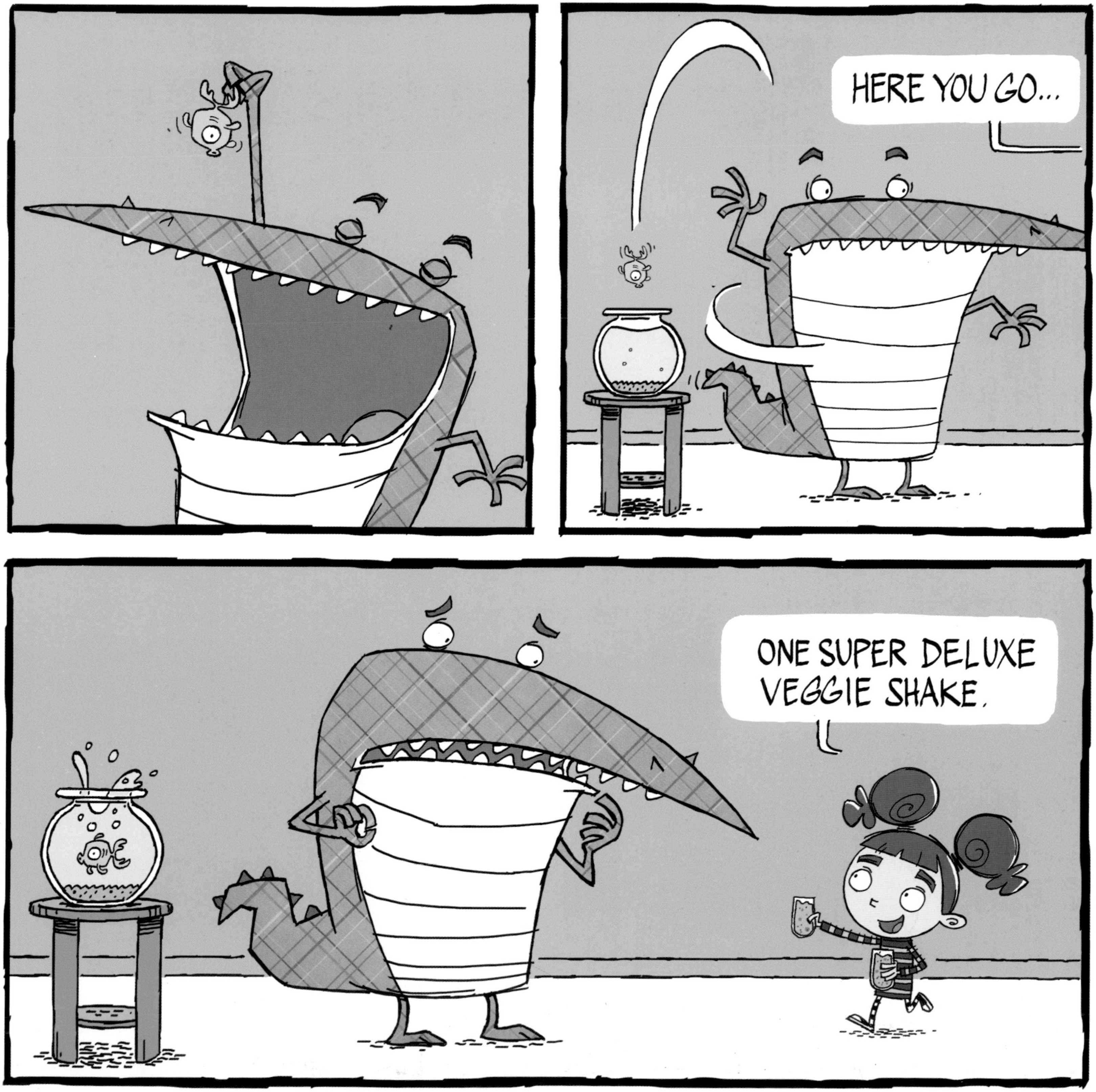
HERE YOU GO...
ONE SUPER DELUXE VEGGIE SHAKE.

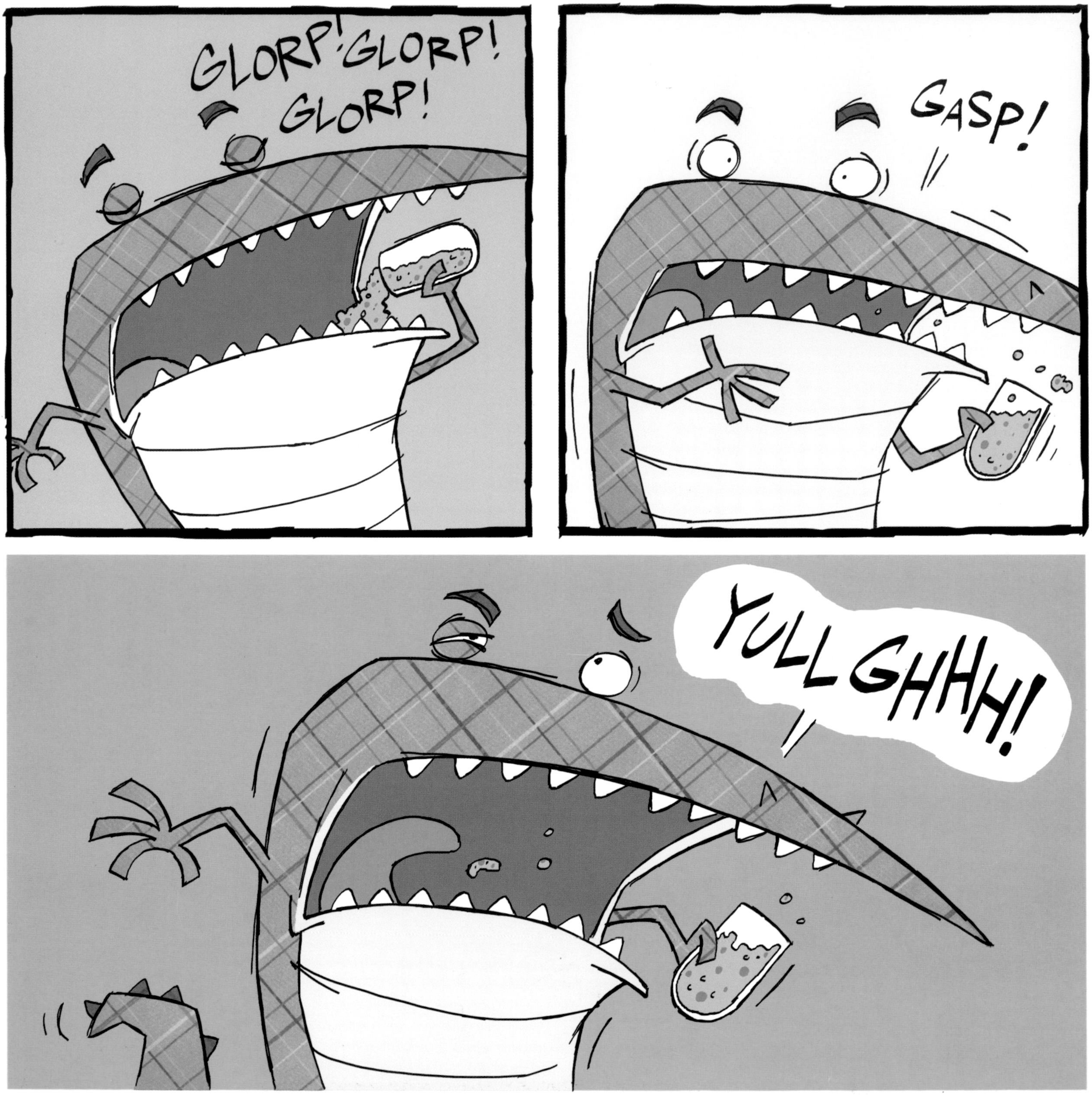
GLORP! GLORP!
GLORP!
GASP!
YULLGHHH!

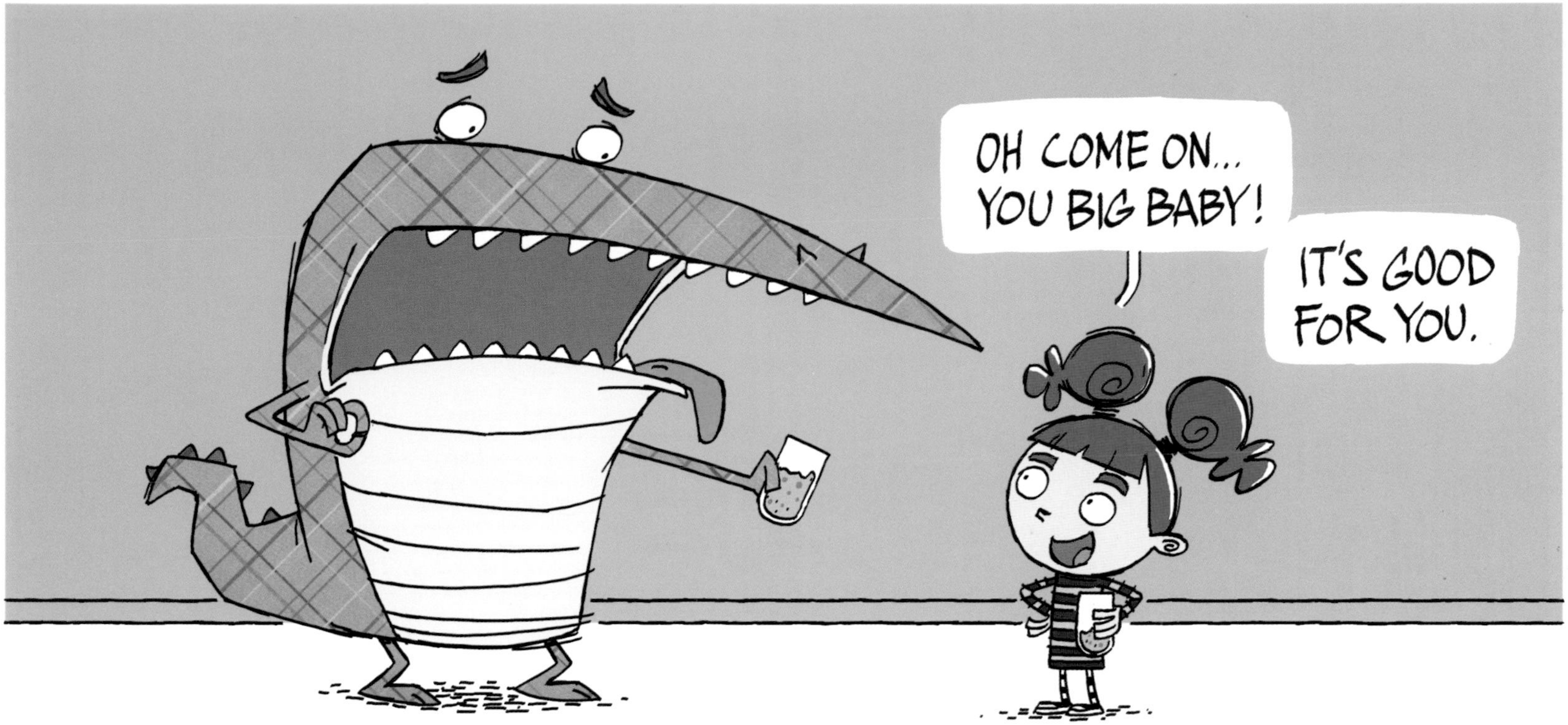
OH COME ON...
YOU BIG BABY!
IT'S GOOD
FOR YOU.

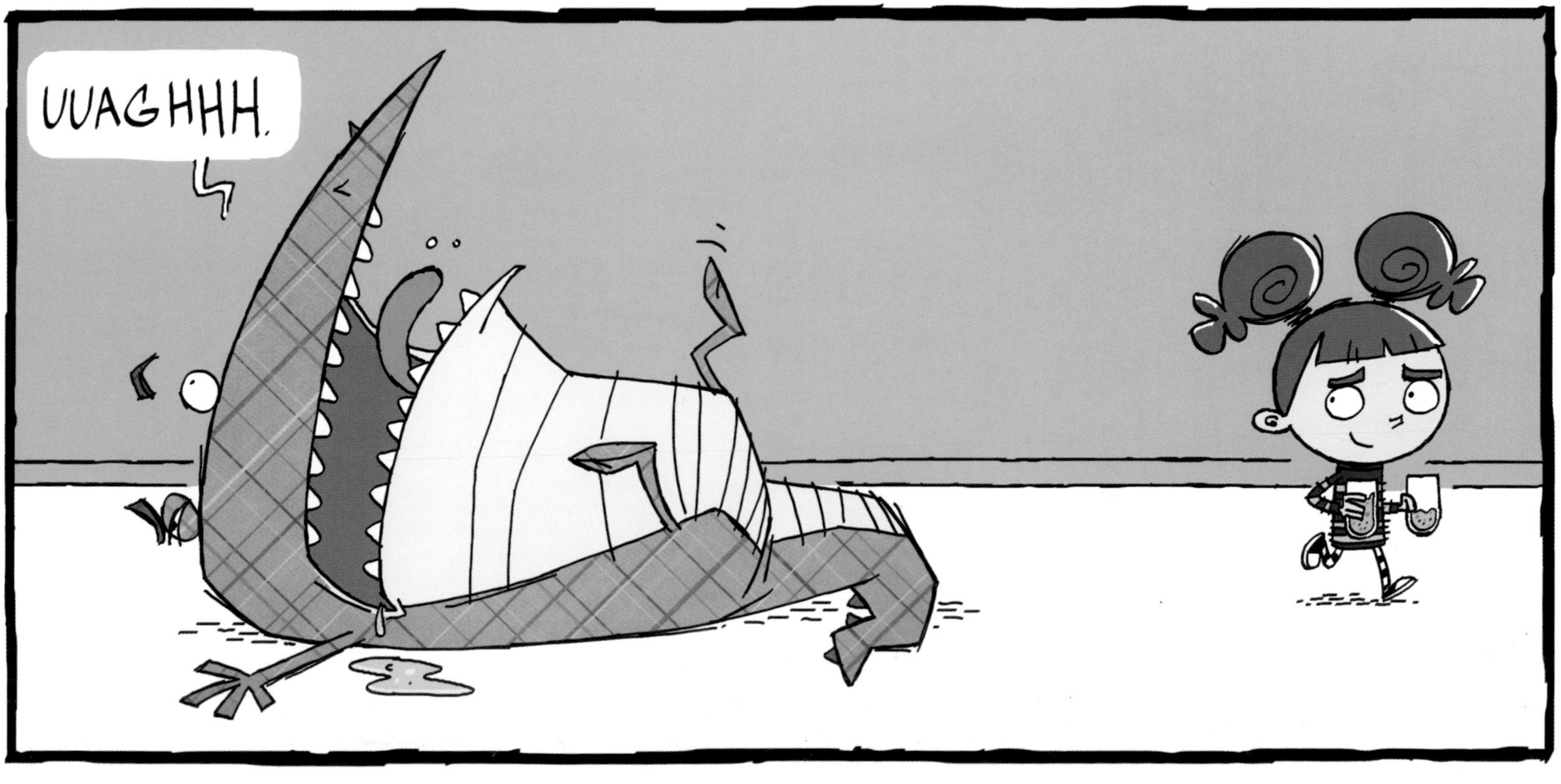
UUAGHHH.

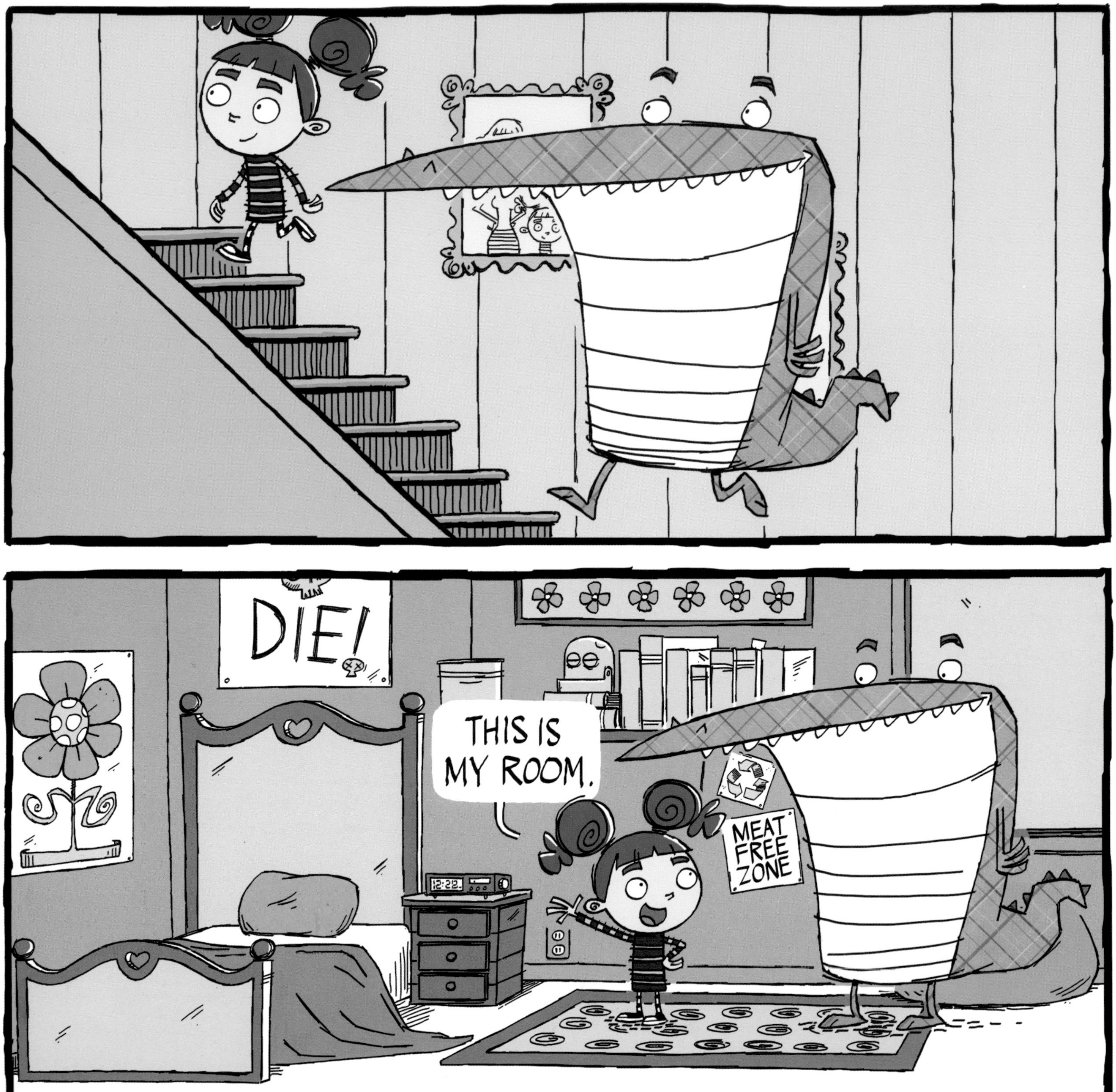
DIE!
THIS IS MY ROOM.
MEAT FREE ZONE
12:22

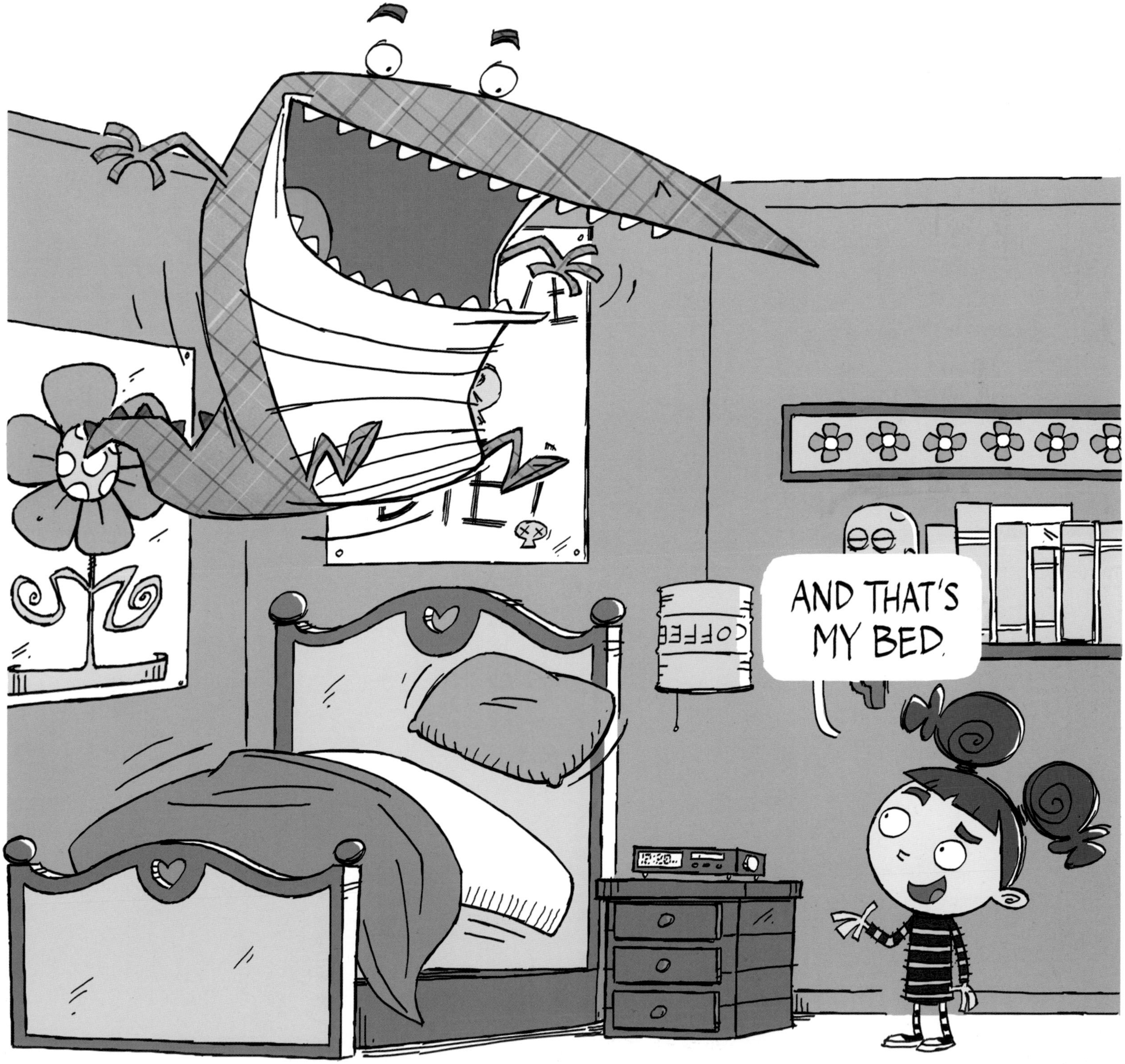
AND THAT'S MY BED.

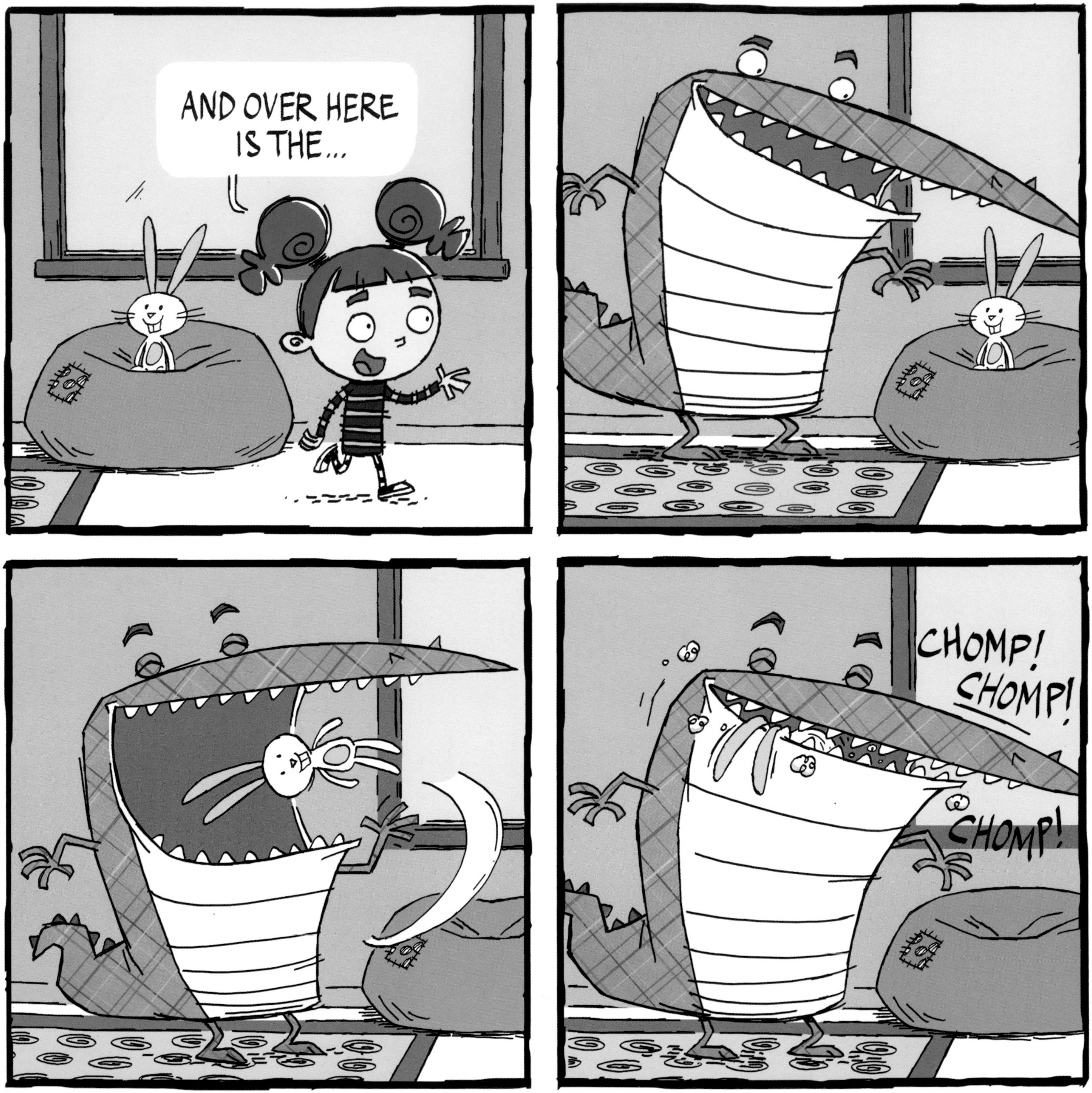
AND OVER HERE IS THE...
CHOMP!
CHOMP!
CHOMP!

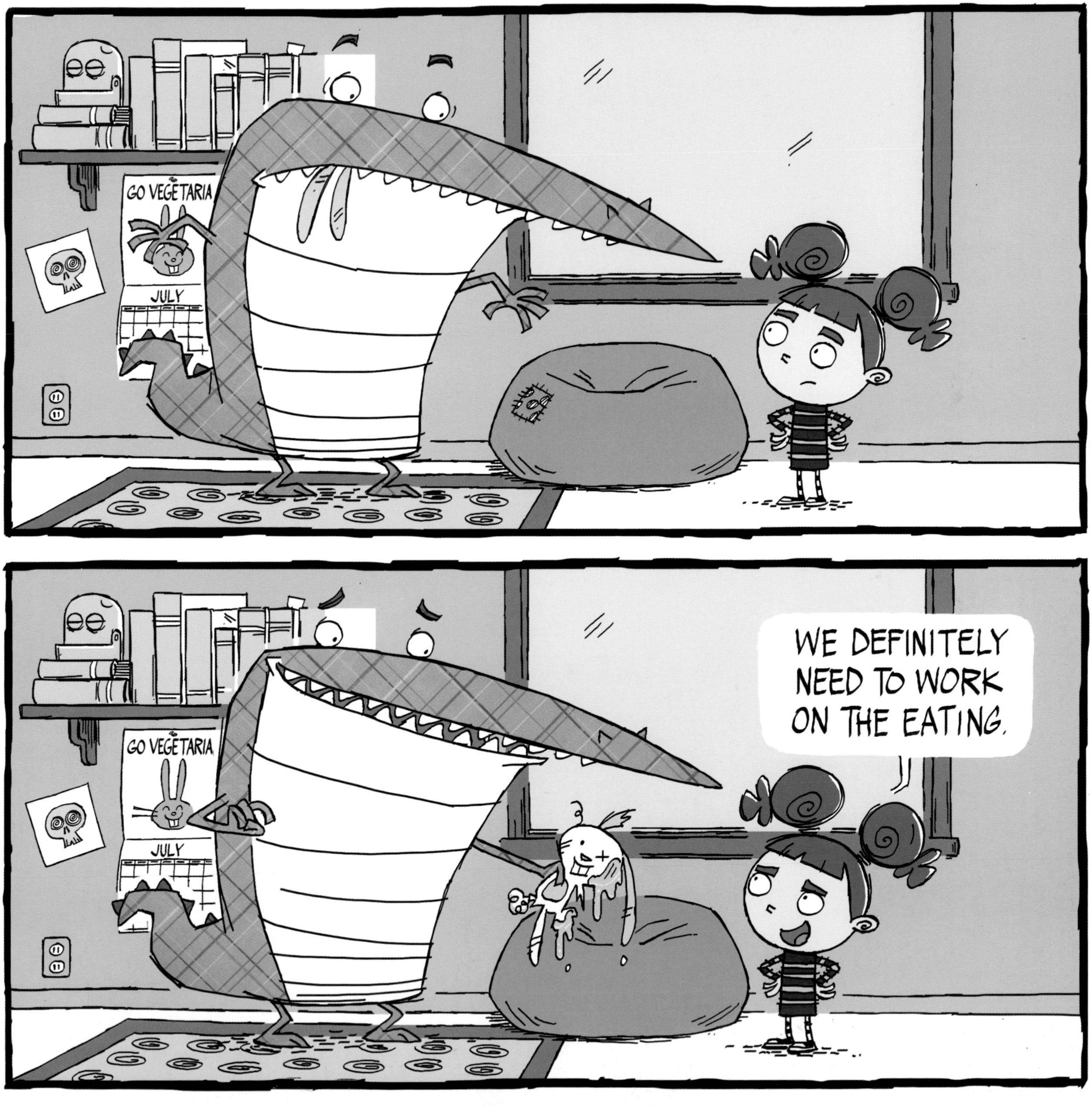
GO VEGETARIA
JULY
GO VEGETARIA
JULY
WE DEFINITELY NEED TO WORK ON THE EATING.

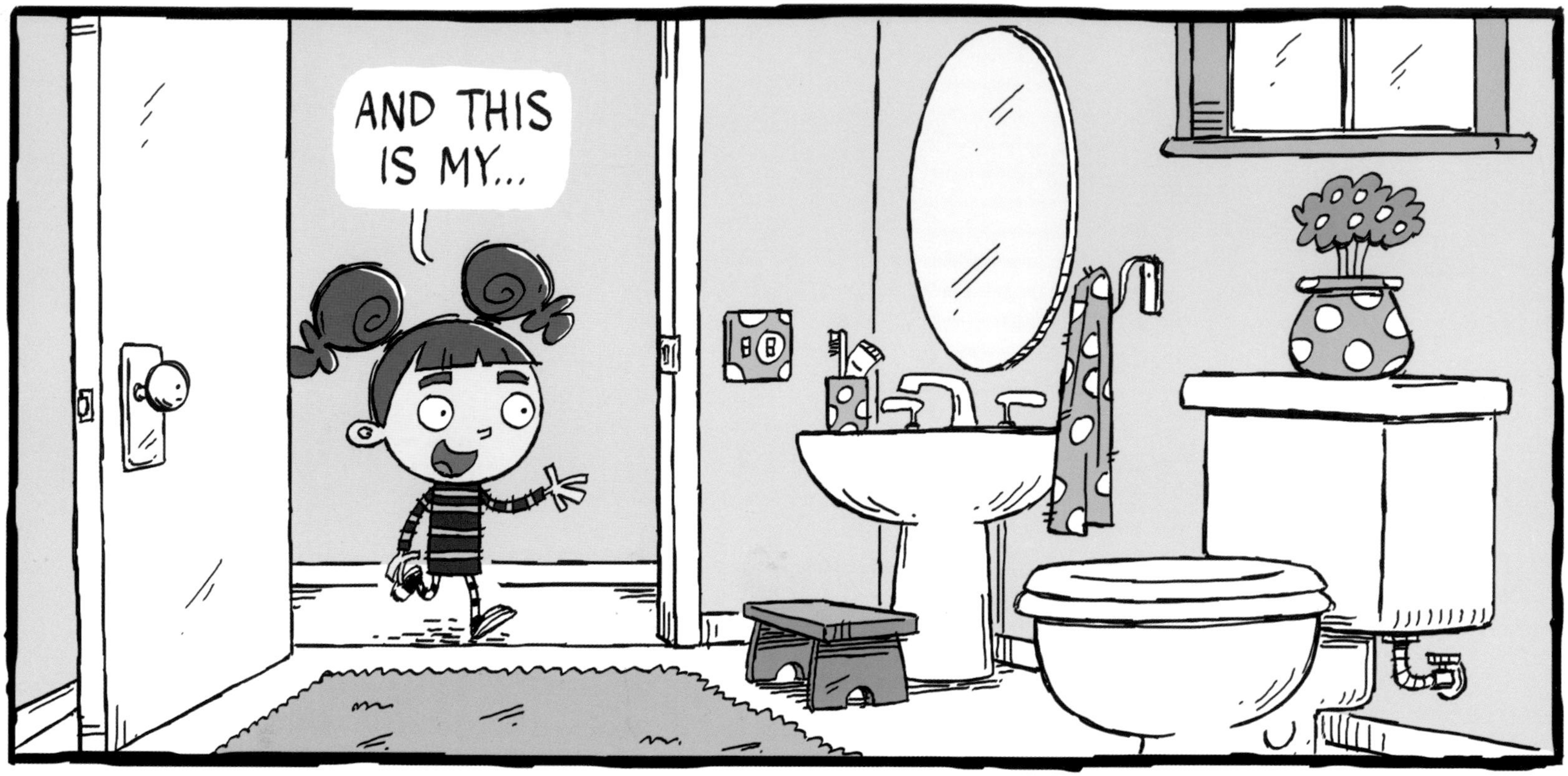
AND THIS IS MY...

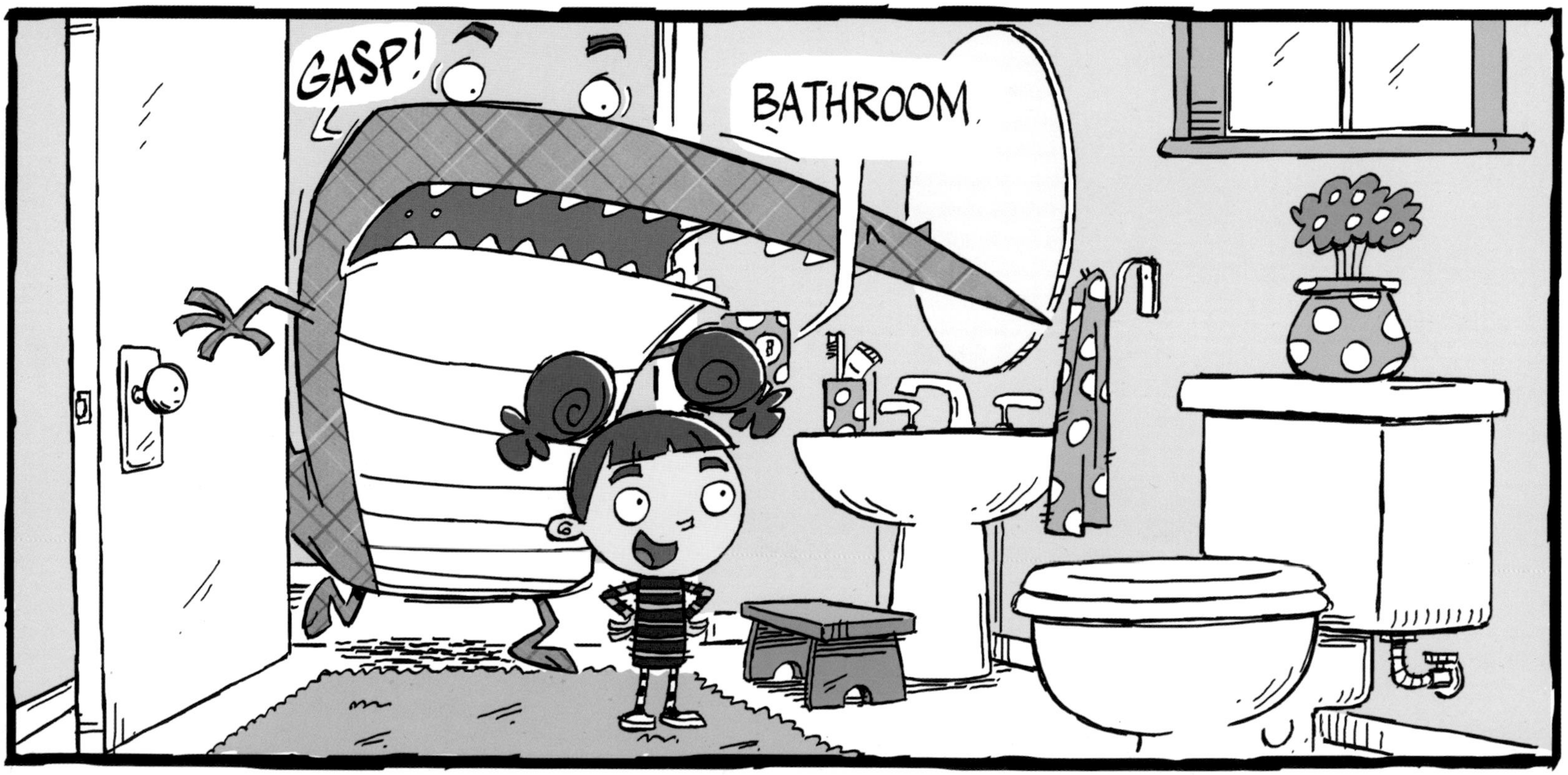
GASP!
BATHROOM.

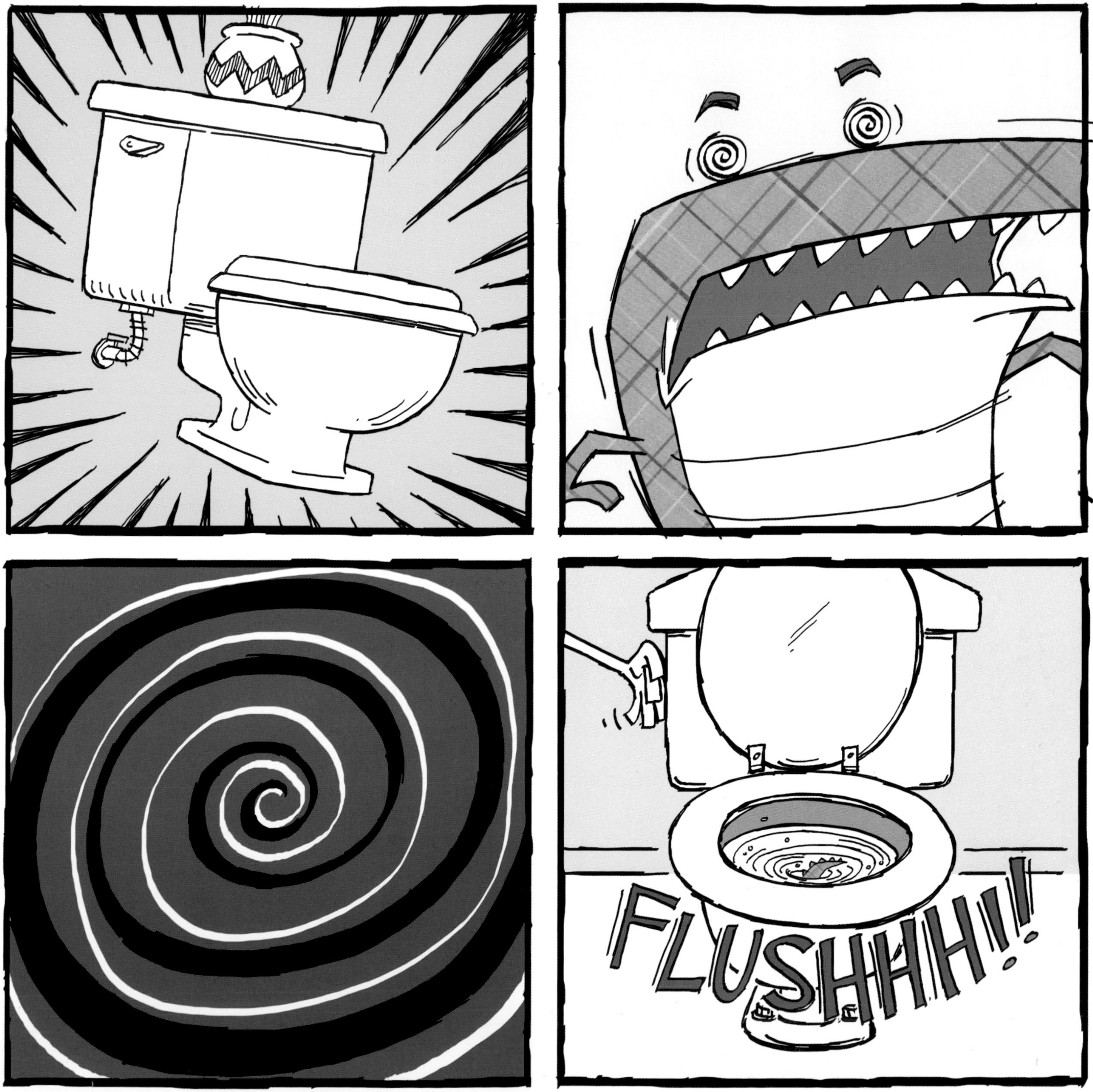
FLUSHHH!!

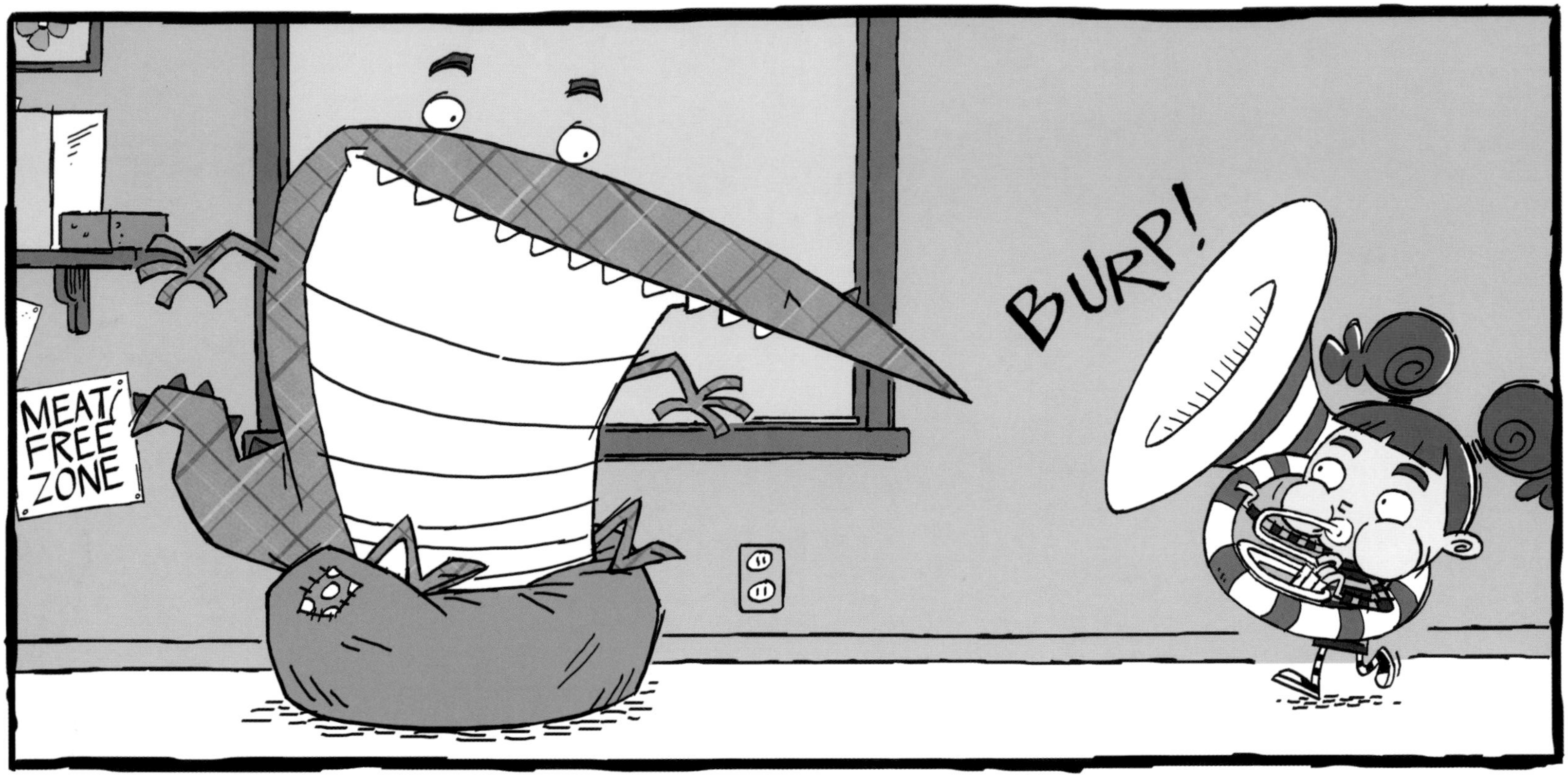
MEAT FREE ZONE
BURP!

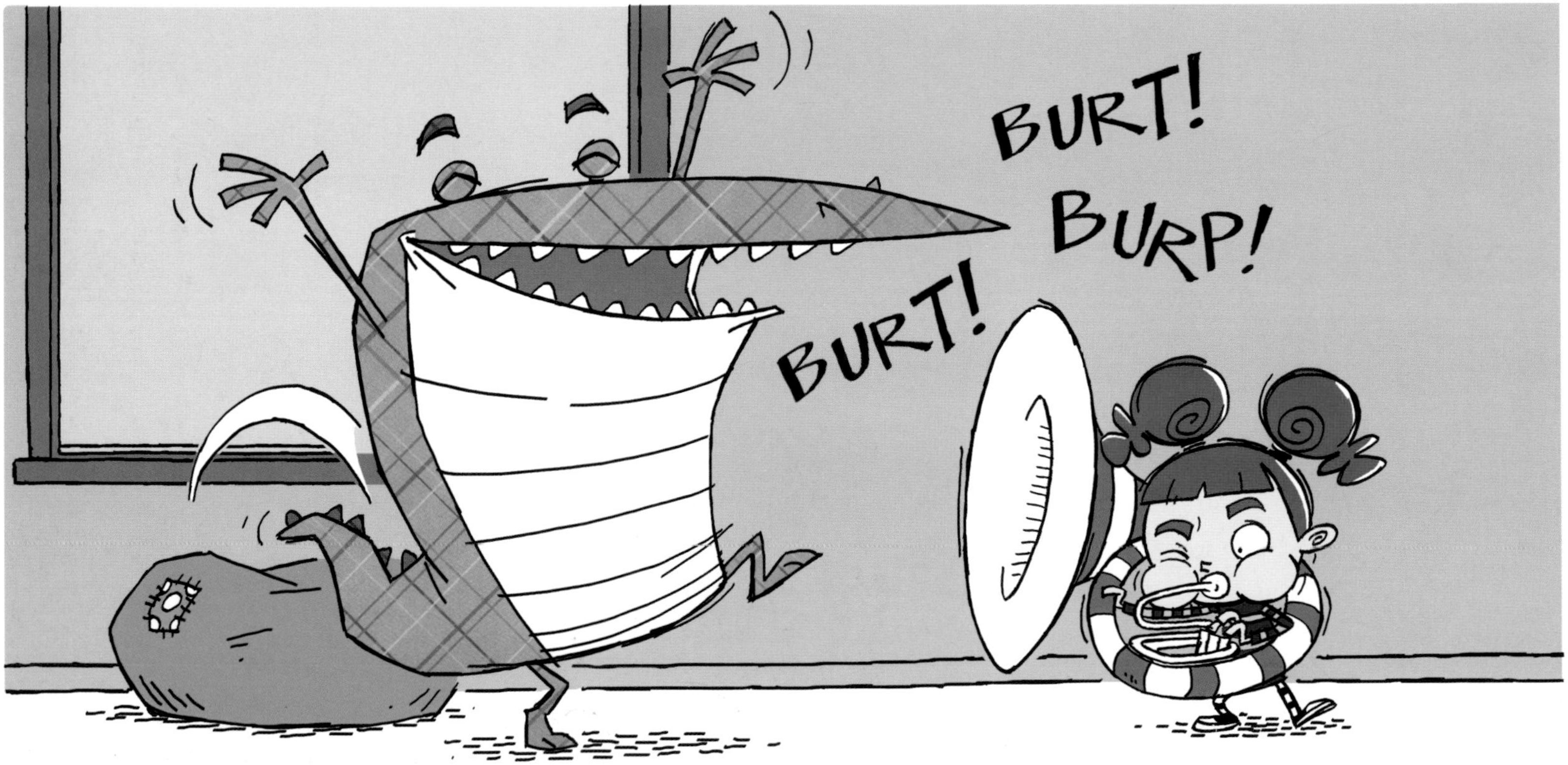
BURT!
BURP!
BURT!

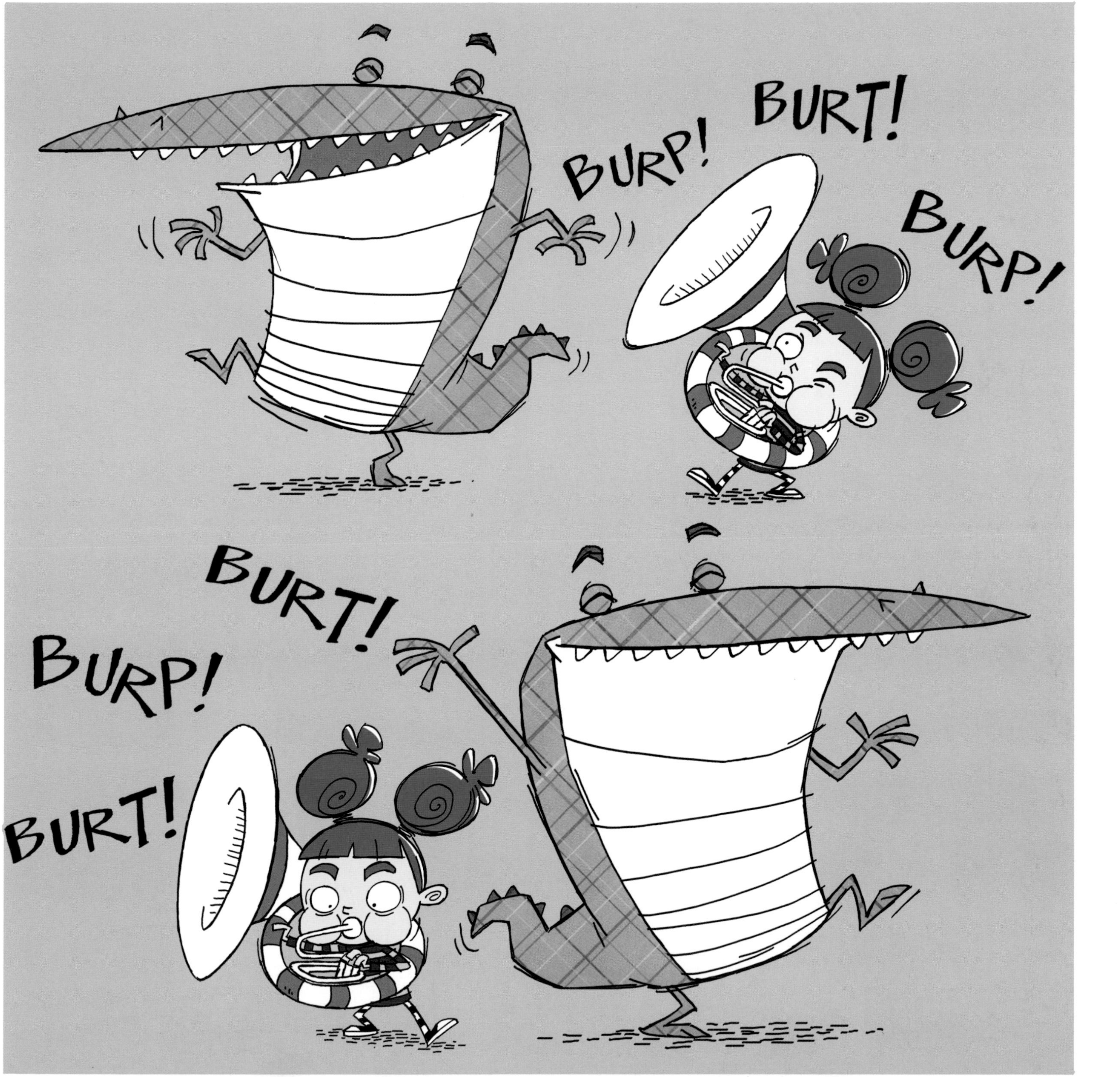
BURP!
BURT!
BURP!
BURT!
BURP!
BURT!

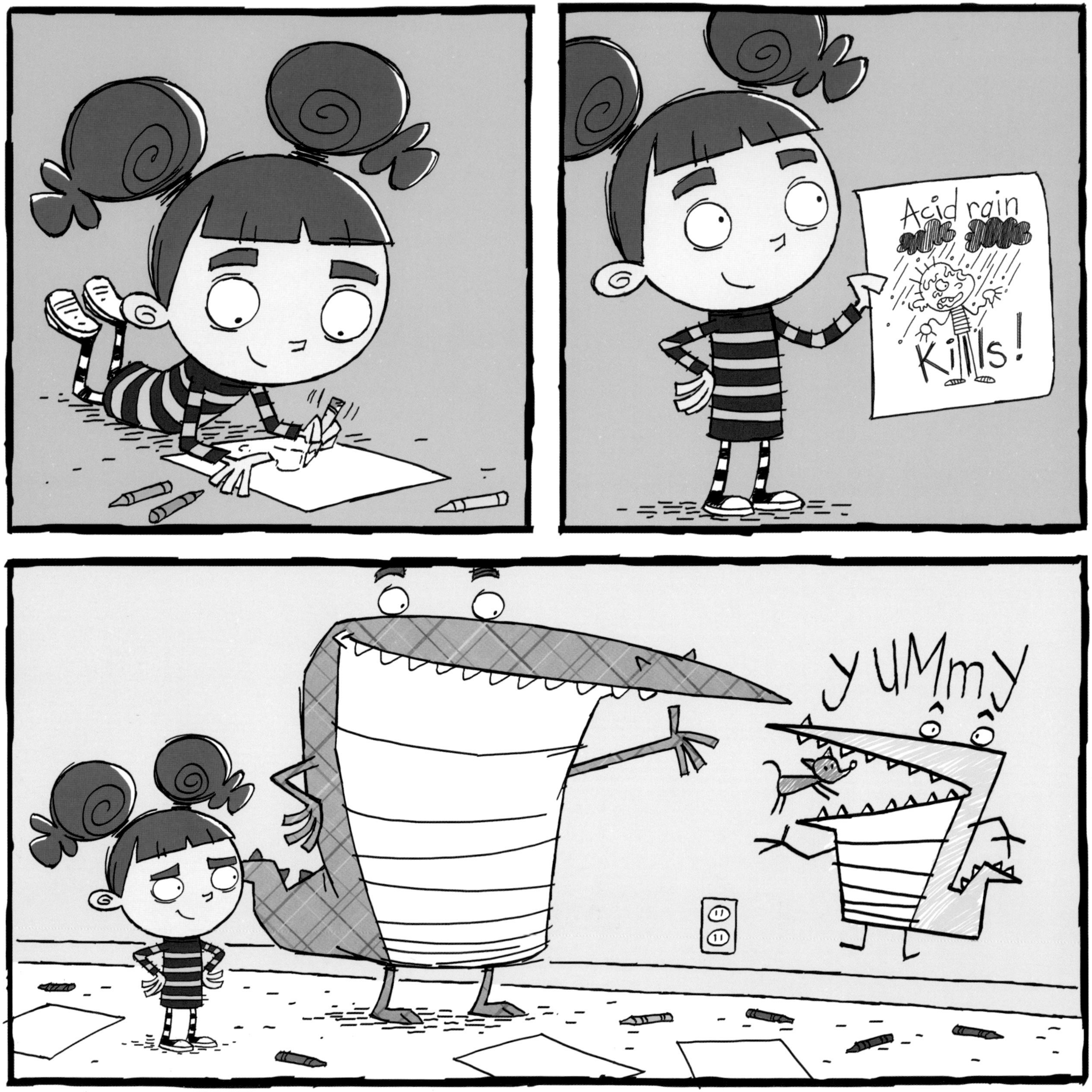

Acid rain
Kills!
yUMmy

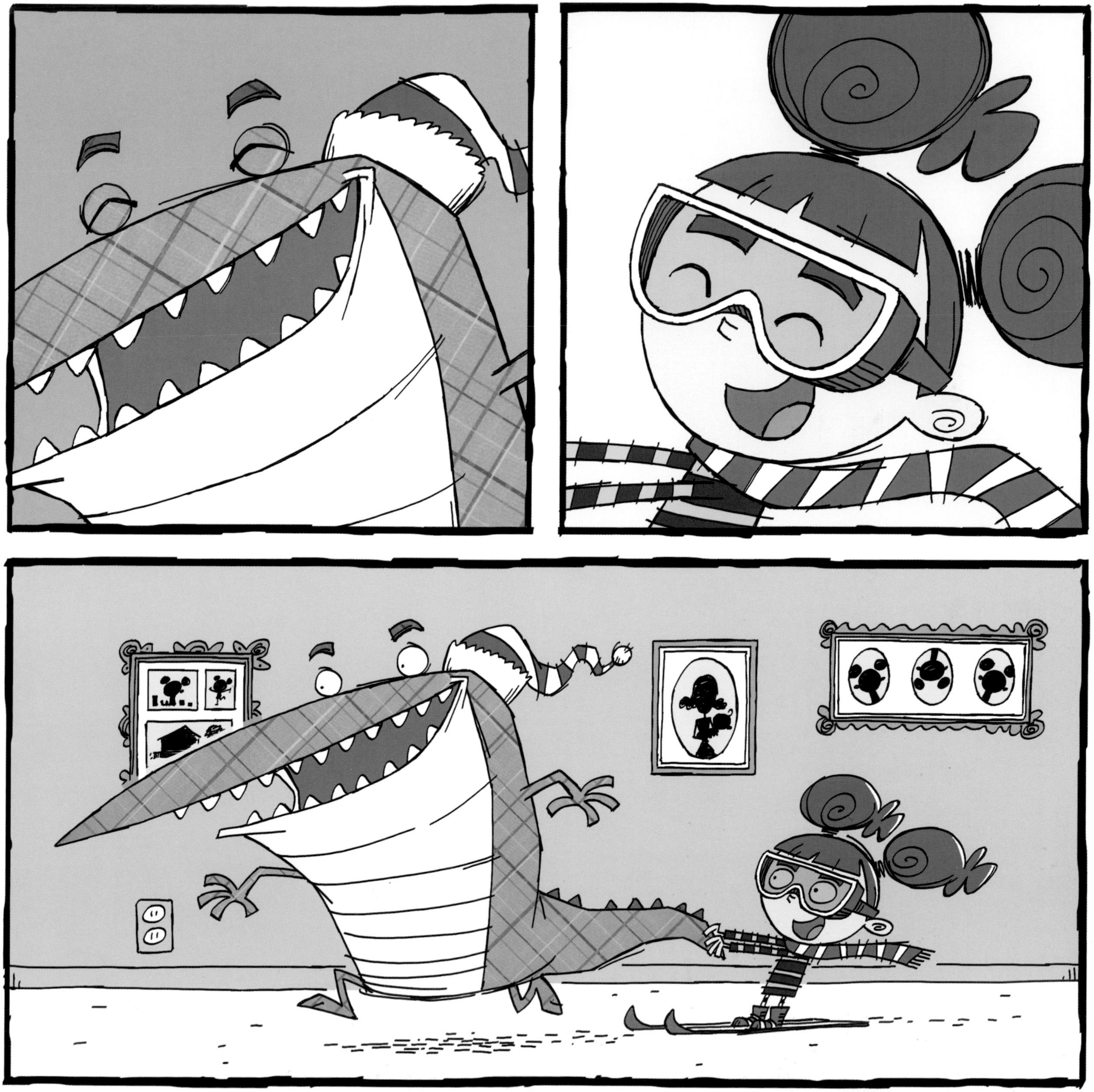

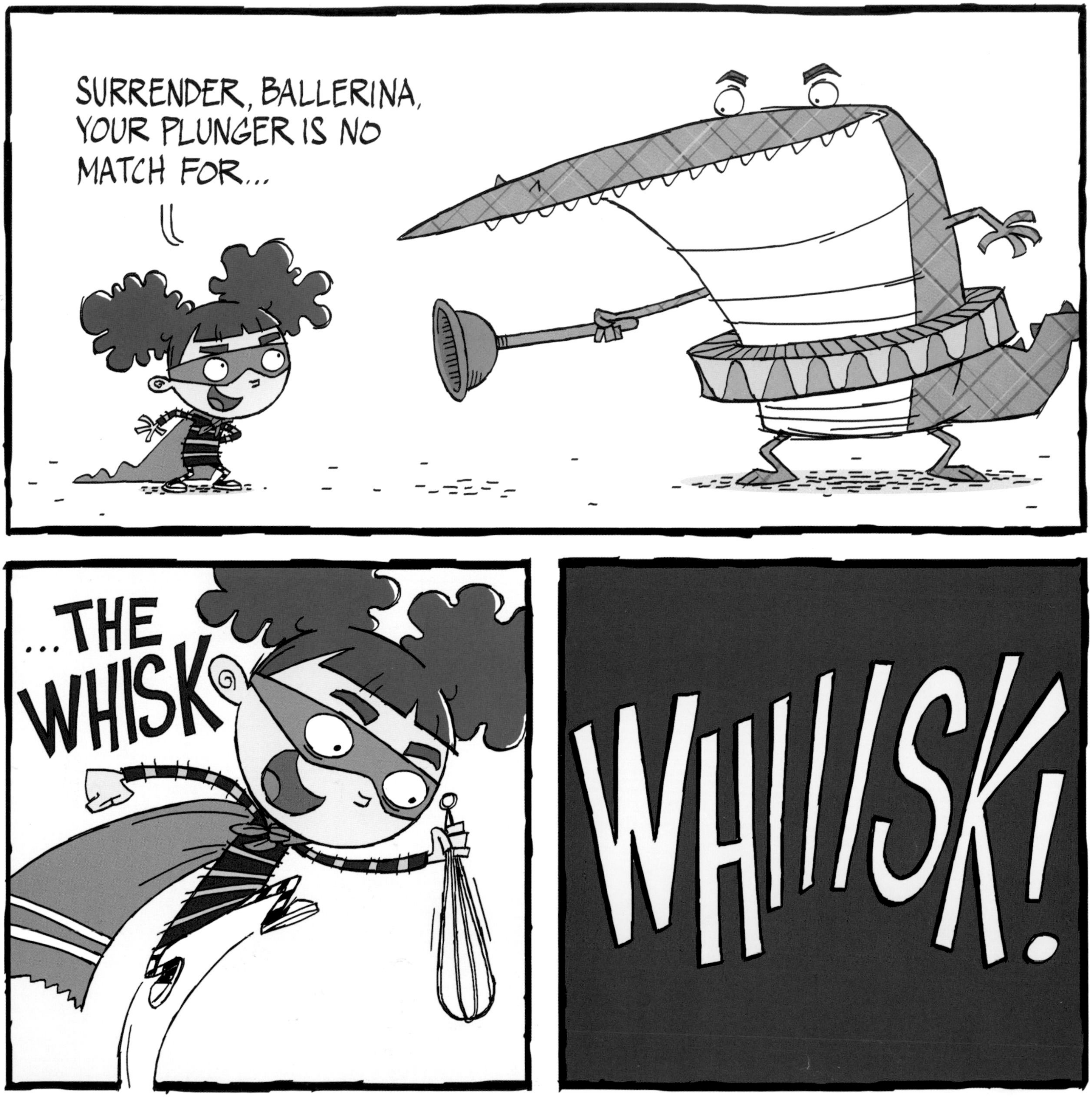
SURRENDER, BALLERINA, YOUR PLUNGER IS NO MATCH FOR...
...THE WHISK
WHIIISK!

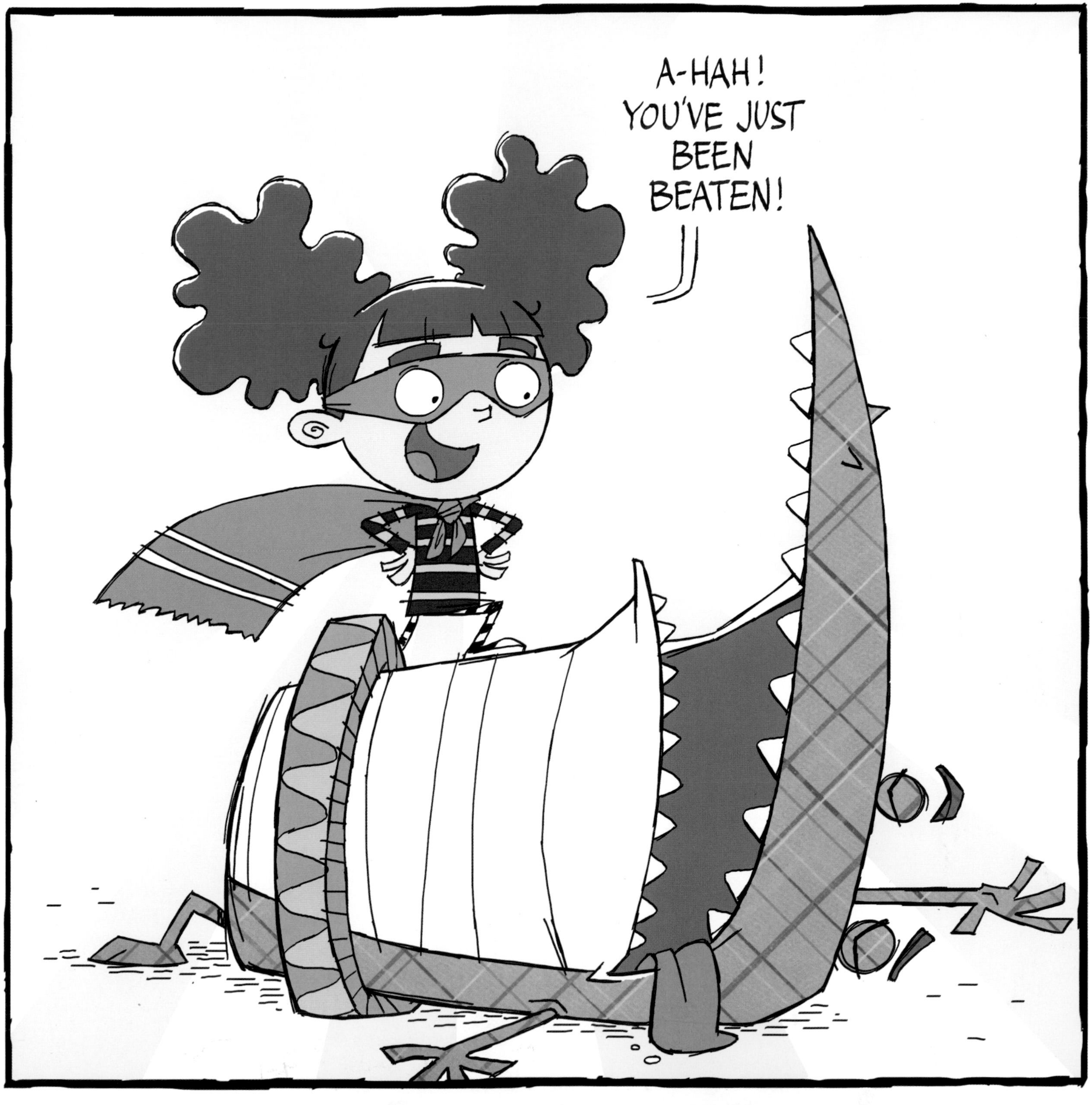
A-HAH! YOU'VE JUST BEEN BEATEN!

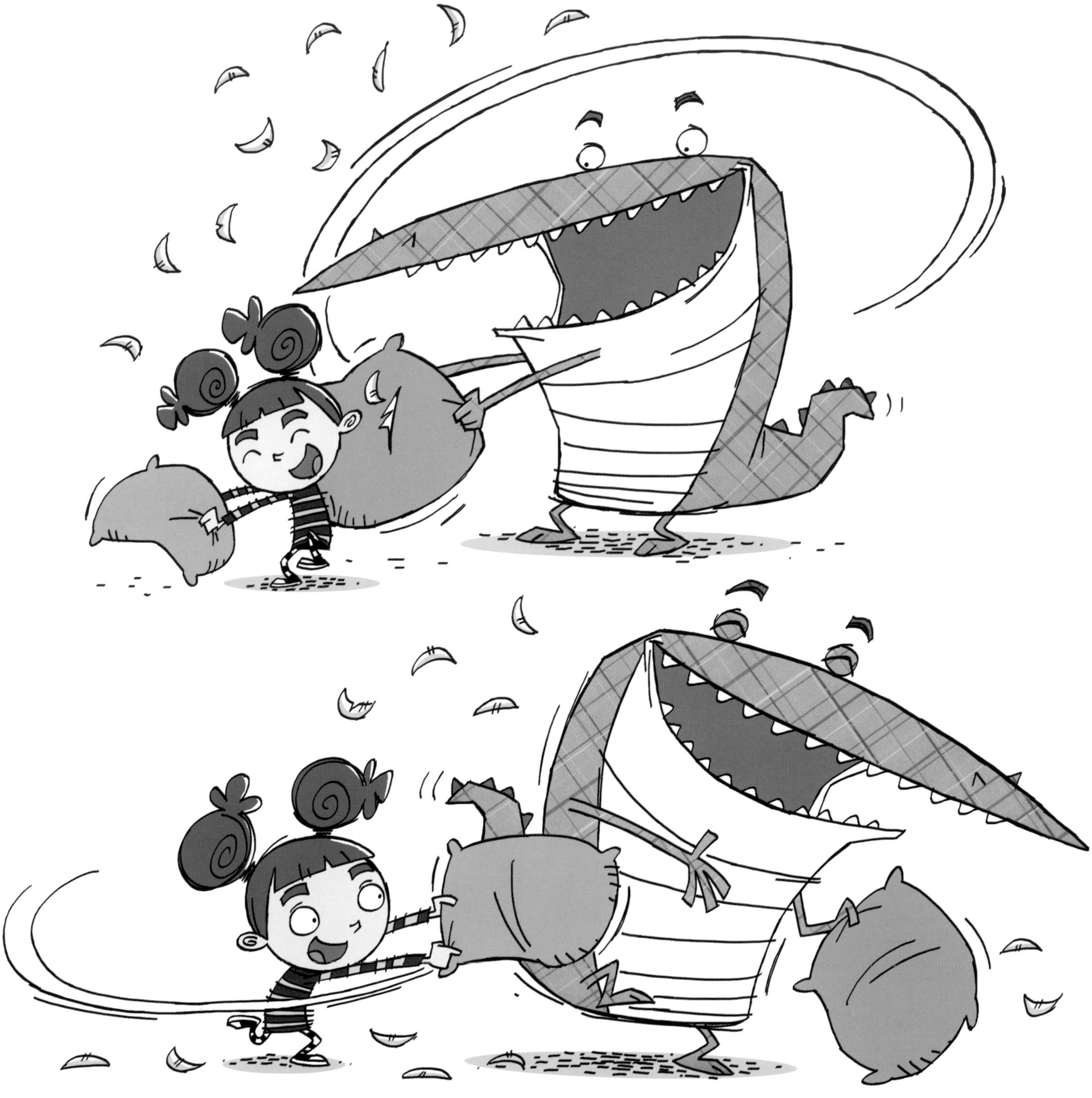

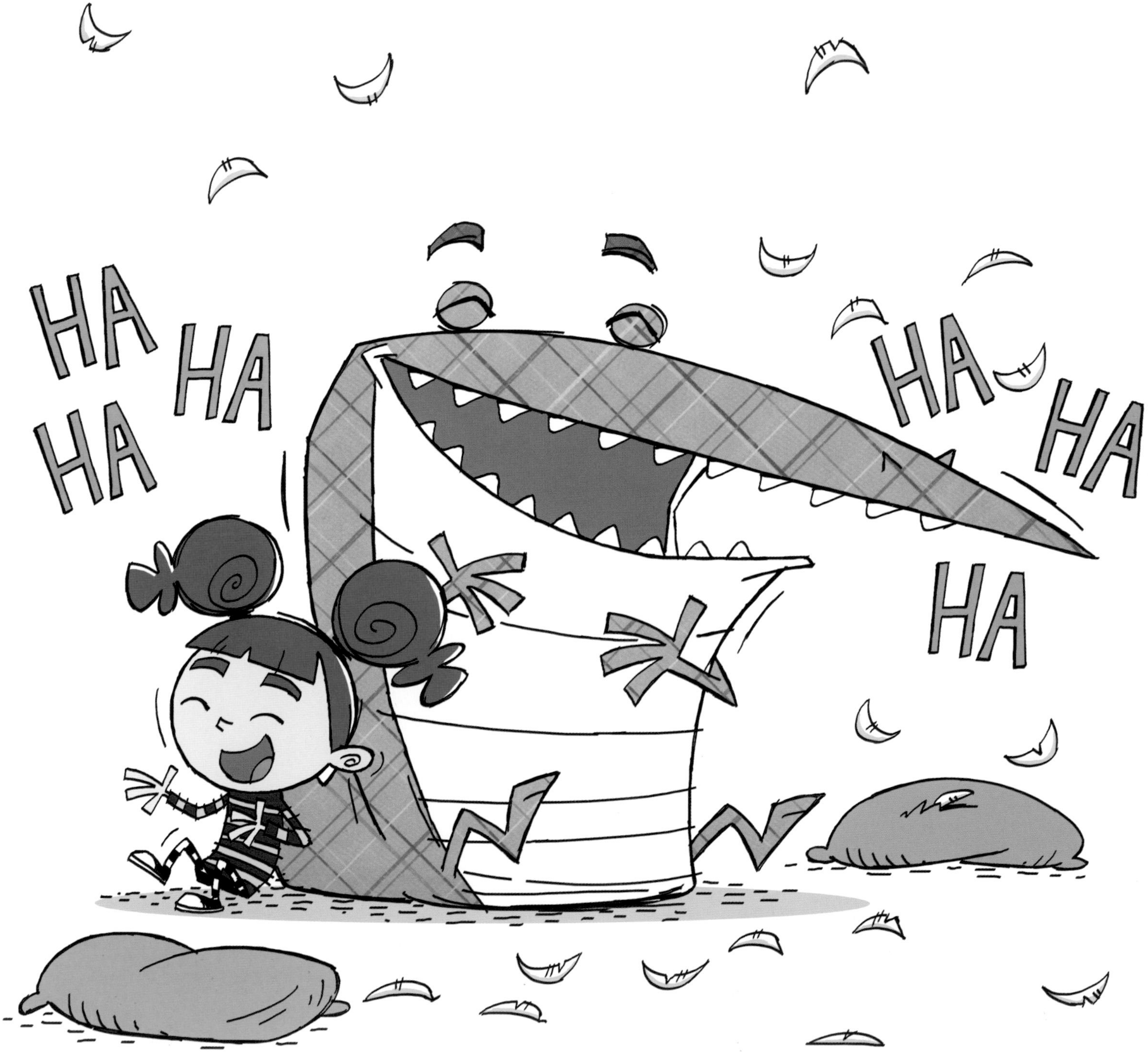
HA
HA
HA
HA
HA
HA

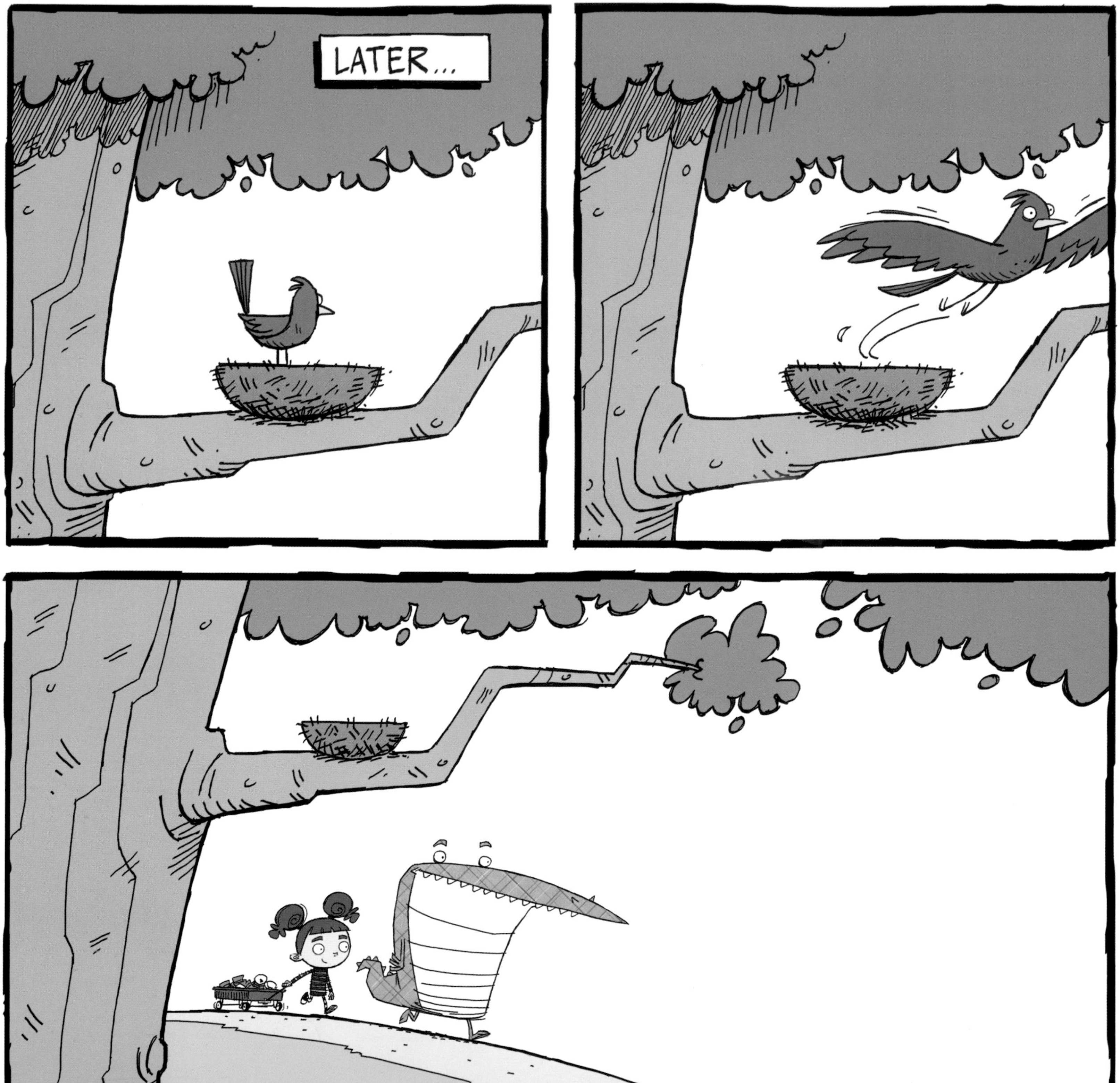
LATER...

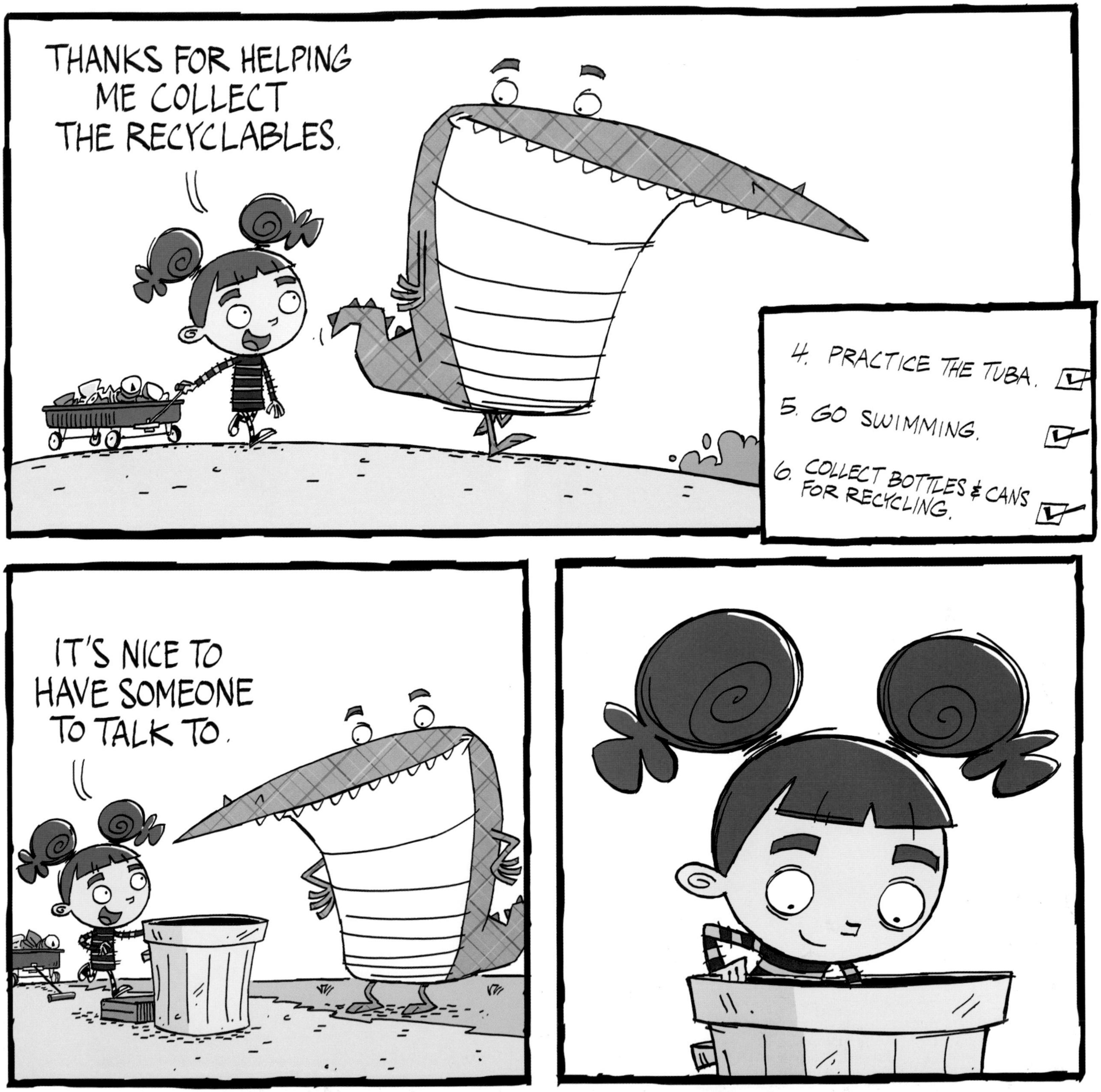
THANKS FOR HELPING ME COLLECT THE RECYCLABLES.
4. PRACTICE THE TUBA.
5. GO SWIMMING.
6. COLLECT BOTTLES & CANS FOR RECYCLING.
IT'S NICE TO HAVE SOMEONE TO TALK TO.

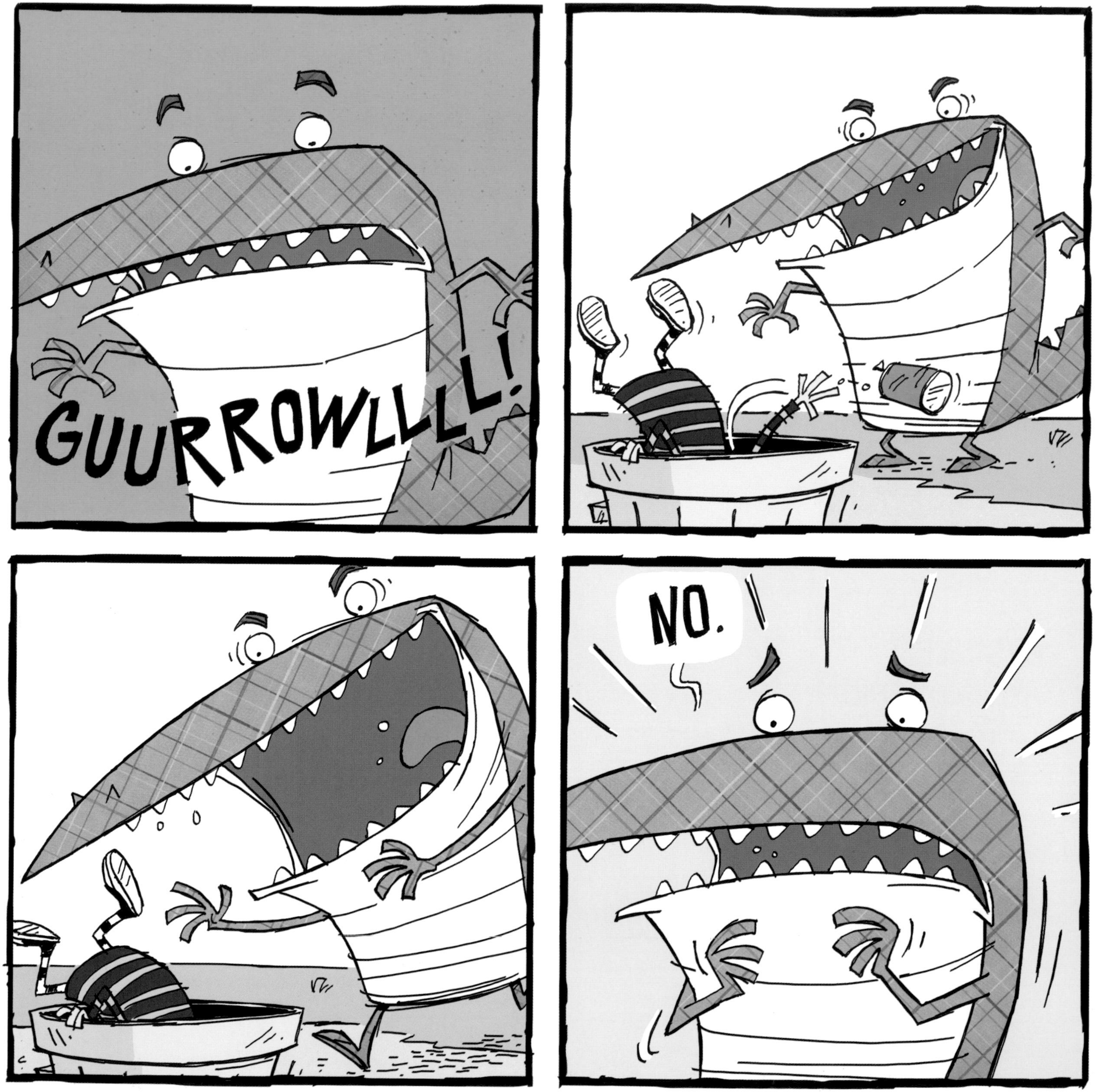
GUURROWLLLL!
NO.

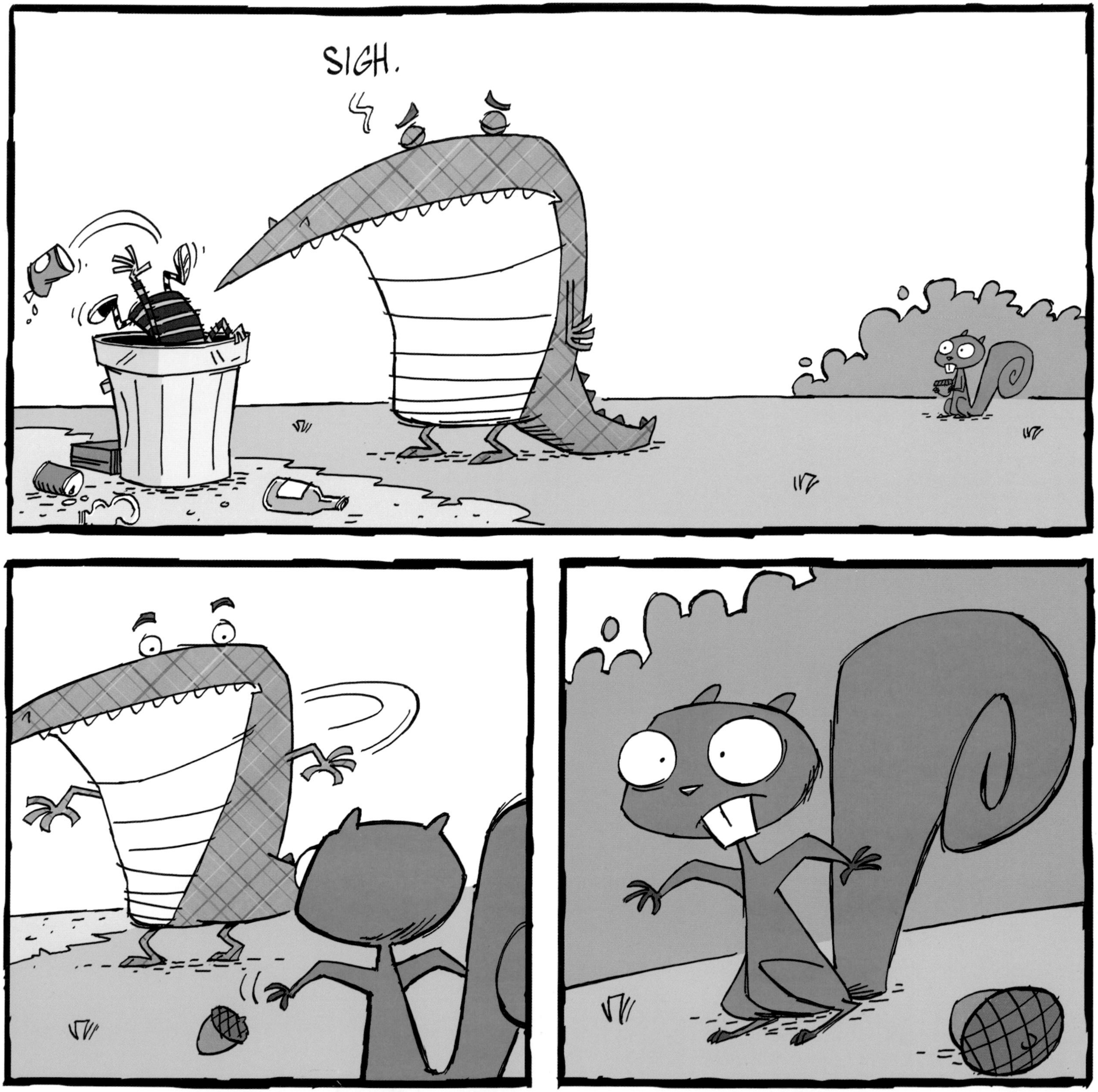
SIGH.

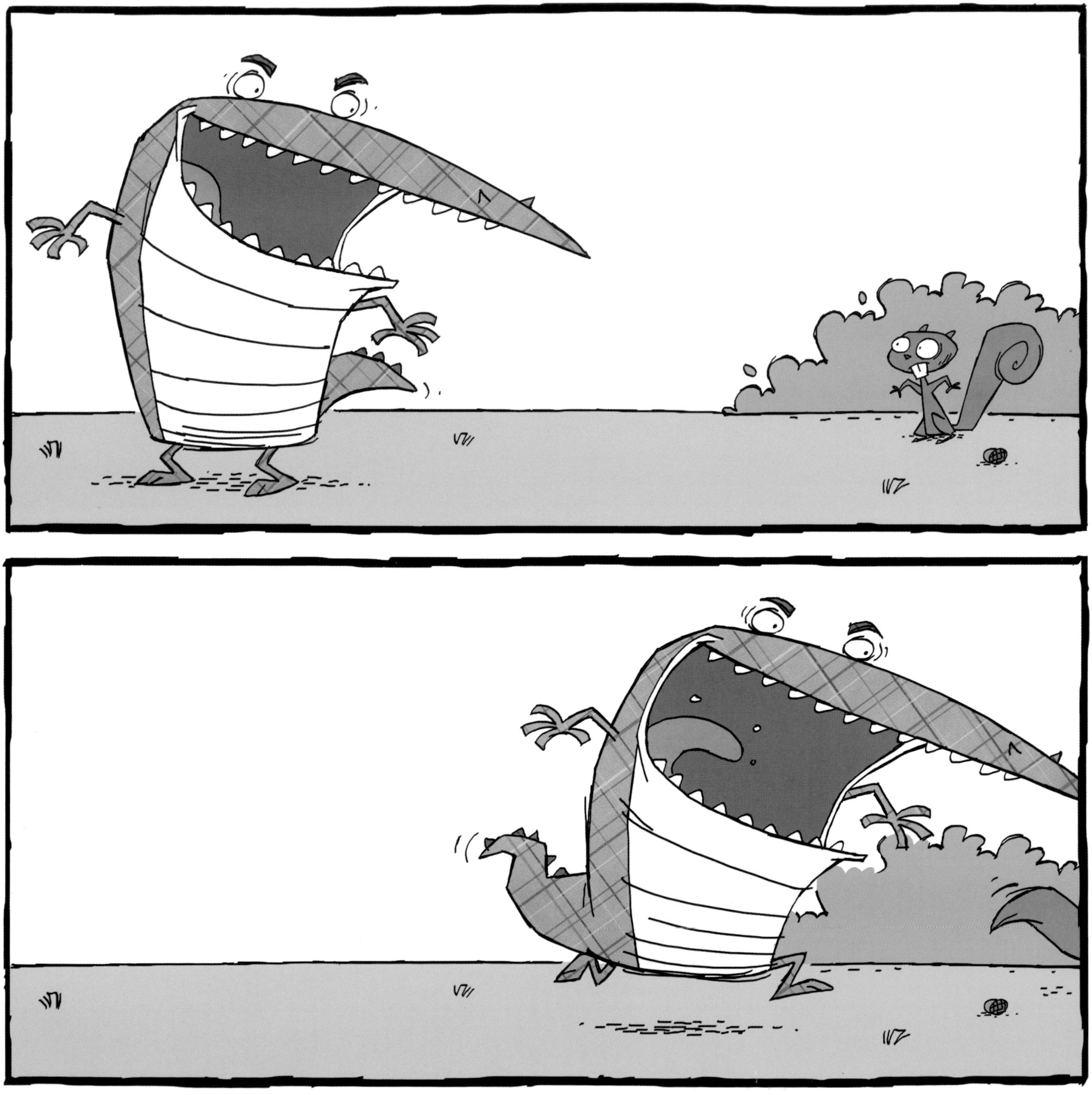

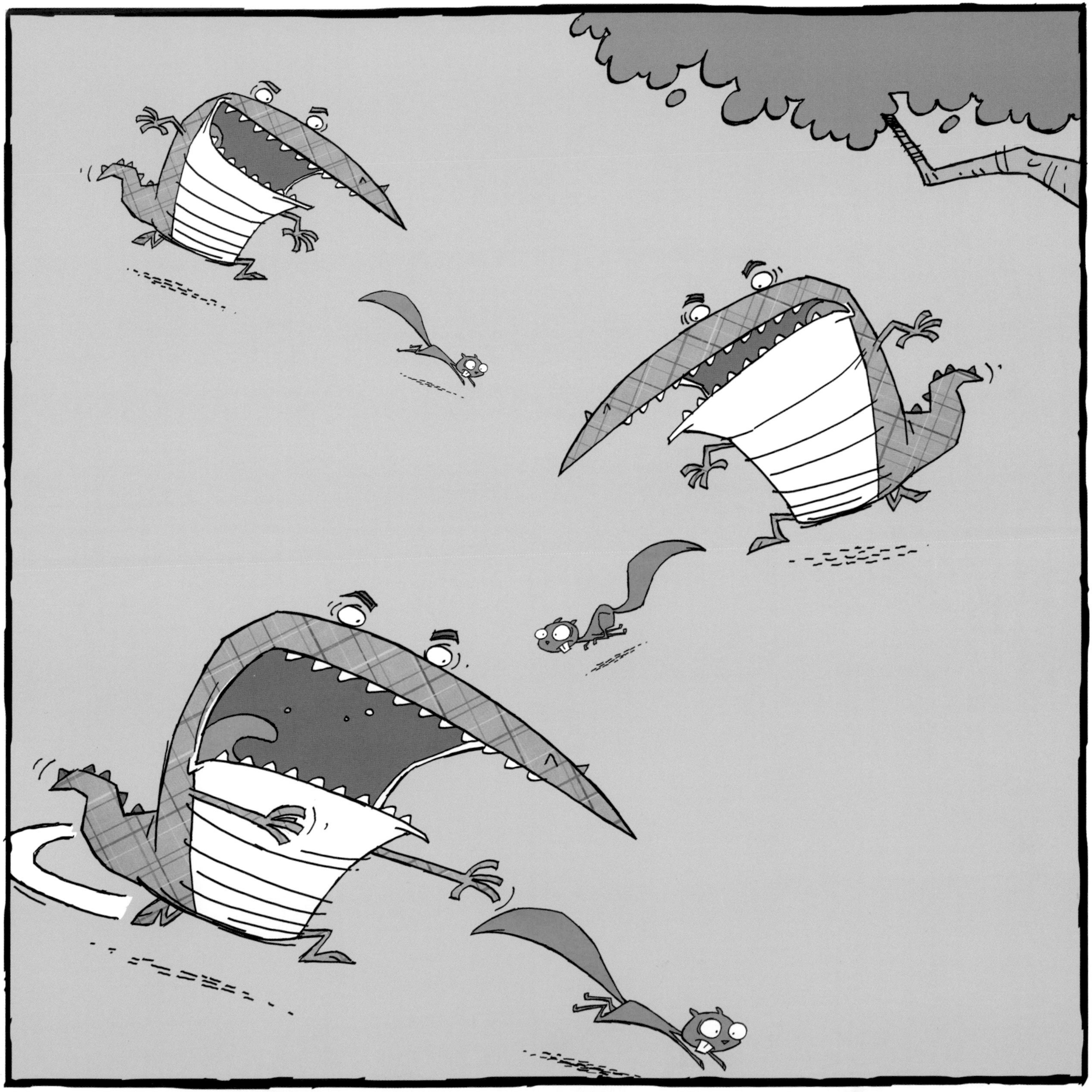

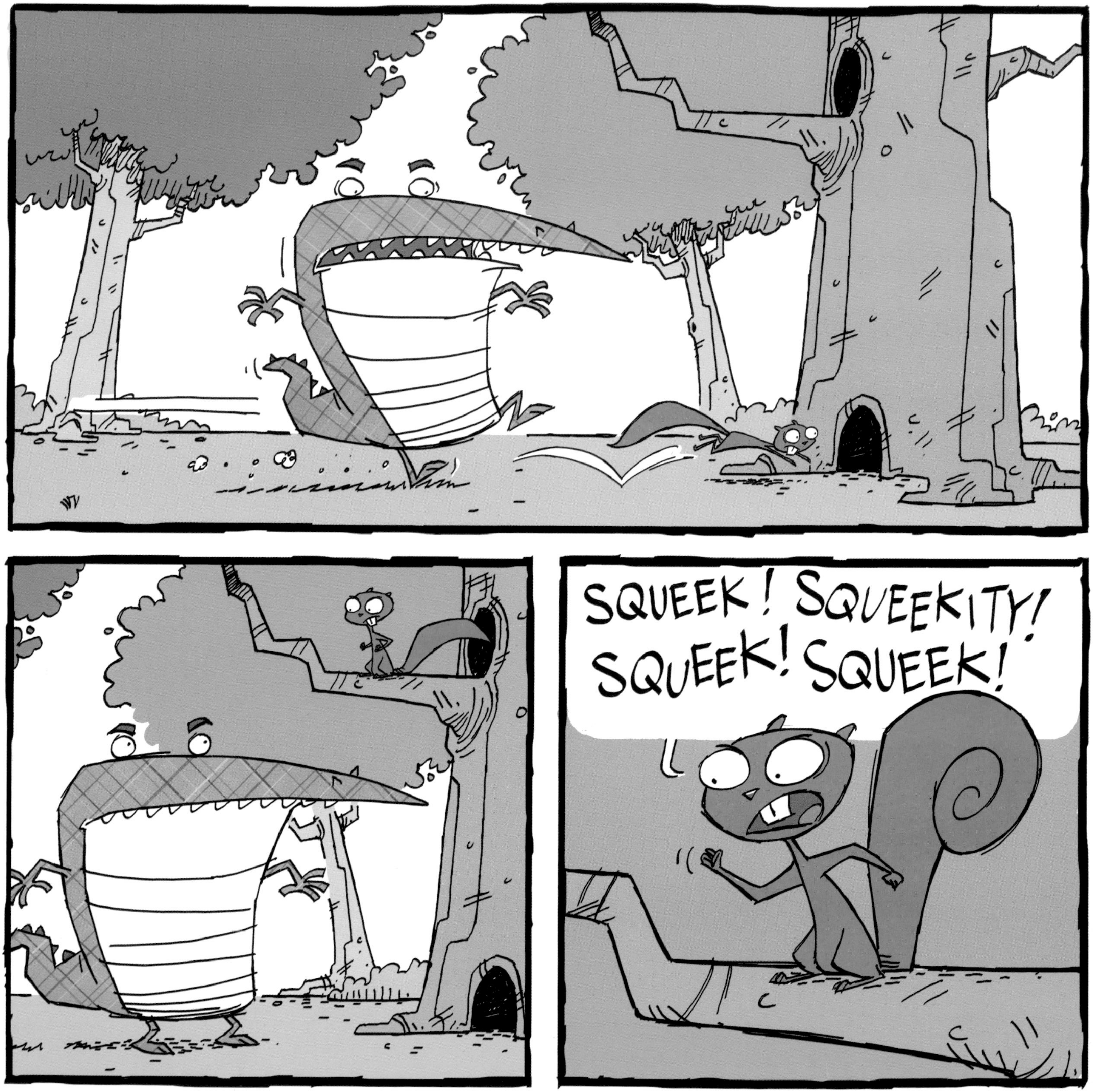
SQUEEK! SQUEEKITY!
SQUEEK! SQUEEK!

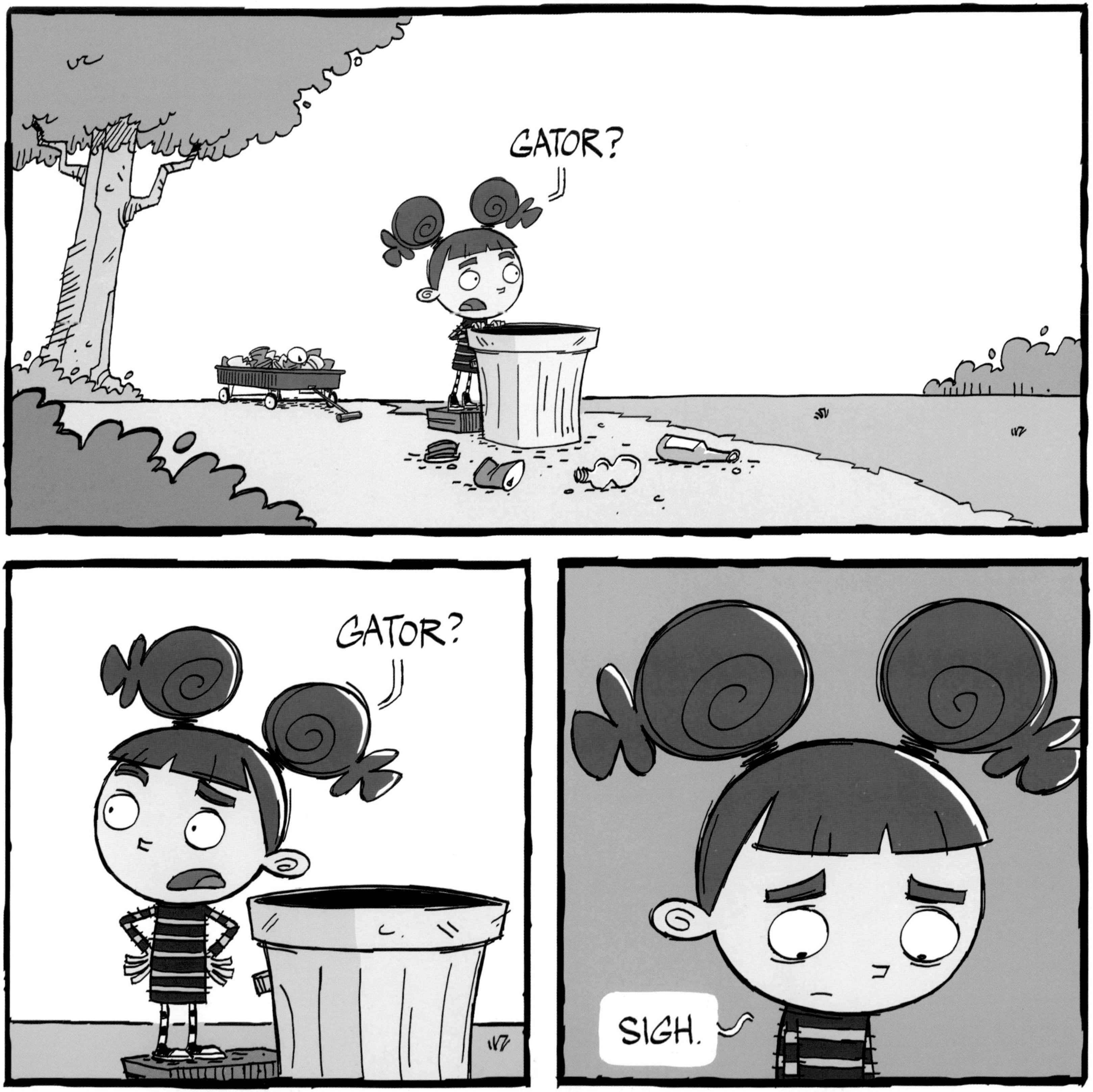
GATOR?
GATOR?
SIGH.

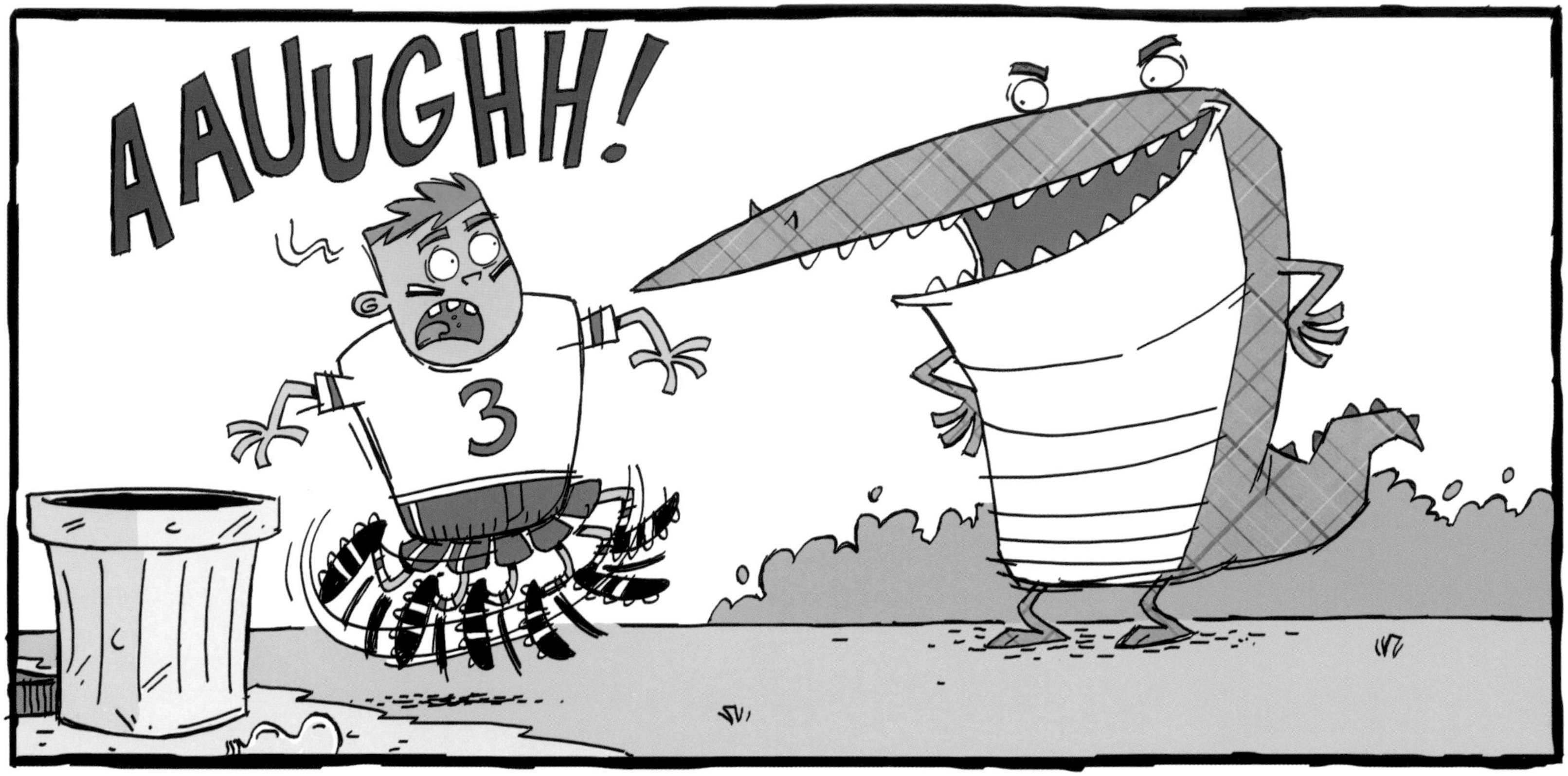
AAUUGHH!

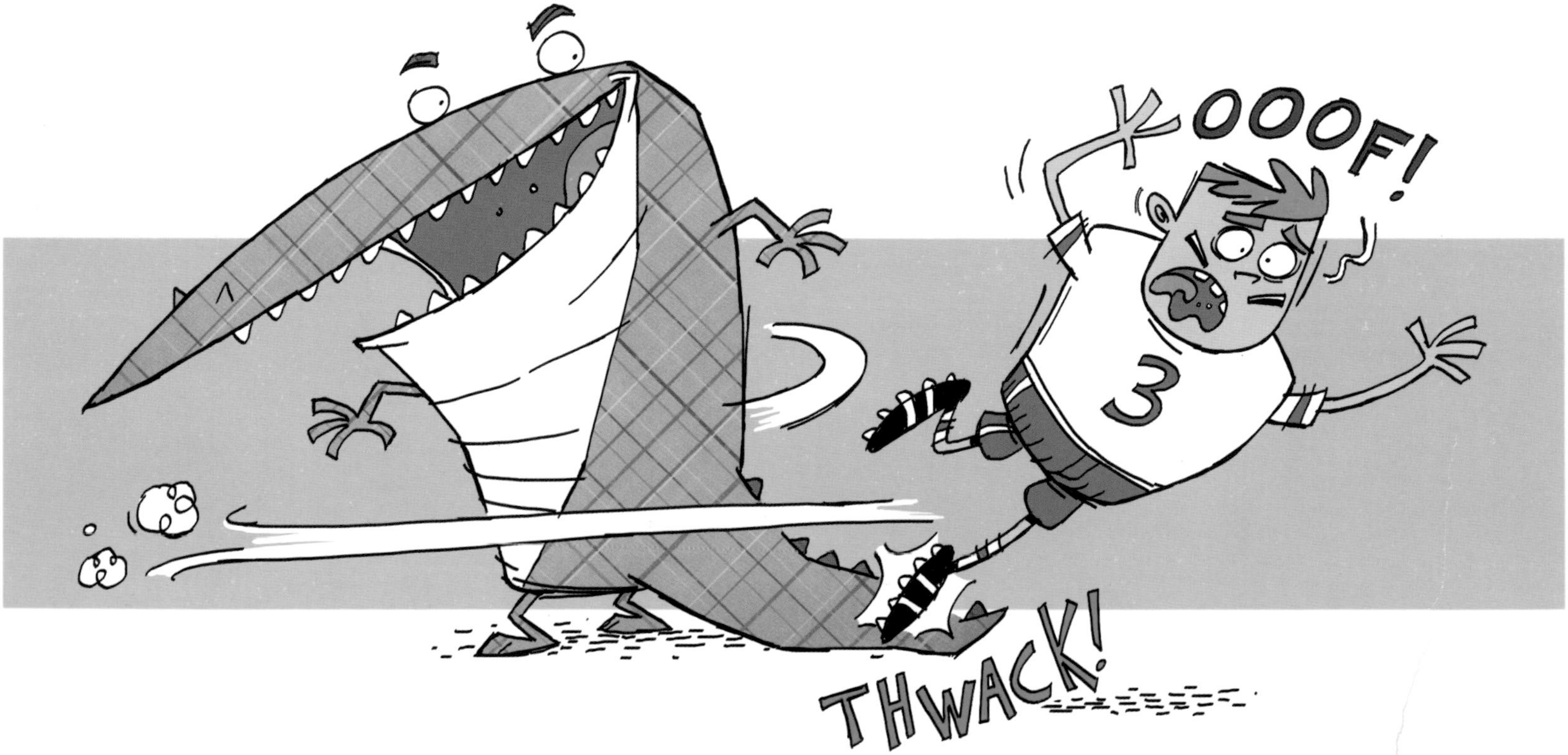
OOOF!
THWACK!

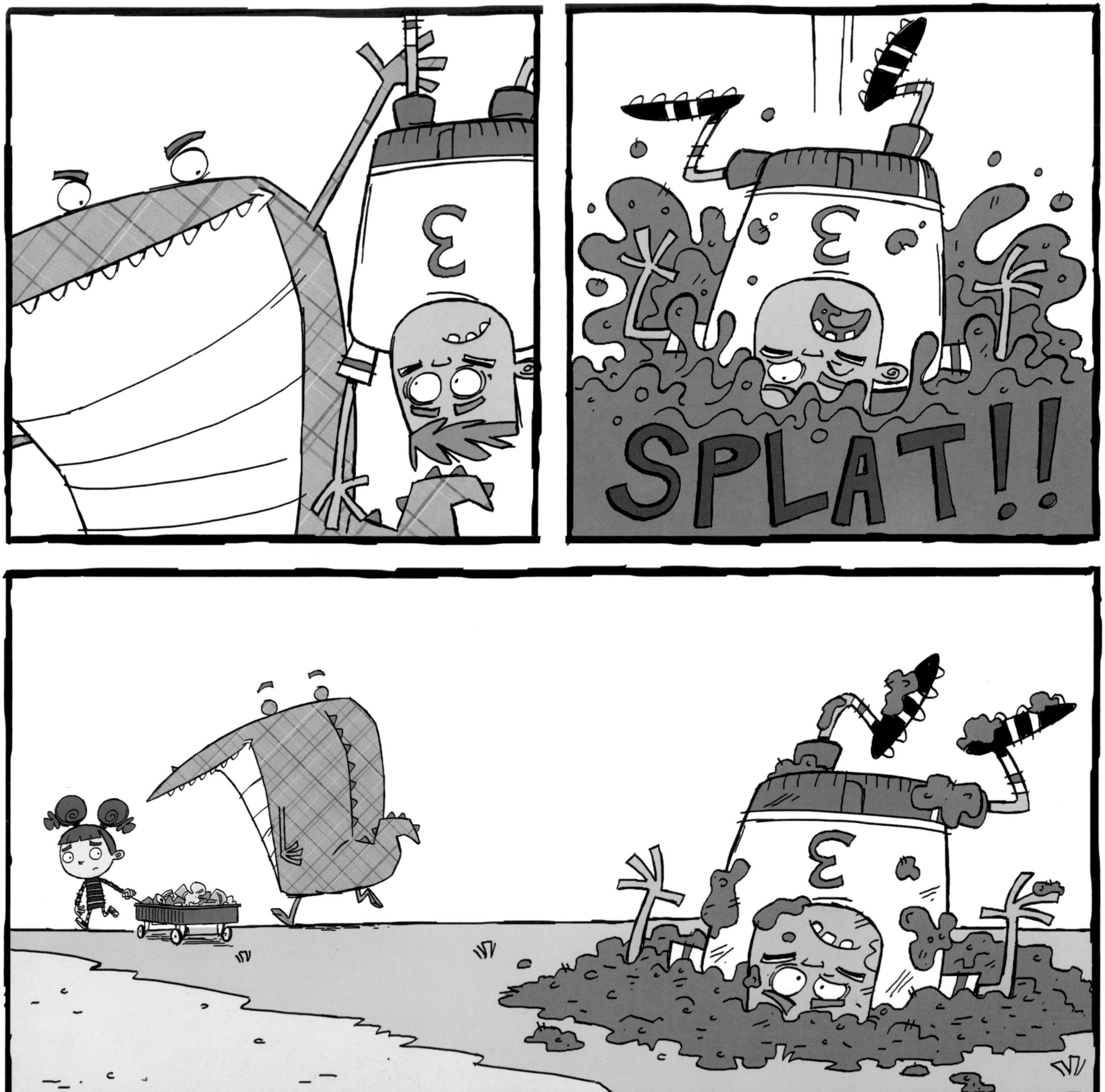
SPLAT!!

AREN'T YOU A LITTLE TOO OLD
TO BE PLAYING IN THE MUD?

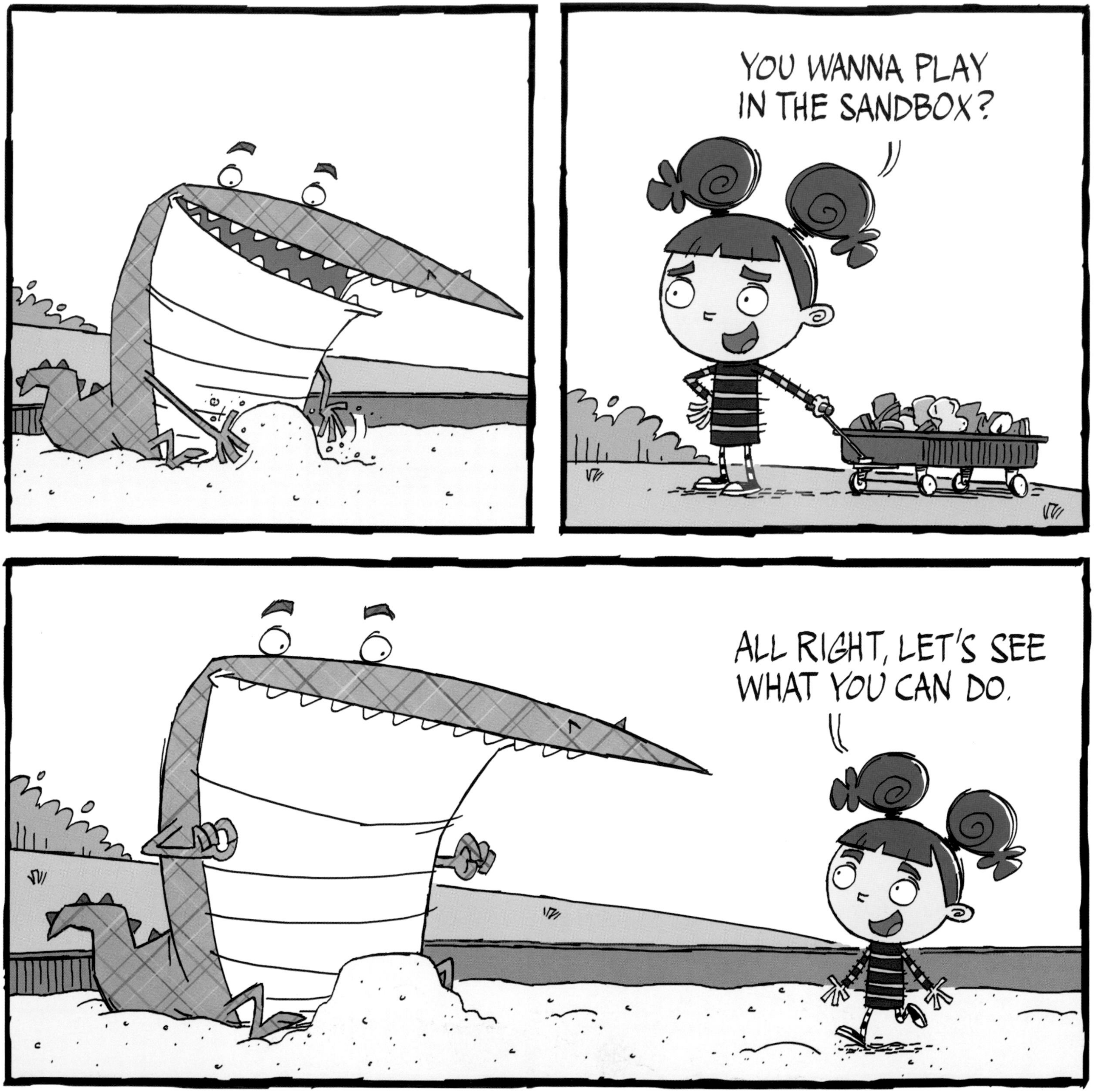
YOU WANNA PLAY IN THE SANDBOX?
ALL RIGHT, LET'S SEE WHAT YOU CAN DO.

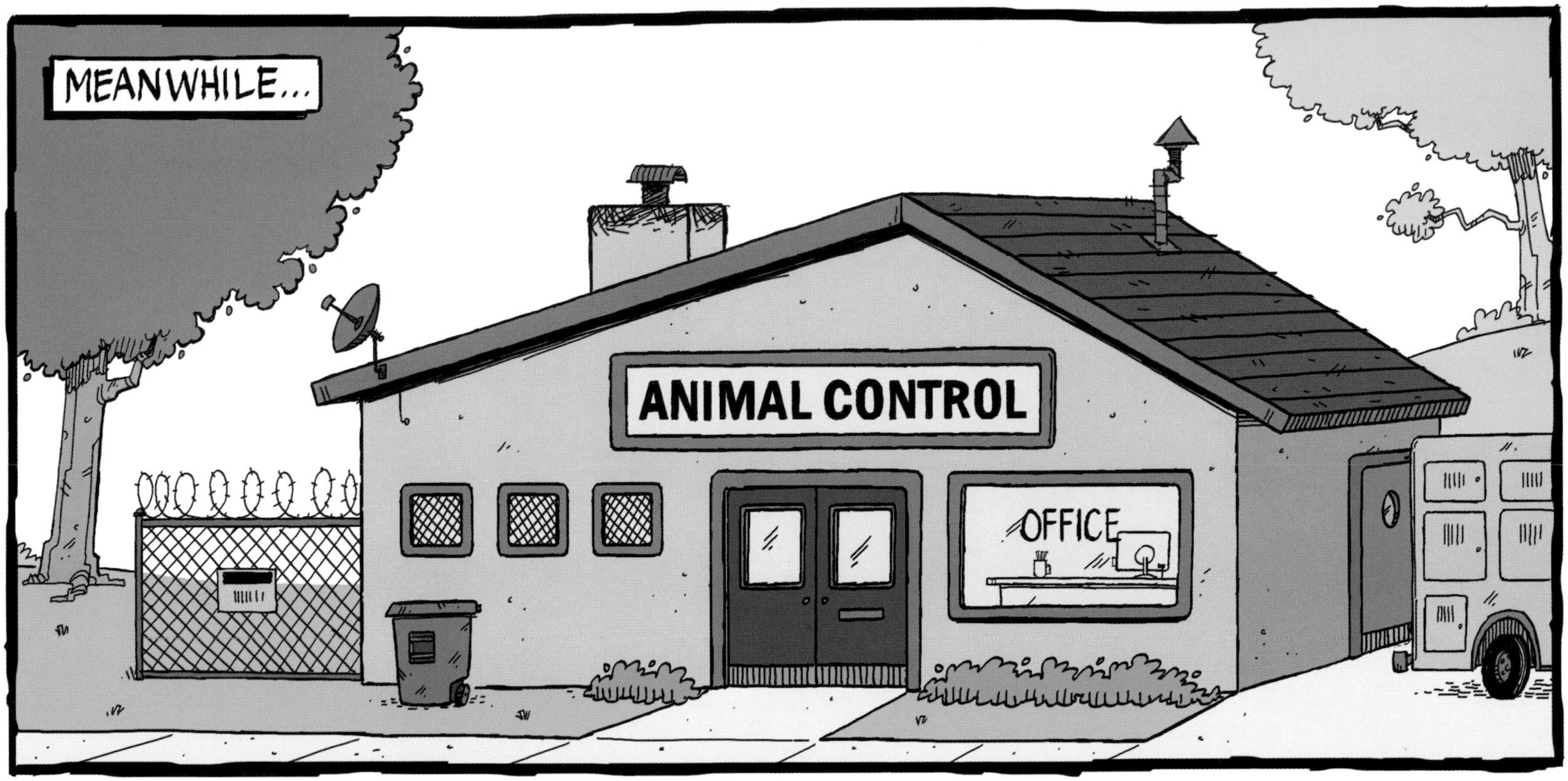
MEANWHILE...
ANIMAL CONTROL
OFFICE

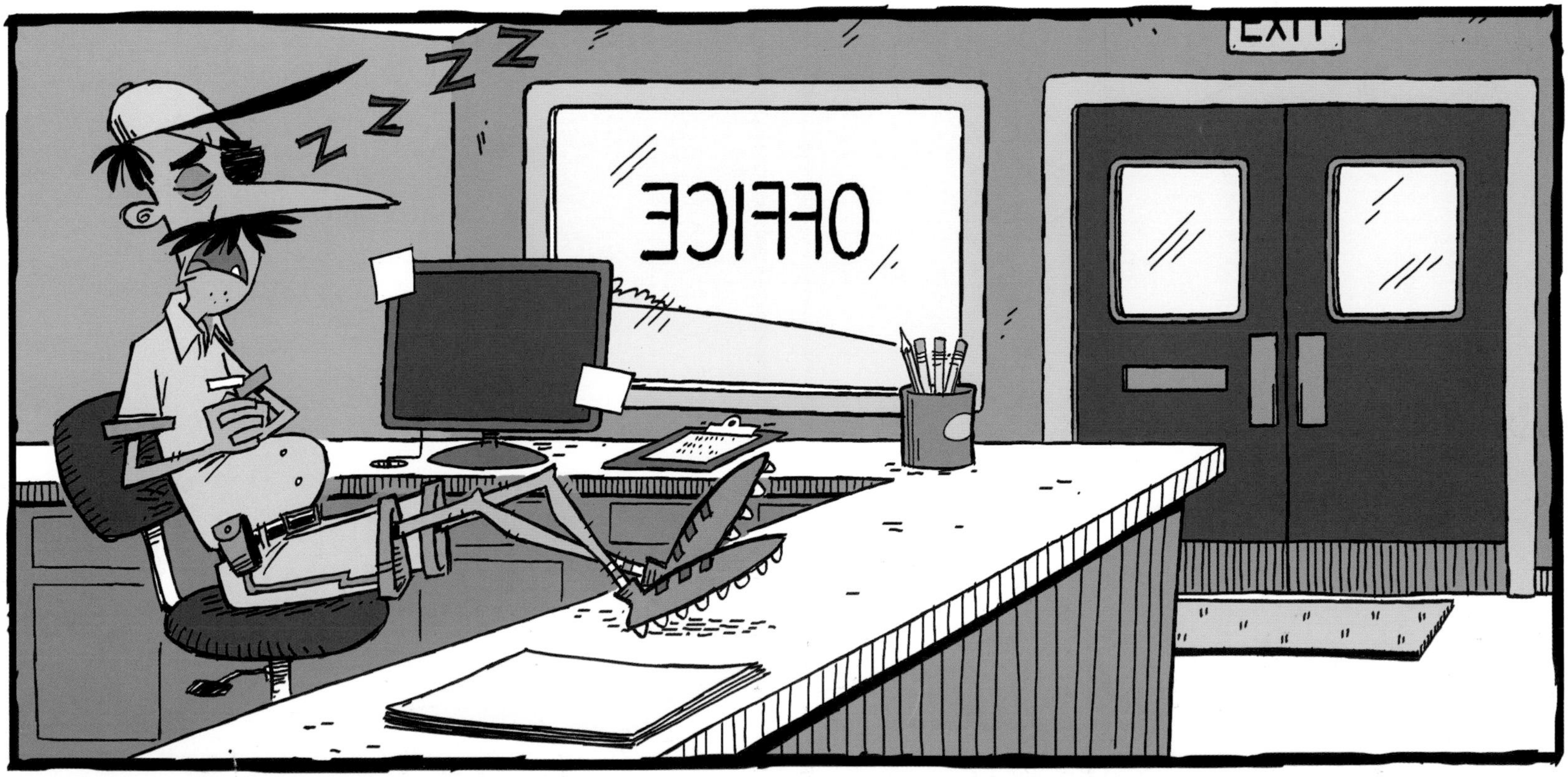

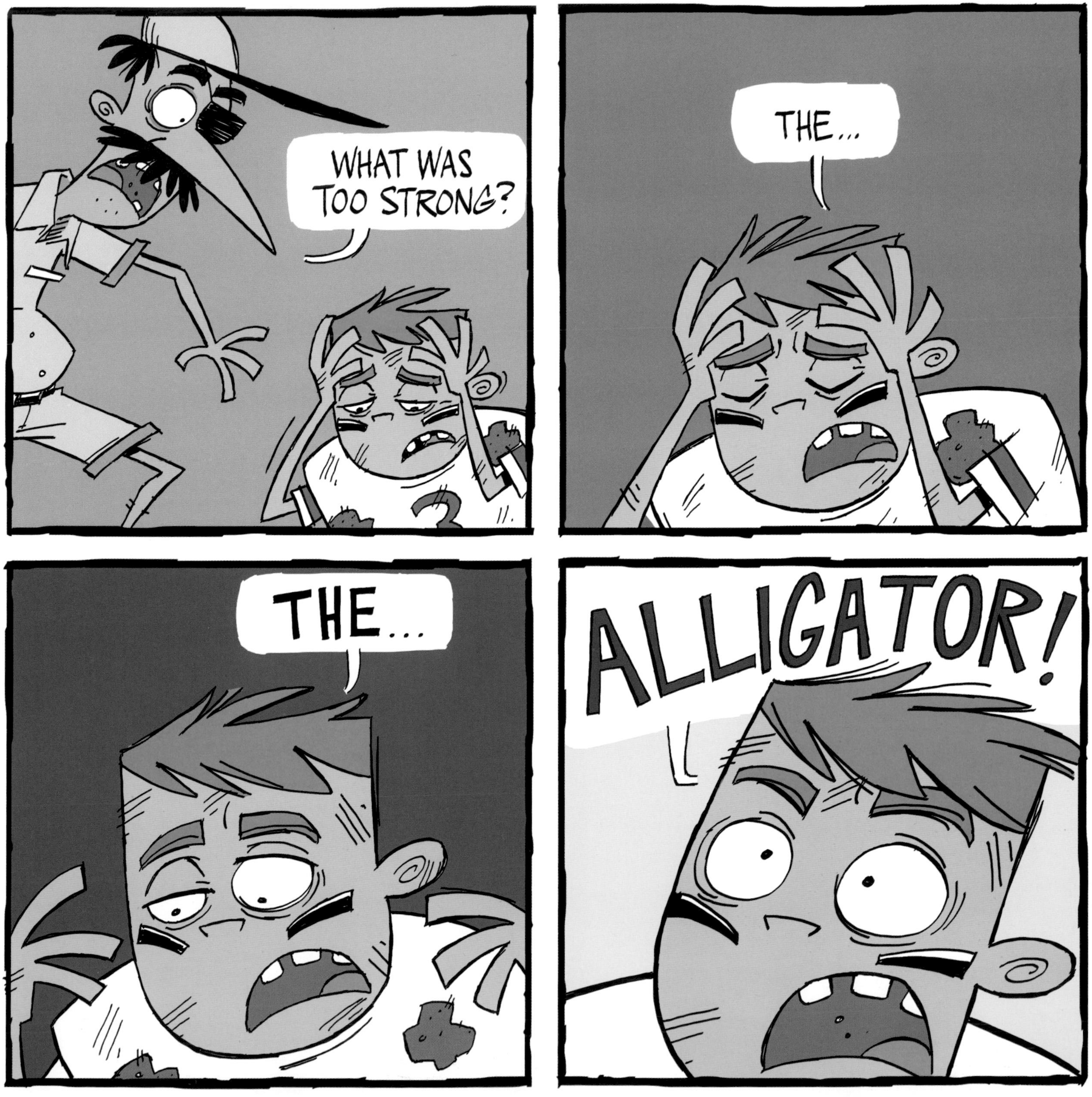
WHAT WAS TOO STRONG?
THE...
THE...
ALLIGATOR!

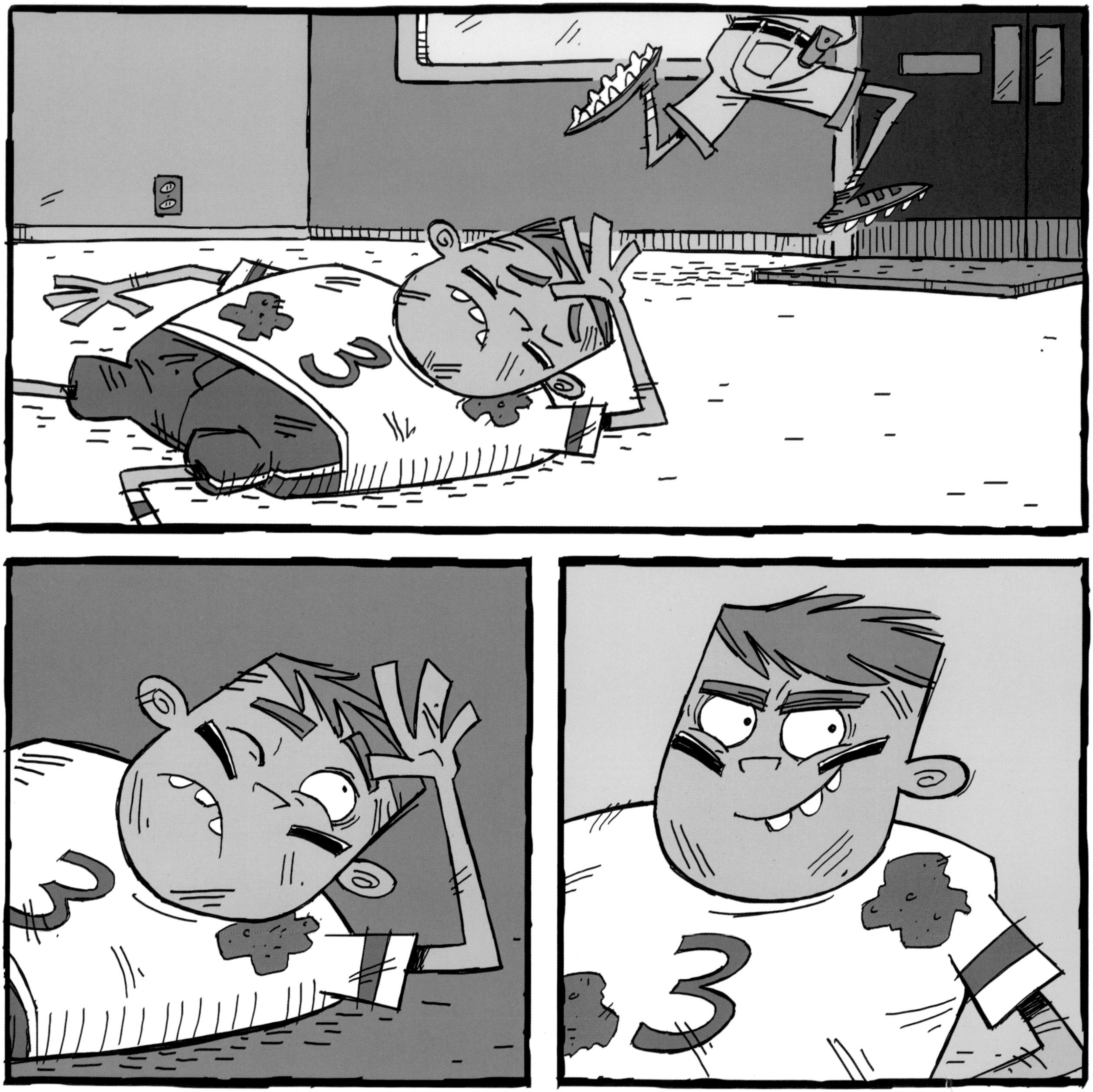

TA-DA! IT'S THE SAND CASTLE OF THE FUTURE.

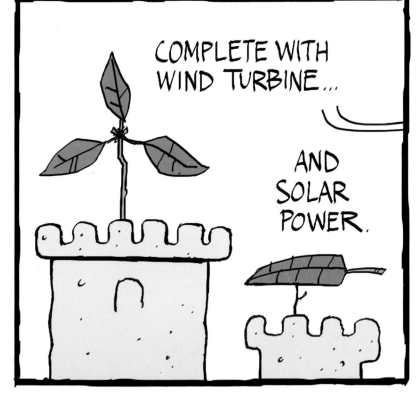

COMPLETE WITH WIND TURBINE...

AND SOLAR POWER.

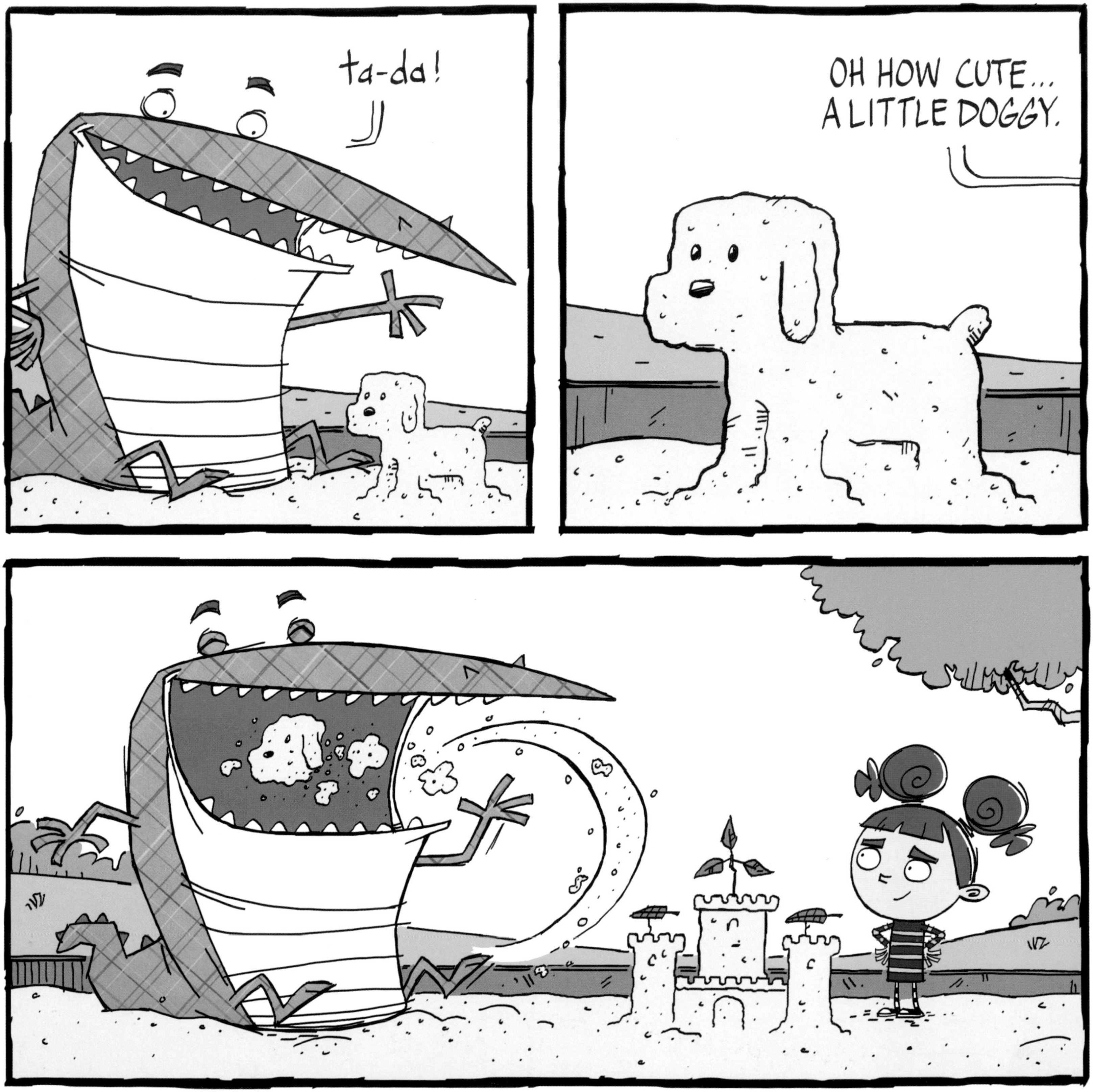
ta-da!
OH HOW CUTE... A LITTLE DOGGY.

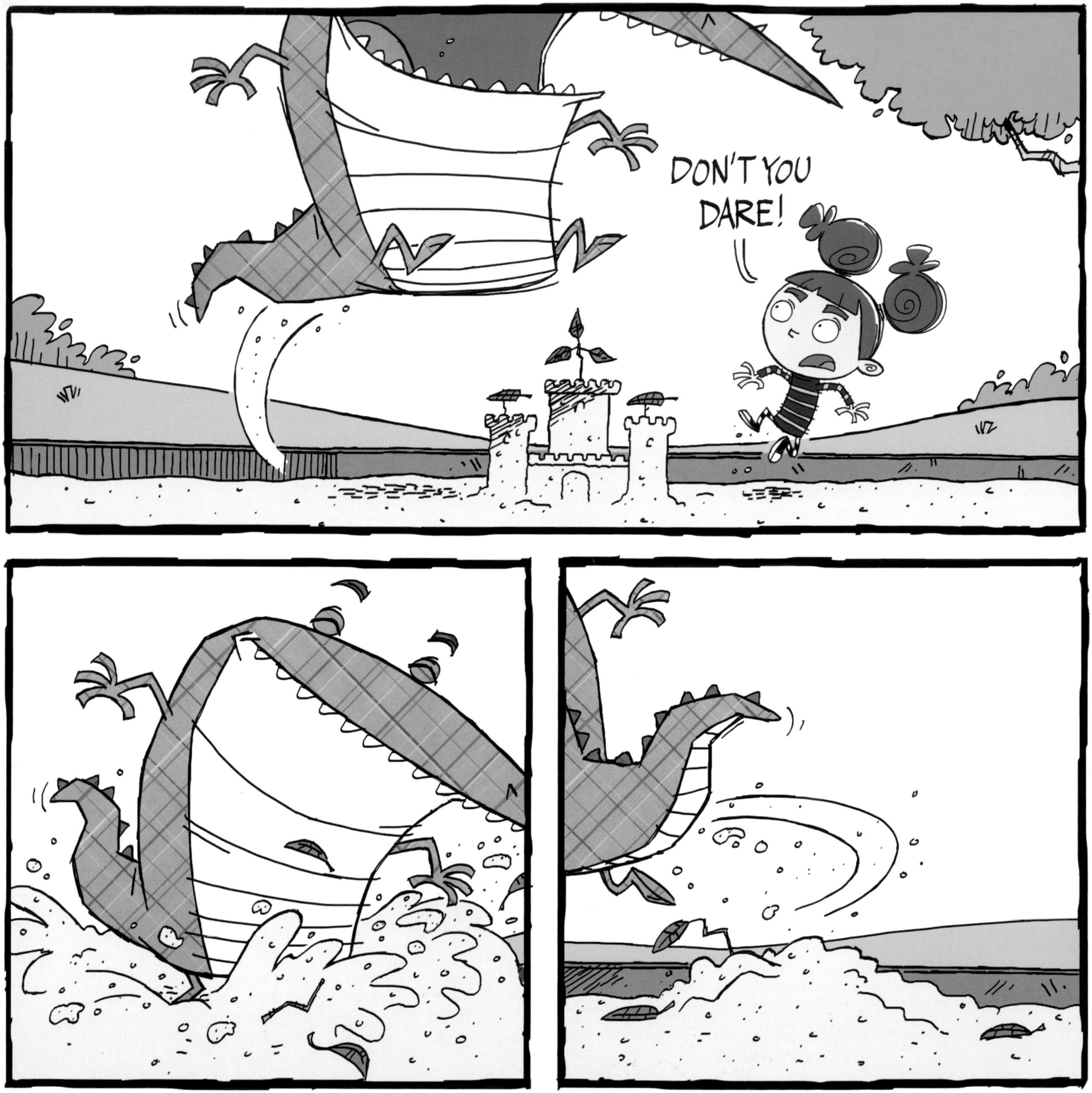
DON'T YOU DARE!

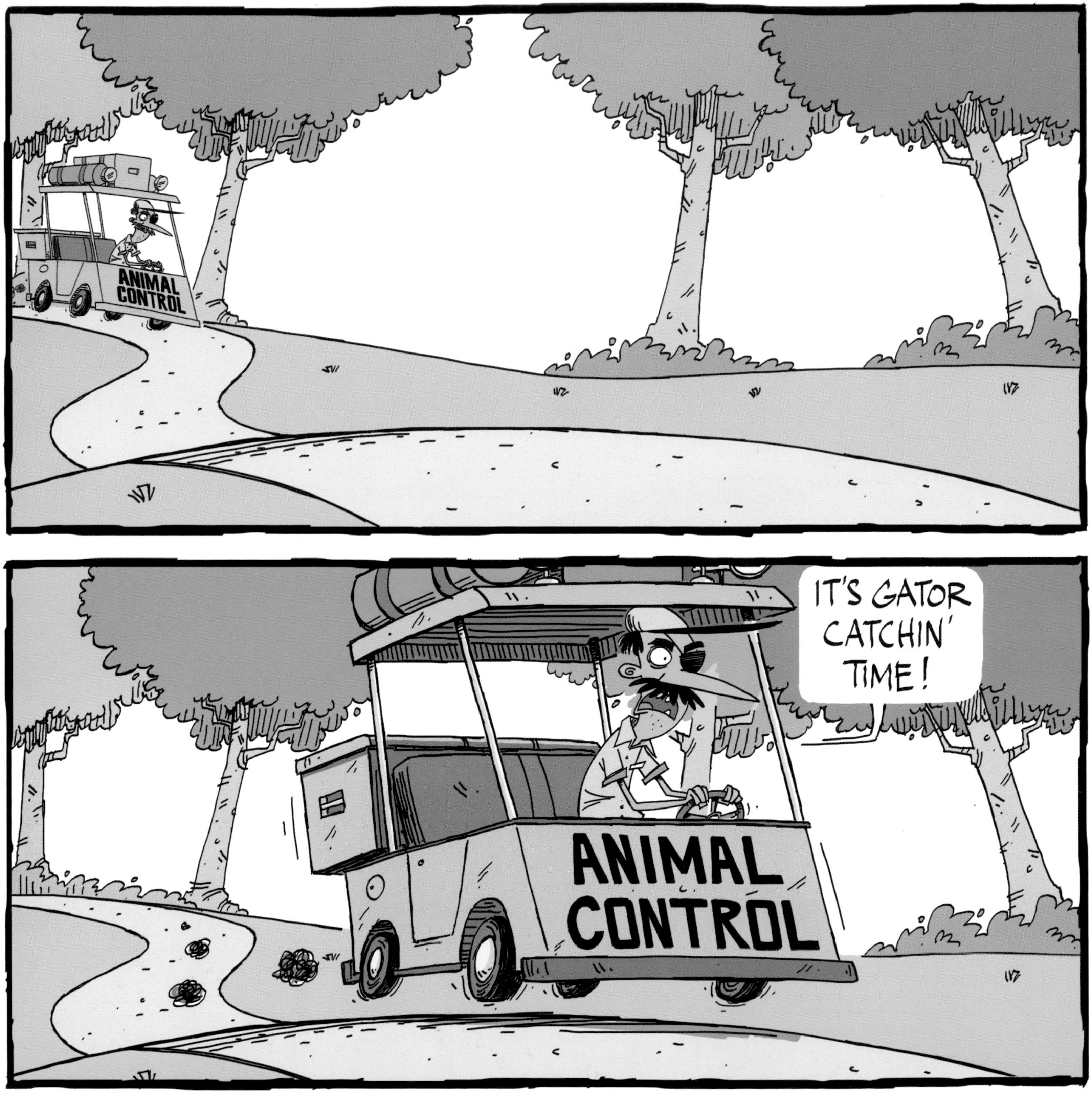
ANIMAL CONTROL
ANIMAL CONTROL
IT'S GATOR CATCHIN' TIME!

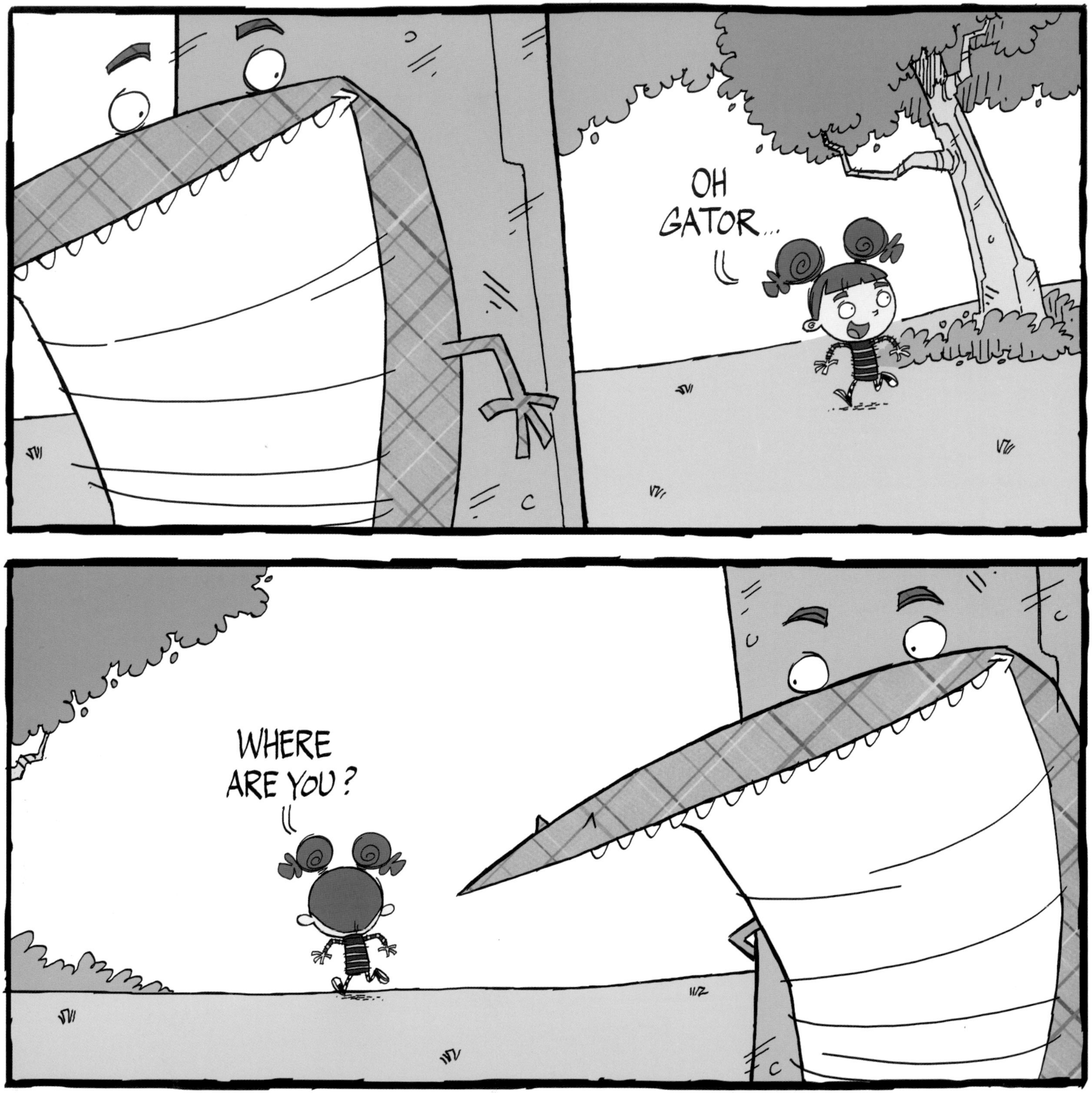
OH GATOR...
WHERE ARE YOU?

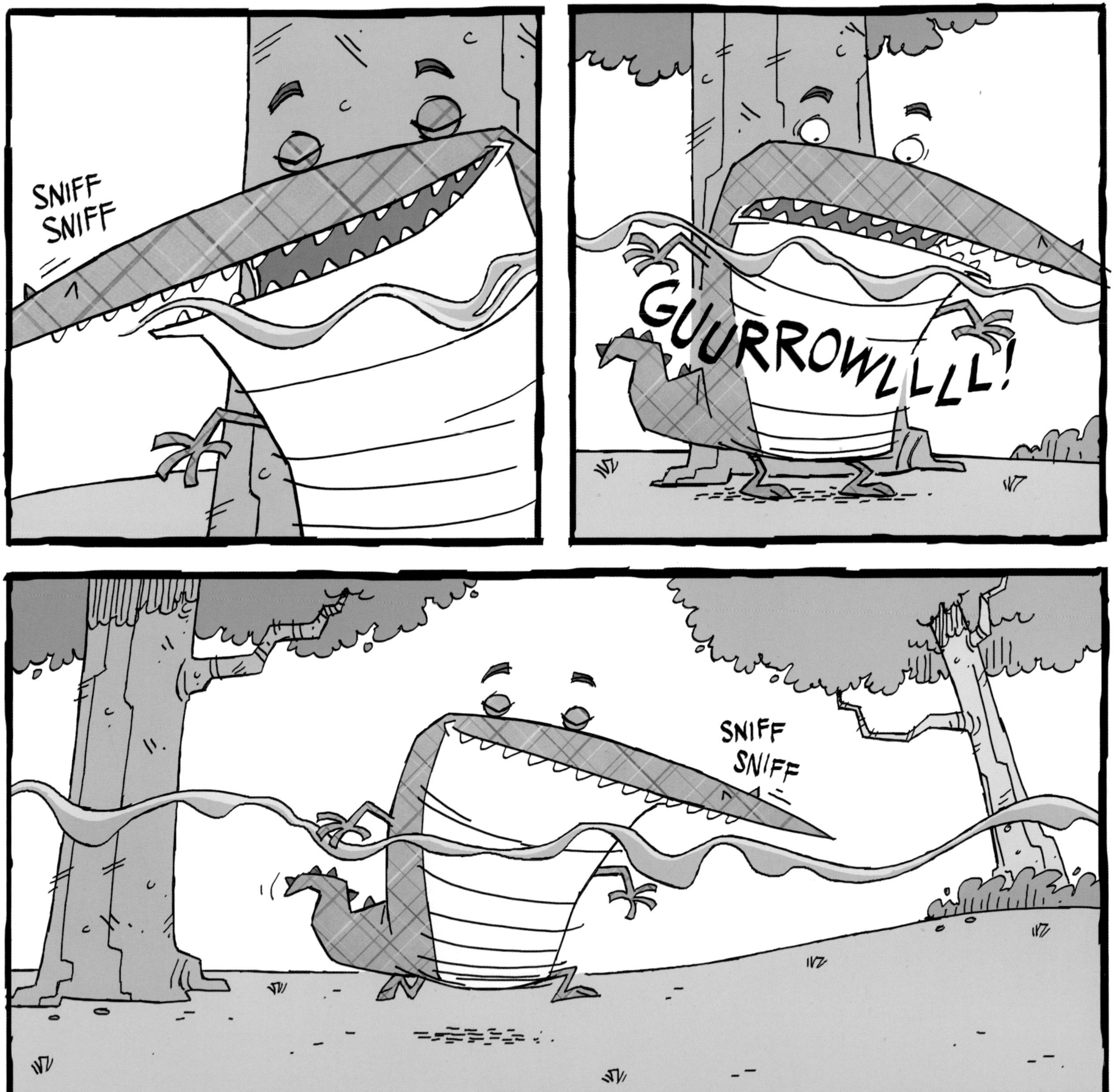
SNIFF
SNIFF
GUURROWLLLLL!
SNIFF
SNIFF

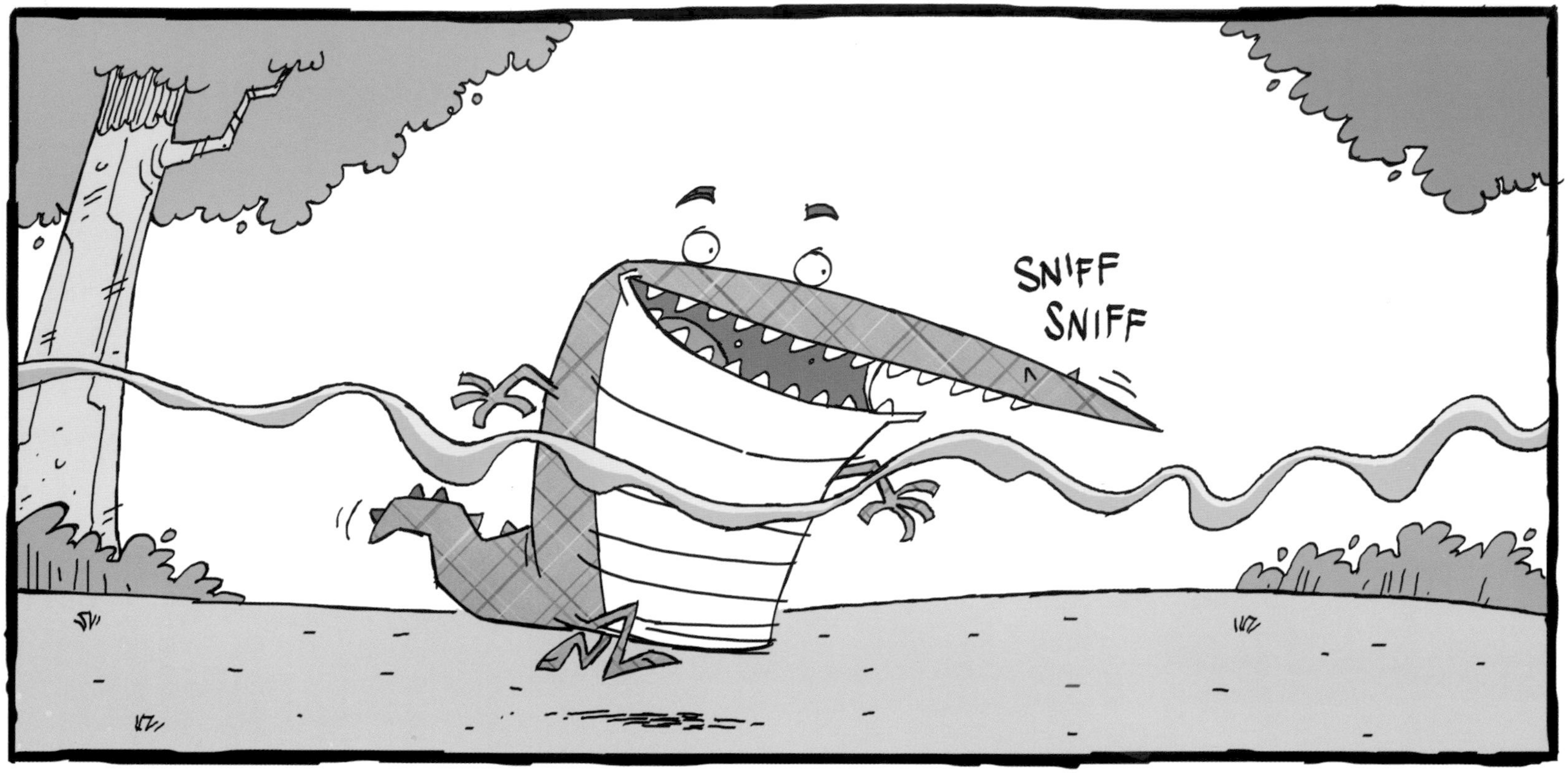
SNIFF
SNIFF
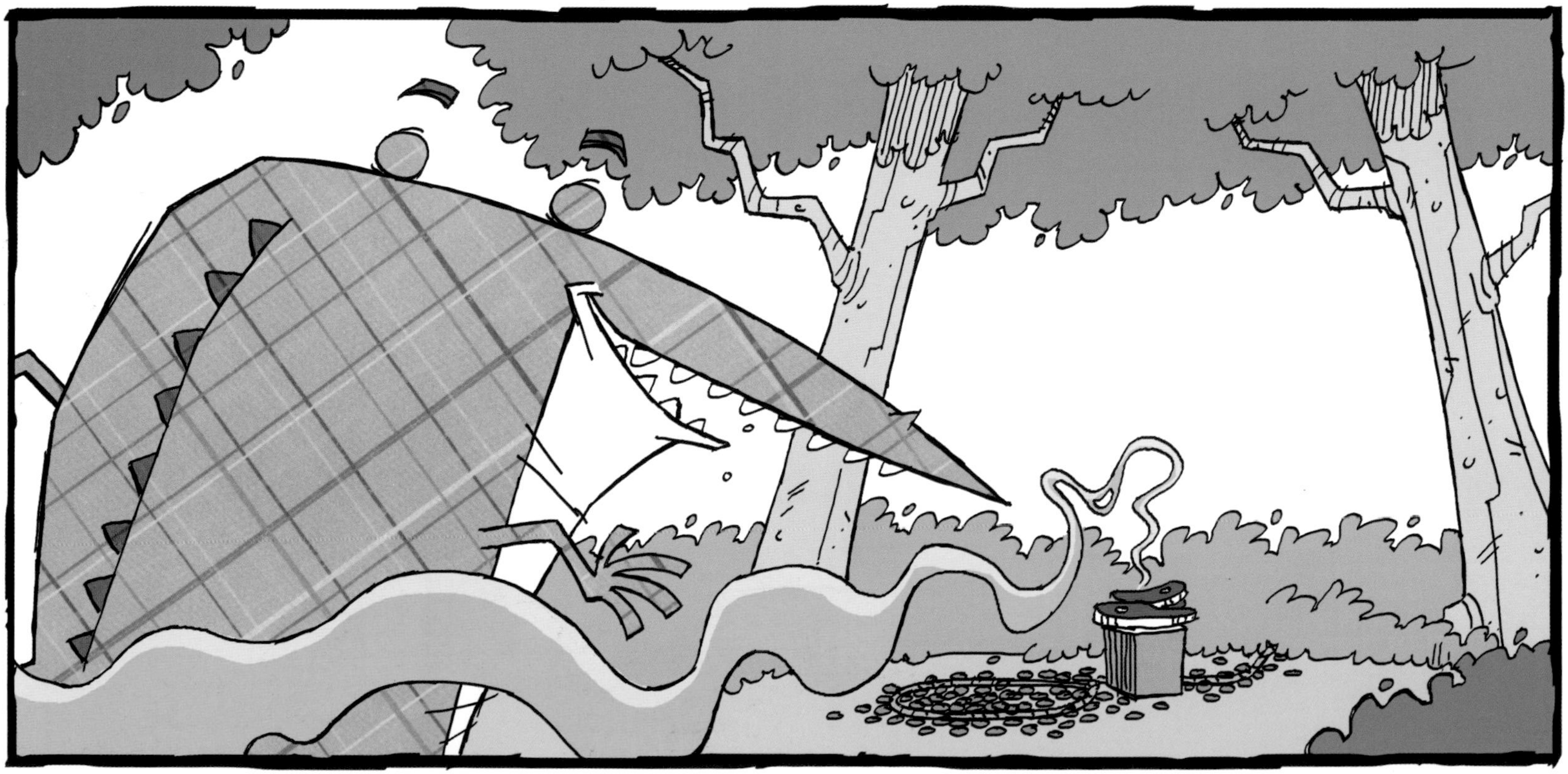

SLURP!

NNZIP

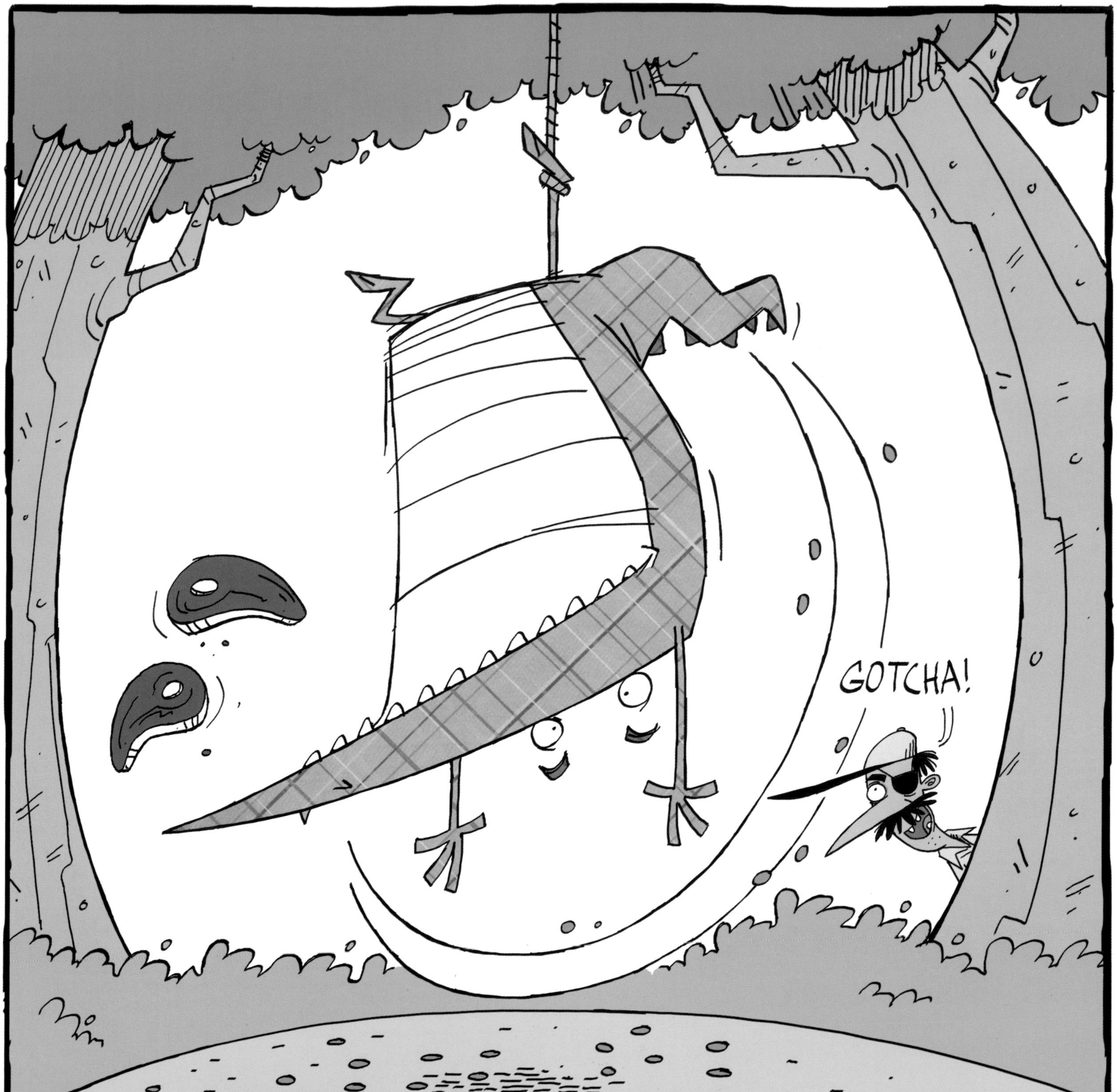
GOTCHA!

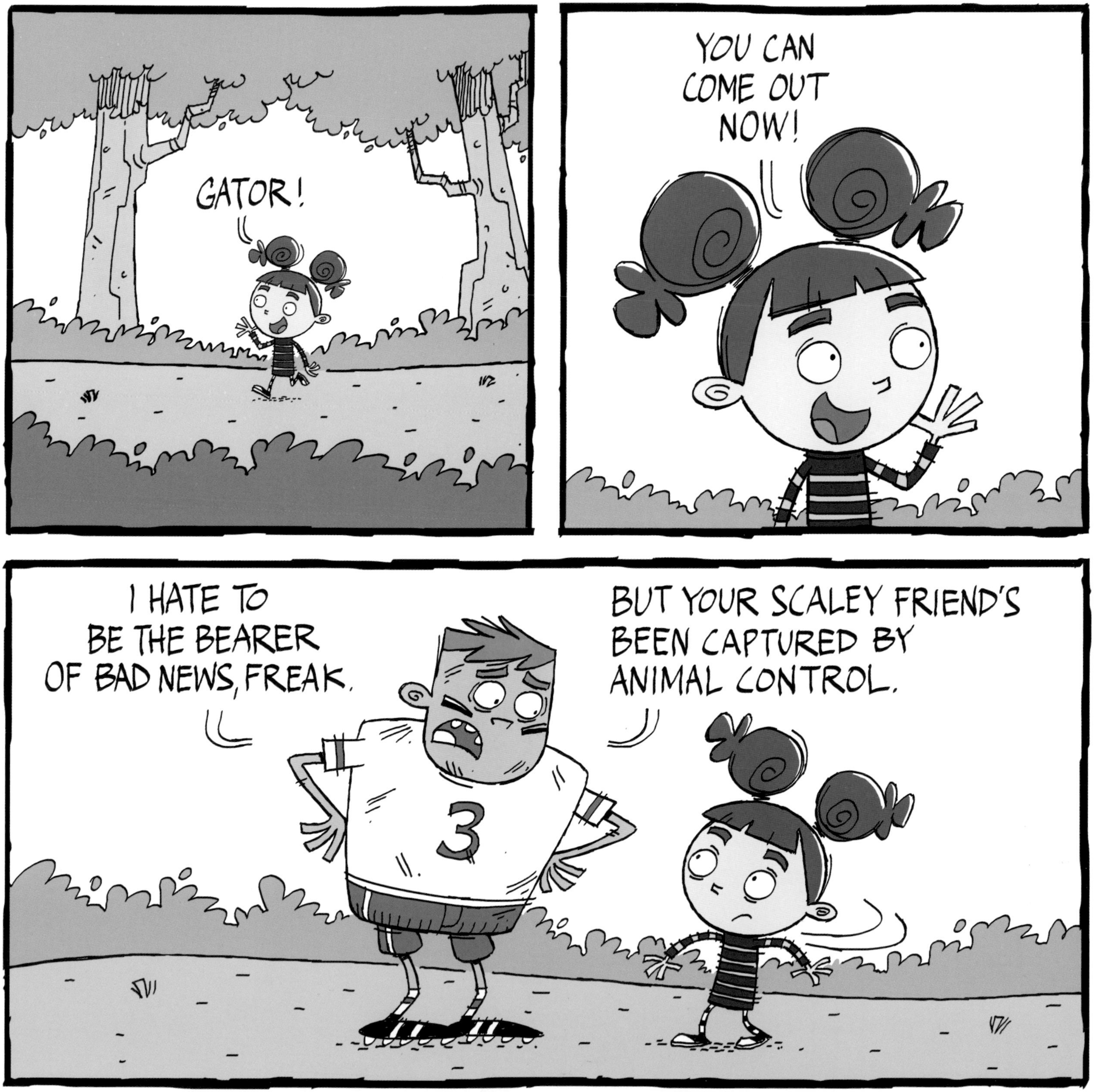
GATOR!
YOU CAN COME OUT NOW!
I HATE TO BE THE BEARER OF BAD NEWS, FREAK.
BUT YOUR SCALEY FRIEND'S BEEN CAPTURED BY ANIMAL CONTROL.
3

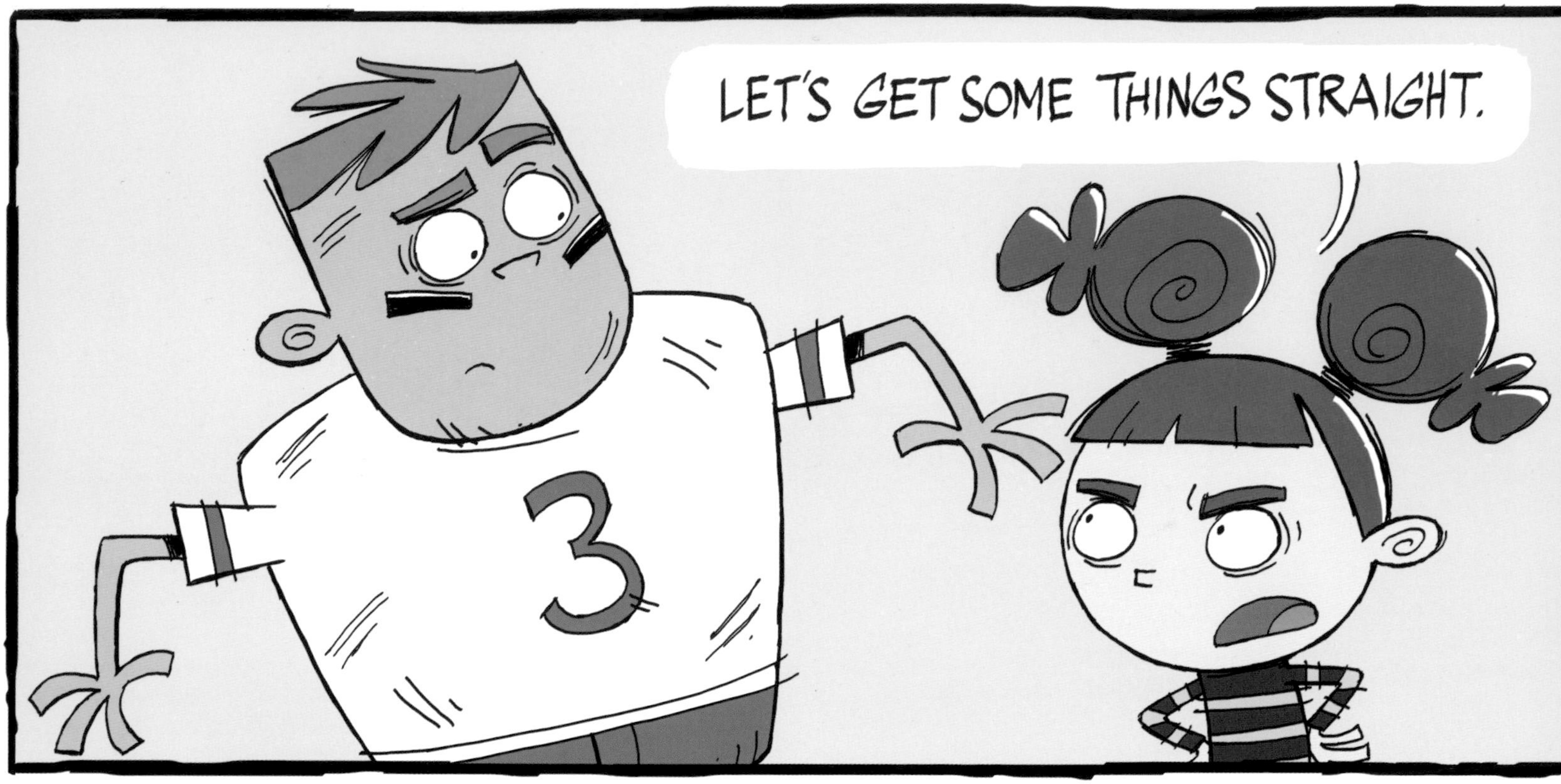
LET'S GET SOME THINGS STRAIGHT.

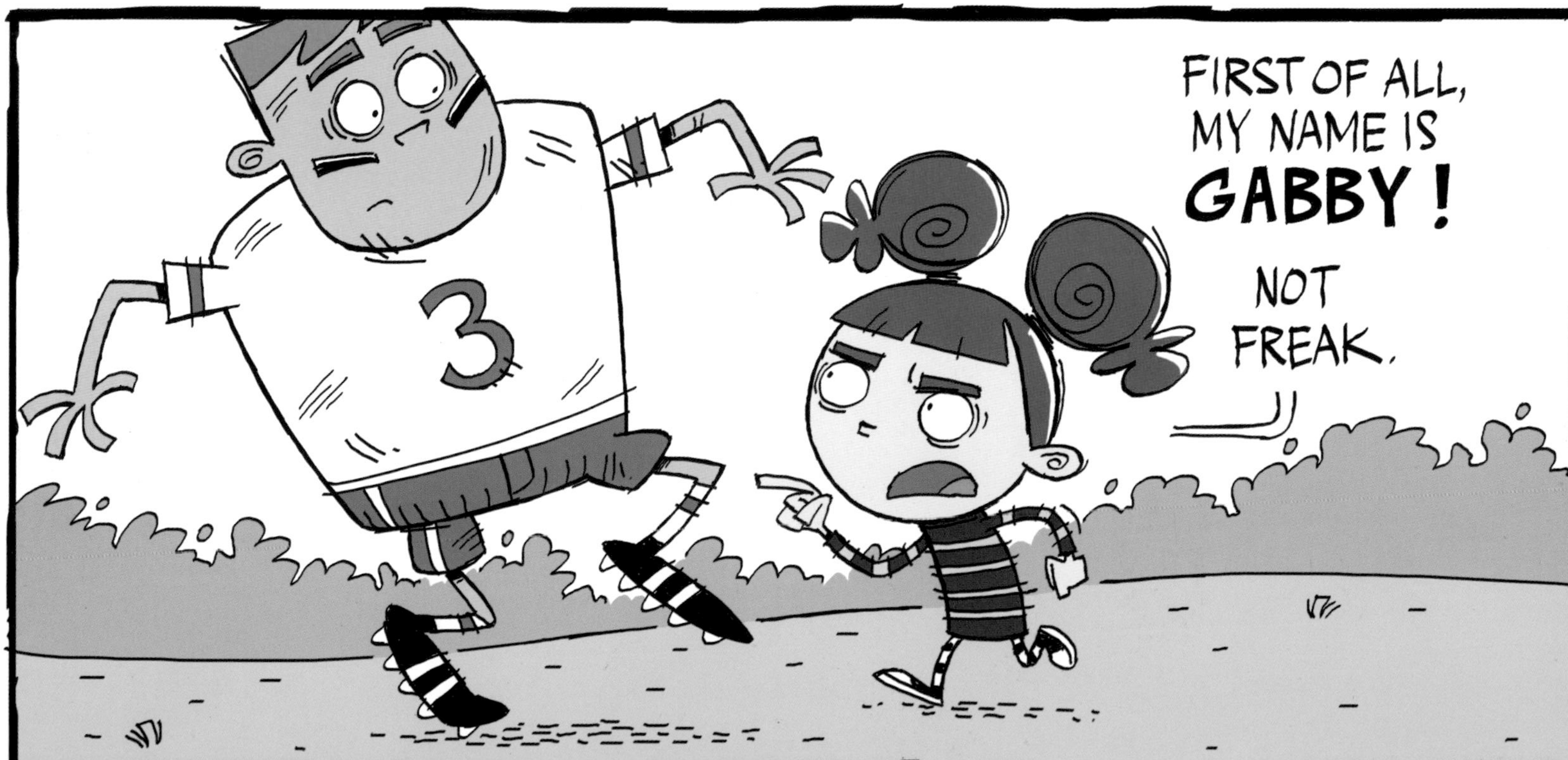
FIRST OF ALL, MY NAME IS **GABBY!**
NOT FREAK.

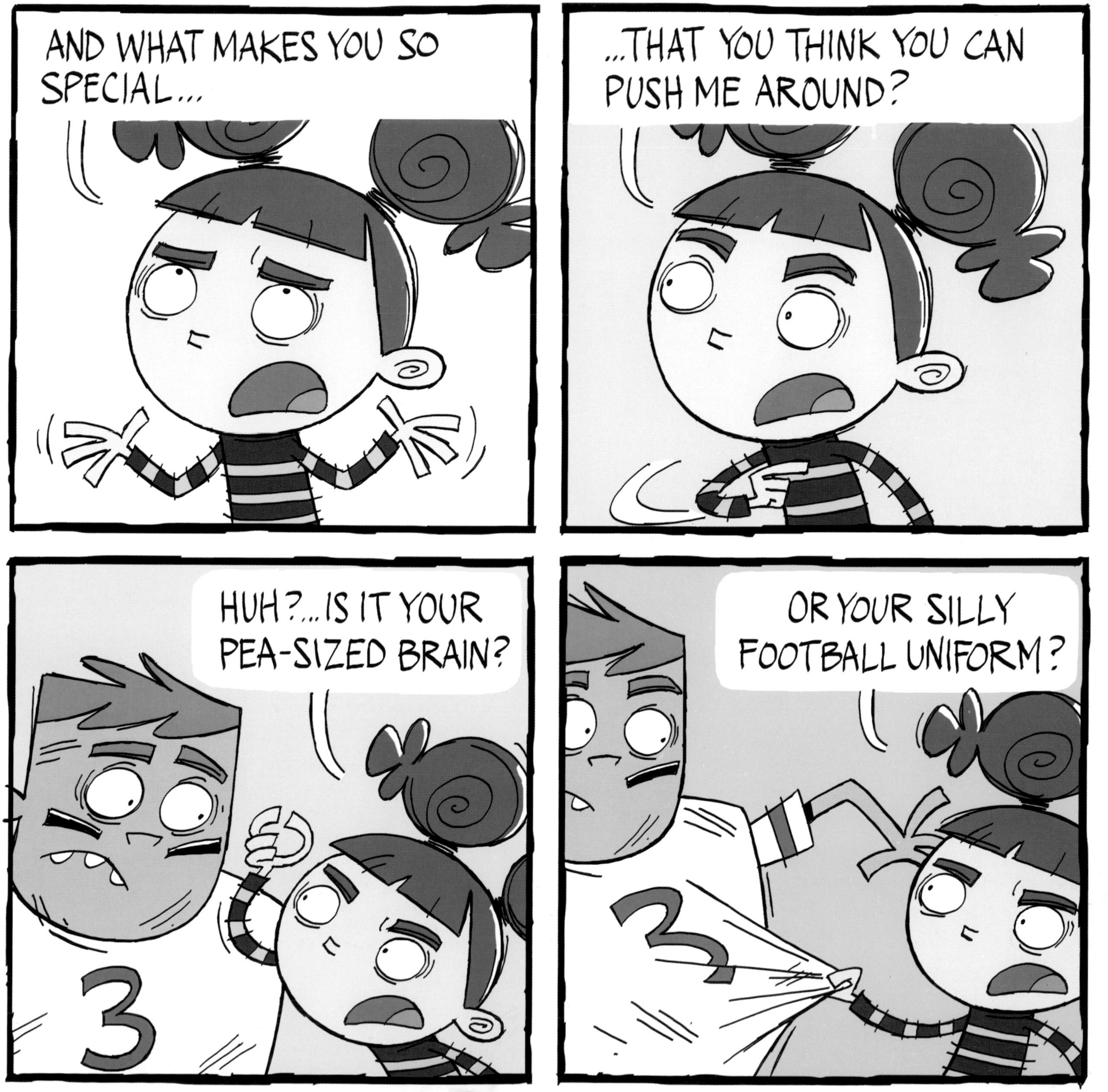
AND WHAT MAKES YOU SO SPECIAL...
...THAT YOU THINK YOU CAN PUSH ME AROUND?
HUH?...IS IT YOUR PEA-SIZED BRAIN?
OR YOUR SILLY FOOTBALL UNIFORM?

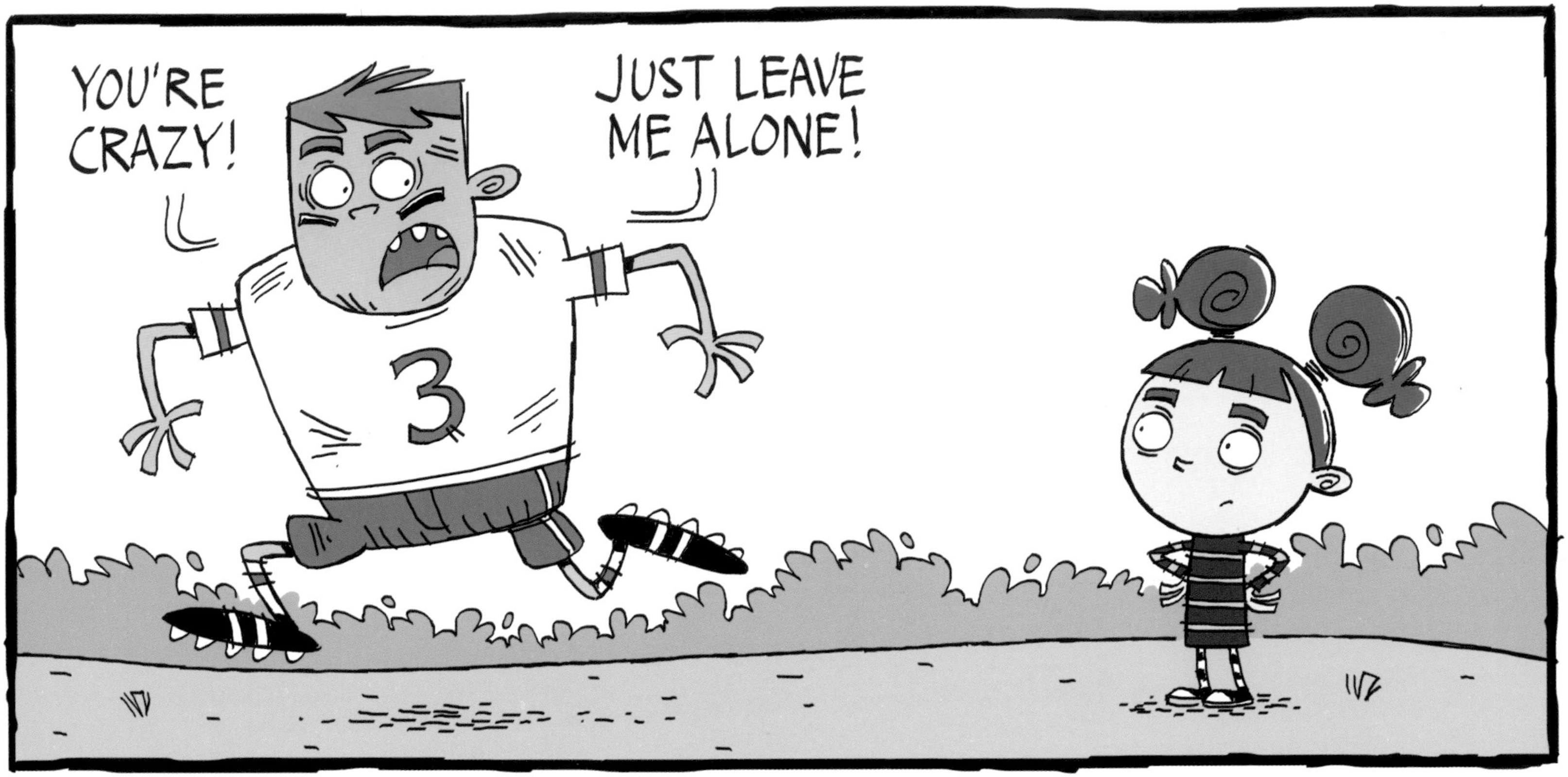
YOU'RE CRAZY!
JUST LEAVE ME ALONE!

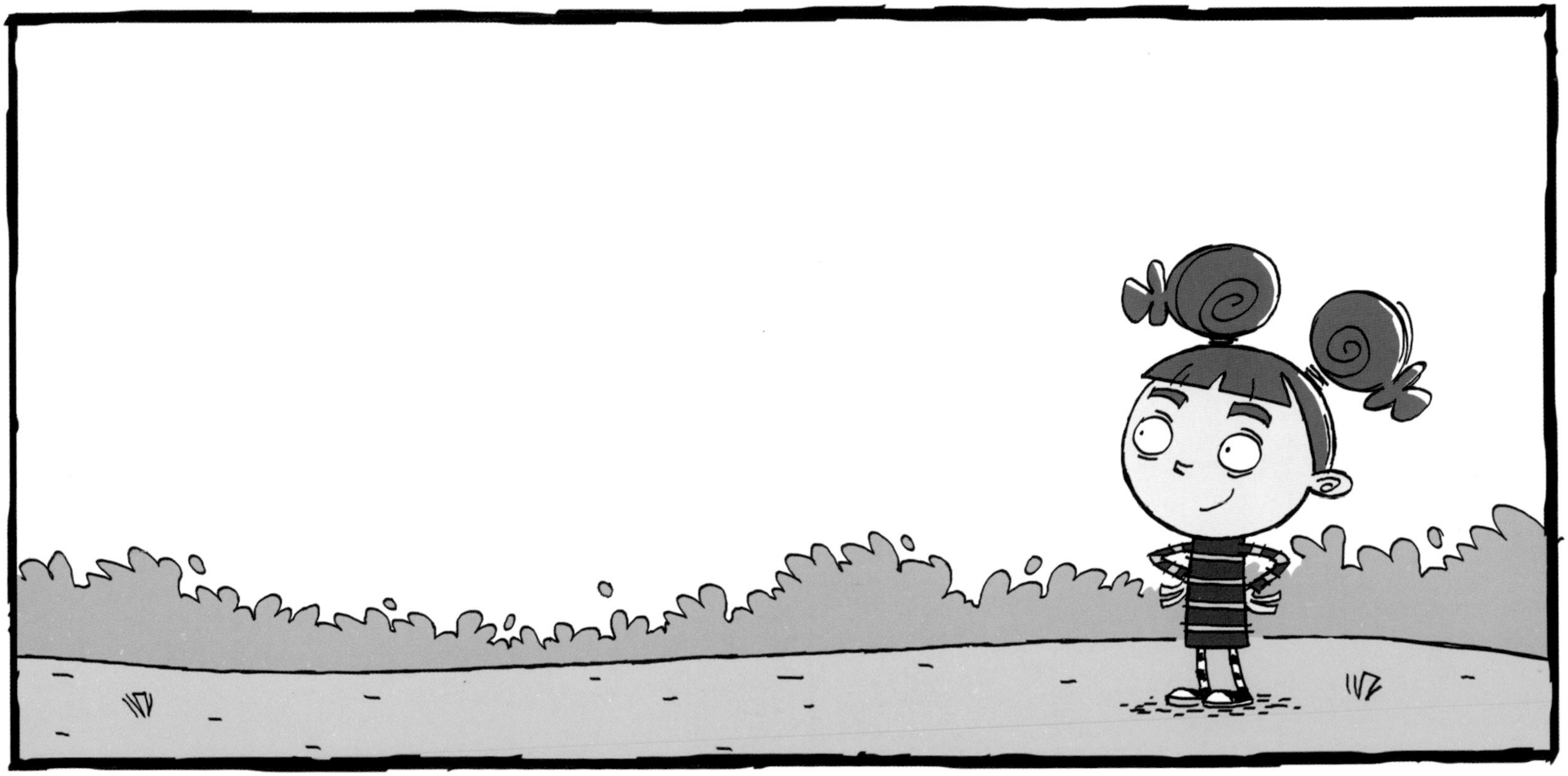

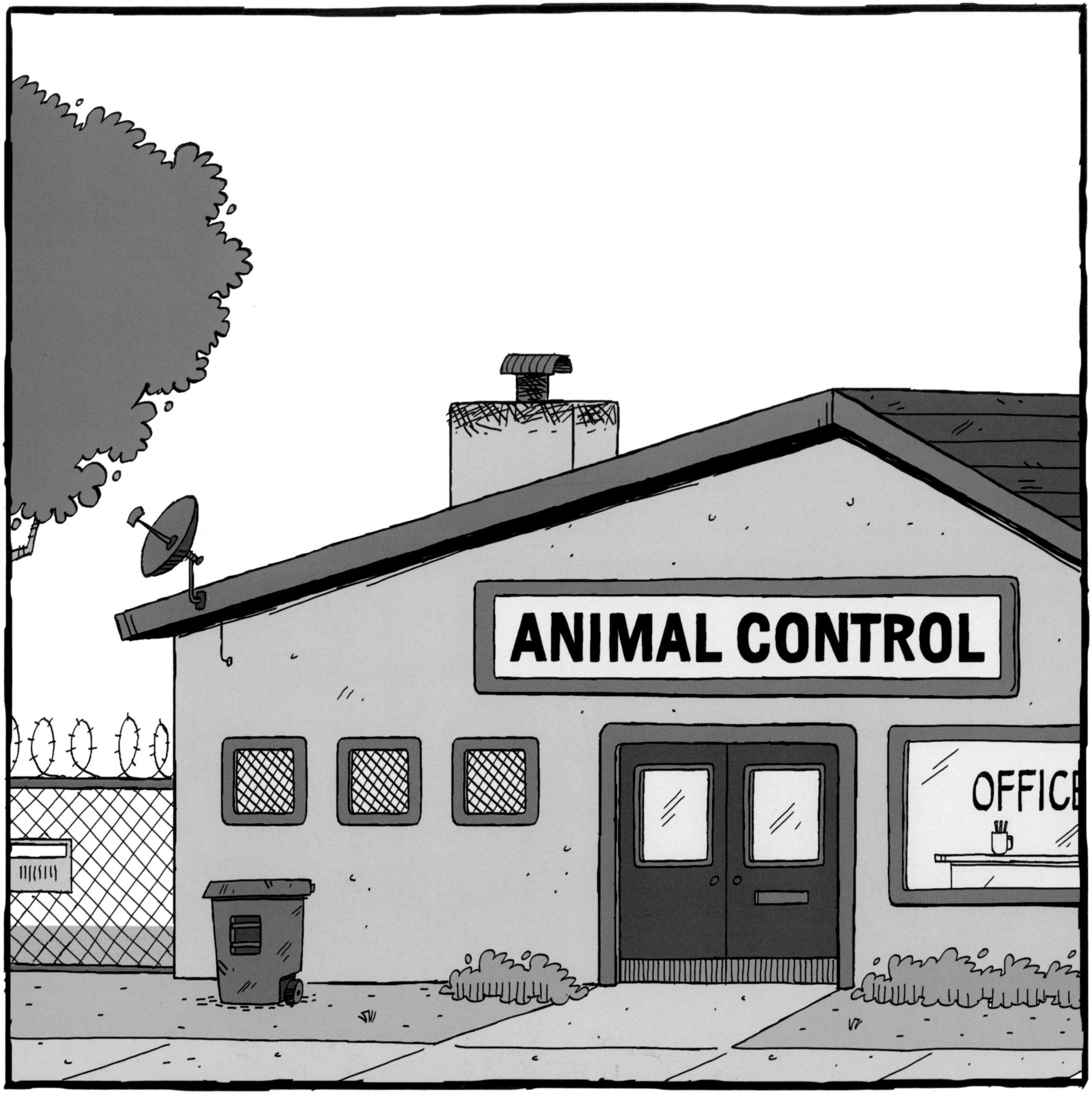
ANIMAL CONTROL
OFFICE

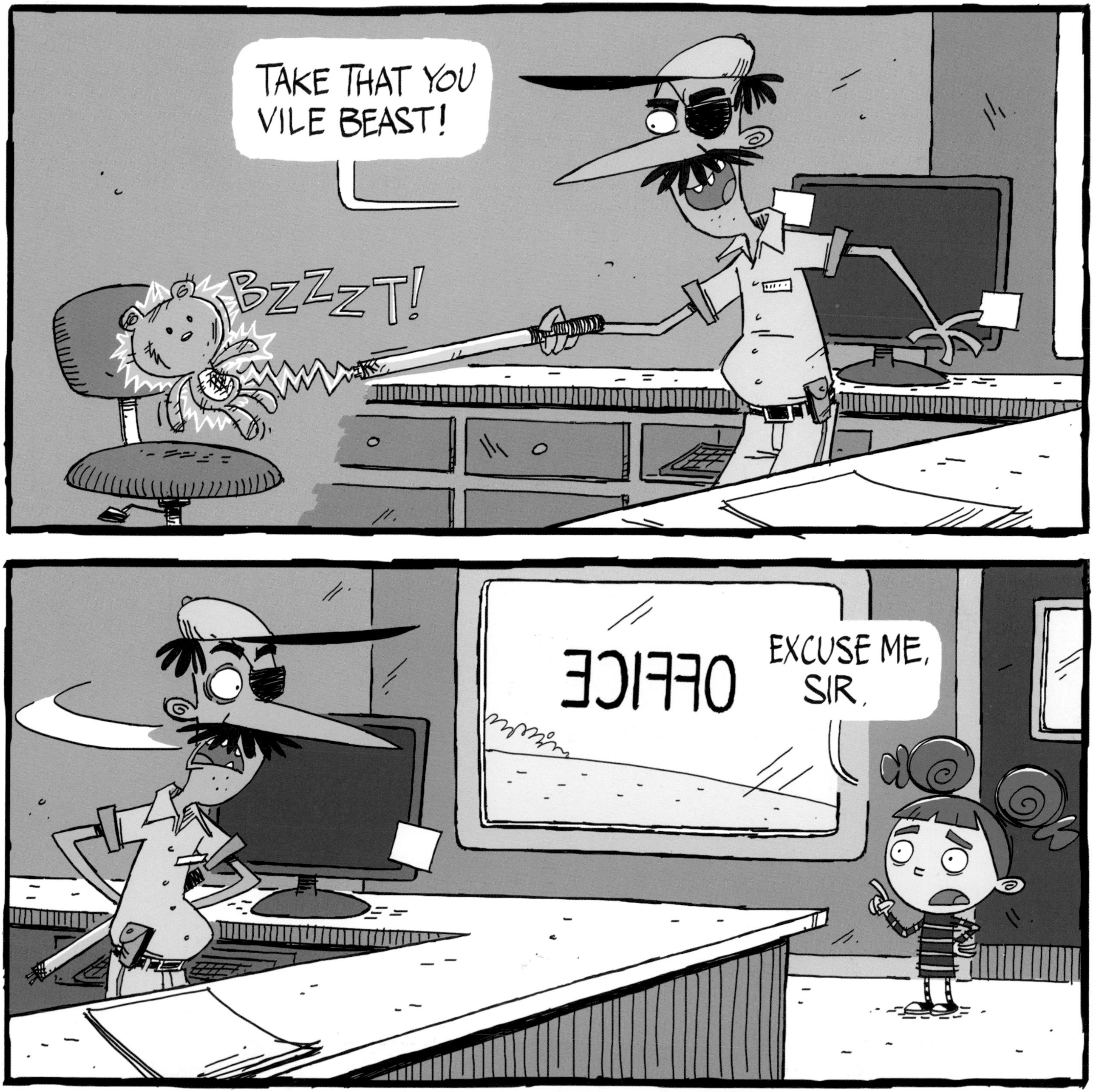
TAKE THAT YOU VILE BEAST!
BZZZZT!
OFFICE
EXCUSE ME, SIR.

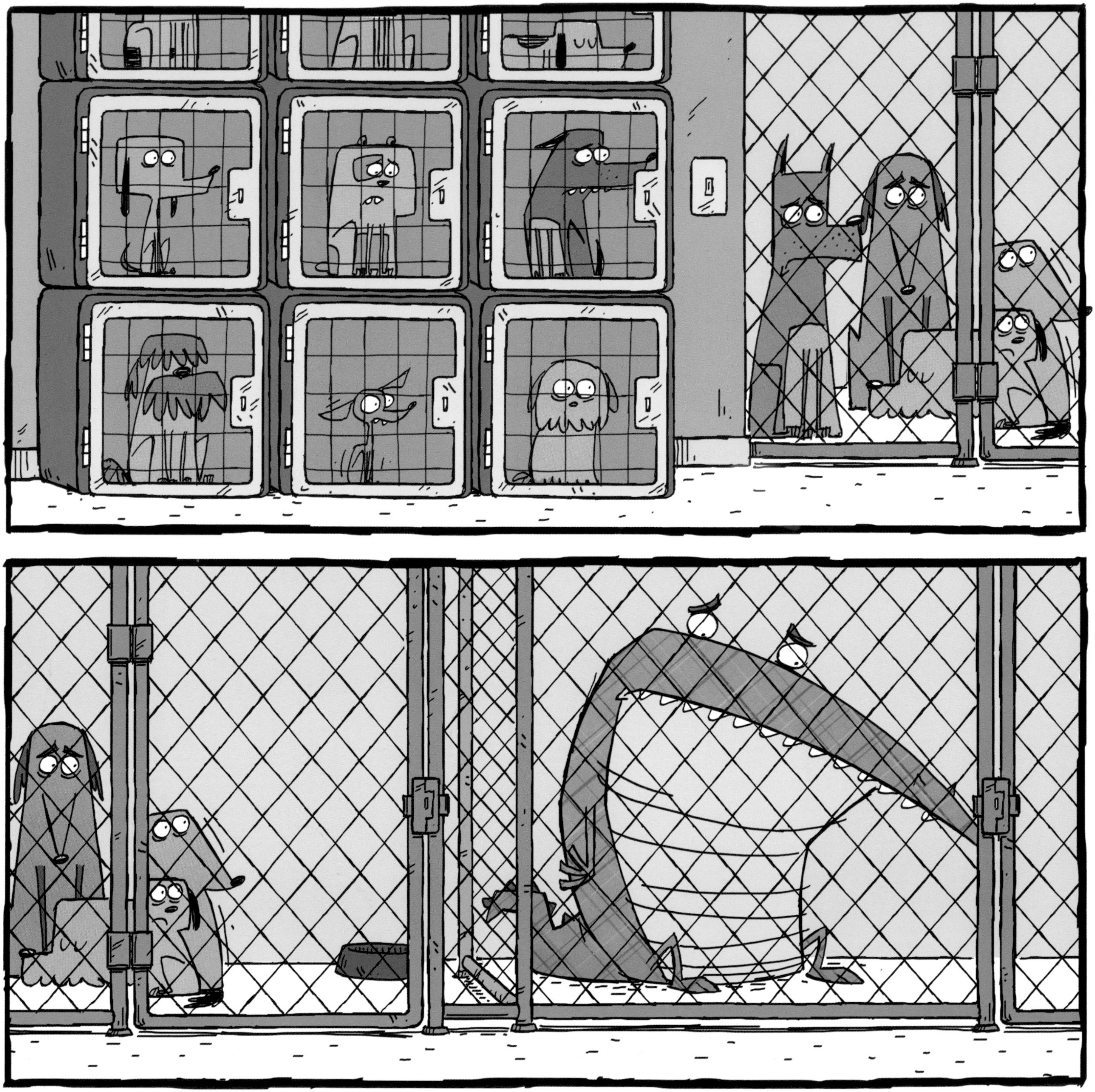

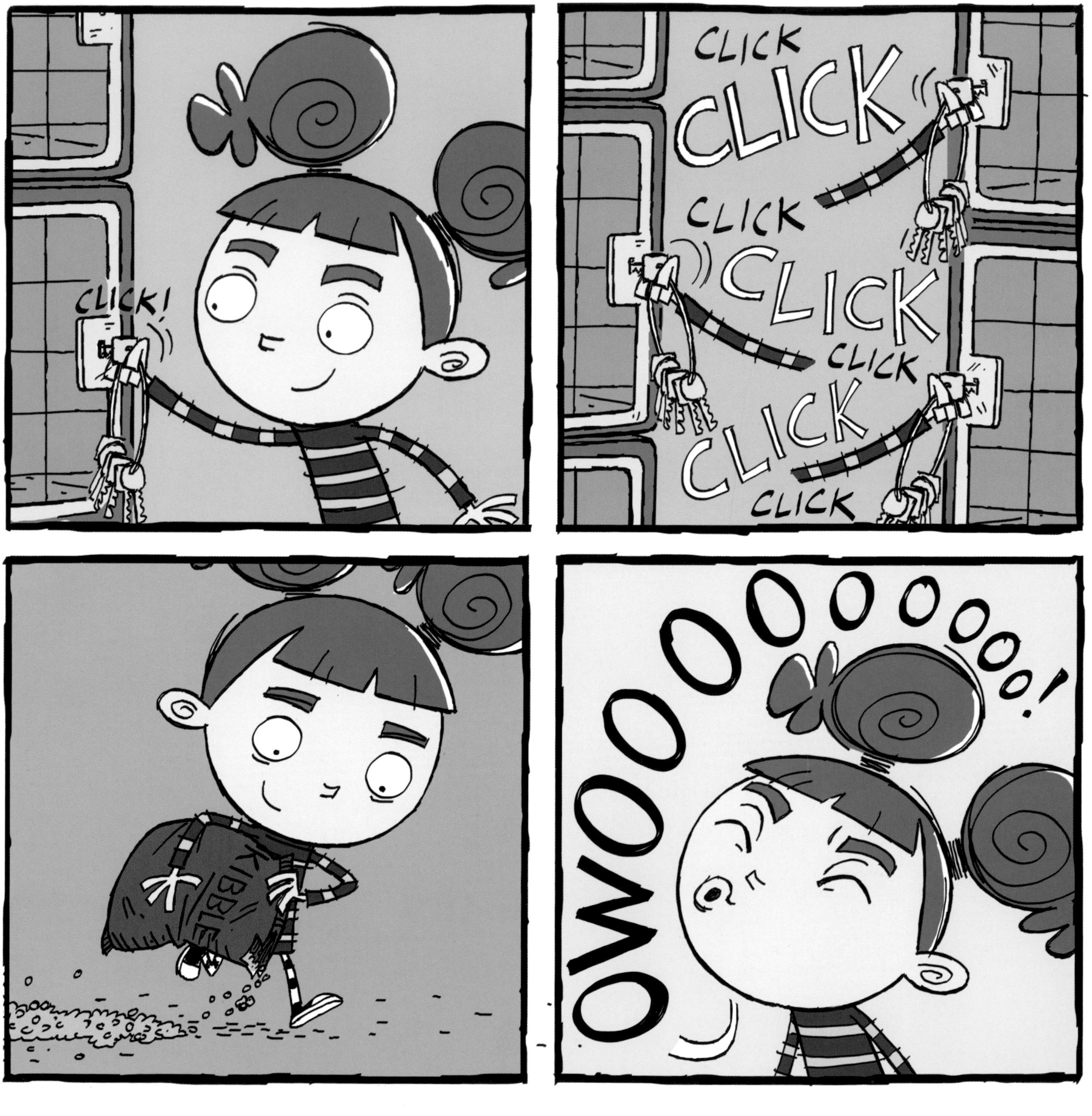
CLICK!
CLICK
CLICK
CLICK
CLICK
CLICK
CLICK
CLICK
KIBBLE
OWOOOOOOOoo!

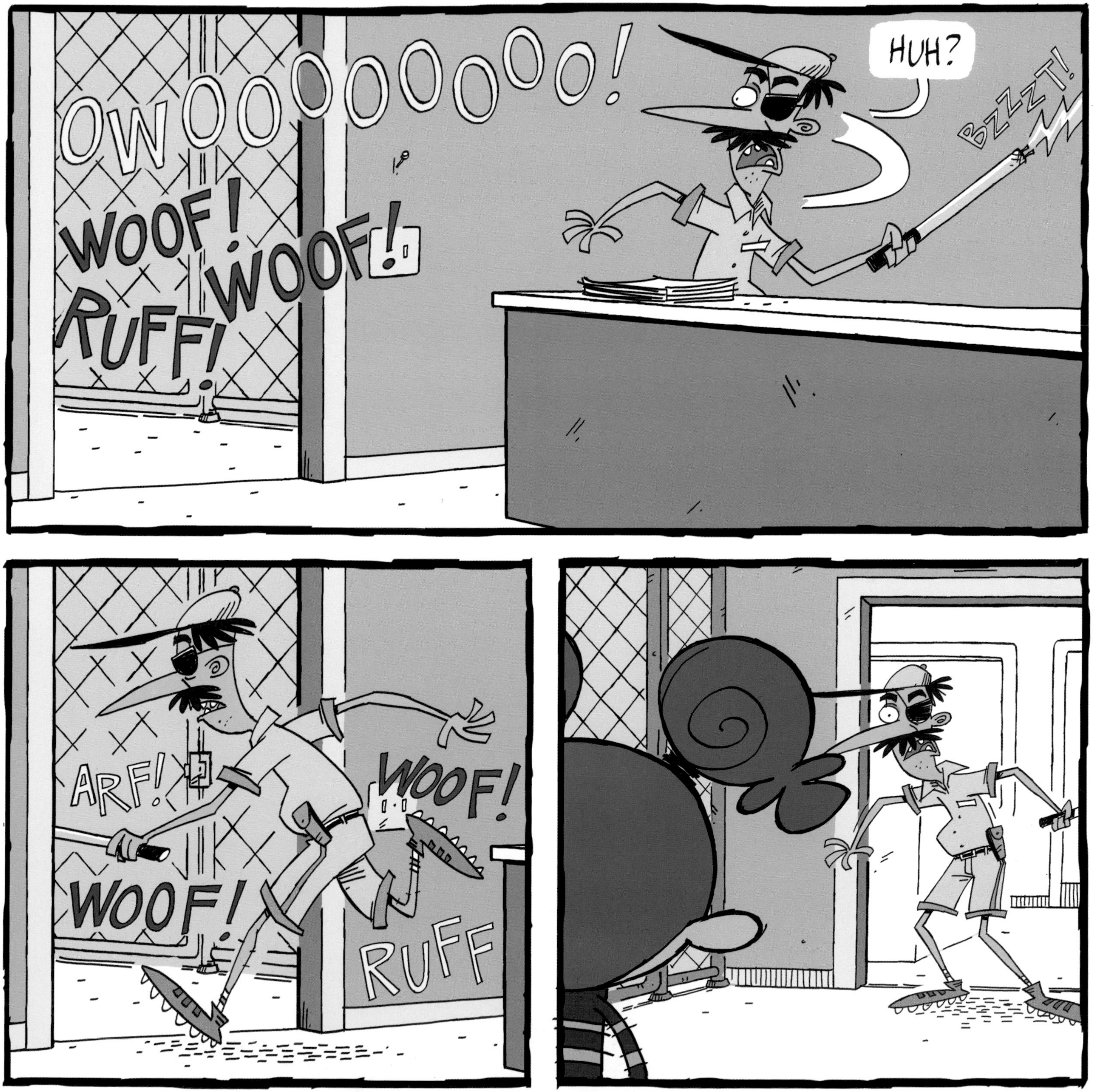
OWOOOOOOOOO!
HUH?
BZZZT!
WOOF!
WOOF!
RUFF!
ARF!
WOOF!
WOOF!
RUFF

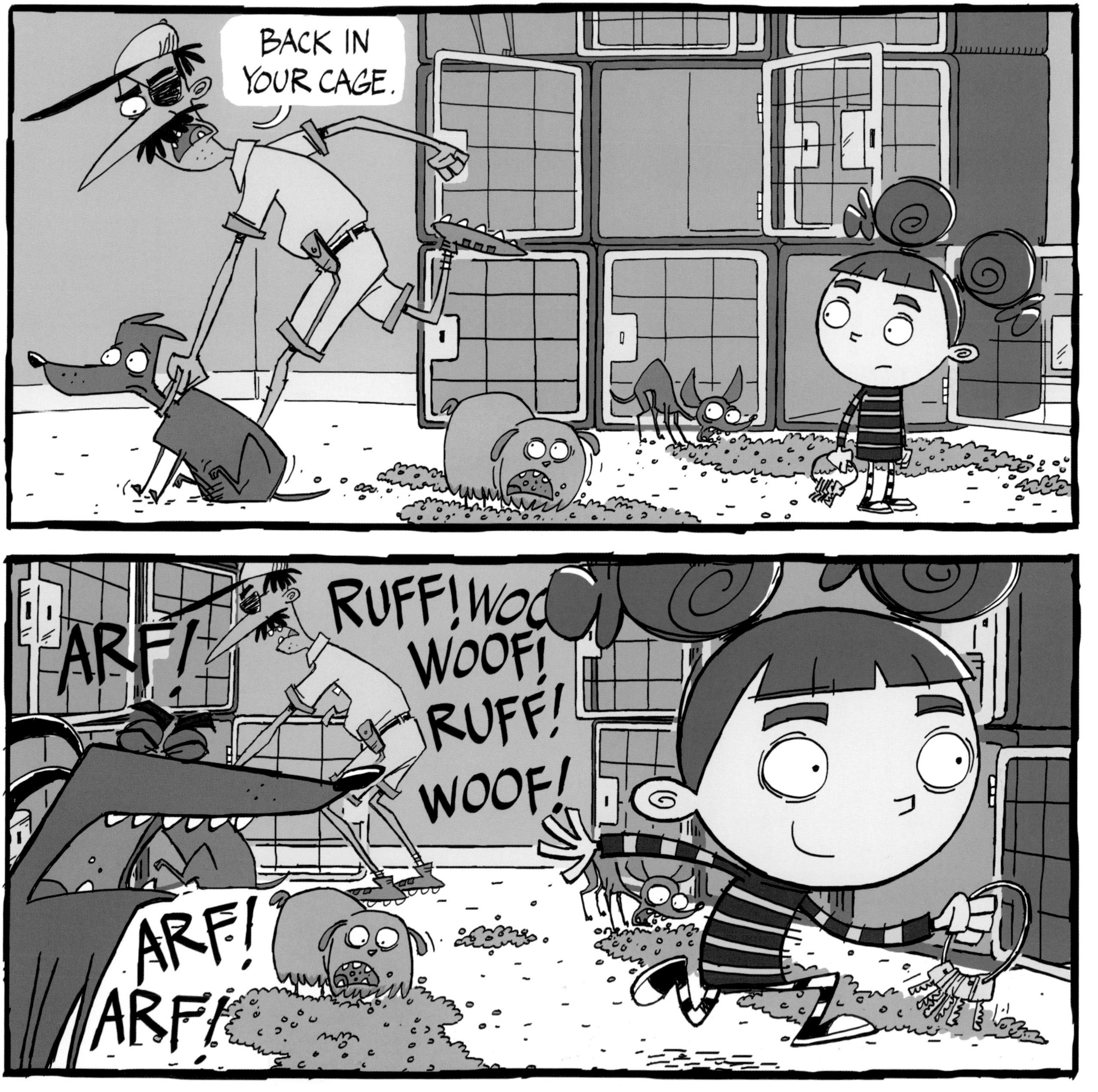

BACK IN YOUR CAGE.
ARF!
RUFF! WOO
WOOF!
RUFF!
WOOF!
ARF!
ARF!

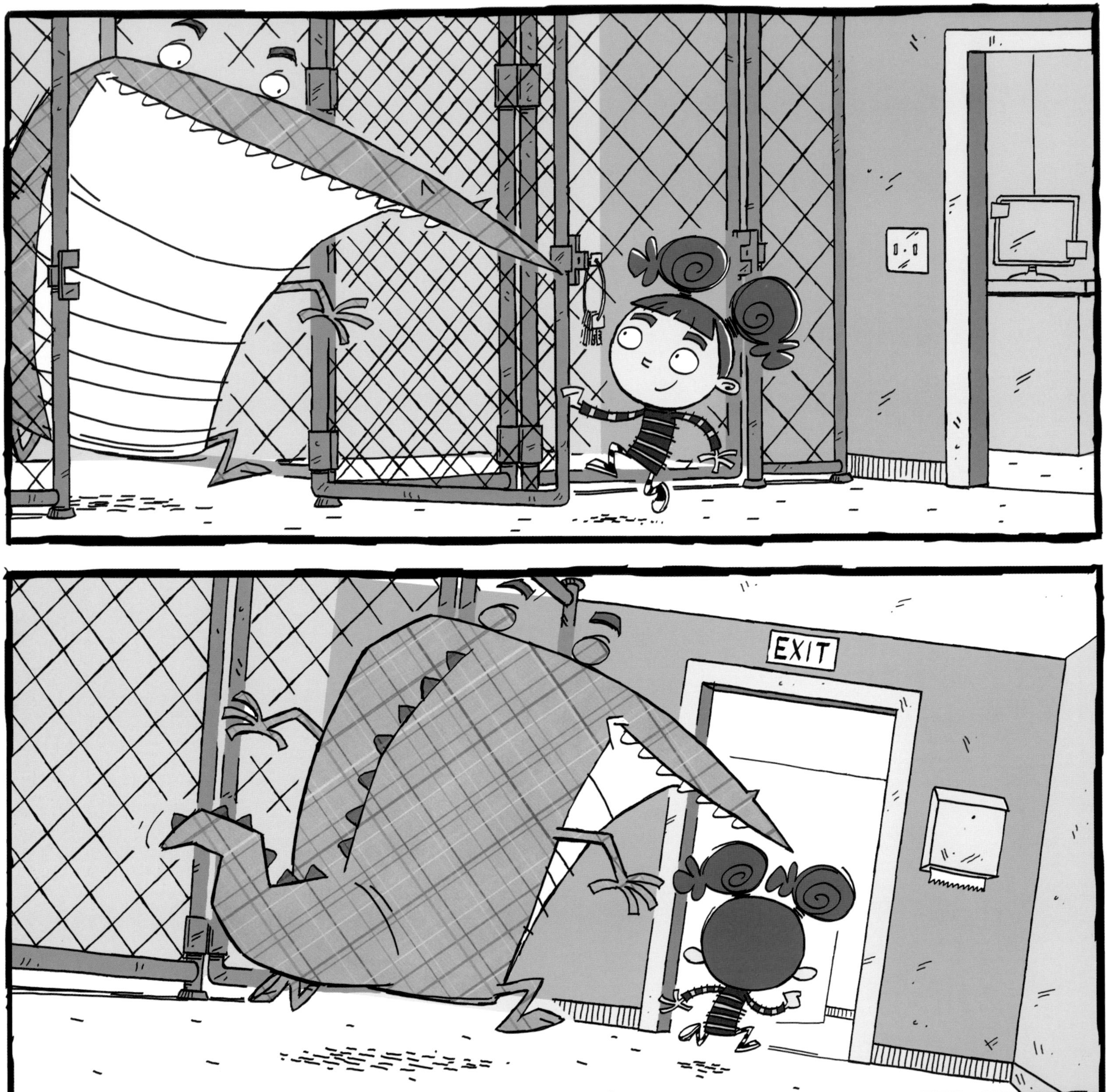
EXIT

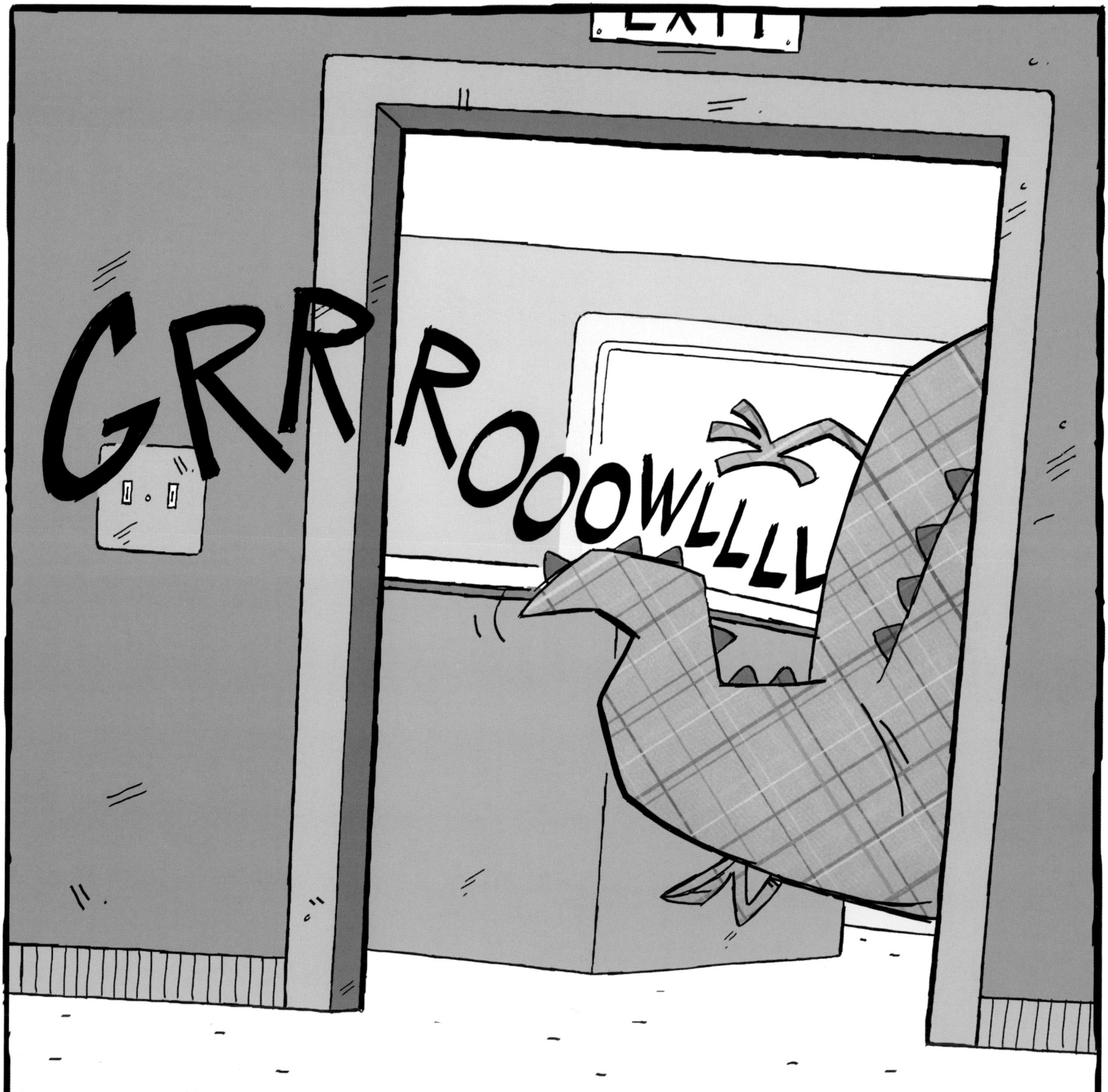
GRRRROOOOWLLLLL

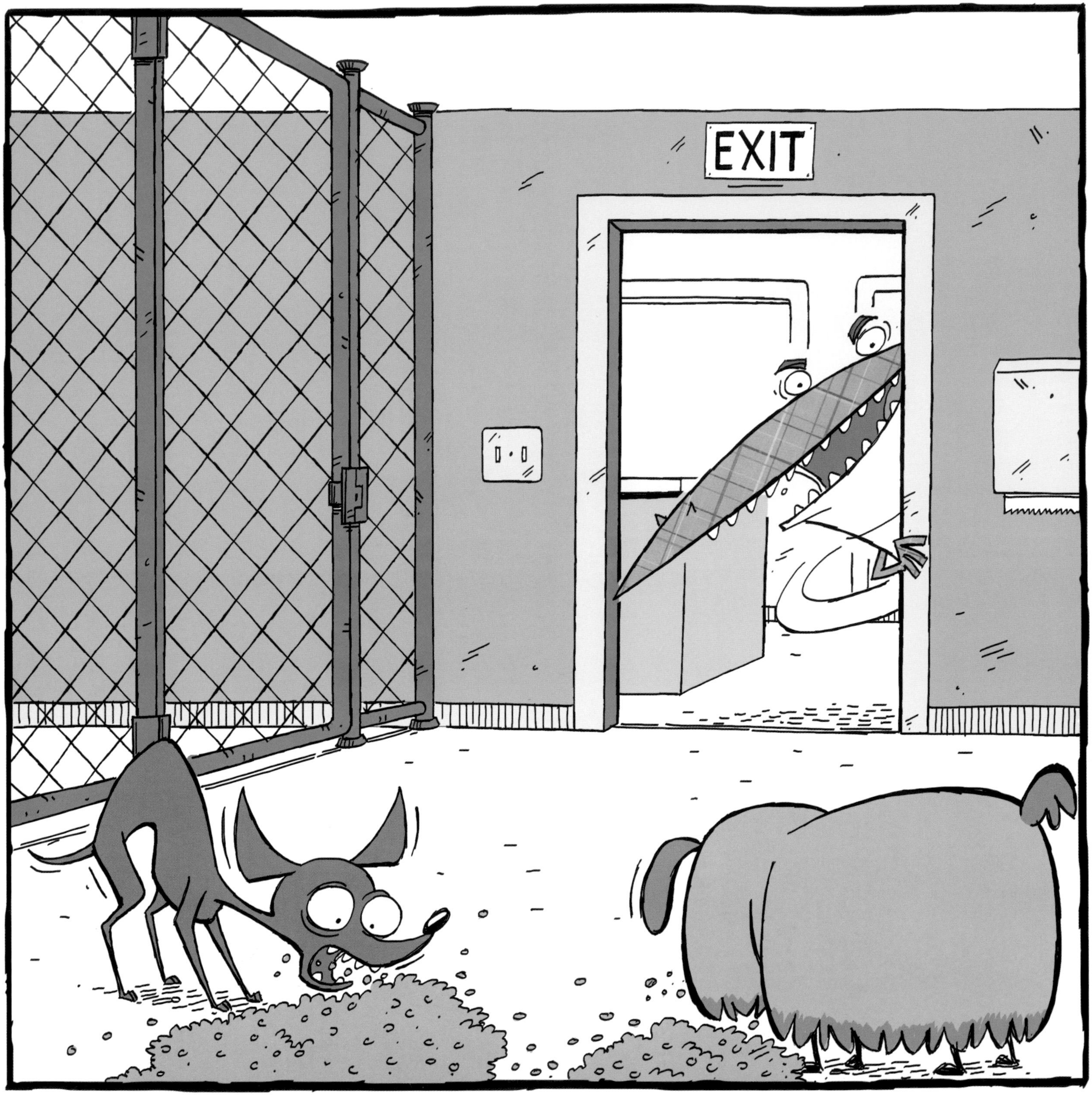
EXIT

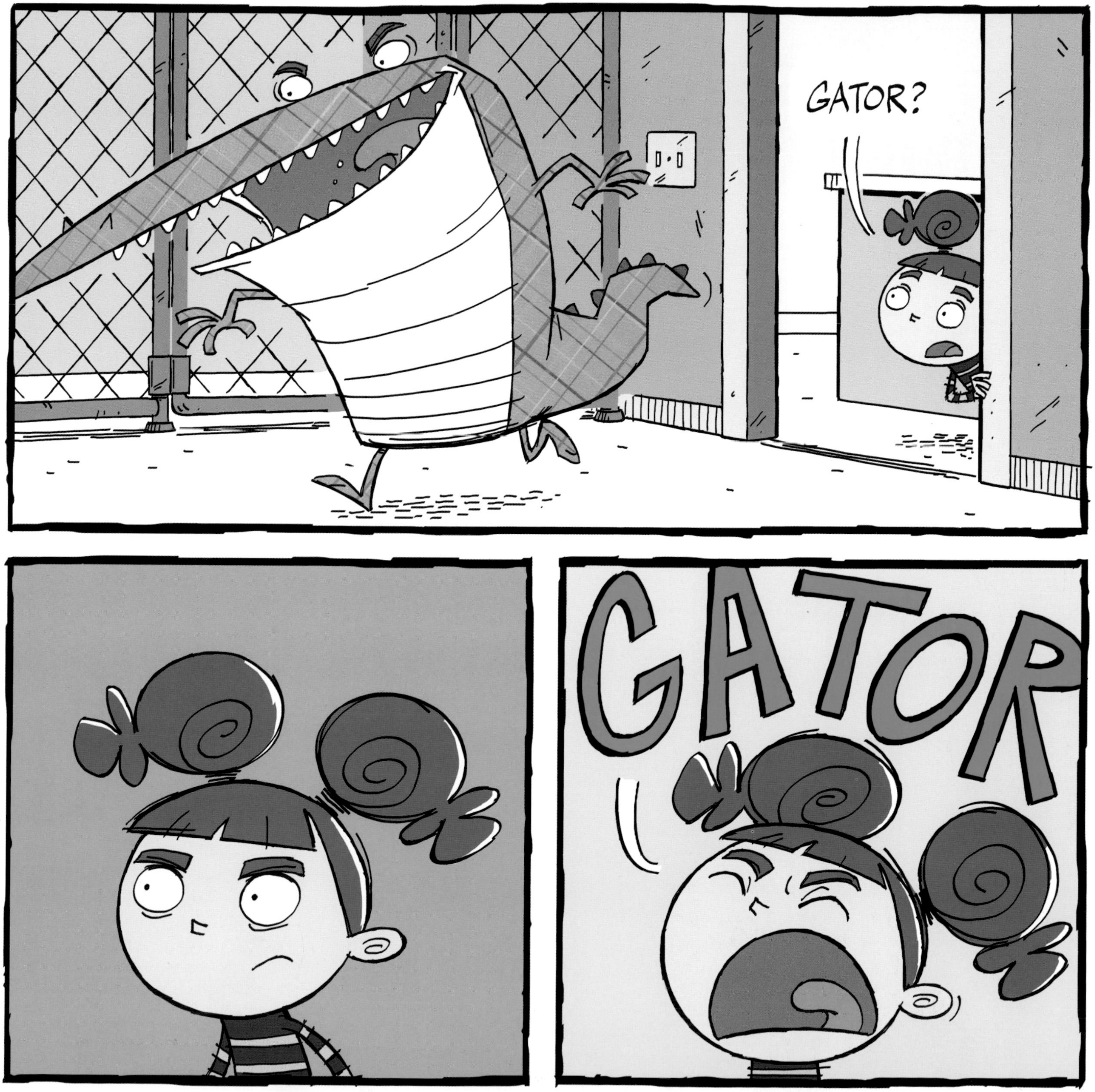
GATOR?
GATOR

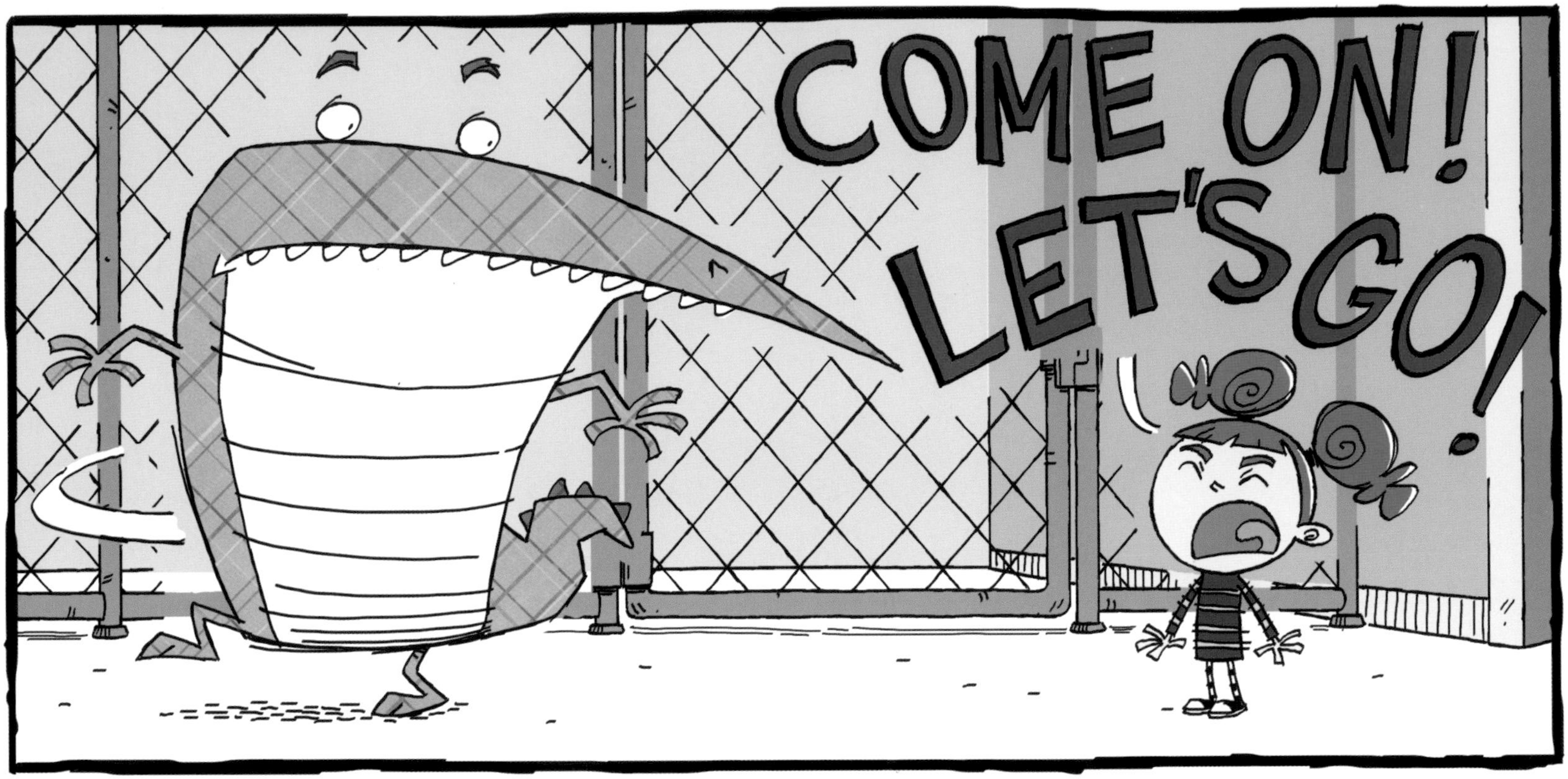
COME ON! LET'S GO!

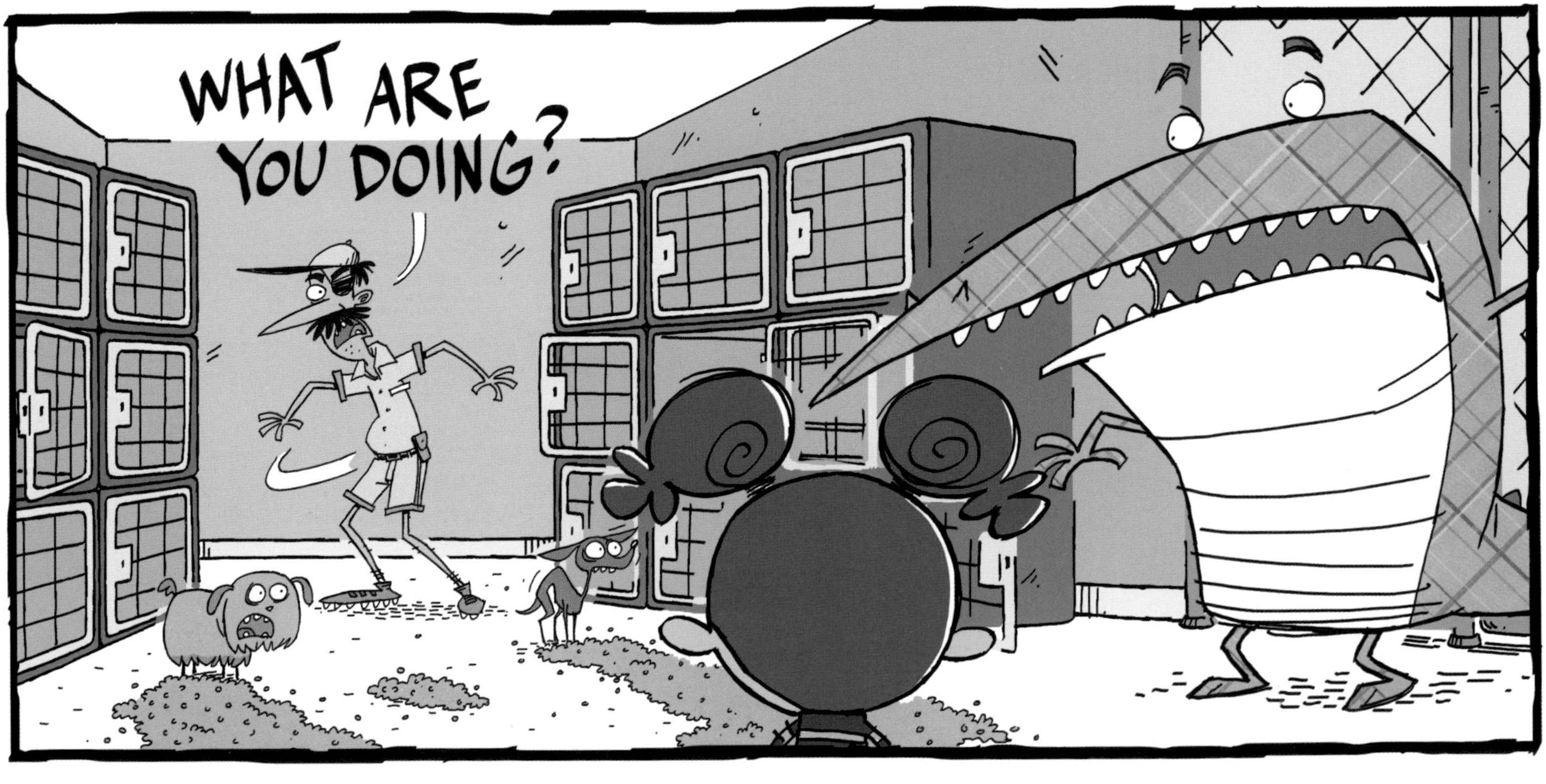
WHAT ARE YOU DOING?

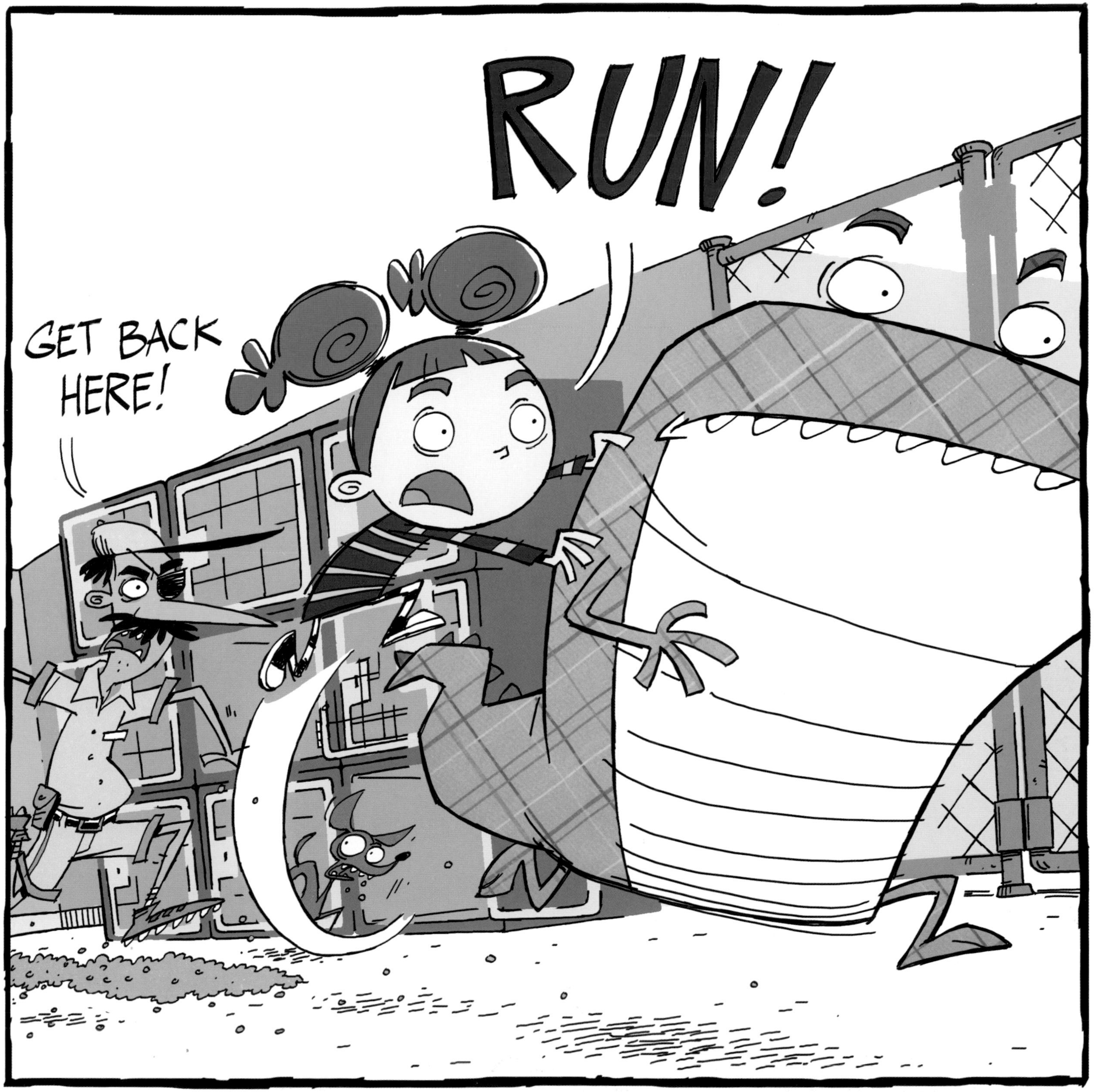
RUN!
GET BACK HERE!

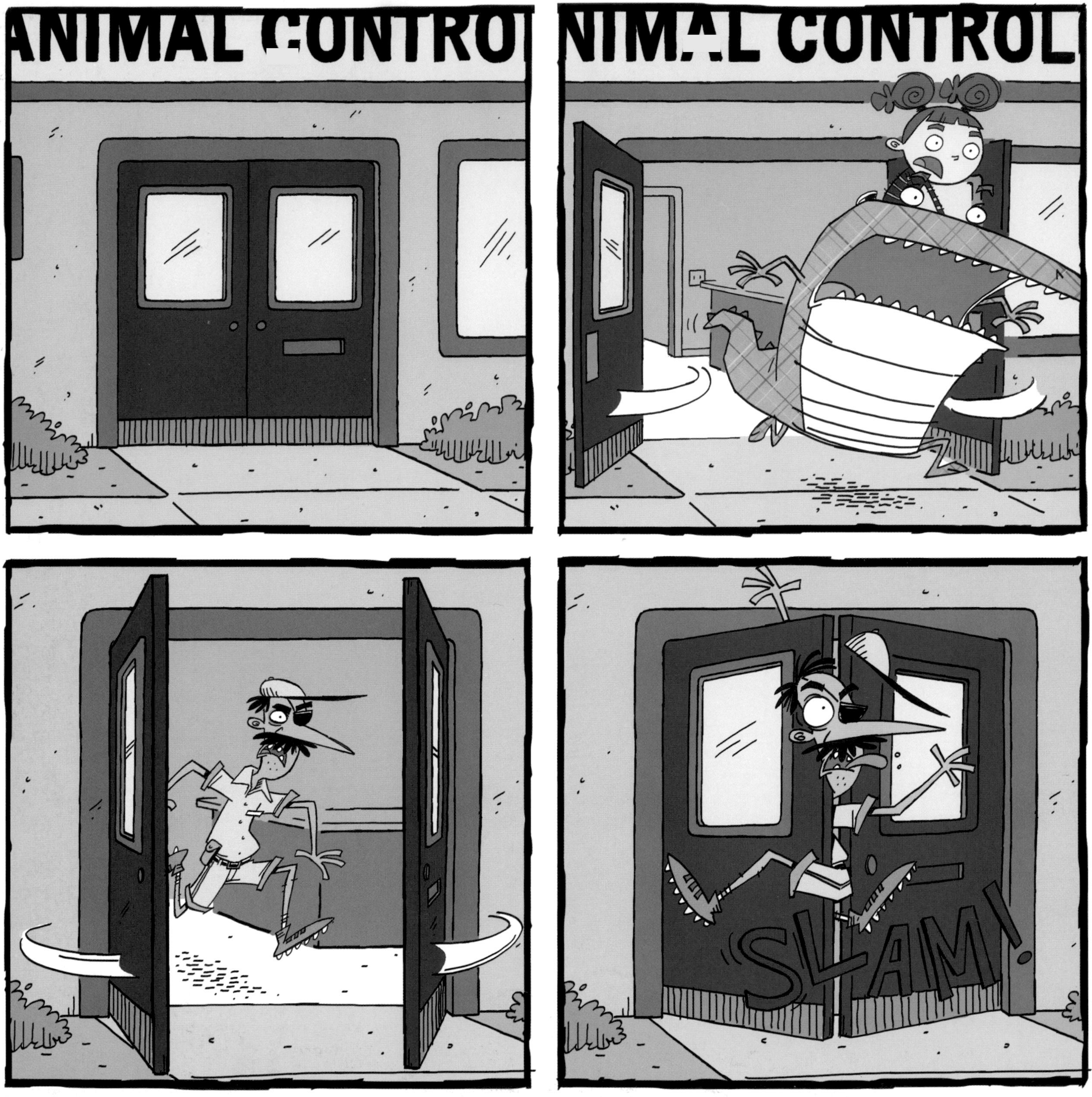
ANIMAL CONTRO
NIMAL CONTROL
SLAM!

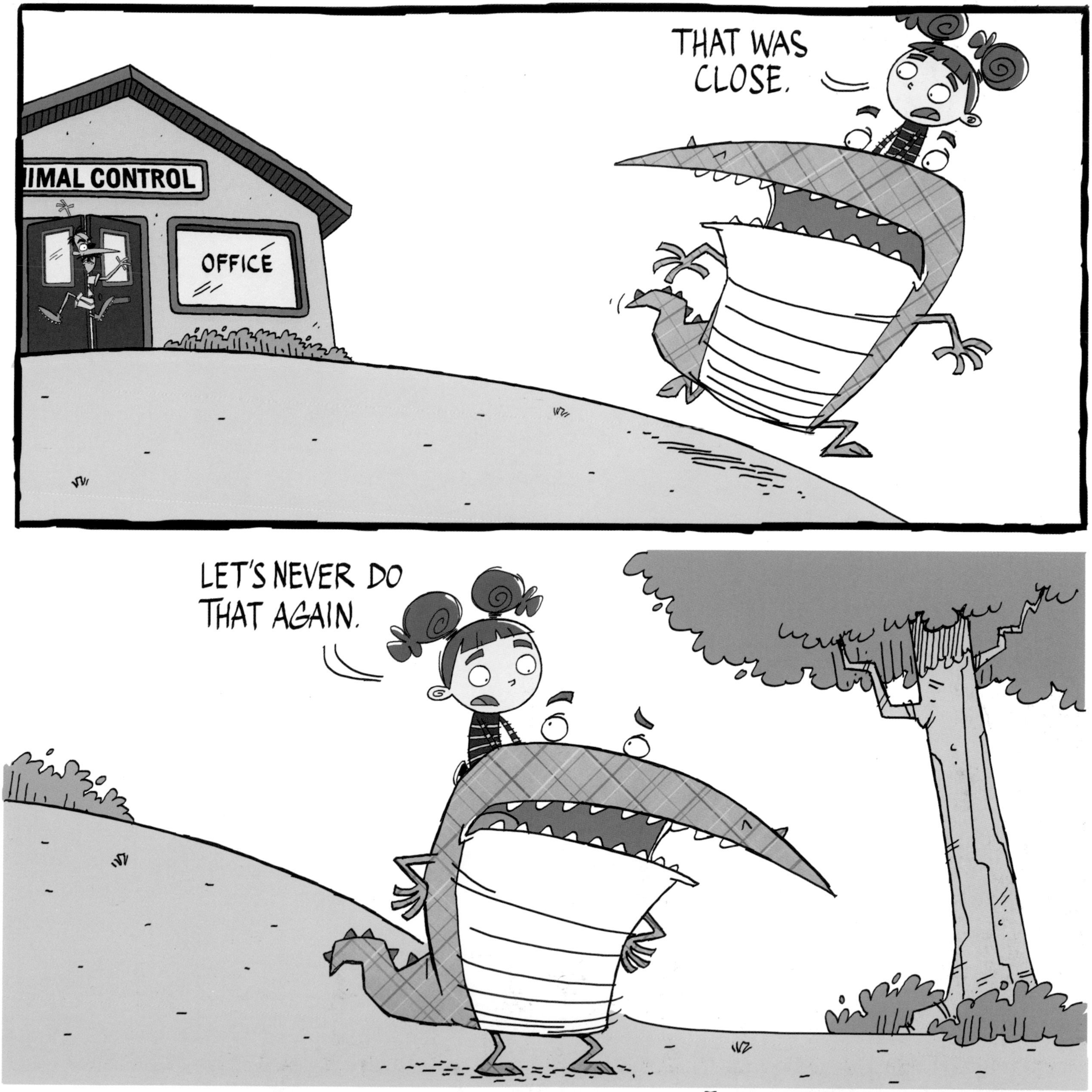
THAT WAS CLOSE.
IMAL CONTROL
OFFICE
LET'S NEVER DO THAT AGAIN.

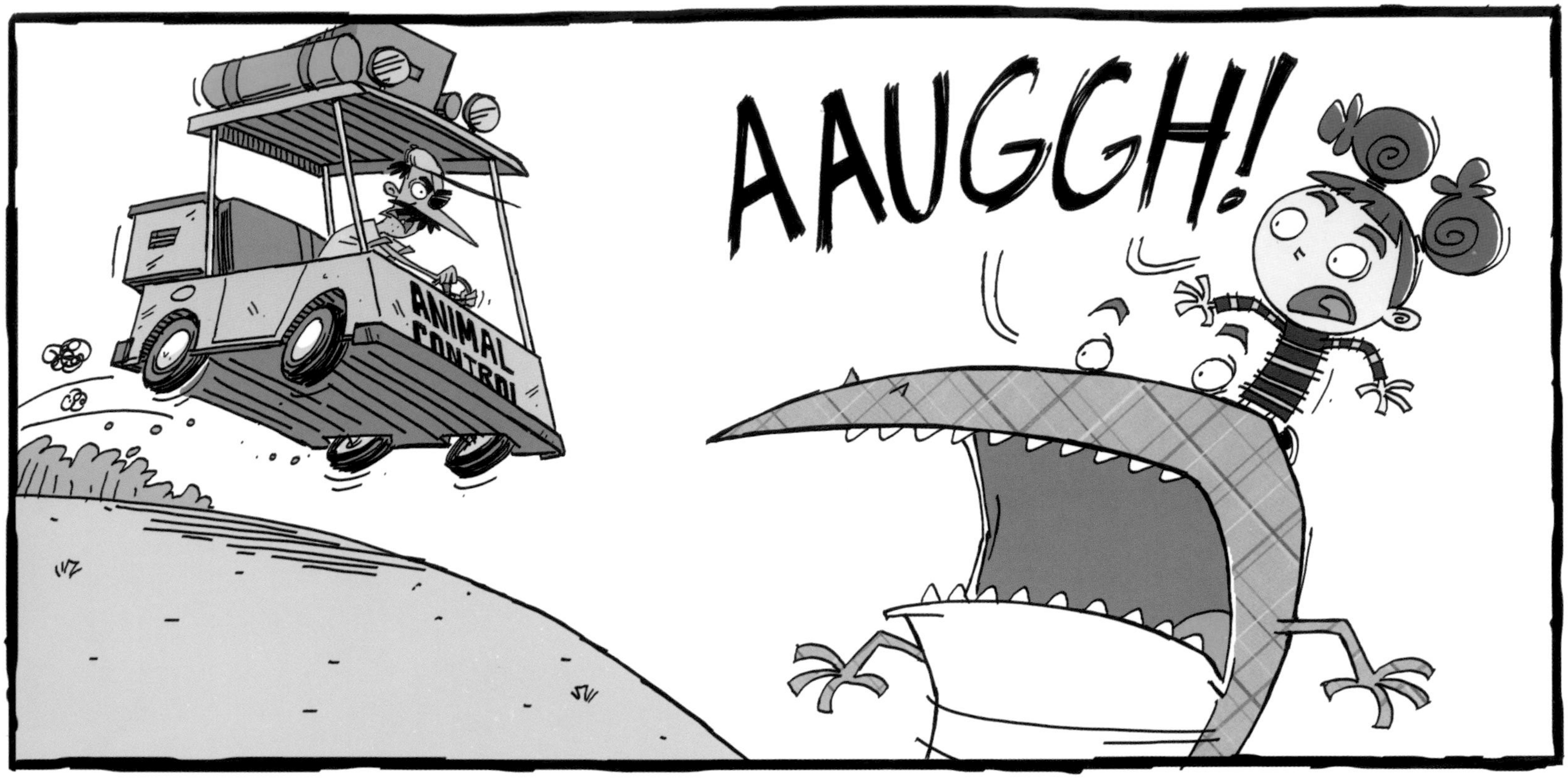
AAUGGH!
ANIMAL CONTROL

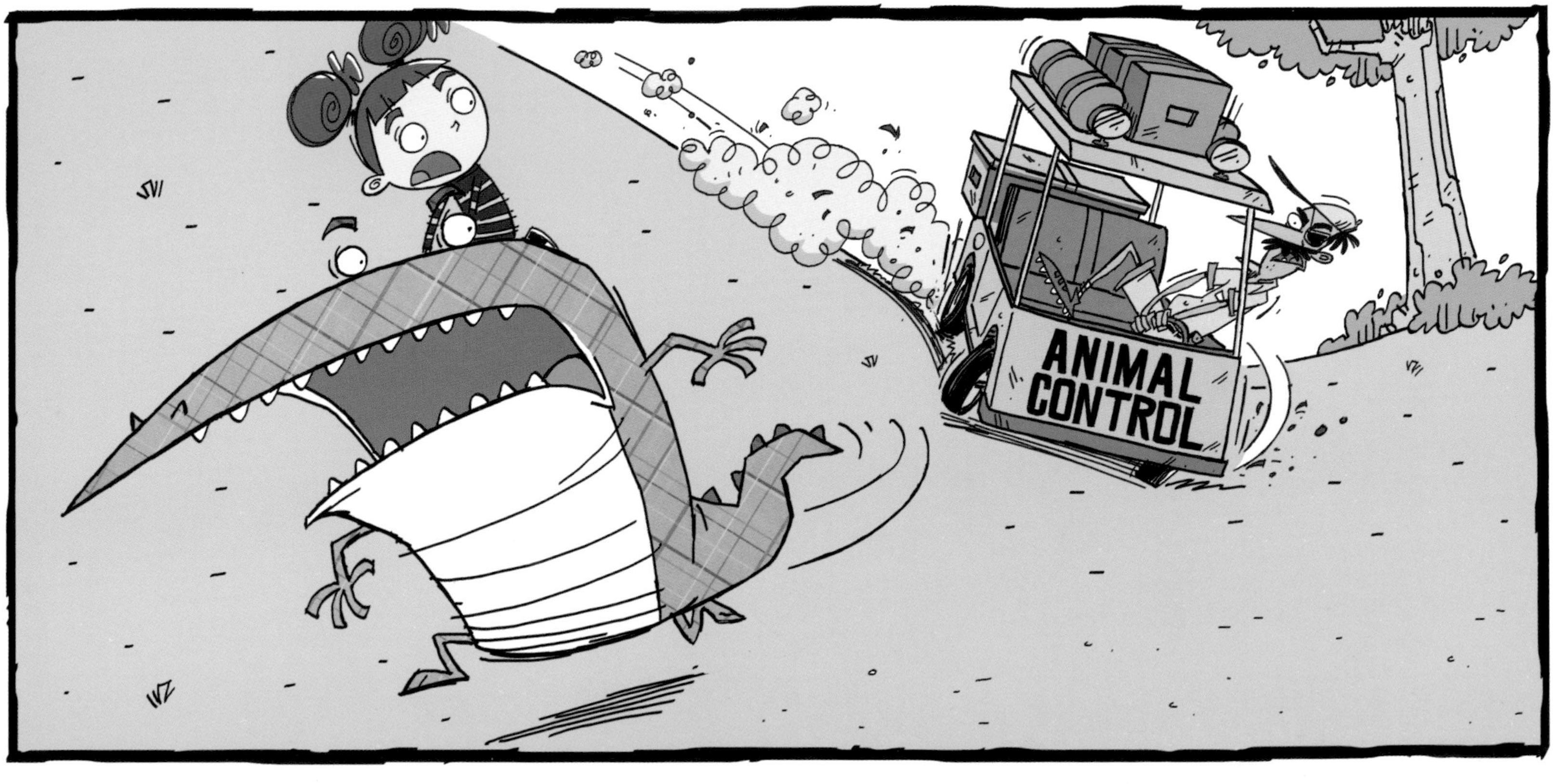
ANIMAL CONTROL

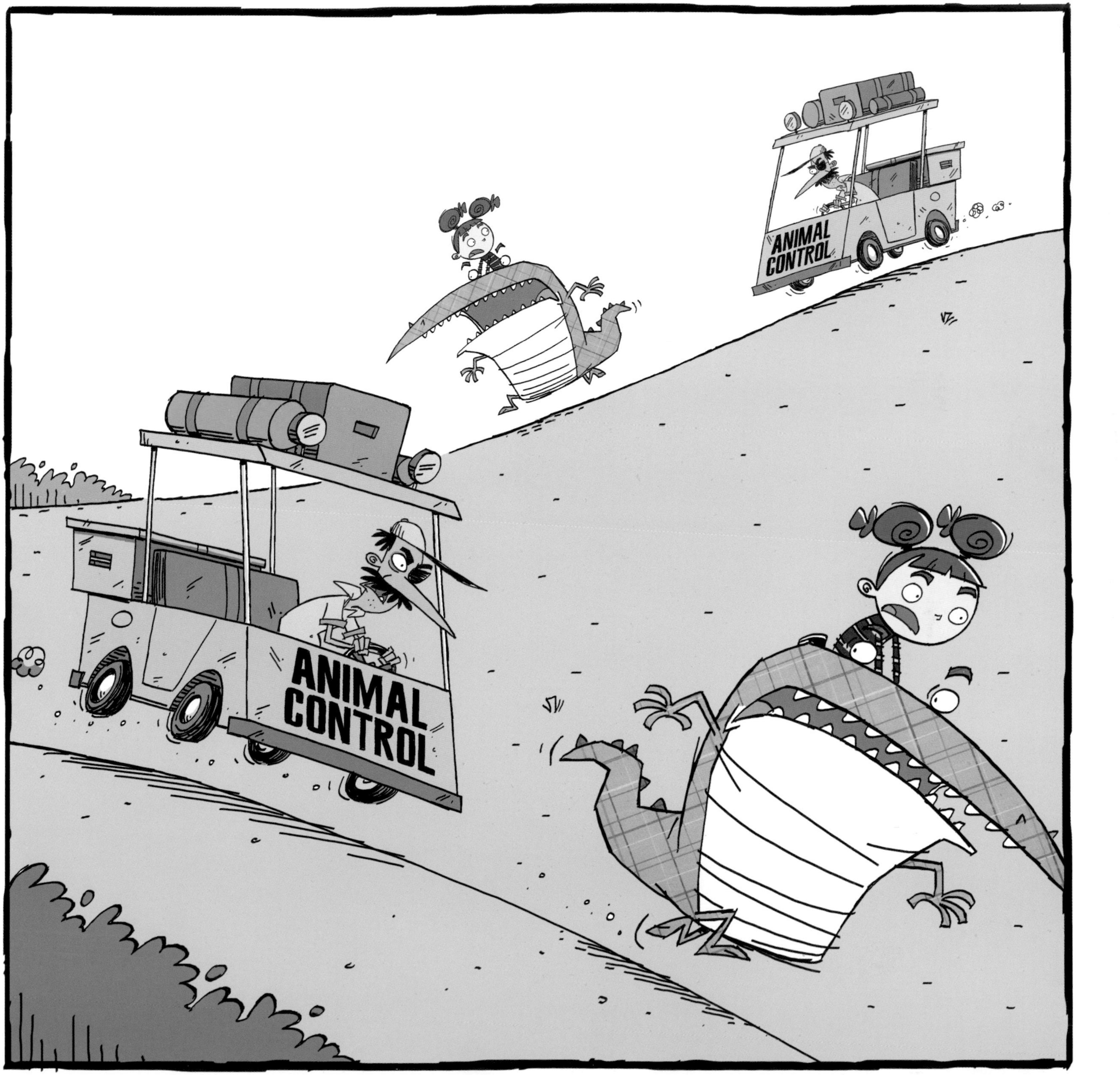
ANIMAL CONTROL
ANIMAL CONTROL

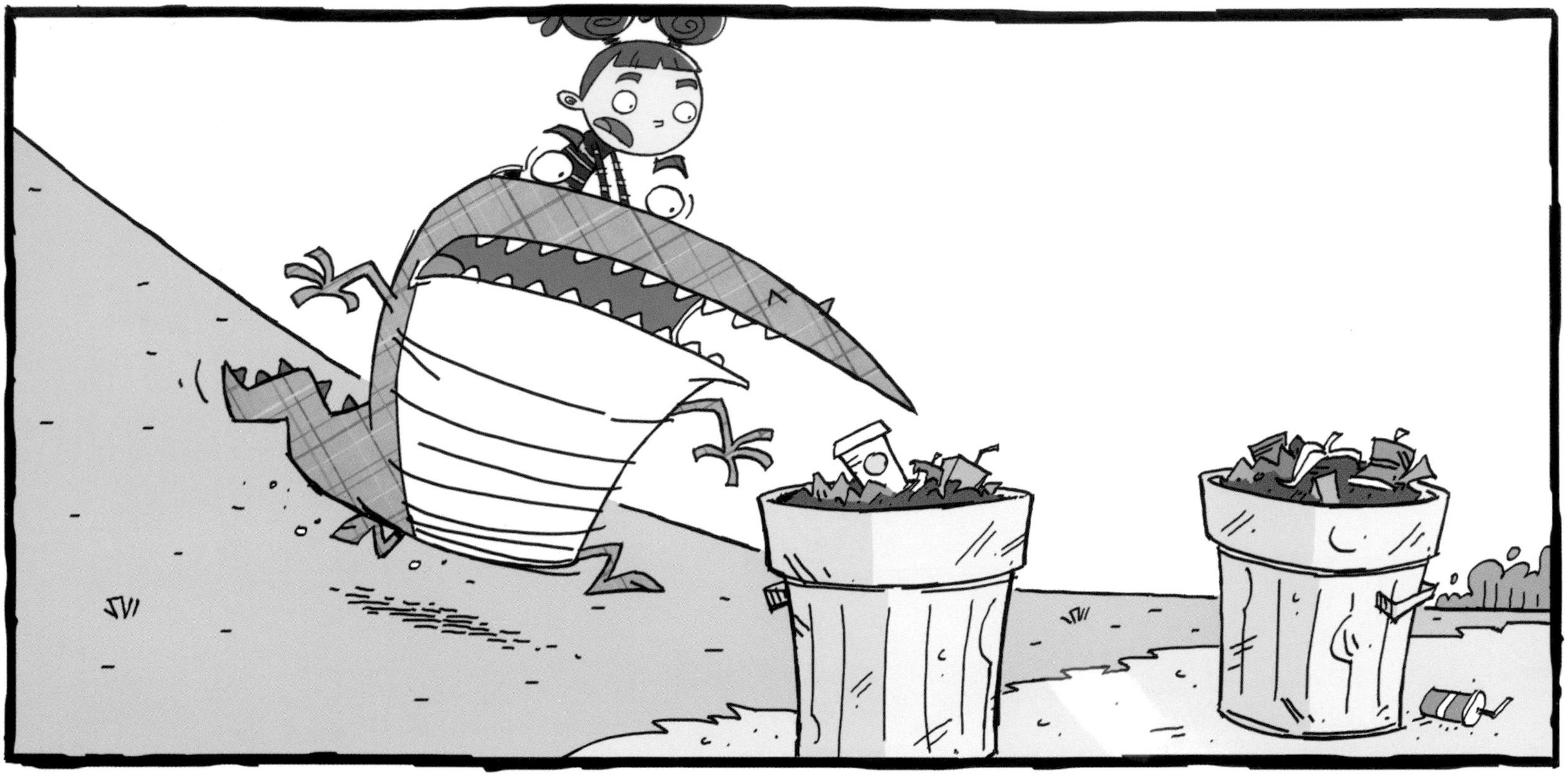

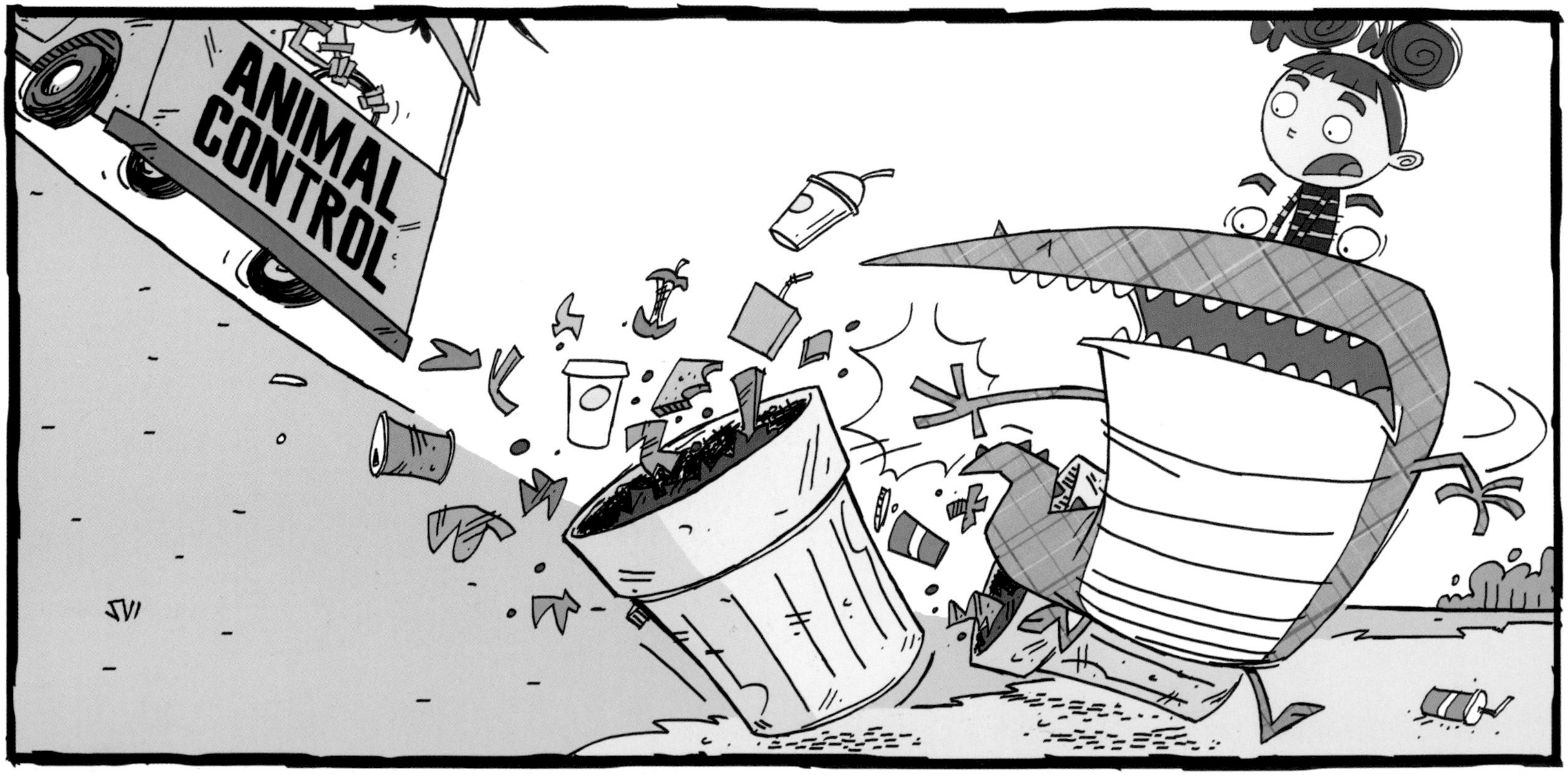
ANIMAL
CONTROL

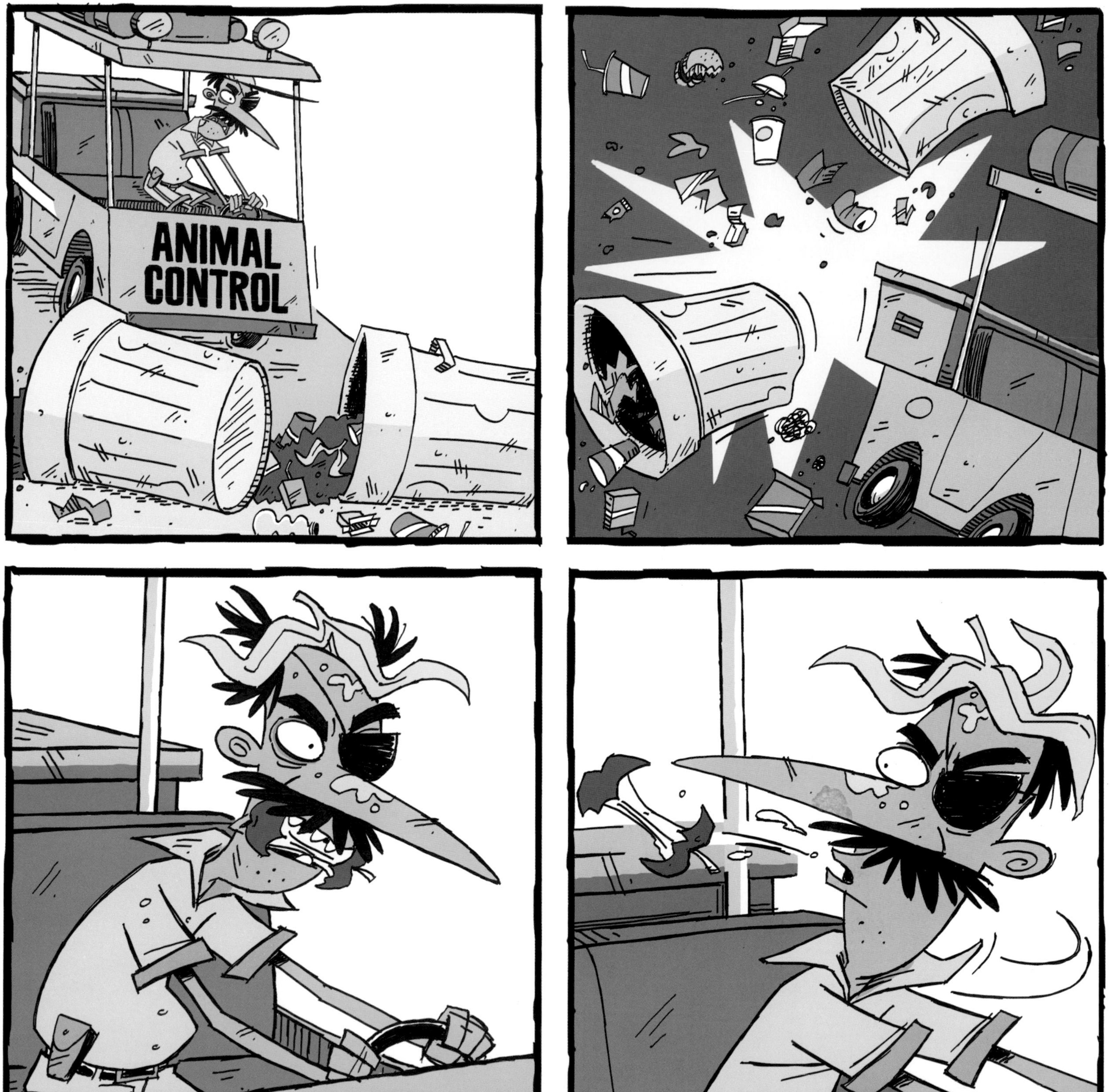
ANIMAL
CONTROL

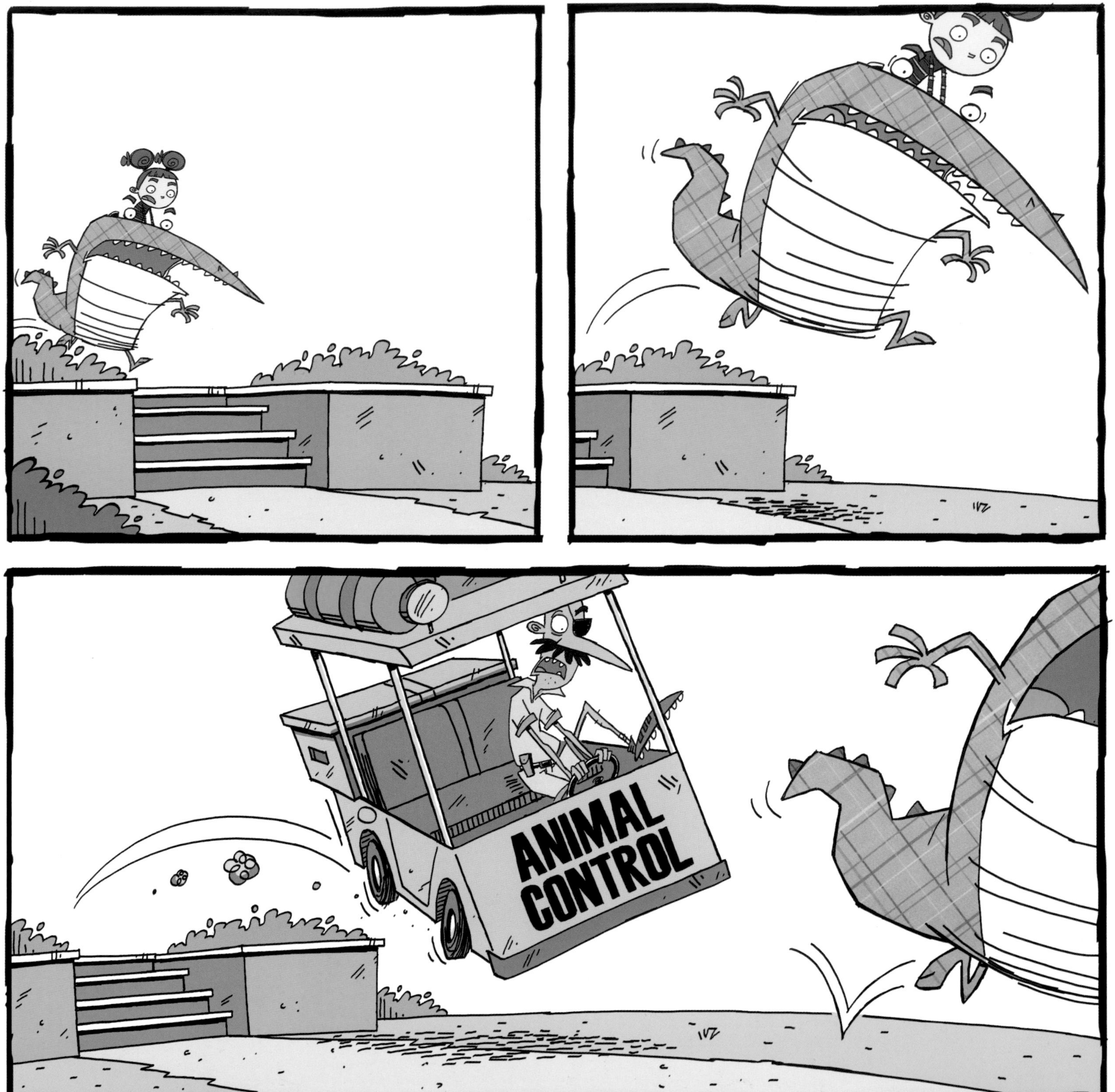
ANIMAL CONTROL

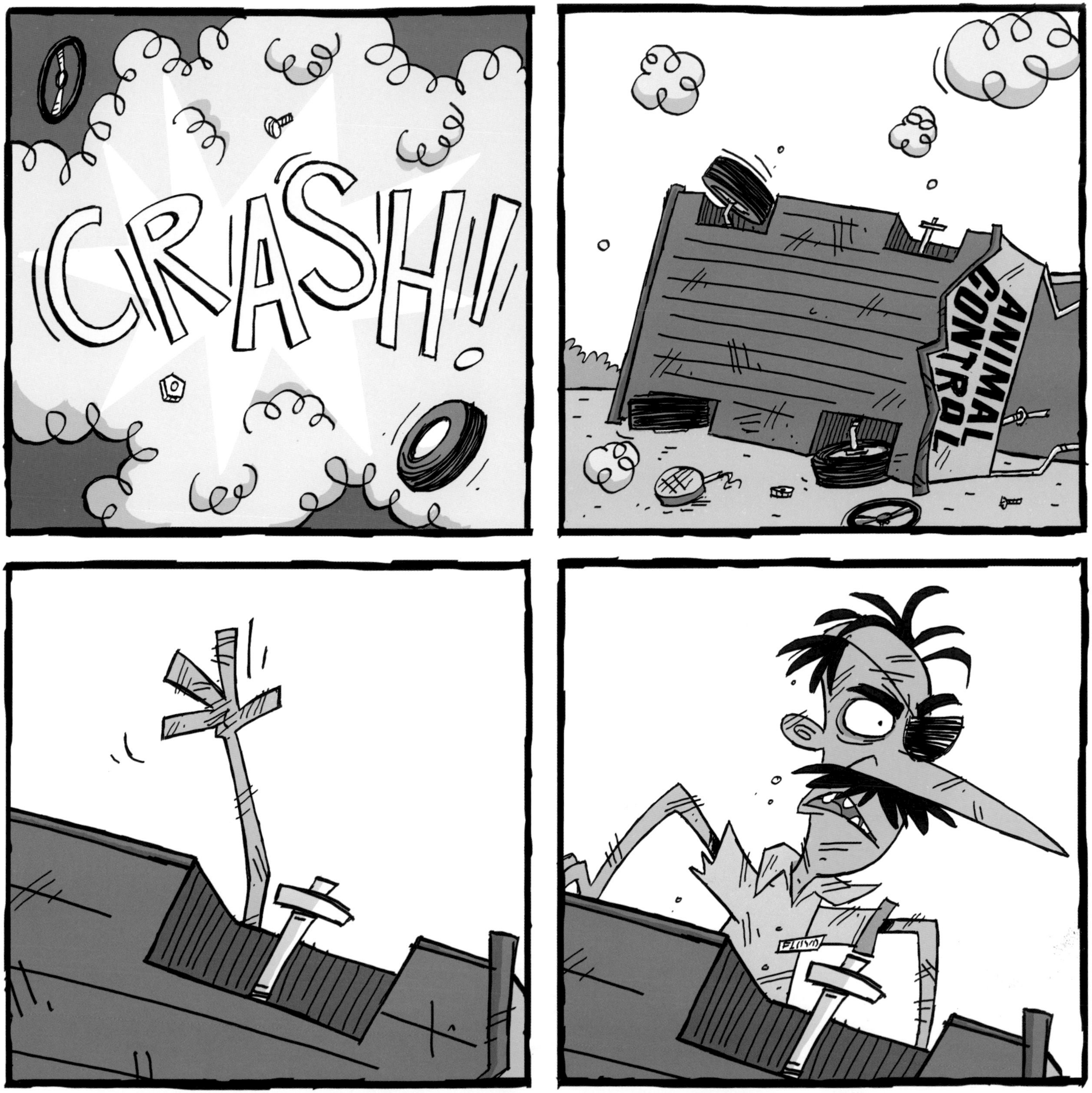
CRASH!!
ANIMAL CONTROL

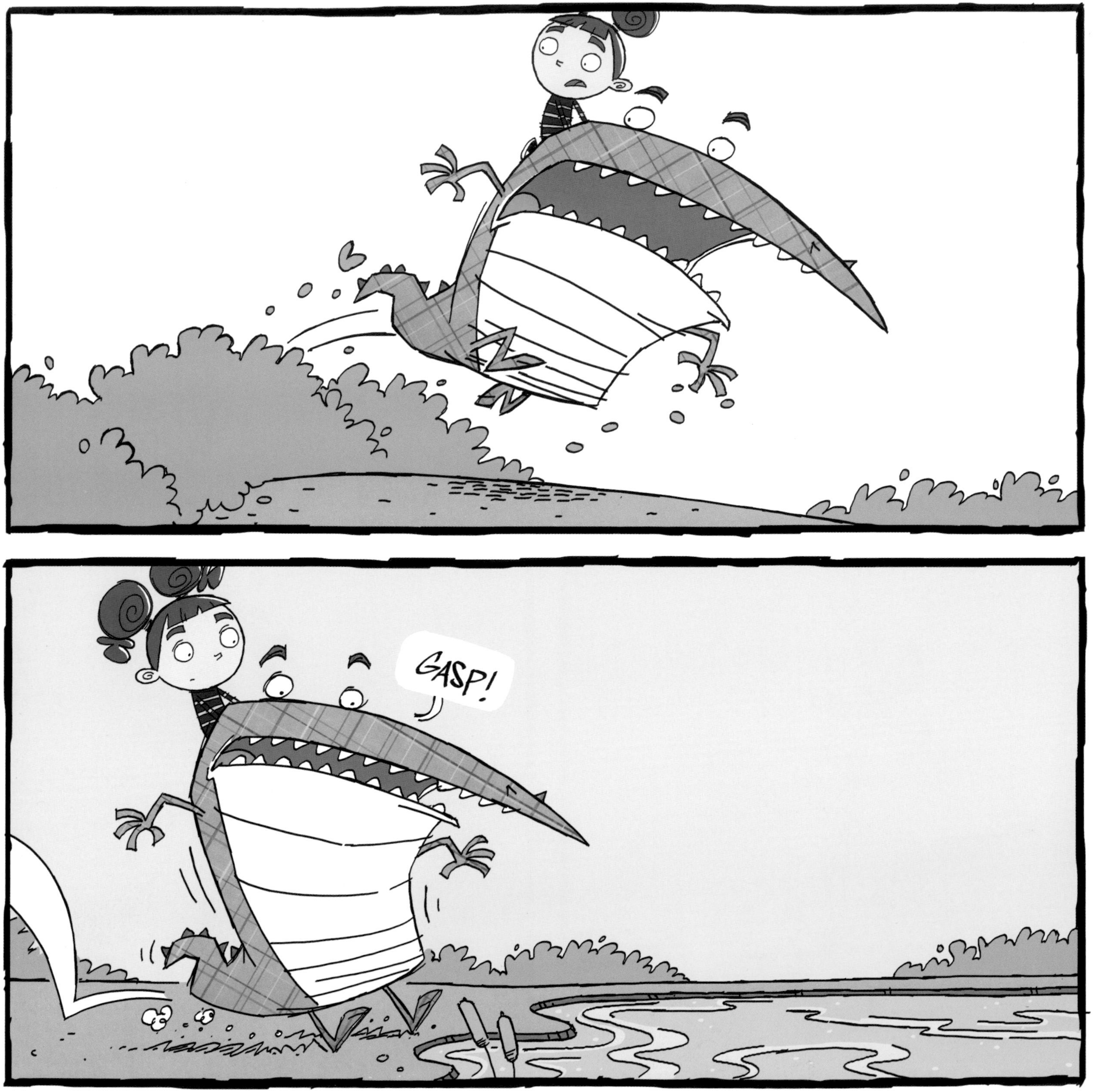
GASP!

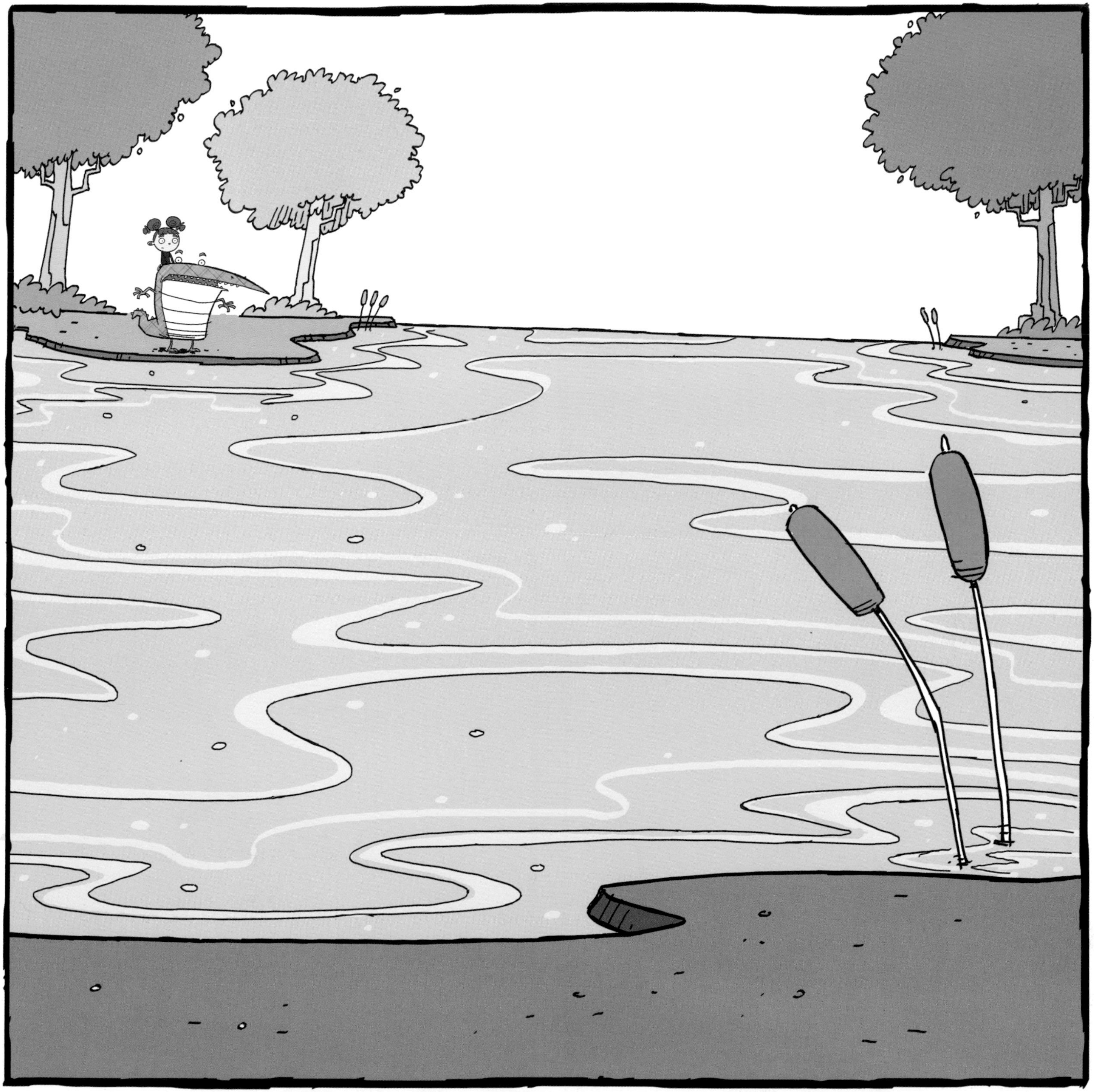

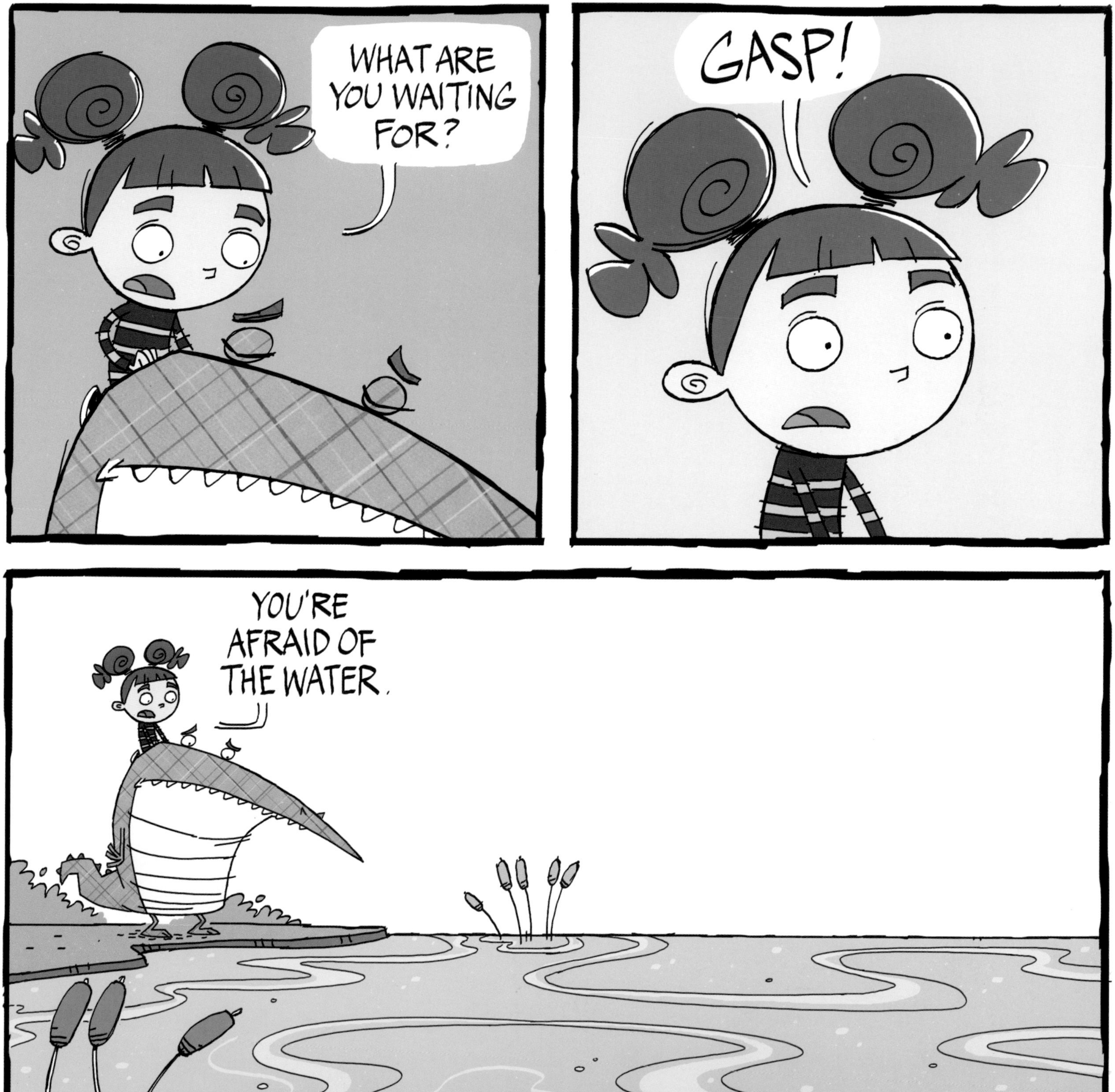
WHAT ARE YOU WAITING FOR?
GASP!
YOU'RE AFRAID OF THE WATER.

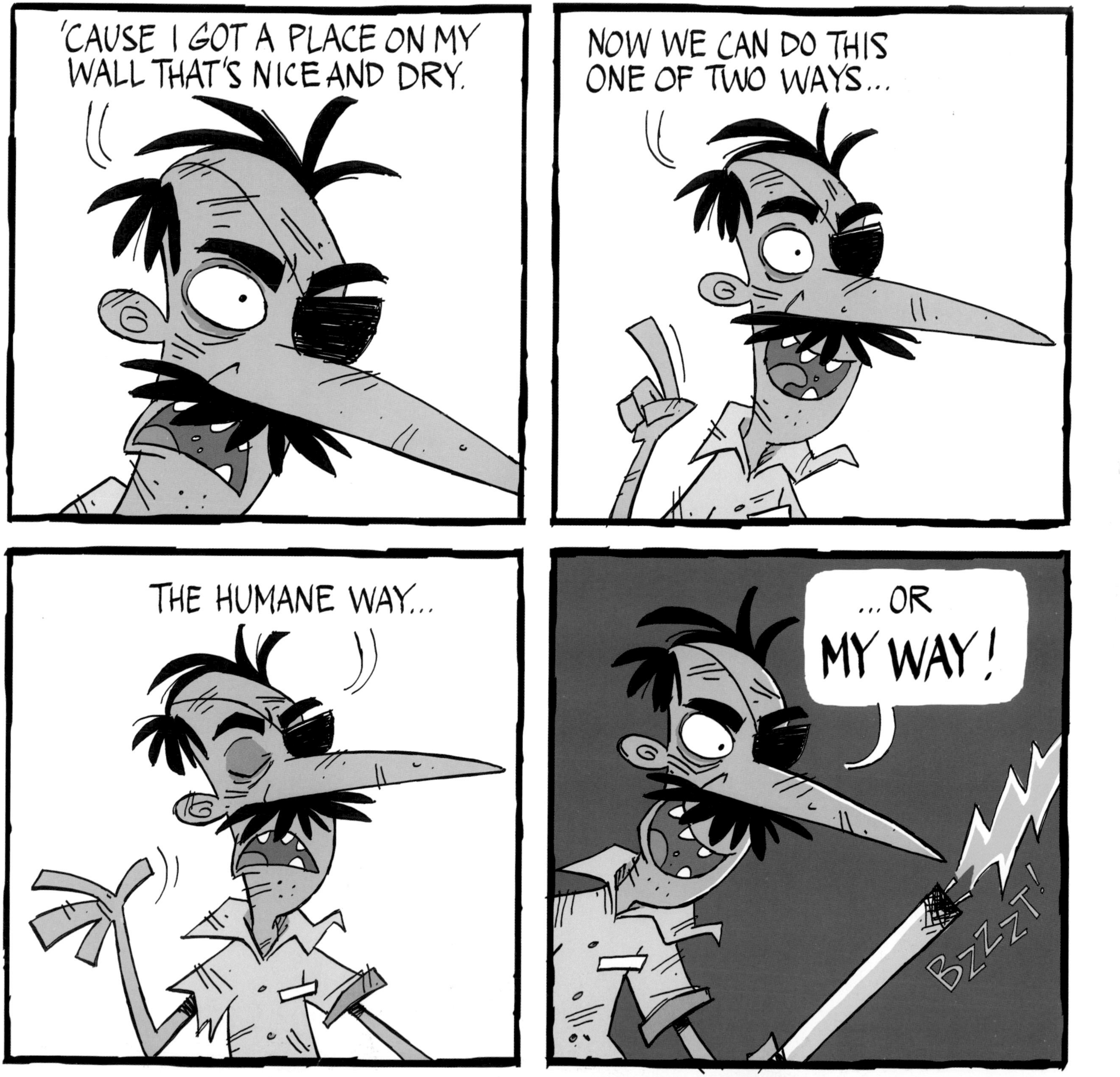
'CAUSE I GOT A PLACE ON MY WALL THAT'S NICE AND DRY.
NOW WE CAN DO THIS ONE OF TWO WAYS...
THE HUMANE WAY...
...OR MY WAY!
BZZZT!

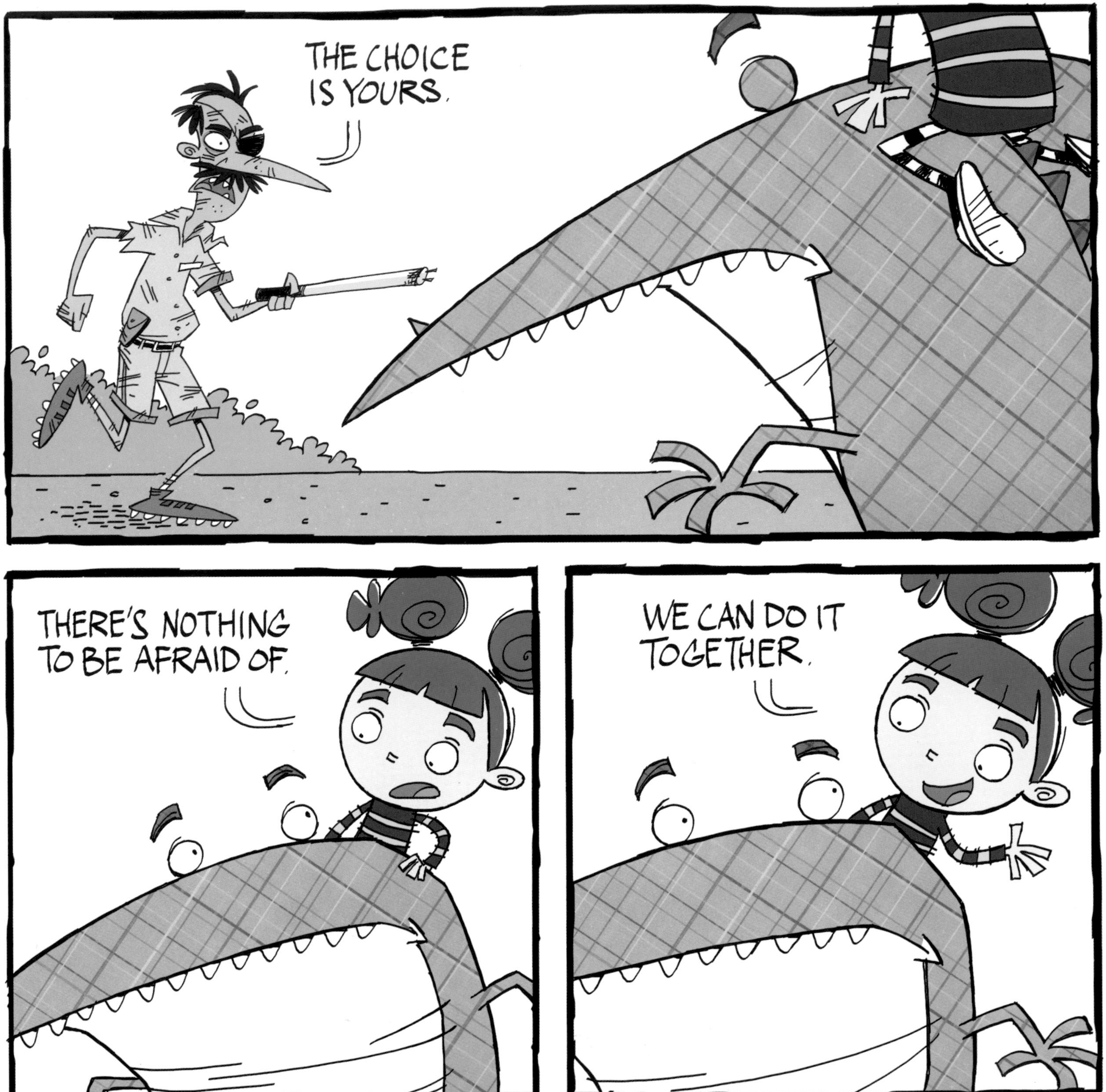
THE CHOICE IS YOURS.
THERE'S NOTHING TO BE AFRAID OF.
WE CAN DO IT TOGETHER.

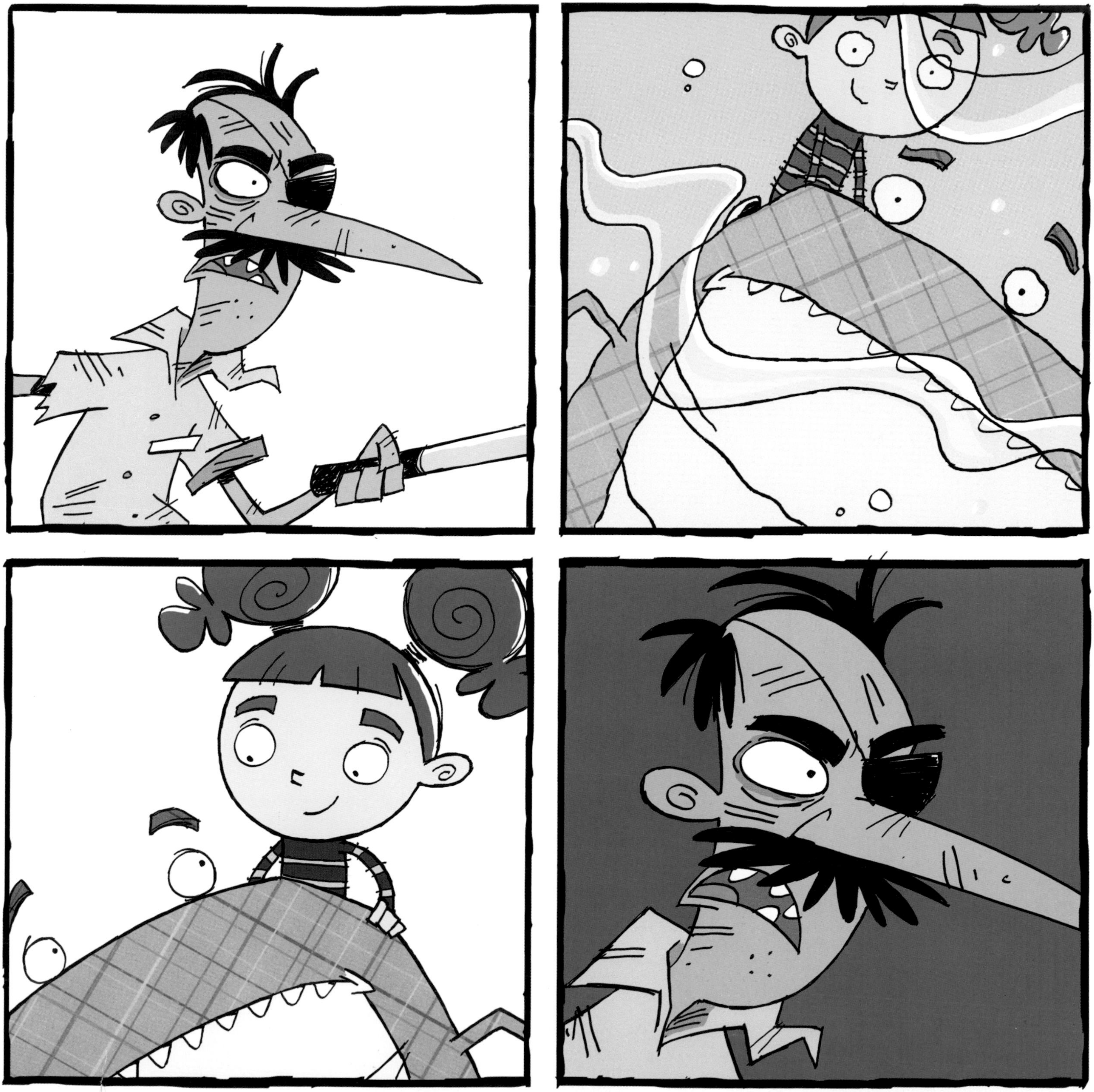

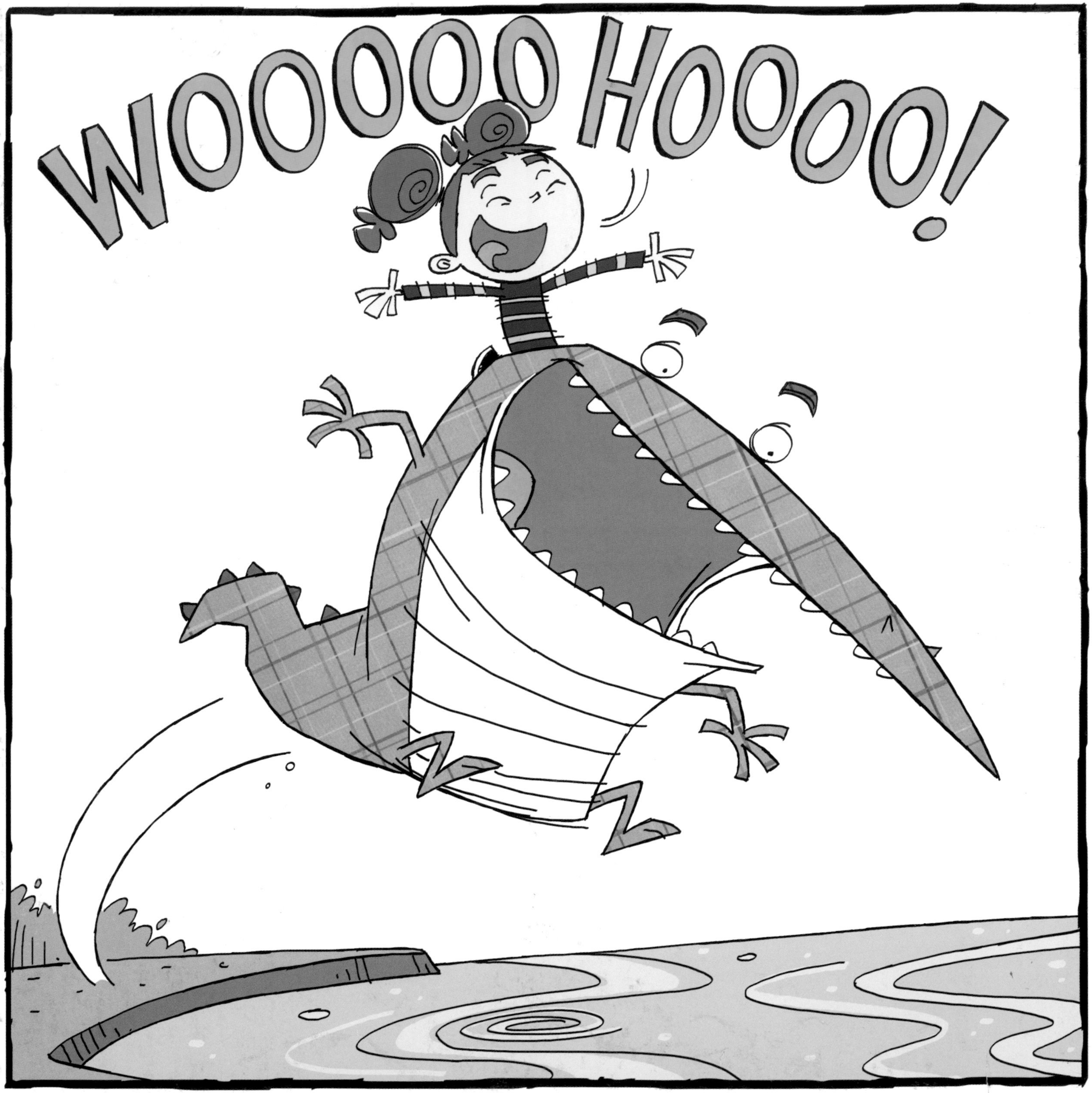
WOOOOO HOOOOO!

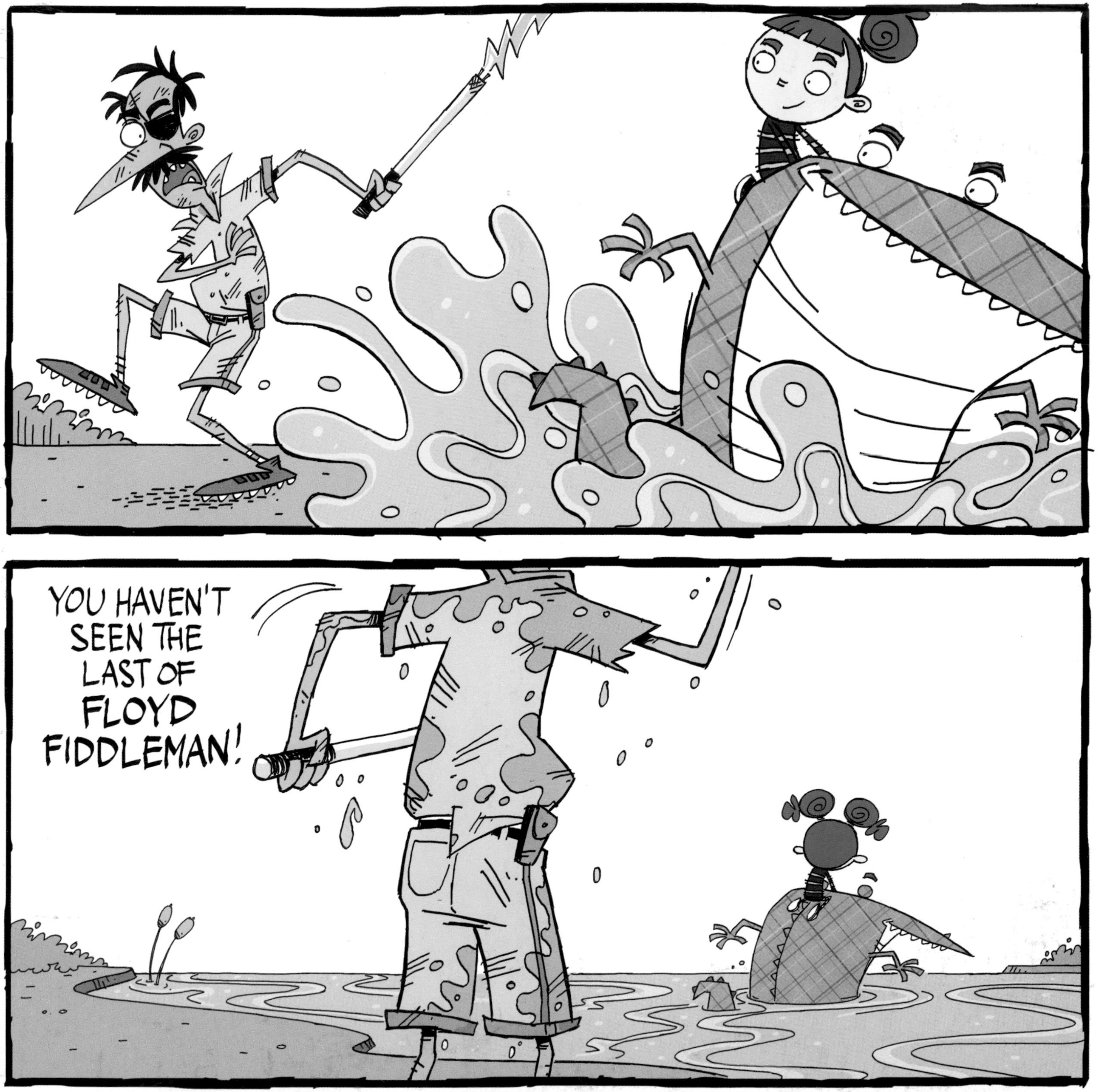
YOU HAVEN'T SEEN THE LAST OF FLOYD FIDDLEMAN!

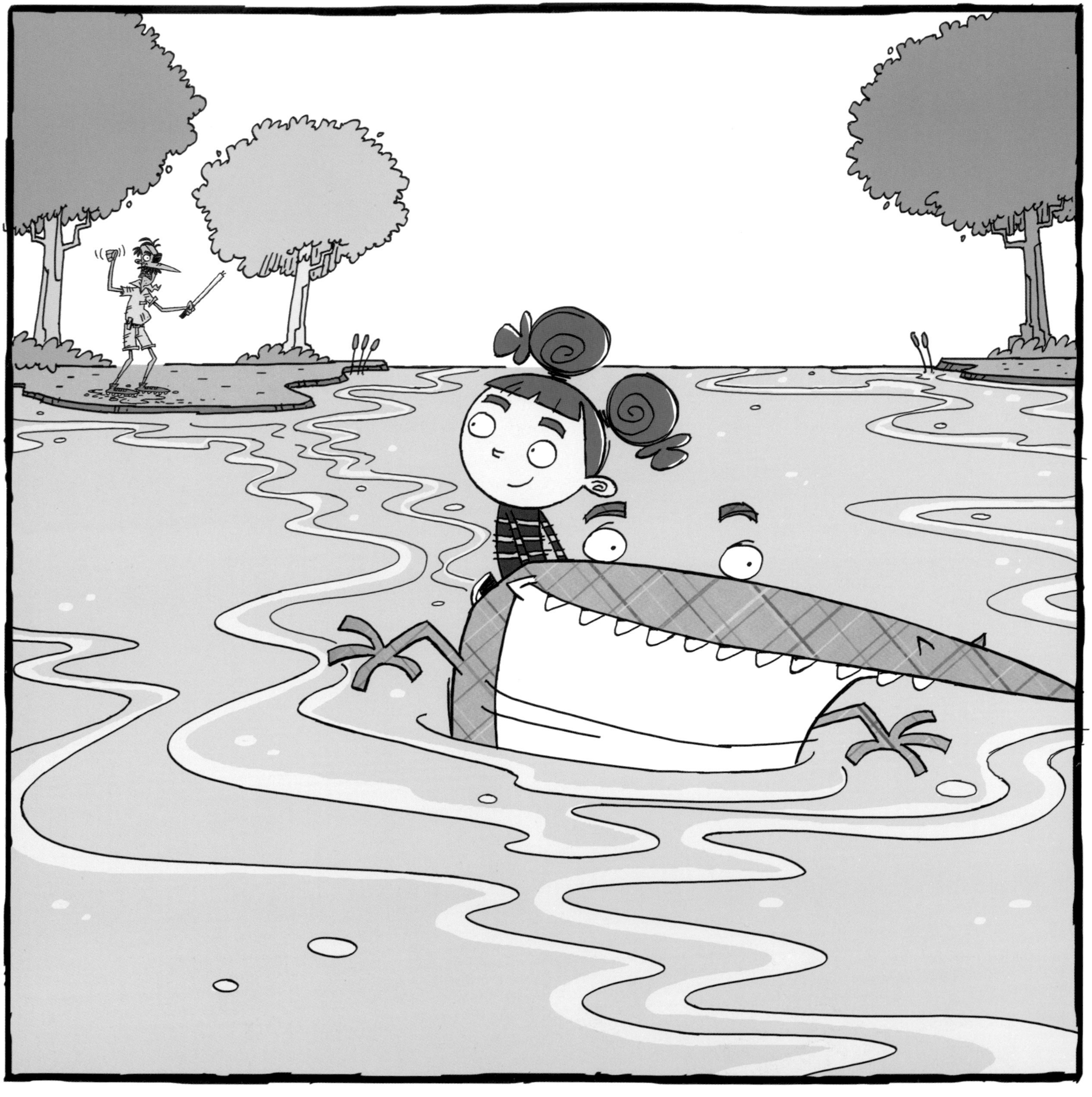

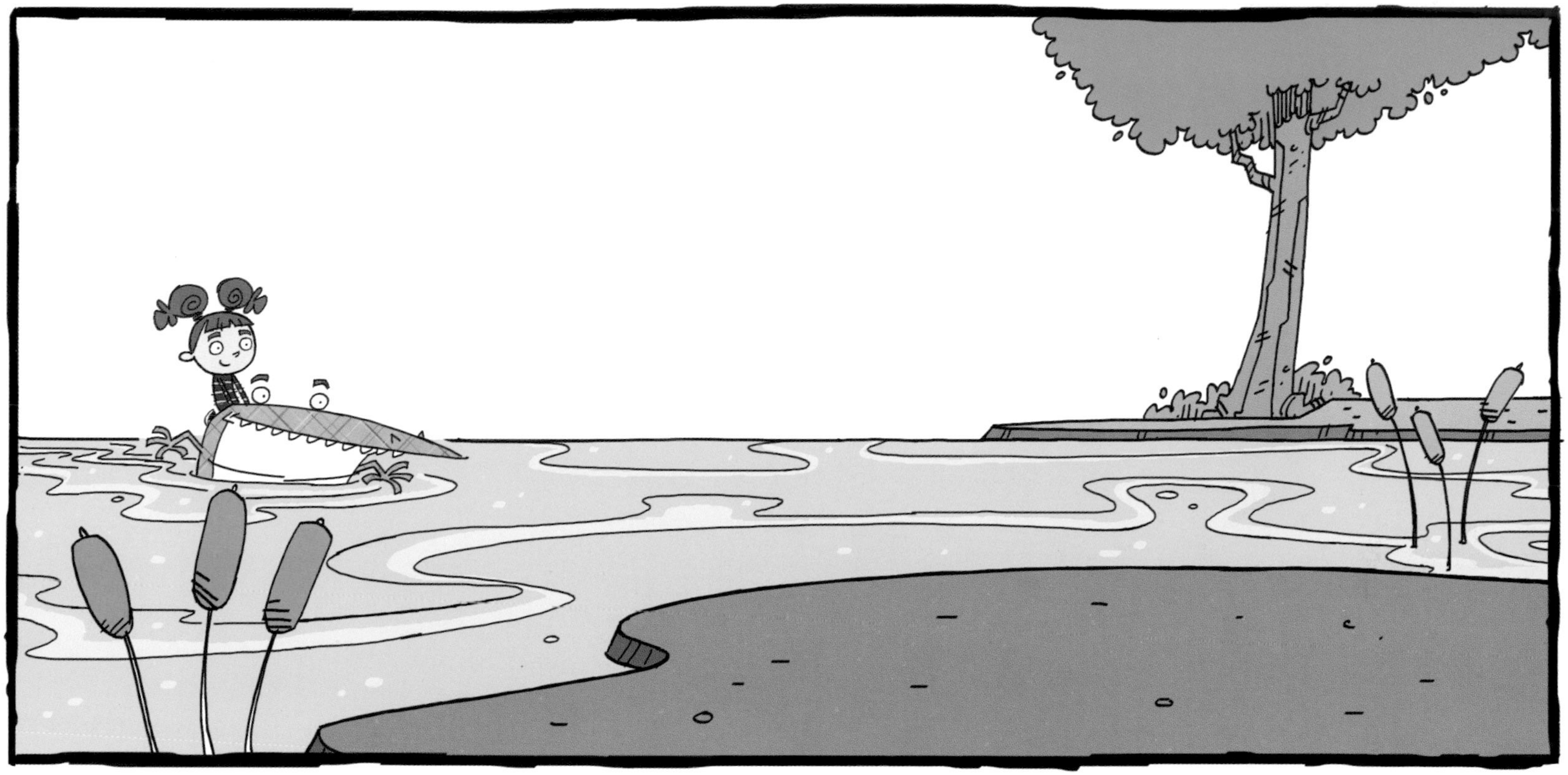

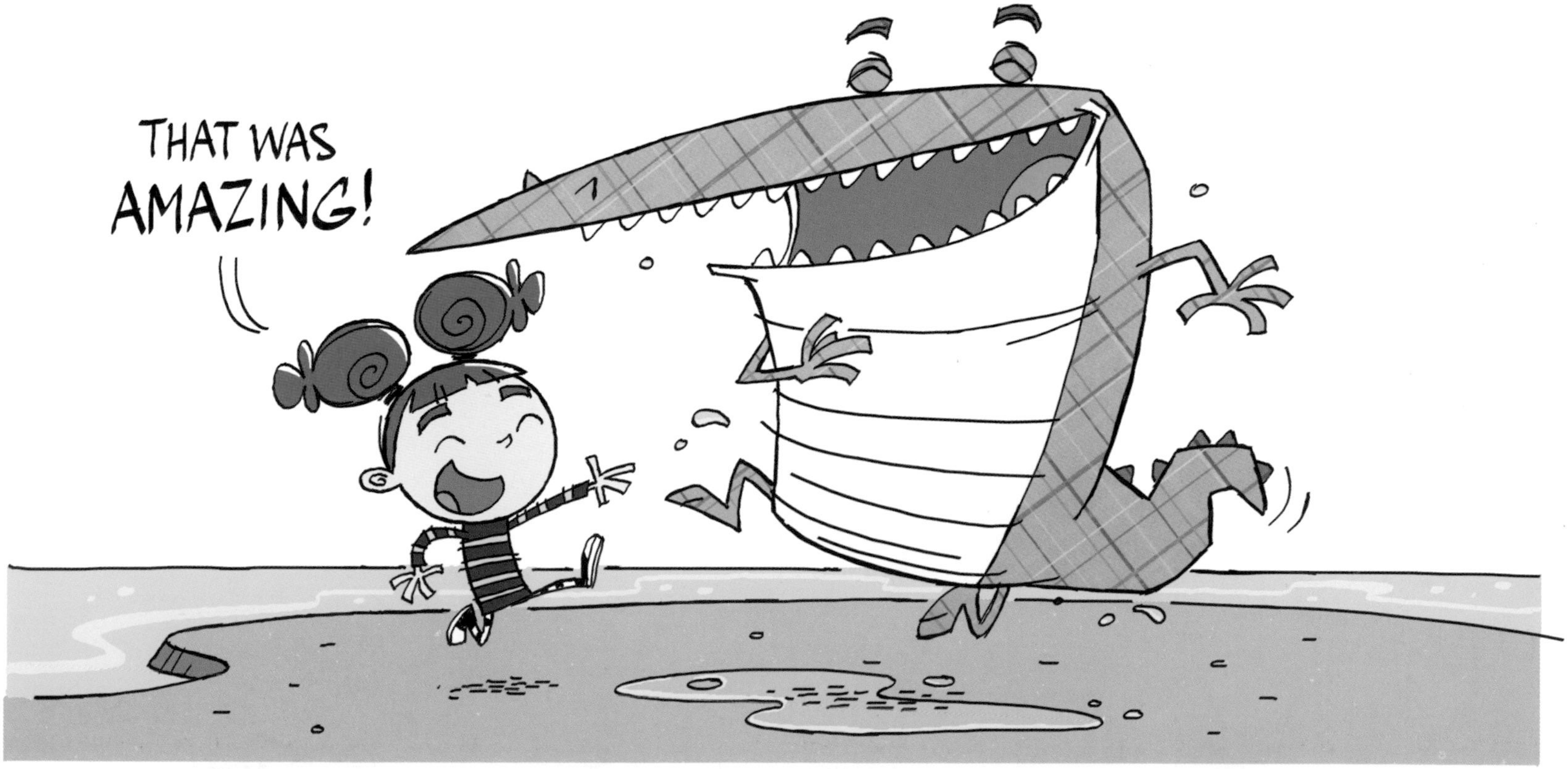
THAT WAS AMAZING!

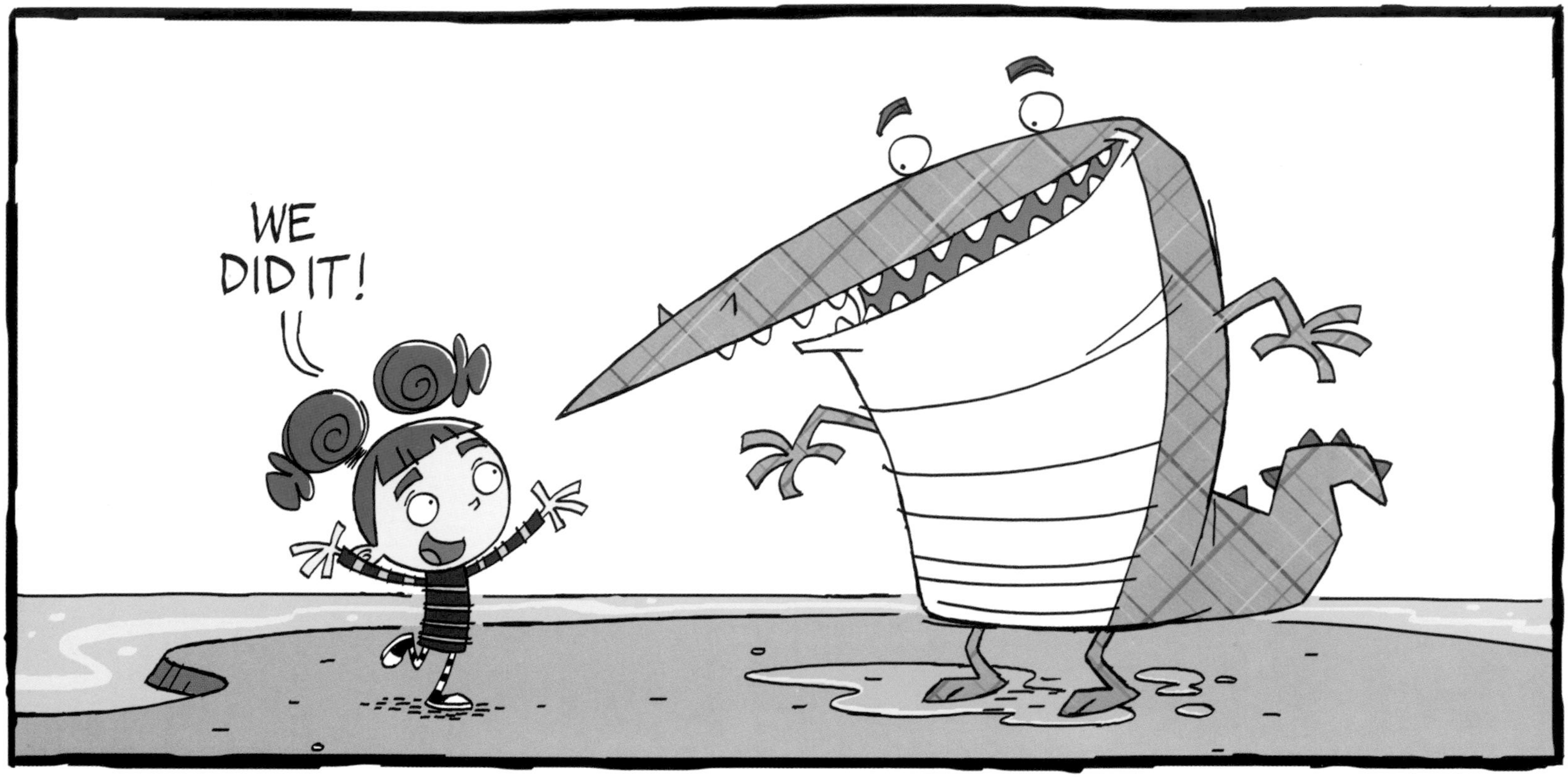
WE DID IT!

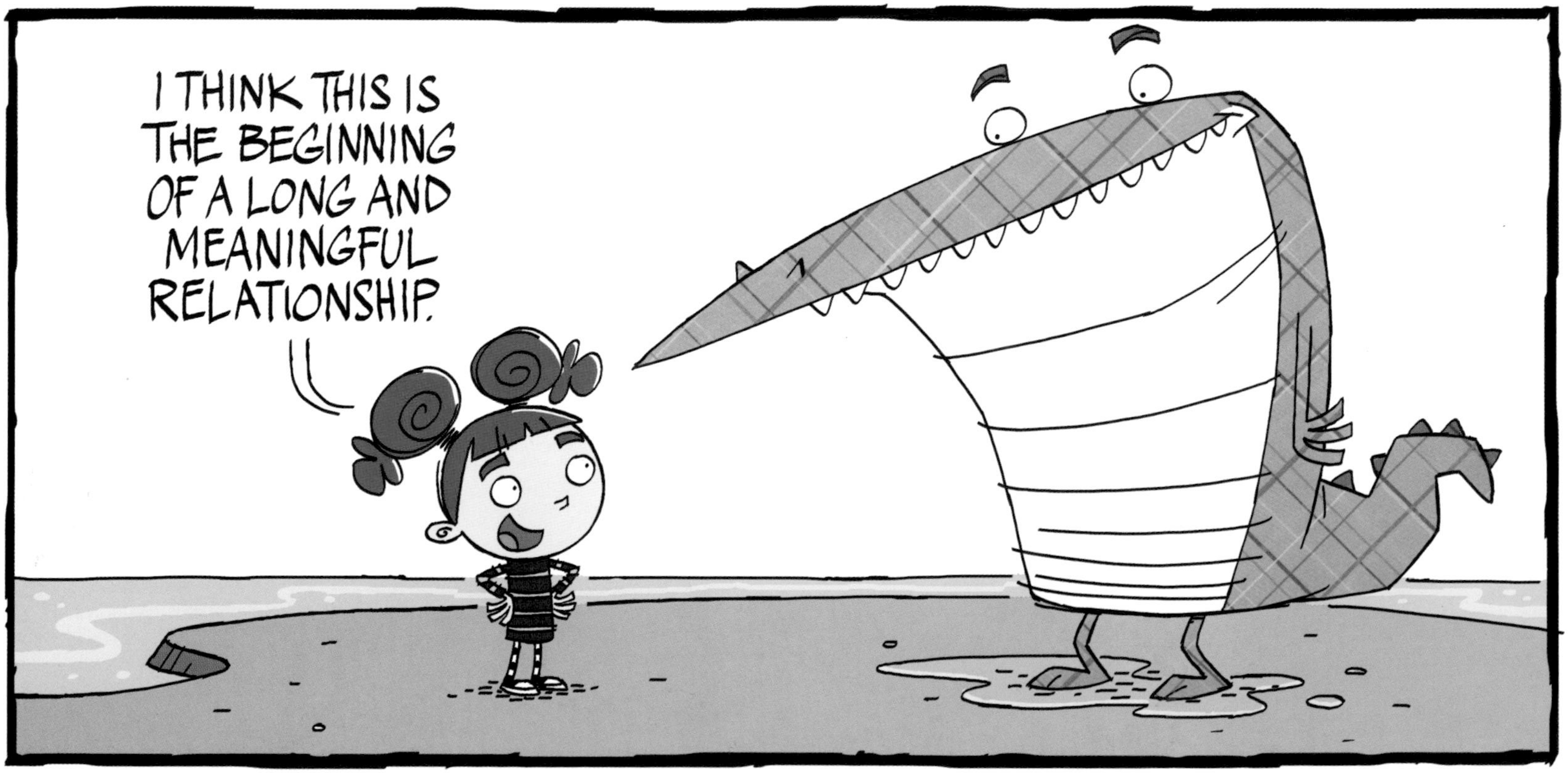
I THINK THIS IS THE BEGINNING OF A LONG AND MEANINGFUL RELATIONSHIP.

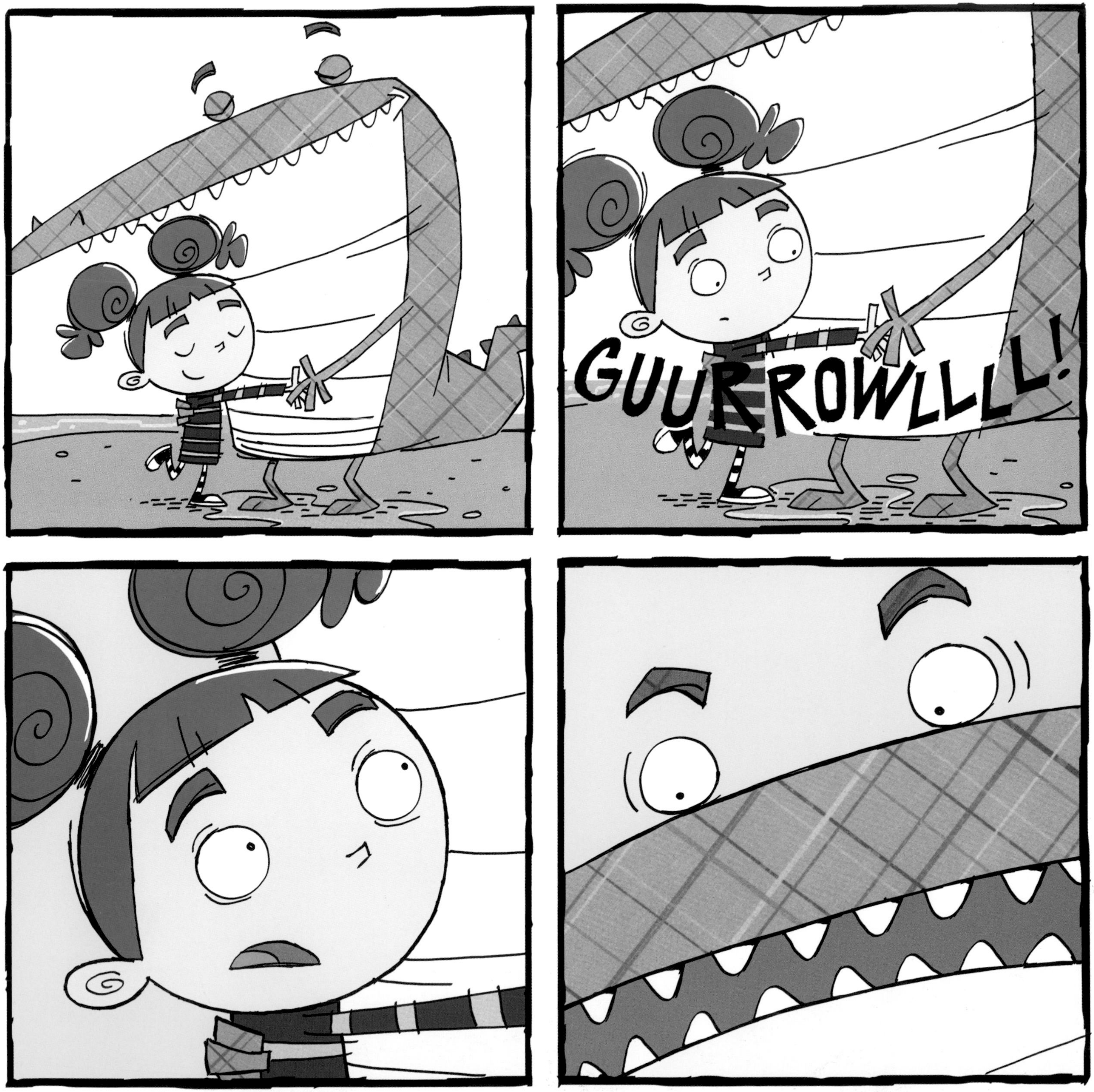
GUURROWLLLL!

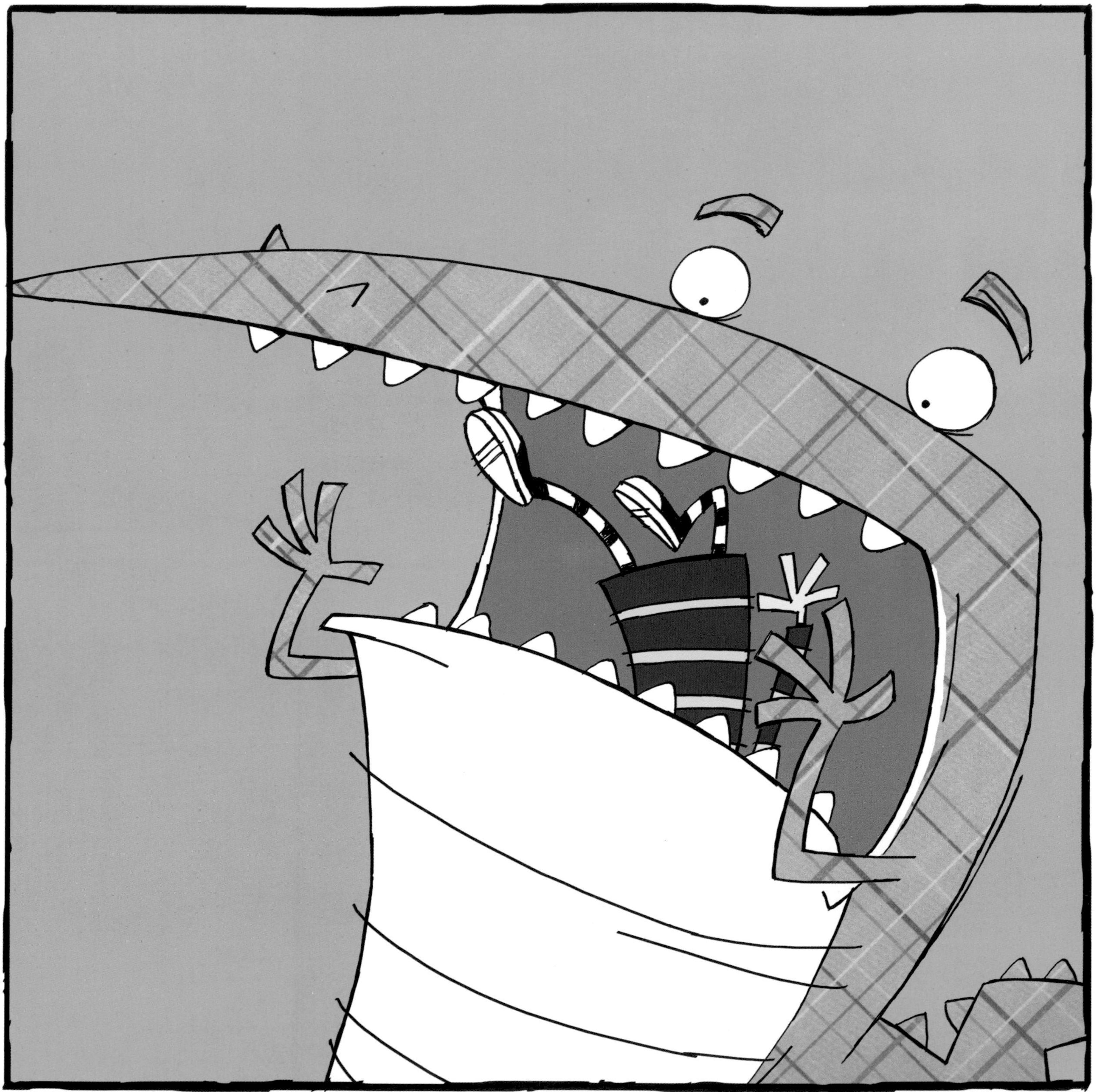

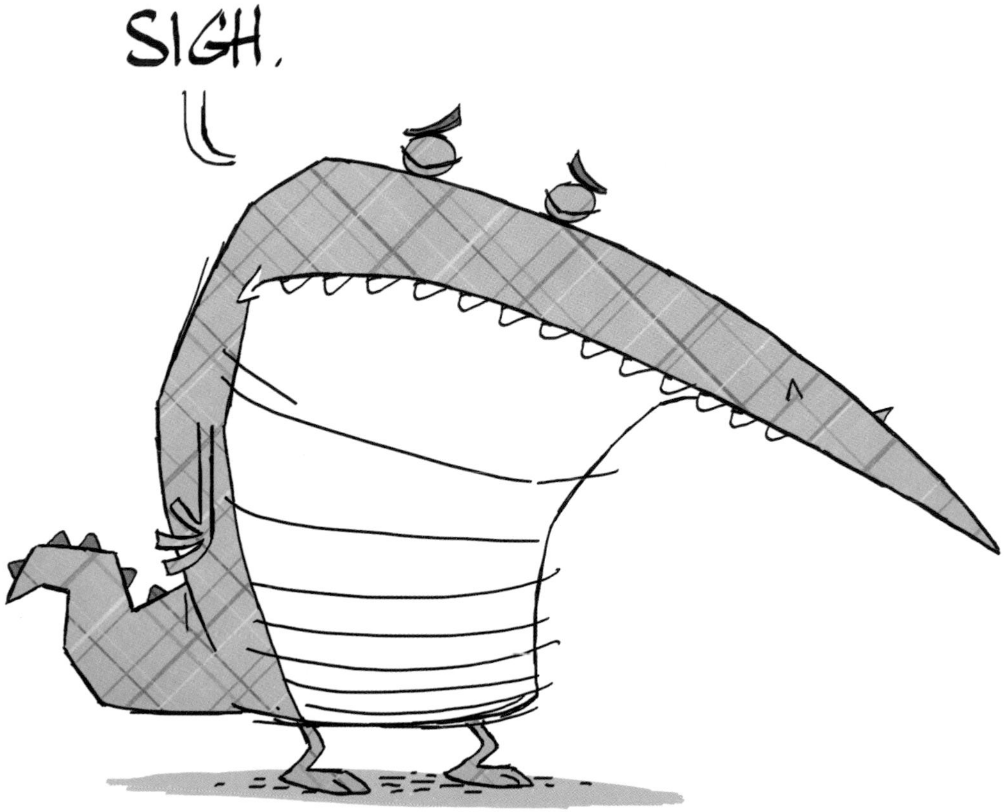
SIGH.

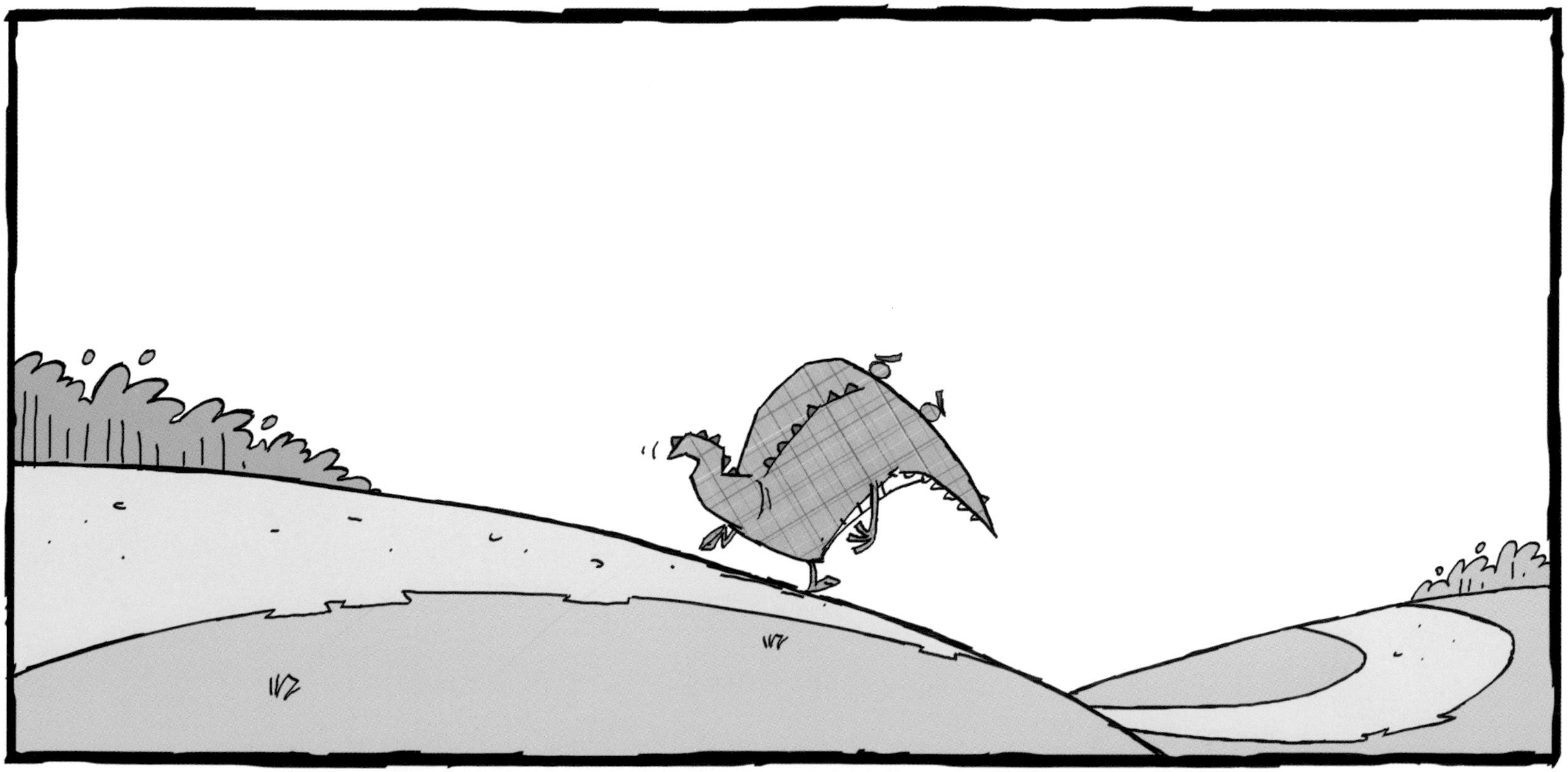

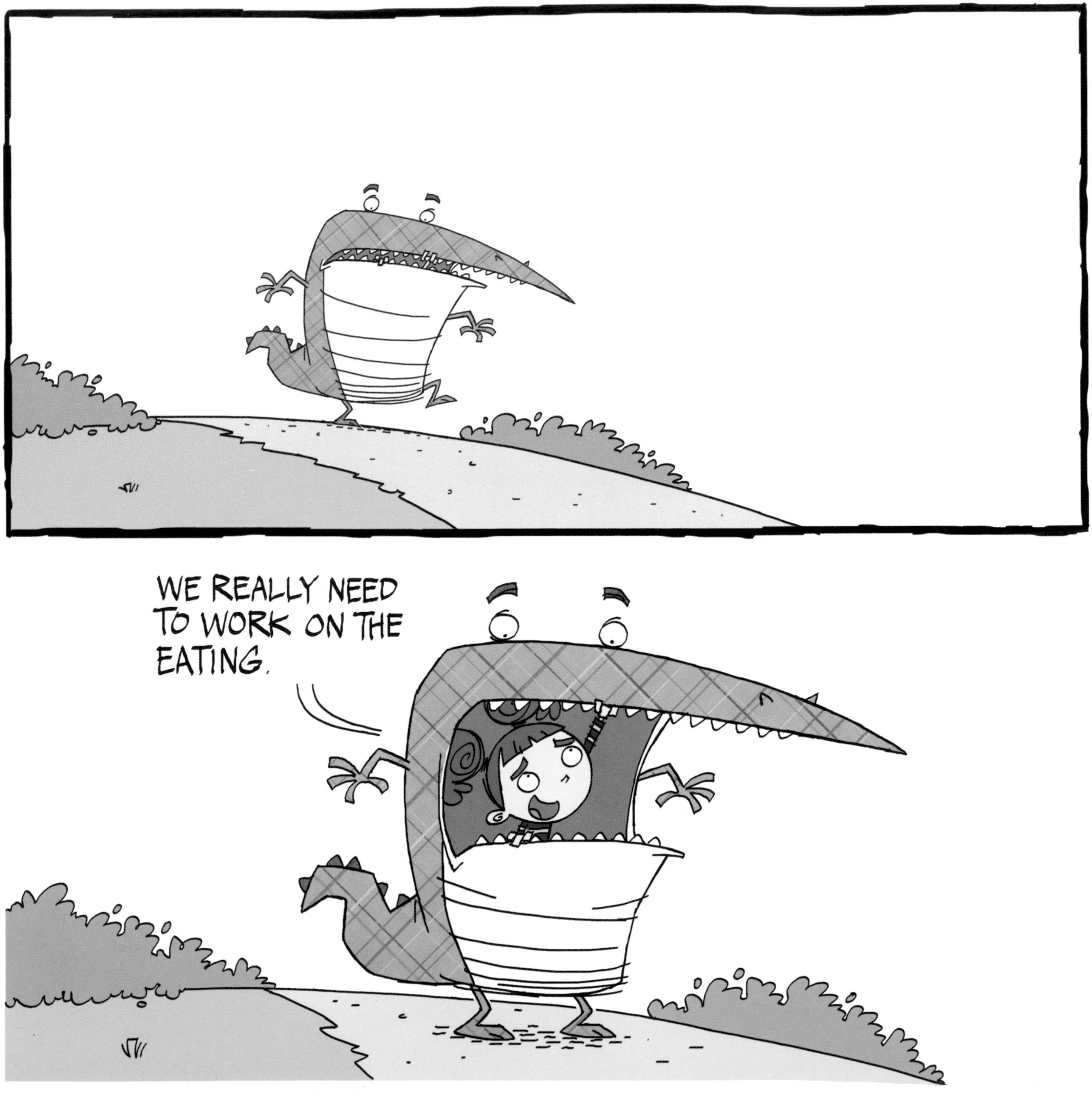
WE REALLY NEED TO WORK ON THE EATING.

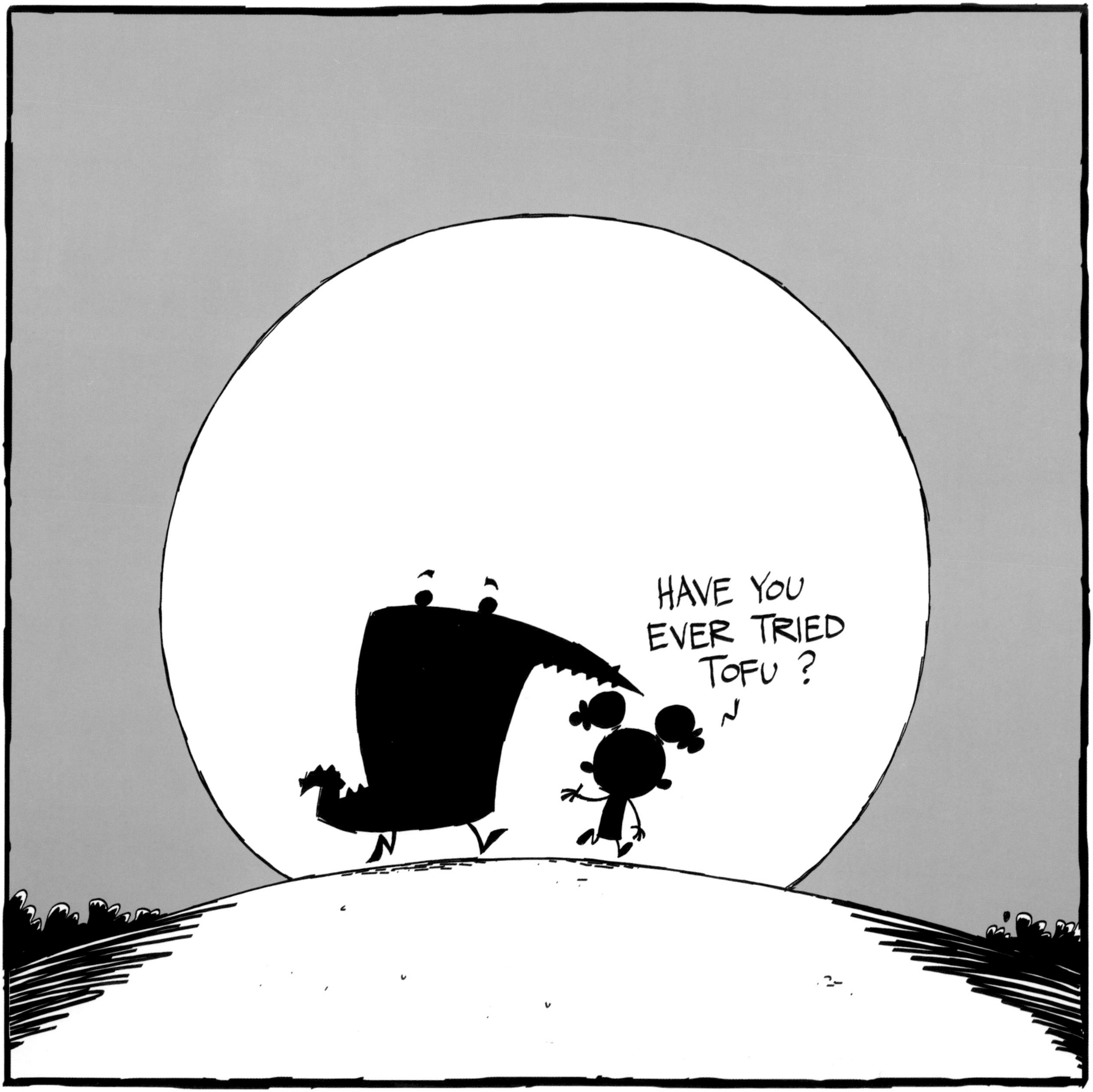
HAVE YOU EVER TRIED TOFU ?

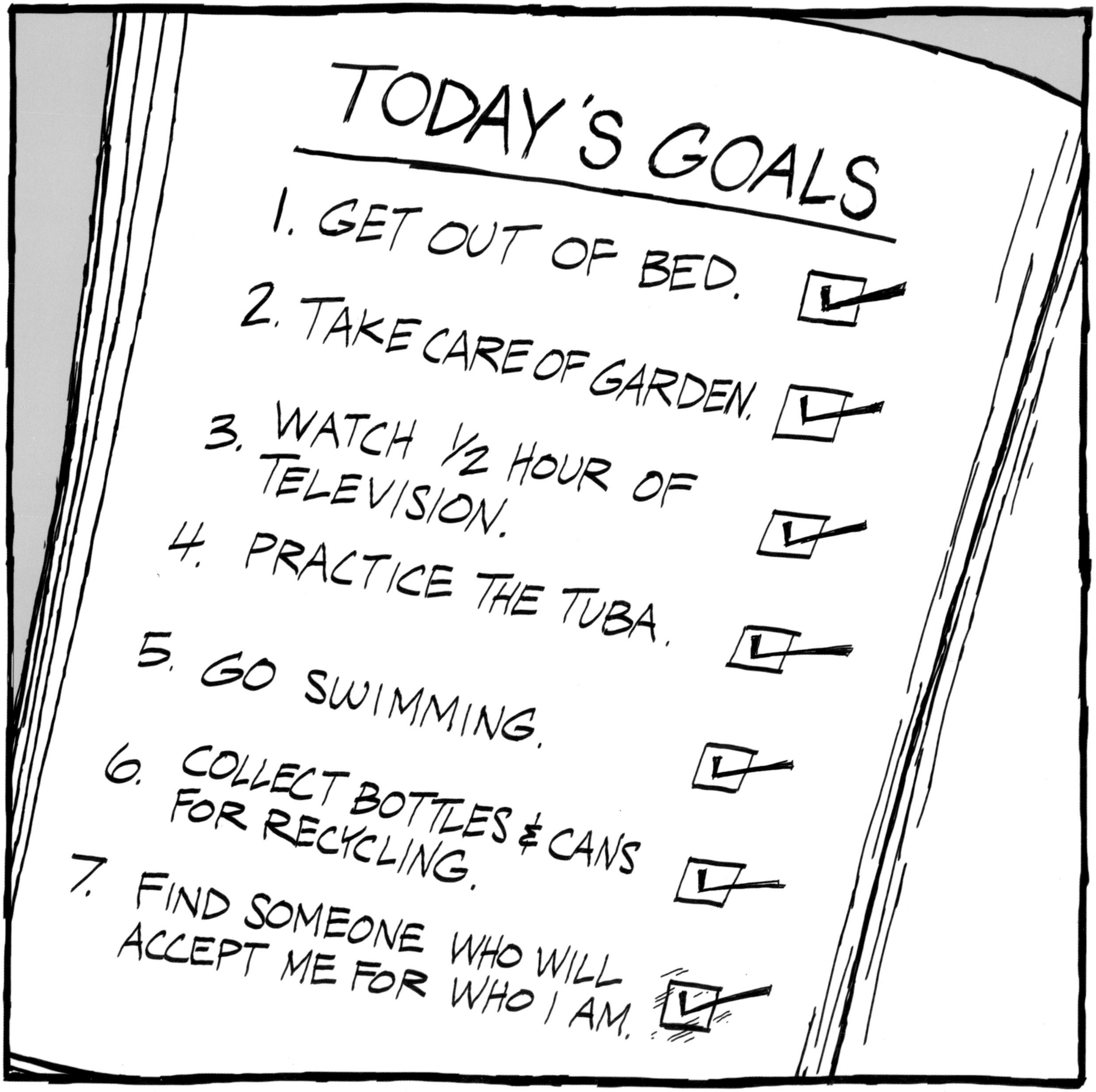
TODAY'S GOALS
1. GET OUT OF BED.
2. TAKE CARE OF GARDEN.
3. WATCH 1/2 HOUR OF TELEVISION.
4. PRACTICE THE TUBA.
5. GO SWIMMING.
6. COLLECT BOTTLES & CANS FOR RECYCLING.
7. FIND SOMEONE WHO WILL ACCEPT ME FOR WHO I AM.

[redacted]

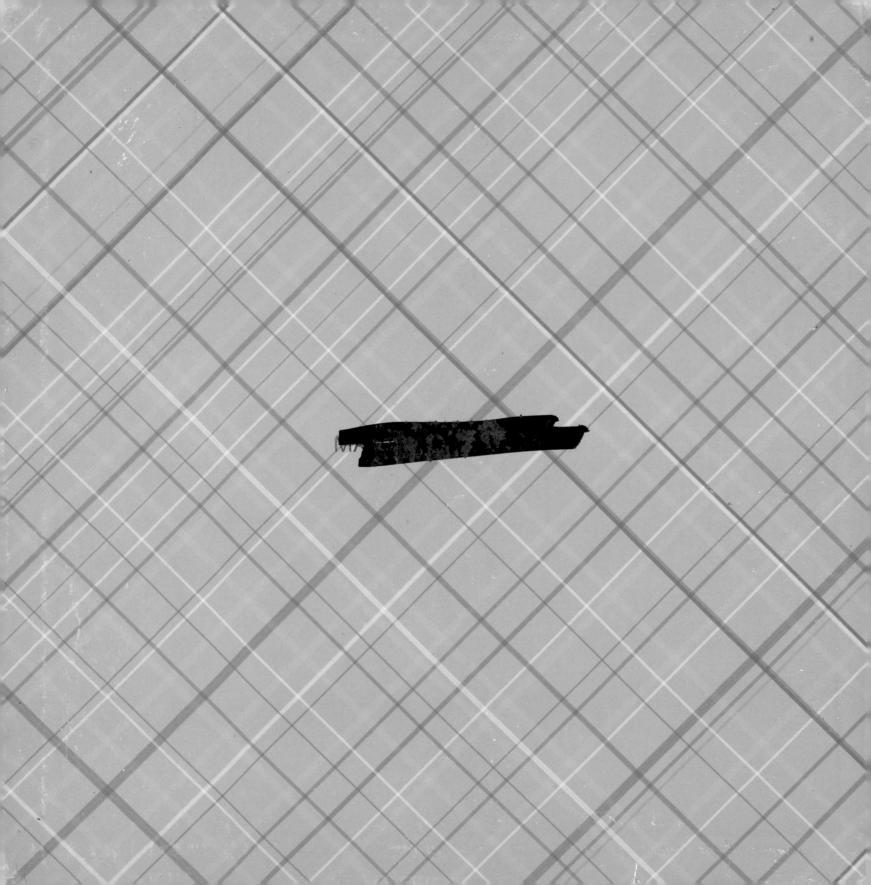